The Elders Chronicles:

Collision

Division

Revision

The Elders' Chronicles:

Collision

Division

Revision

By: Keith Imbody

Copyright © 2022 Keith Imbody

All rights reserved.

This book or any portion thereof

may not be reproduced or used in any manner whatsoever

without the express written permission of the author

except for the use of brief quotations in a book review.

Cover art created by Alecia Witbart

The Elders' Chronicles: Collision

The Elders' Chronicles:
Collision
By: Keith Imbody

Copyright © 2020 Keith Imbody

All rights reserved.

This book or any portion thereof

may not be reproduced or used in any manner whatsoever

without the express written permission of the author

except for the use of brief quotations in a book review.

Cover art created by Alecia Witbart

Preface

The idea for this story started in a somewhat different way than you might think. My thought was to write down three sentences and then post them in a group on Facebook as a round robin story. I'd write some of the story, then others would write some of the story. After writing the three sentences, however, I decided that I wanted to write this story myself. I never ended up posting it on Facebook. About a week or so later, I had written an entire story, about twenty-five thousand words, on my phone. That's right, this entire story was typed up on my smart phone. It's funny, the editing process has taken much longer than writing the story itself.

The character's names are completely made up from my mind. Though I'm sure the different TV shows, stories and names I've seen throughout my life have impacted not just the characters, but the story itself, and my overall love for Science Fiction.

Keith Dunbady

Acknowledgments

To my family:

My sister has helped me with editing, creating the cover of the book and the formatting that needed to be done. The formatting alone was daunting, so I'm very grateful that I didn't have to worry about that. Thank you, Alecia.

My parents listened to my story and gave me feedback throughout the editing process. Self publishing doesn't mean you have to do everything by yourself, thank God. Thanks, mom and dad.

To the reader:

Thank you for taking the time out of your day to check out my book. I hope that you find a character that you love, that maybe reminds you a little bit of yourself or someone you know. Thank you for reading my book. Without you, the reader, reading itself wouldn't exist, now would it?

The Elders' Chronicles: Collision

By: Keith Imbody

Table of Contents
Chapter 1. The Newcomer
Chapter 2. Groundfloor
Chapter 3. Catching Up
Chapter 4. Frozen
Chapter 5. Chance Meetings
Chapter 6. The Holograms
Chapter 7. Answered Questions
Chapter 8. The Forest
Chapter 9. The Rock
Chapter 10. Splitting Up
Chapter 11. Scanning for Answers
Chapter 12. Zot
Chapter 13. Reinforcements
Chapter 14. Flashback
Chapter 15. The Plan
Chapter 16. Gloria
Chapter 17. Missing Pieces
Chapter 18. Loose-leaf
Chapter 19. Descending
Chapter 20. Savior
Chapter 21. The Gift
Chapter 22. Second Chances
Epilogue

Chapter 1
The Newcomer

This story takes place on a distant planet similar to our own. Think of Earth, but instead of humans inhabiting the planet, there lives an alien race that all have superpowers. All of them, except this one Newcomer, who just seemed to appear out of nowhere.

Dazed and confused, this Newcomer seemed to stumble around for a bit, trying to find his footing. His bearings. Just trying to stand.

"Hello?" he said, in a gruff, confused voice. "Can anybody help me?"

He looked around, and saw these other beings flying around. Running around. Chatting. Playing games.

"DOES ANYBODY EVEN SEE ME?" The Newcomer said again.

Looking around, this Newcomer, who looked remarkably like a human, started to take in the view of his surroundings. The beings that he had previously observed started to look familiar.

"They look... human?" The Newcomer said. "What's a human?"

A group of these aliens stopped what they were doing and sneered at The Newcomer.

Another group looked at him.

One of them walked over to The Newcomer and looked at him closely. "Who are you?" it said. "I haven't seen you around here. What do you know of the 'humans'?"

"I, I don't know," The Newcomer said.

"Do you have a name?" the alien asked.

"Not that I can remember..." The Newcomer thought for a minute. "No, unfortunately."

Confused, the alien looked back at the group he was with and waved them over.

"My name is Clory."

"Well, Clory, I hope it is nice to meet you. But I'm rather confused at the moment. Where am I?"

Clory's friends started to come over. There were three of them. Clory himself had short blue hair. He wore what a human might call jeans and a long sleeve yellow shirt.

Clory's first friend to walk over had long green hair. She was also wearing jeans and a thick, fuzzy, purple jacket over a plain yellow shirt. Walking up, she said, "What do we have here, Clory?"

"Oh, this is our new friend!" Clory said. "He needs a name…"

She looked at him. "Hello, sir. My name is Trolk! I've never seen you around here! Welcome! What is your superpower?"

Trying to take in what was going on, The Newcomer looked closely at Clory and Trolk. Somehow, they looked like humans. He knew they looked like humans. But he didn't even know what a human was! Or did he?

"Hello," The Newcomer said.

"He needs a name!" another of Clory's friends said. "Hey dude! My name is Gleck!" Gleck was wearing a hat. The first thing The Newcomer noticed, was the hat. His attire was different than Clory's. His jeans were more faded and older looking. He also wore a black shirt.

"You have some interesting names!" The Newcomer said. "What is on your head?"

"At least we have names!" Gleck laughed, a quite annoying laugh.

Before he could answer the question about his hat, Clory's third friend finally caught up. She looked around, and said with a laugh, "Are you guys trying to add a fifth member to our group?"

She was wearing black shorts, and a yellow t-shirt. "Is anybody going to introduce me???" she asked.

"You could introduce yourself!" Gleck said with a smirk.

Trolk shot Gleck a look. She looked at The Newcomer and simply said, "This is Glor."

"Yes, my name is Glor. Not Gloria. Glor. Please don't add to my name. It's not cool. My name is Glor."

"It's okay, Glor," Clory said. "He understands."

"Actually, I'm very, very lost!" The Newcomer said. "How does everyone have names except me? Who am I? Where did I come from?"

16

Clory looked at The Newcomer, then at his friends. "Should we tell him?"

"No!" Glor said. "You don't even know him! He might be The Destroyer that we've heard about. Sent to destroy us. The powerless--"

"Enough talk!" Trolk yelled. "If you think him to be SO dangerous, why are you telling him about The Destroyer?!"

"Wait, who is The Destroyer?" The Newcomer asked.

"Hopefully not you!" Glor said, with an untrusting look on her face.

"Who are you people?" The Newcomer looked past them and saw something. "What is that?!"

A fiery rock came flying towards them.

"BEWARE THE DESTROYER!" someone screamed.

"The Destroyer has arrived!" Another alien started running around like crazy. Everyone got nervous.

"Oh, not this again!" Clory sighed. "Glor, Trolk, Gleck, meet us at the Groundfloor!"

Before The Newcomer could take in what was happening, Clory took his hand and they transported away from the madness.

Chapter 2
Groundfloor

The Newcomer quickly backed away from Clory. "What have you done? Where am I now?!"

"It was about to get dangerous out there," Clory said.

"But why?! Who is this Destroyer? Who are you?"

"My name is Clory!" Clory smiled. "And you just met my friends, Trolk, Gleck and Glor."

"But who are you?" The Newcomer asked again.

"Maybe we should try and figure out who you are!" Clory looked at him. "Who are you?"

"I seriously don't know. I don't remember anything before today. This very day. All I remember is today."

"Then how are you speaking? There is knowledge in there. In your mind."

"It's not like I'm forgetting this on purpose!"

Clory sighed. "Let me make you some soup. Maybe that will help."

The Newcomer looked around. "Is this the Groundfloor?" he asked. "It looks nice." He saw a stove and a sink. He turned around and saw some nice portraits on the wall.

"Who are those people?" he asked.

Clory's face saddened. "My parents."

"Where are they now?" The Newcomer asked, curiously.

"I don't know." Clory frowned. "Anyways, I've got some soup here for you, let me just heat it up."

He turned on the stove and poured out the soup from a can into a pot. The writing on the can didn't look familiar. But since he was already so confused, The Newcomer just shook off the thought.

"Who is The Destroyer?" The Newcomer asked again.

"It's legend."

"What?"

"Legend tells us that once every fifty-seven years, The Destroyer comes and wipes out the entire planet."

"If the planet is wiped out just once, how are any of you here?"

"Don't ask me! But the Elders have clocked us at about fifty-seven years. Tomorrow will be exactly fifty-seven years, according to them."

"And this, Destroyer. Why does he destroy?"

"I don't know anything more than what the Elders have written."

"You keep saying 'the Elders'. Where are they? I want to speak with them!"

"Though I appreciate the enthusiasm, you don't even know your own name, friend. How do you expect to enjoy council with the Elders? Besides, no one has seen them in quite some time."

"Interesting."

"What is interesting?"

"That the very ones who are foretelling your doom are absent when this Destroyer is supposed to arrive."

"Your soup is ready, Newcomer."

Clory brought the soup to a table in the middle of the room, sat down and called The Newcomer to join him. He took some soup out of the pot and poured it out into two bowls.

"Come, let's regain some strength."

He handed The Newcomer a spoon, and they both sat there in silence, eating the soup Clory had prepared for them.

The silence was broken by a loud clang, clang, clang!

"What was that?!" The Newcomer started coughing on his soup.

Before Clory could answer, Trolk came through the ceiling, as if there was nothing in her way.

"Gleck and Glor!" Trolk said, frantically. "I don't know where they are!"

Clory looked worried.

"After you teleported away," Trolk started to cry, "The talk of The Destroyer caused mad chaos. And this newcomer caused everyone to panic. We all tried to get to safety. But I quickly got separated from Gleck and Glor. I tried to find them, but the confusion only made everything worse."

"Gleck finally just got control of his powers. And Glor? Well, we don't want to talk about the last time she got upset," Clory said.

"Clory. The fire that was being thrown at us, started coming from every direction. Like the entire planet had turned against us at once. I flew up to get a better view of what was going on. I saw Gleck turn invisible, like he does, and Glor was following what I assume was Gleck. I tried to follow them, but I had to avoid an oncoming fireball. After trying to fly around it--"

"How do you all have powers?" The Newcomer interrupted.

"Excuse me?" Trolk scoffed.

"It's just, it doesn't seem normal. You can fly, Clory can teleport, Gleck turns invisible... what does Glor do?"

Trolk just stared at him. "Sir, my friends are missing. It's not my fault you don't know who you are, and that you don't have powers. All this trouble started when you showed up. So, forgive me, if I don't trust you." She turned back to Clory. "What have you told him?"

"Not much," Clory said. "What were you saying about the fireball?"

Trolk looked at The Newcomer, then back at her friend. "It just barely missed me. And when I looked back towards Glor and Gleck, I lost them. So I immediately came here, hoping they would already be here."

Again, The Newcomer heard a clang, clang, clang!

"Is that them?!" Trolk was hopeful.

Clory looked at The Newcomer, who was confused. "The 'clang, clang, clang' that you're hearing, is our groups secret call. Something that lets us know that everything is okay."

"Clory! Don't tell HIM!" Trolk scolded him.

"Trolk, I trust him." Clory sighed. "I don't know why. But I trust him." He continued, "The first three clangs you heard were Trolk. So, I'm sure that what you just heard, was Gleck and Glor!"

Just as Clory had spoken these words, there was another clang, clang, clang. The Newcomer looked around the room. He saw a door near the stove. It opened but no one was there. There were pots hanging by the stove as well. They fell off the wall, and Gleck appeared on the ground by them.

"Nice one, Gleck!" Trolk laughed. "Where's Glor?"

Glor came walking in the doorway. "So, have you found out his name yet?"

Clory shook his head. "I'm glad we all made it! I think we all need to talk about what just happened. What we all saw. Gleck and Glor? Trolk caught us up to when Gleck turned invisible and Glor was following him. What happened after that?"

"You might want to sit down for this," Gleck said.

Chapter 3
Catching Up

Gleck continued, "You and The Newcomer disappeared. Sorry, 'teleported away'. What appeared to be fireballs started coming at us in every direction. Trolk flew up to try and get a better look at who might be leading this attack. But one of these fireballs came flying towards me. I turned invisible and told Glor to follow me. I had to keep talking so she knew where I was. After we avoided the fireball, I stopped for a second, turned visible again, and asked Glor if she saw you, Trolk. Neither of us could see you. So Glor looked at me."

Glor interrupted Gleck, "I told him we had to get to the Groundfloor. But before he could answer, someone came running up to us. He looked like a hologram. Or, a projection. Almost like the shadow of a person, but with more detail! I said he, but I suppose he could be a she. Or maybe it was just the trick of the light. Maybe the fireballs cast a shadowy hologram projection that--"

"Glor!" Clory said, interrupting her. "What happened next?"

Gleck answered, "This hologram creature looked directly at me and Glor. It simply said, 'The Destroyer has arrived.' It then blipped out of existence. Or, at least out of our eyesight."

"Gleck turned invisible again, grabbed my hand, and we started running as fast as we could until we couldn't run anymore."

"Glor," The Newcomer interrupted, "What is your superpower?"

"You ask too many questions!" Glor snapped. "Why is he here?"

"Glor, it's okay," Clory said, reassuringly. "Go on with the story."

"Gleck stopped, out of breath. He turned visible again. We were in the middle of the forest at this point."

"Groundfloor is by the forest," Clory said to The Newcomer. He looked at his friends. "Since we teleported here, I thought The Newcomer could use some context."

"He really needs a name," Glor said. "Anyways, since we were in the forest already, we were pretty close to Groundfloor. But we wanted to make sure we weren't being followed."

Gleck started talking, "I told Glor to look around. We both looked around quickly, to make sure we were alone. After we thought we were all clear, we started walking this way. We heard a loud noise. A stray fireball came flying near us and landed just in front of us."

"Just then, Gleck and I saw another hologram projection! It blipped on and off this time. It was weird. Like it was out of range, or the signal was jammed. Anyways, it appeared right in front of us. And it said, 'The Destroyer has arrived! The Destroyer is here! Find The Destroyer!' and POOF! It was gone again!"

"After that, we walked for maybe five minutes. And that's when we stumbled our way down here," Gleck laughed, that annoying laugh.

Glor continued the story, "We got through the three puzzles that Clory set up to make sure no unwanted people find the Groundfloor! I still don't know why he's here." Frowning, Glor looked at The Newcomer. "Clang, clang, clang!" Glor said, "The secret code that everyone knows about now! That's when Gleck, turning invisible, thought he'd try to sneak up on you guys."

"I thought it might be funny!" Gleck said.

"Hilarious," Trolk said. "The entire world may have turned on us, so let's scare the only friends we can trust. Good one, Gleck." She rolled her eyes.

Glor said, "You're no fun, Trolk."

"Is that when you tripped, fell towards the pots on the wall, knocked them off the wall and then you turned visible again, ashamed, on the ground?" The Newcomer said.

"That was implied!" Glor looked at him. "He states the obvious a lot, doesn't he?"

"She really doesn't like me," The Newcomer said.

Just then, a flaming fiery rock came flying through the door of the Groundfloor.

23

Everyone backed away from it, and before they could react any further, a hologram like creature appeared in front of the fiery rock.

"The Destroyer is here. The Destroyer must be destroyed before it's too late!"

"Hey, guys?" The Newcomer said. "That fiery rock is ticking! We better get out of here!"

The hologram looked directly at them and started counting down. "Five... four... three... two..."

Chapter 4
Frozen

"STOOOOOOOP!" Glor yelled. She closed her eyes, expecting nothing but demise, and doom.

Nothing.

Glor opened her eyes. Everything had stopped. Everything. "Clory?" she looked at Clory, who seemed to be frozen. "Gleck? Trolk? What is happening?"

She looked and saw that all her friends had frozen. The fireball still stood in the middle of the room, but it too had frozen. As did the hologram creature.

"What have you done?" Glor heard someone say. She looked over to see The Newcomer. He apparently had not been frozen.

"Of course," Glor said, annoyed, "Of all the people to not get frozen in this room, I got stuck with you."

"I could say the same thing!" The Newcomer said. "What did you do to them?"

"What do you mean? I did nothing to them!" Glor stared at The Newcomer. "Who are you? Where did you come from?!" she demanded.

"Look," The Newcomer said, "I don't remember anything before today. I think we should concentrate on getting everyone out of here safely. What did you do, freeze time?"

"What?"

"Everyone has superpowers here, it seems," The Newcomer continued, "but no one ever told me what your powers are."

"I don't have powers!" She frowned. "Are you happy?! Now you know!"

"Why don't you have powers? That doesn't make any sense."

"You don't have powers either, Newcomer. Unless it was, in fact, you that froze time."

Confused, The Newcomer looked around the room. The hologram creature started to move. It moved its face to look directly towards The Newcomer and Glor.

"Yeah, I think we better get out of here," The Newcomer said.

Glor ran over to Clory and tried to move him, then to Gleck and Trolk. Nothing. The hologram creature seemed to be regaining strength. It started to speak.

"The Destroyer. Must. Be. Destroyed." It flickered on and off a couple times and then vanished into thin air. The glowing fireball stopped glowing. After five seconds of confusion, Trolk, Gleck and Clory started to move.

"EVERYBODY RUN!" Gleck screamed.

Clory was about to teleport himself and Trolk to safety, when The Newcomer spoke up. "Everyone, look!"

They all stared at the now non-fiery rock. Standing in the middle of the room was a rock. Just that. A big, boulder sized rock.

"What just happened?" Clory asked, confused.

Gleck walked towards the rock. "Be careful, Gleck!" Trolk scolded him, "It may not look dangerous, but we don't know what is going on!"

"Ask Glor," The Newcomer said, in a somewhat mocking voice.

"Glor?" Trolk said. "What just happened here?"

"I don't know!" Glor cried. "Time just froze or something!"

Clory stared at her. "What did you just say?"

"Time, froze," Glor said. "The hologram counted down to two, and I yelled stop. And everything stopped. Everything. I tried to wake you guys up. But I don't think freezing time was my doing. I think The Newcomer had something to do with it. I… I don't have powers." Glor frowned.

"Me neither!" The Newcomer said. "But before you guys came to, the hologram creature started to come to. He looked at Glor and me and said once again, 'The Destroyer. Must. Be. Destroyed.' He then flickered in and out, and ultimately vanished. The fiery rock started to lose its glow, and then you guys all woke up. Time started again."

Clory looked concerned. "Glor, I thought you didn't have powers."

"I don't!" said Glor. "It's The Newcomer!"

Gleck stared at the rock, then looked at Clory. "Wait," he said. "Everything was frozen, except The Newcomer, Glor and eventually, the hologram creature, right? So that would make me think that the powers would have come from one of those three."

"Really, Gleck?" Glor huffed. "You have known me for three weeks. This Newcomer is here for what, three hours, and you take HIS side?!"

"No!" Gleck exclaimed. "I'm trying to figure this out!" He stared at the rock again.

"You've only known Glor for three weeks?" The Newcomer asked.

Clory sighed. "She is the newest one in our friend group, yes."

The Newcomer looked at her, then at Clory. "Then how do you know anything about her? What if she is this 'Destroyer' you keep talking about?"

Glor was furious. She yelled, "Seriously?! YOU COME OUT OF NOWHERE INTO OUR LIVES AND START ACCUSING ME OF--"

"Calm down!" Clory said to Glor. "Everyone, calm down!"

"NO!" Glor screamed. "I PROVE MYSELF EVERY DAY! YOU, YOU, NEWCOMER. I AM SO SICK OF YOU JUST THINKING YOU'RE ALLOWED TO COME HERE AND START ACCUSING ME OF STOPPING TIME! HOW DARE YOU?!"

The room started to shake. Clory looked at Glor. "Glor, that's enough!"

Glor stared directly at The Newcomer. "GO AWAY!" she screamed. "NEWCOMER! JUST. GO. AWAY!"

The Newcomer vanished from their sight.

Chapter 5
Chance Meetings

The Newcomer found himself alone, outside, in a forest.

"What just happened?" he thought.

He started to walk around until he heard a noise by a nearby tree.

"Hello?" he said. "Who's there?!"

"I could ask you the same thing!" a voice said.

The Newcomer stared towards the direction he heard the voice. Suddenly, he heard someone behind him. He turned around quickly. "I demand you tell me who you are!" The Newcomer suddenly had the courage he lacked two minutes prior.

"Maybe you should find out who you are before you find out who I am!" the voice said. "Do you want to know who you are?"

"Of course I do!" The Newcomer said. "But how do I find out who I am?!"

"Isn't that easy?" the voice said. "Just remember!"

"Just, remember? Don't you think I've tried that already?!"

"Have you?"

Just then, The Newcomer appeared back with Clory, Gleck, Trolk, and Glor, back at the Groundfloor.

"So sorry about that," Clory said to The Newcomer. "Glor, I think you have something you need to say to The Newcomer."

"I'm so sorry that I made you vanish. Whatever," Glor said, unapologetically.

"Where did you go?" Gleck asked.

"I'm not sure." The Newcomer said. "Glor sent me to--"

"He's still blaming me for all of this!" Glor said, annoyed.

Gleck started to speak, "You have to admit--"

Clory interrupted him, "Where were you, Newcomer?"

"In a forest," he said. "Maybe outside the Groundfloor? I've never been outside the Groundfloor."

"What happened while you were gone?" Trolk asked.

"There was a voice," he said. "I thought it was coming from in front of me. Then, behind me. I was trying to find out who was there."

Clory was curious. "What did the voice say?" he asked.

"It told me to find out who I was before trying to find out who it was," The Newcomer said. "It told me to remember."

"Remember what?" Gleck asked, before anybody else could.

"I have no idea! Maybe, who I am? I have no memories before today."

"See?" Glor interrupted. "Isn't THAT concerning? It probably is him with these powers! Not me!"

"You speak and things happen!" The Newcomer said, angrily. "How is this so complicated?!"

Glor looked away from him, then at Trolk. "Trolk, I want to go somewhere else. Can we go outside?"

Trolk looked at Clory, who nodded. "We'll be careful out there," Trolk said.

"At the first sign of any fireballs, anything weird at all, come back inside. Don't go too far," Clory advised.

Glor and Trolk walked outside.

The Newcomer looked at Gleck and Clory. "How do you all know each other? How did you all meet?"

Clory looked over at the rock, that still seemed dormant. Empty. "I guess we're okay to talk, just for five minutes. Then we must figure out our next move. Sit down, Newcomer. Let me tell you how I met my friends."

"You met me first!" Gleck said.

"Yes, about ten years ago, I met Gleck," Clory started the story. "I had been on my own for a while. Life on this planet is normal, usually. You know, when The Destroyer isn't at our doorstep. I had a normal life. A job. I even had a girlfriend." Clory sighed. "I miss her."

"What happened to her?" The Newcomer asked.

"She left the planet," Clory said, saddened.

"Left?"

"She got a job offer on a planet three light-years away. But enough about her. I was just living my life, alone. I didn't want anything to do with anybody. I just wanted to go to work, go home, and live a life of solitude. I started studying my planet's history. I found out a lot about the Elders and The Destroyer.

Though The Destroyer was about ten years away at that point, I figured I should know my enemy. My planet's enemy."

"That's when he met me!" Gleck said. "We worked at the same place. I noticed his interest in the Elders and The Destroyer when I saw him reading an old book about our planet one time, during a break at work."

"We started talking about our planet's history, and our mutual interest and fascination did the rest," Clory said. "We've been friends ever since!"

"Our place of work may have changed buildings since we met that day, but our friendship has remained constant throughout all the changes life throws at us," Gleck added.

"I personally miss the old building we worked at," Clory admitted. "There was something special about it."

"How'd you meet Trolk?" The Newcomer asked.

Just then, the guys heard someone scream. Trolk and Glor came running back inside.

"Clory!" Trolk said. "Come outside, quickly!"

They all ran outside, to see twelve hologram creatures, and an enormous fiery rock floating high in the sky.

Chapter 6
The Holograms

Clory looked up at the fiery rock, then down at the holograms. "What do you want?" he demanded.

"The Destroyer must be destroyed!" they all said, in unison.

"Who is The Destroyer?" Clory asked the holograms, not expecting much of an answer.

All the holograms turned and looked at everyone in front of them. Their eyes fixated, however, on The Newcomer.

"Destroy The Destroyer!" they screamed. The fiery rock started plummeting towards them. However, it stopped just twenty-five feet before smashing into everyone. The holograms started to walk towards The Newcomer.

"I have no powers!" he yelled. "How am I The Destroyer? What would I possibly want to destroy?!"

The holograms stopped. They looked at each other. Then back at The Newcomer. One hologram walked right towards The Newcomer. Clory, Gleck, and Trolk were ready to help him if need be. However, Glor just watched, wondering what was about to happen.

"Newcomer?" the hologram said. He had a device in his hands. It was square. Half gold and half silver. He scanned The Newcomer with it. "Born on unknown planet. Time spent on current planet, five hours. Age thirty-five. What planet are you from?"

"He doesn't remember!" Clory said. The hologram turned to Clory. Before anybody could react, he scanned Clory. "Clory. Born on this planet. Age, seventy-eight years."

"Seventy-eight?!" The Newcomer was shocked. "You look like you're no more than thirty!"

"I'm not seventy-eight!" Clory said. "I think I know my own age. And no one on this planet has ever lived past fifty-seven. Because of The Destroyer! I am thirty-nine, by the way, Newcomer. Thank you for the compliment."

The hologram now scanned Gleck. "Gleck. Born on this planet. Age thirty-nine."

"Sounds right to me!" Gleck laughed. "Clory and I are the same age!" he stated the obvious.

Trolk walked towards the hologram. "Go ahead, scan me. You'll find nothing special here."

The hologram looked at her. "Your courage is admirable." It scanned her. "Trolk. Born on this planet. Age thirty-seven."

Glor tried to hide behind Gleck but startled him in the process. He turned invisible and jumped out of the way, like it was a reflex to do so.

The hologram's attention quickly turned towards her because of this. She was about to run away, but the hologram already had the information on his scanner.

"Glor. Born on unknown planet. Time spent on current planet, three weeks. Age unknown. Are you friends with The Newcomer?"

Glor looked at the hologram in disgust and went to stand by Gleck, who had become visible again. "Sorry," Gleck said, "you scared me!"

"We have found the one we were looking for," the lead hologram said. "We will bring him with us."

Just knowing they meant him, The Newcomer was afraid, and braced himself for the worst.

The holograms started to disappear. One by one. Until only the leader remained. He started to walk away. He then turned back.

"You will come with us. And we will not harm your friends," The hologram said.

"He doesn't even know us!" Glor said. "Take him away!"

The rock that had been dormant for a while in the Groundfloor came floating outside and joined the other fiery, floating rock. Nearly a dozen other rocks appeared out of nowhere. As if they were cloaked the whole time.

The hologram looked at everyone and smiled. "I'm glad you're letting your friend go so easily. The Destroyer must be destroyed."

He disappeared, and the twelve floating rocks were now all lit up fiery red and orange.

Not ready to let The Newcomer go, Gleck, Trolk and Clory were still ready to protect him.

The twelve rocks formed a huge molten boulder looking ship. The hologram's voice could be heard clearly by all of them.

32

"Clory!" it said. "Come fulfill your destiny!"

Everyone shared a look of confusion. Clory looked at all his friends then immediately disappeared from everyone's sight.

The Newcomer, Gleck, Trolk, and Glor looked on, in shock, as the ship flew away at a speed they had never seen, with their friend, Clory.

Chapter 7
Answered Questions

Trolk immediately took charge. "Everyone, back inside the Groundfloor." Everyone listened.

"I have so many questions!" The Newcomer said.

Gleck looked concerned. "Why did they say Clory was seventy-eight? If he were seventy-eight, he would have lived through the last time our planet got destroyed. He would have been twenty-one. He would remember that."

"Why did that hologram say Glor wasn't from this planet? Why did it say she's only been here three weeks? Isn't that when you met her?" The Newcomer questioned them.

"Because I'm just like you, okay?!" Glor said, frustrated. "I appeared on this planet, out of nowhere, just like you. I don't really know who I am, where I come from, and seeing you like that just reminded me how lost I was three weeks ago. How lost I still am now."

The Newcomer wasn't sure what to say. Trying to lighten the mood, he simply asked, "How'd you get a name then?"

Glor, though frustrated, found herself trying not to smile. "I remembered my name. Who forgets their name?"

The Newcomer frowned, then looked at Gleck, who was staring straight ahead.

Trolk also noticed. "Gleck?" she said. "Are you okay?"

"I've known Clory for ten years. Now I feel like I don't know him at all."

"Because of what The Hologram creatures said?" Trolk asked. "I'm not sure they are trustworthy."

"All their other information seemed accurate," Gleck answered. "Should we even try to save him? Is he where he's supposed to be? Is he safe? Are we safe? Is The Destroyer going to end us all soon anyways? Does anything even matter anymore?"

The Newcomer looked at Trolk. "How many years have you known Clory?" he asked. "How did you meet?"

Trolk stared at him. "Is now really the time for stories?"

"Humor him," Gleck said. "I need a minute to think."

Trolk rolled her eyes. "Fine. I met Clory and Gleck at a local event."

"What kind of event?" The Newcomer asked.

"What do you think?" Trolk laughed. "A speaking event about our planet's history."

"And you attended this event too?" The Newcomer said.

Gleck laughed. "Attended! You could say that."

"I was the one speaking at the event!" Trolk laughed. "After I speak, I talk to anybody who wants to learn more. Clory, Gleck and I talked for hours after the event. That was nearly two years ago. We've been friends ever since."

Gleck smiled, as if he forgot his current worry, but just for a split second.

"Glor," The Newcomer said, "I'm sorry if I shouldn't ask, or if it is painful, but how exactly did you meet these three?"

Glor sighed in frustration.

"Maybe it will help him, or you, if you tell the story, Glor," Trolk said, reassuringly.

"Okay. All I remember is appearing out of nowhere, at a birthday party. I looked around, and everyone was singing to the birthday girl. Trolk."

Trolk smiled.

Glor continued, "I walked up to Trolk. Even though she had no idea who I was, she asked me if I wanted some cake. She asked me my name. I told her my name was Glor and asked her where I was. Before she could answer, Gleck and Clory called Trolk over to open a gift they got her."

"This necklace." Trolk pulled a necklace out of her pocket.

"Why aren't you wearing it?" The Newcomer asked.

"It reminds Glor of that first day we met her," Trolk said.

"I'm sorry," Glor said to Trolk. "You really should wear it. It's alright."

Trolk smiled and put the necklace back in her pocket. "Anyways," Trolk said, "now you know how we all met, Newcomer!"

Gleck looked at everyone and said, "I have an idea! Let's go back to where it all started!"

"Where you held the party?" Glor asked.

"Or where you met me?" Trolk said.

"No," Gleck looked determined, "where I met Clory. We have to go to the building we worked at ten years ago. I don't know why, but we have to go there."

Chapter 8
The Forest

"Gleck," Trolk asked, "didn't your work move from that old building to a newer one a couple of years ago?"

"Yes," Gleck said, "but the building is still there. After they shut that building down, I guess nothing really became of it. They were going to tear it down last year and build a completely new structure, but demolition on the old abandoned building was suddenly halted the exact same day it was scheduled. Still don't know why."

"You have superpowers," The Newcomer said. "Why haven't you checked into this sooner?"

"There was really no need to," Gleck admitted.

Trolk looked around at the Groundfloor and said, "I guess we better leave this old place for now and see if we can make our way to the abandoned building!"

"What a speech!" Glor laughed. "But are you sure it's safe to go to this old abandoned place?"

"Not at all!" Gleck said seriously. "But are we even safe here anymore?"

Everyone finally agreed, Trolk leading the charge, Gleck following behind, then Glor, then The Newcomer.

They simply walked out the front door. They figured those fiery rock wielding hologram creatures already had what they needed, apparently that was Clory. So at least they wouldn't be waiting for them outside. But with all the uncertainty, and all the talk of The Destroyer basically at their doorstep, they were ready for anything.

It was a boring, eventless walk for about thirty minutes. Until The Newcomer found himself in a familiar place. "Déjà vu," he said.

"What?" Trolk asked.

"He said, days are through," Gleck added.

"No," Glor said, "he said Déjà vu. It's the feeling that one has lived through an event that is currently happening."

"How... do you know that?" Gleck asked.

"I don't know." Glor said, confused.

"Do you guys hear that?" The Newcomer asked.

"Hear what?" Trolk asked.

"I think I do!" Glor said.

"I don't hear anything!" Gleck said, wishing he had.

"Glor," The Newcomer asked, "what do you hear?"

"'Remember.' That's all it's saying. 'Remember. Remember.'"

The Newcomer heard the same thing.

"When Glor yelled at me earlier and told me to go away, I appeared here, in this forest. There was this voice that Glor and me are currently hearing. It told me to remember."

"Remember what?" Trolk asked.

Just then, Glor became startled when she thought she saw something. She quickly yelled, "Wait! Everybody wait! I need to concentrate!"

Everyone stopped moving, except for her and The Newcomer.

"Glor, did time stop again?"

"I don't know what's happening," Glor admitted. "I'm sorry for sending you here if it was me. I'm not convinced it was, but I don't know."

"REMEMBER!" The voice said, loudly. It seemed to be coming from every direction.

"Glor, do you need to remember anything?"

"Besides my entire life before three weeks ago, no, I'm good," she said, sarcastically. "Why don't you remember your name? Maybe that will help."

"How could remembering my name help anybody but me?" The Newcomer said. "My name is Bob!" he yelled, confidently.

"Seriously?" Glor said.

"Of course not!" The Newcomer sighed. "How am I supposed to just remember something?"

"Just, try!" Glor said.

"REMEMBER! REMEMBER! REMEMBER! REMEMBER!" The voice was echoing the entire forest, until The Newcomer finally yelled out, "I CAN'T REMEMBER!" The voice stopped, for maybe a moment.

Out of nowhere, a humanoid figure appeared in front of Glor and The Newcomer. "Why don't you remember?" it asked. "You need to remember!" It was basically pleading with them at this point. "Please!" It disappeared.

"Do you remember anything?" Glor asked. "It was looking at you!"

"How could you tell?! It didn't even have a face!" The Newcomer cried.

"Trolk? Gleck? Come back!" Glor said.

"I think it only works when you're angry," The Newcomer guessed.

"I'm still not convinced it's me!" Glor scolded him. "What is the meaning of this? Why do I remember my name and you don't? If we both appeared here the same way, are we from the same place?"

"Remember…" The Newcomer started to think.

He was interrupted by Glor, "Newcomer. Look." In front of them, was what looked like another rock. It was like the rock they encountered earlier, after it had become dormant. Possibly a spaceship, or part of a spaceship. Glor walked towards it in curiosity. Forgetting they were still frozen, Glor yelled, "Gleck, Trolk, come over here!"

Without missing a beat, Gleck and Trolk came to and walked over to the dormant rock.

The four of them stared at it, unsure of what they should do next.

Chapter 9
The Rock

"Okay, what did we miss this time?" Trolk said, knowing she and Gleck had been frozen. "You have got to stop doing that!" she joked, looking at Glor, who wasn't amused.

Gleck stared at the rock. "They all look similar," he said.

"They are rocks," Glor said.

The Newcomer had been staring at the rock the entire time, trying to make sense of anything.

"Glor?" he said. "Look at this!"

Glor looked where he was pointing. To her shock, there was something scratched into the side of the rock. Just two words. "Find Glor."

"What does this mean?!" Glor cried.

Gleck stared at the rock. He looked at Trolk. Then at Glor and finally at The Newcomer.

The Newcomer stared at the words. Without even thinking about it, he took Glor's hand and touched the message. Glor looked at The Newcomer, and also without thinking, she too put her hand on the rock. Instantly, what appeared to be a door on this huge rock opened. The Newcomer quickly let go of Glor's hand, as if he regretted taking it in the first place.

"So sorry," he said to Glor, "I don't know what came over me."

Confused about everything, Glor decided to say nothing in return.

Gleck and Trolk stared at the rock, and the door. "Is this your ship?" Gleck asked.

Trolk looked at Gleck with wide eyes in disapproval.

"Someone had to ask!" Gleck said.

Trolk wanted to go into the ship, but instead, she looked at The Newcomer and said, "Maybe it would be best if you or Glor went and checked this out. I love adventure. But I have no idea what this is."

"It's weird," Gleck laughed.

Before anybody could say anything else, The Newcomer had stepped into the rock. Inside, was a chair, a bunch of controls and a viewing screen. He quickly sat down on the chair. He pressed a button and heard a familiar voice.

"Hello! Hello! If this message is being played, you need to listen up. You need to listen! We encountered a problem flying by this planet. We are merely travelers. We mean no harm. This planet seems to be headed for collision with another planet. We tried to turn our ship around, but we were too late. The planet pulled us down towards it. After careful consideration, we, as a crew, decided to split up the ship, as it was designed this way for emergencies. Each crew member will take an escape pod and hopefully land safely on this planet. Unfortunately, there are not enough escape pods for everyone, as we have picked up a few new crew mates along the way these last few months. Some of you will travel in pairs so everyone has a chance of survival. Once we have all landed, we will find each other and unite. We must act carefully, quickly, and accordingly. Our ship will break up into twenty-four pieces. Twenty-four rocks. We are all aware of the consequences and sacrifices about to be made. Some of us will make it out of this one alive, but I fear not all of us will. Whatever awaits us, I, the captain, am giving this final order. You will all look out for each other. You will all find each other. And we will, to the best of our abilities, try and survive this one. I'm uploading this message to every escape pod. With an additional, more personal message to follow, for each individual escape pod. Godspeed, my beloved crew." The message ended.

The Newcomer turned around. He saw Glor standing there. "Glor, did you hear that?"

"Yes," she said. "Play the other message."

The Newcomer tried to hit the button again. Nothing. He tried to hit other buttons. Nothing.

Outside the ship, the rock had started glowing, just a little bit.

"That voice sounded so familiar. And I think I know why. I think that was my captain! And this, this must be my ship!" He started to cry. "Glor, who am I?"

Glor wasn't sure what to say, except, "This ship does look so familiar. He said some had to travel in pairs. What… what if… I don't even want to say it. But I have to. What if this was our escape pod?"

Taken aback, The Newcomer stared at Glor in confusion, and for the first time, he unintentionally just looked into her eyes. "I remember…" he said softly.

"Hey guys?" Trolk said. She and Gleck were standing just outside the ship. "The rock is glowing. And not to break up whatever this is but I think I may have another more pressing reason why that voice sounded familiar."

Gleck agreed with her. Trolk continued, "The voice of your captain, that was the exact same voice of the lead hologram. The hologram that took Clory."

The Newcomer literally fell off the seat he was sitting in, in shock. He must have hit a few buttons during this because a message started playing. It was the same voice.

"To Glor and Quo. I'm sure you two of all people will somehow survive. Quo. One of my first crew members. And Glor, one of my newest crew members. Somehow you two have become remarkably close friends in a matter of months. Godspeed you two. Save us all."

Glor looked at The Newcomer. "Quo?" she asked.

"That's what I remembered," he said. "That's my name. That's me he was talking about. Hello, Glor." Turning to look at Gleck and Trolk, he said enthusiastically, with tears in his eyes, "Hello. It is very nice to meet you. My name is Quo!"

Chapter 10
Splitting Up

"I am so glad you finally have a name," Gleck admitted, as him and Trolk walked onto the ship, "but why does your captain sound exactly like the evil hologram leader that took Clory away from us? Also, I believe what your captain was describing, all of the escape pods coming apart from the ship? Yeah, I think half of your ship found each other and reassembled. We witnessed that earlier today too. I'm not sure what the deal is here, but I'm starting to worry."

"Gleck," Quo assured him, "I promise. We mean you no harm."

Glor agreed. "I'm not sure what's going on with all of that, but we'll find that out soon enough!"

Trolk and Gleck walked closer to the consoles and the chair. They were taking in the wonder of this small ship. Four people were inside an escape pod ideally made for one. It was roomier than you might think, but after being there for a minute Gleck was ready to get off the escape pod. Trolk followed behind him.

Glor heard a small noise, but looking around, she didn't see what had made the noise.

Now off this small ship, Gleck was trying to feel better, but he just felt like he should get away from there altogether. "Hey, I still need to get to that abandoned building. Trolk, maybe we should leave these two here and--"

Trolk interrupted him, "Gleck, I was kind of thinking the same thing."

"Do you still want us to come with you?" Glor said, excitedly, now looking out the door of the ship.

Trolk looked at the still glowing rock, at Quo and finally at Glor. "I'm sorry. I think Gleck needs it to be just us two."

Confused, Glor watched as Gleck and Trolk walked away from them. "I hope they find the building." She looked back at Quo, then noticed something on the floor of the ship, glowing. "Quo!"

"What is it?" Quo asked.

"I think Trolk dropped this!" She picked up the necklace Clory and Gleck had given Trolk for her birthday just three weeks before. "Hey, was it glowing before?"

Quo and Glor stared at the necklace. Glor ran outside to call for Trolk, but they were long gone by now. She looked back at the ship and noticed something weird. "Quo, come out here!"

Quo, though he didn't want to leave the pod, ran outside. "Is that…?"

They stared at the rock and the necklace, as they seemingly glowed in unison. As the light outside the pod went dim and turned brighter, the necklace itself did the exact same thing.

"That is so weird and beautiful!" Glor said.

"Should we follow Gleck and Trolk?" Quo asked.

Before she could answer, their gaze was turned upward as another fiery rock like escape pod came hurtling towards them. "Into the pod!" Quo yelled. She put the necklace in her pocket.

He and Glor went running back on to the ship and closed the door. Quo turned on the viewing screen to watch the oncoming rock. It landed no more than twelve feet away from them, causing their pod to shake. After it completely landed, Quo and Glor waited a minute to see if anybody would come off of this pod. After no one did, they got out of their pod to look closer at this one.

"Is that one of our friends?" Glor asked.

"I don't know," Quo said. "But things are starting to make more sense."

"What do you mean?"

"No one was ever hurtling fiery rocks at us!" he exclaimed. "Our ship has been breaking up and falling into this atmosphere for nearly a month! I suppose some of us just landed more quickly than others."

"If we were in this same pod, why did I make it out three weeks before you? That still doesn't add up," Glor said.

"Think of it this way," Quo said. "These were made to hold one passenger. One. So when we were both crashing in this pod, it tried to sustain two life forms. When we crashed, maybe it revived you, but it took a while to save me. You must have stumbled out of the ship and found your way to Trolk's birthday party."

44

"Speaking of that, what is up with this necklace?" Glor asked.

"I'm not sure about that one. But I think I may be able to answer one more question," Quo said, proud of himself. "Once I found my way off the ship, I must have remembered your name. Because who else would have scratched 'Find Glor' on the side of the ship?! Everything is starting to come together now! And that makes sense. You remember your name. I guess I remembered your name too. But with the ship being designed the way it is, sustaining one life form, that must be why I couldn't remember my own name! After finally regaining my own strength, I eventually made it to Clory and his friends. And to you."

Beaming, Quo's smile quickly turned to a frown.

The other pod's door opened and what he saw made him weak. There were three passengers just inside, by the door, blocking the entrance, but none of them were moving. Quo looked closer, and gasped.

"CLORY?!?!"

Chapter 11
Scanning for Answers

Glor looked inside the pod and saw Clory. "Wait, who are the other two passengers?" she asked.

Getting closer to one of them, Quo flipped it over and jumped back. "What in the world?!"

"Quo, that's... that's the lead hologram!"

"But, if that's the lead hologram... Glor, does he look familiar to you?"

"I'm not sure. Why?"

"Because if that was in fact the lead hologram, and he had the same voice as our captain, wouldn't that make this our captain?!"

Taken aback by this, Glor looked at the third body. "These pods were made for one passenger," Glor said. "We barely survived with the two of us. Who, knowing anything about our technology would allow THREE people on one of these?!"

"Maybe, maybe whoever was flying this one didn't know anything about our technology. Clory. Clory! I need you to wake up!" Quo said, trying to move him. He wouldn't move.

Stepping around the bodies, Quo went inside the pod, followed by Glor. Inside, there was a bunch of sparking and loose wires. "Be careful," Quo said to Glor, "this doesn't look good."

Looking closer at everything, Quo noticed a difference in the controls on this ship, like they had been modified or changed. He looked at the chair, which was quite similar to the one on his pod, but there were more buttons on the arms of the chair. Quo sat down in the chair. He pressed a button on this new looking control panel and heard a voice. "THE DESTROYER MUST BE DESTROYED!" it said. Quo jumped.

Glor thought she saw something outside, so she slowly peeked out the pod door. "Quo? Hit that button again!"

He obliged. Glor saw a hologram appear outside. It said, "THE DESTROYER MUST BE DESTROYED! DESTROY THE DESTROYER!"

"Quo?" she said. "Try some other buttons!"

Pressing other buttons, Glor gasped when she saw a hologram of Quo himself, standing outside.

"Glor!" the hologram said. "What do you see now?"

"I see... you! Standing out here."

"That is amazing!" Quo was excited. "Even though I'm sitting, it is projecting a hologram of me standing?!"

"I guess so..." Glor laughed. "But is that what we should be focused on right now?"

Quo laughed, then pressed another button. "What is happening now, Glor?" Glor heard a different voice this time. But a familiar one.

Glor turned back into the pod. "Quo. What did you just do?!" she said, frantically.

"I hit this button and started talking! Why?"

"You just sounded like the lead hologram. Like the voice that was recorded on our message on our pod! Like, The Captain!"

Shocked, Quo realized, "So that guy was using our captain's voice?! We have to tell Gleck and Trolk!"

"Does this pod have a message?" Glor asked, walking back towards Quo. "If all the pods had a message, maybe we can find out whose pod this is!"

As they were pressing buttons that weren't familiar to either of them, Glor reached into her pocked and pulled out the necklace. "Where did Clory and Gleck get this necklace?" she asked.

Looking on the ground, Quo noticed something. "Glor! Look!" He got out of the chair and picked something up off the ground.

"That's the device that was used to scan us!" Glor said.

"And it apparently works via hologram!" Quo exclaimed, as they were all scanned by the hologram with this device. This square silver and gold device.

"Wait a minute..." Quo had an idea. He walked over to the bodies that were on the floor, and said to Glor, "Let's find out about our friends over here!"

He looked at Clory, the lead hologram, and the third body. He decided to scan the lead hologram's body first. He pressed a button that was nearly hidden on the device.

The device sparked a little, and then like a computer screen, loaded up the details. Quo stared at it in disbelief.

He read out loud, "'Smedge. Born on this planet. Age seventy-eight.'" He looked at Glor. "But how is that possible, if The Destroyer comes every fifty-seven years?"

He turned to Clory. "Let's make sure this is our Clory." He scanned him. "'Clory. Born on this planet. Age seventy-eight.' He is the same age as this Smedge fellow? But he said he was thirty-nine."

Confused, Glor said, "Scan that last body."

"Wait," Quo said. "Whenever this device scans someone from this planet, it recognizes them. That means that this Smedge fellow was just using our captain's voice."

"That doesn't make sense! He was using the captain's voice, but his own body to project the hologram?"

Still confused, Quo finally scanned the third body.

"'Zot. From unknown planet. Time spent on current planet: three weeks. Age fifty-seven. Captain of ship 'The Boulder''"

"Captain Zot!?" Glor exclaimed.

"Captain Zot," Quo agreed. "Glor, I believe we just found Clory, the captain of our ship and possibly the one behind all of this."

Just then a few sparks started to fly from the control panel, and a message finally started to play from the pod. It was the same voice the lead hologram, apparently named Smedge, had stolen. The voice of Captain Zot.

48

Chapter 12
Zot

"This message is a message to myself. Thirty-nine of my crew members have hopefully made it safely to this planet. Though I didn't agree, the crew insisted I take a pod for myself. I tried to share a pod with someone so someone else had a better chance of survival, but the crew held a united front on the matter. Flattering, I must say. They said I still needed to lead them, so my safety was crucial. I really do love my crew. I have just landed, though it was a bit rough of a landing. I hope I didn't cause too much of a commotion. I'm about to open the door of my pod and step outside. Here's hoping the locals are friendly."

"Is that the end of the message?" Glor asked.

Unsure, Quo waited for a minute and then said, "I guess so."

But just as the words left his mouth, the control panel sparked, and it started to play another message from Zot. "I've been here two hours, and I've met some lovely people. I was a bit dizzy when I stepped off the pod, but I found myself crashing a birthday party!" The Captain laughed. Glor's mouth dropped open.

Zot continued, "I met this lovely fellow. And for some reason, I felt the need to give him this necklace. This necklace that has been in my family for generations. But I didn't want to crash a birthday party empty handed. So, I walked over to this fellow. He was with another fellow. I can't quite remember their names. I'm fairly sure the impact on this planet is messing with my crew and I. Something like Cory, and his friend Glock. I gave it to them, and said, 'Give this to the birthday girl. But I take no credit for this gift.' I still don't know why I gave a family heirloom to a stranger, but it just felt right at the time."

Still holding the necklace, Glor started to remember something. "Quo?" She started shaking, as the message continued.

"I've been invited to an event later," Zot said. "Something about The Destroyer. I think I'm glad we landed on this planet. Sounds like these guys could use some help. Funny, a planet of what appears to be superheroes. Everyone seems to have powers here, I found out quickly. And they might need the help of a simple, normal being. I'll be seeing Cory and Glock tonight. They are going to tell me more of this planet's intriguing history. And about this Destroyer."

They heard a weird noise come from the message. "Hello?" Zot said, still recording. "Who's there?!" Quo and Glor heard a man say, "Captain Zot. You are needed immediately." They heard another weird noise, and a thud.

"Is that it?" Glor asked. "No more messages?"

Quo pushed a couple buttons, and sighed. He then saw one of the buttons blinking. He pressed it. Lightning like energy went through the entire control panel. Quo and Glor were about to run off the pod, when they heard something start to play.

"We have taken measures out of The Destroyer's hands," The message said. They didn't recognize the voice.

"Perhaps that's the main hologram's real voice?" Quo asked.

It continued. "Modifying this ship to our own preference. We have found numerous ships like these around the city. We have captured and converted them to be used for good. For the cause. The Destroyer is coming, and we will destroy him. Clory was foolish to trust this man and his technology from the skies. As Elders, it is our duty to protect this planet from The Destroyer at all costs."

"As Elders?" Quo questioned. "Clory is an Elder?"

The message completed, "THE DESTROYER MUST BE DESTROYED!"

At that, the sparks on the ship increased, and it became dangerous to stay on the pod.

"We have to move The Captain and Clory to safety!" Glor said.

"What about him?" Quo asked.

"What about him?" Glor stared at him.

Just then, with all the commotion, The Captain started to wake up. "We really have to get out of here!" Glor said, nervously.

The outside of the ship was glowing brighter than it had been before. Glor looked at the necklace, still in her hand. "Quo, the necklace is brighter than it has been."

Looking outside, Quo saw his pod, also glowing brighter. "I think it's sending a signal?" Quo guessed. They heard movement by the door. Zot had stood up. Clory started to wake up too. As did Smedge. Confused, everyone just looked around at each other for a split second. At once, there were loud noises that filled the sky.

Everyone stumbled off the pod and looked up, to see a bunch of the rock looking pods up in the sky.

"Nineteen, twenty, twenty-one, twenty-two..." Quo said, in shock. "They are all here!"

Quo looked around. Glor took his hand. Clory backed away from Smedge. Zot looked at everything and said, "My ship! Where is my crew?!"

Smedge smiled and said, in a loud voice that was his own, "THE DESTROYER MUST BE DESTROYED!"

Chapter 13
Reinforcements

"You all landed safely?!" Captain Zot cried, looking at Quo, Glor and then at the twenty-two floating rocks.

Smedge looked at The Captain and said, "They are all under my control, Zot, as were you these past three weeks."

The Captain looked at Smedge, unknowingly. "Three weeks? What have you done? Who are you?!"

"Captain," Smedge said mockingly, "I slowly found and captured all these ships and the crew on them. Well, all except for those two." He pointed at Quo and Glor. "They aren't under my control. Yet."

Clory looked at Smedge, then at Quo.

"Clory, you're an Elder?" Quo looked upset.

"Of course not!" Clory said. "I'm not nearly old enough to be an Elder!"

Smedge started laughing.

Clory looked at him. "What are you laughing at?!"

"Oh, nothing," Smedge stared at him. "Seriously, even I'm amazed at my power."

"Your power?" Clory asked.

"No matter," Smedge continued. "The Destroyer must be destroyed!" Laughing, he looked at Clory again. "The look on your face. Oh, that look."

Clory started to remember something.

"Go ahead, Clory, remember it all!" Smedge smiled. "I'll allow it."

Memories rushed into Clory's head like a whirlwind, knocking him over. "I… don't understand."

"Come on, Clory, try a little!" Smedge sighed. "Fine. I'll tell you. Brother."

Clory jumped up at that word and remembered everything he had forgotten. "My name is Clory. I am seventy-eight years old…"

"The fake memories. The backstory! Exquisite!" Smedge laughed. "Your girlfriend got a job offer on another planet. That was my favorite part. Especially after what happened to father."

Clory growled, "Smedge, why are you doing this?!"

Quo stared at this all, in amazement. "You two are brothers?!"

"Oh, more than that, my friend," Smedge smiled. "Us two, Clory and I, are in fact, the Elders!"

Now believing it all, Clory stared at Quo and Glor. "Where are Gleck and Trolk?" he asked.

"Why should we trust you anymore?" Glor asked. "You have been lying ever since we met you!"

Quo added, "Ever since you met Gleck ten years ago!"

"Oh, you fools!" Smedge said, "Not that any of this frivolous business matters, he wasn't lying. He was under my mind control."

"For ten years?!" Quo exclaimed.

Clory looked uneasy, as Smedge laughed. "Twelve actually! But who's counting?! Mix that with all the real memories you have made over those years. But enough of this!" Smedge demanded. He looked up at the rock ships, that were all under his control, and said, "Troops, deploy!"

This time, not as holograms, but the real bodies themselves, all appeared from off each pod. "My crew!" Captain Zot cried.

The other thirty-seven of his crew members faced The Captain, Clory, Quo, Glor, and Smedge.

Smedge looked at them, and said once again, "THE DESTROYER MUST BE DESTROYED!"

"WHO IS THE DESTROYER?!" Clory demanded. "Brother, start making sense!"

He halted the now advancing crew. "Do I have to spell everything out for you?" He shook his head. "No wonder I am the stronger brother." He then pointed at Zot. "Look at him. Does he not look familiar to you?!"

Clory stared at him.

"Look into his soul, brother," Smedge said.

Clory's heart nearly stopped. "Father?!" he gasped.

Quo spoke up quickly, "Okay, now even I know that makes no sense," he demanded. "I scanned him earlier with that square device. He's only fifty-seven years old."

"Fifty-seven years old?" Clory said.

"Does that number sound familiar to you, brother?" Smedge growled. "The Destroyer comes every fifty-seven years!"

"But that doesn't…" Clory was interrupted by Smedge.

"Every fifty-seven years. Works quite good for a legend, don't you think?"

Zot looked around, confused.

"Wait, is it not true?" Glor said.

"Why are you all so, uneducated?" Smedge demanded. "Of course it's true! Fifty-seven years ago, The Destroyer came."

"Every fifty-seven years this happens?" Glor asked.

"How should I know?! I'm only seventy-eight!" Smedge said, annoyed. "But the thought of this happening every fifty-seven years should be enough, more than it just happening once, it should have been enough to push everyone to fight back! It wasn't. So, I wrote books. I stayed in hiding. I spread the word. The end was coming. Not many wanted to believe me. Not many wanted to care. They just didn't want to break away from their everyday, mundane, lives! Then eventually, I had to start telling everyone that The Destroyer was coming! For YEARS I have been trying to stop this from happening! But only some wanted to fight back!" Smedge was getting furious. "Do you know how hard it would be to control a whole planet?! No. I needed something smaller scale. Since all of this pathetic race didn't want to listen to their Elders, I had enough. Some were smart enough to join the cause, but it was never enough. Three weeks ago, some of my followers were at this party for one called Trolk. They followed Captain Zot back to his ship, and the rest is history. Still not enough people, but this technology that Zot, our beloved father, brought back to us, could maybe be enough!"

"I'm still lost over here!" Quo cried. "How is fifty-seven-year-old Captain Zot, from MY planet, the one who recruited me on this mission of exploration, how in the world is he your father?! And when I scanned him with that device earlier, it didn't recognize him as being from this planet! Why wouldn't it?!"

Clory looked upset. "Oh no…"

Smedge in frustration, yelled, "WE ARE COLLIDING WITH ANOTHER PLANET. AND IT IS ALL BECAUSE OF THE EVENTS YOU SET IN MOTION FIFTY-SEVEN YEARS AGO, BROTHER!"

Chapter 14
Flashback

"You know what?" Smedge said. "I have time. Not too much time. But since it's all about to end, let's take a minute, shall we?" He looked at Clory. "No? You don't want to tell them? Good. What am I doing? I'm a telepath. Here, everyone, here is the story of how Clory destroyed everything!" He looked at Zot. "Yes, you too, father! You get to remember your other life!"

Smedge telepathically sent the story of what happened on this planet fifty-seven years ago, simultaneously, to Quo, Glor, Zot, and Clory.

[Fifty-seven years ago.]

"Brother," a twenty-one-year-old Clory said, looking at his brother Smedge, who was also twenty-one. "I don't know what we are going to do. A planet full of people with superpowers. And we are powerless without the level of space travel we would need to save everyone!"

Their father, Zot, who was still fifty-seven years old back then, looked at his sons. "I'm sorry," he said. "These last few years, as we noticed our planet heading towards another, we have tried to perfect space travel. We have had our best scientists on this project. For years. And I fear we've just wasted all of our time!"

Smedge looked frustrated. "Father. I am only twenty-one. I was going to do so much with my life. I wanted to be more than this. A fool that has lived the last years of his life in fear. Fear that I am going to die. Fear that my name, Smedge, will never be remembered."

Zot looked at Smedge. "I'm sorry, son," he said.

Clory looked at his father. "You tried your best, father. It's just, with only one perfected space pod, how in the world could we ever choose?"

"It should be me!" Smedge demanded.

"Smedge," Clory said, "we are a race of so very many. We can only choose one of us to save. Only one."

"And I SHOULD BE THAT ONE," Smedge yelled. "I DID NOT LIVE MY LIFE IN FEAR FOR IT TO JUST END LIKE THIS."

"I am so sorry, sons," Zot said again. "We had a meeting the other day, the Elders and I, and we all have chosen. We must save one. Someone who is smart and knowledgeable on our planet's history. But also, someone young enough to survive the journey. We hope there is a planet close enough to land this ship we created. But even with our best scientists, we aren't too sure what is out there, past our planet."

Smedge looked at his father. "And who did you choose, that fits that description, out of our entire race?" he said, hopeful. Him and Clory had spent their entire lives studying the planet's history. Becoming stronger in the knowledge. Speaking a lot with the Elders.

"Smedge, I'm so sorry," Zot began to say.

Smedge shook his head.

Zot continued, "Clory, you are the chosen one. Your selflessness and your knowledge combined have proved you worthy of this."

Smedge started screaming, "ARE YOU SERIOUS? I AM SELFLESS. CLORY HAS ALWAYS BEEN YOUR FAVORITE, FATHER." He knocked a chair over, and huffed out of the room, still screaming.

"Me?" Clory said, shocked. "You have chosen me?"

"Yes, my son," Zot said. "We are running out of time. Our planet is due to collide with this other planet as soon as tomorrow evening. Gather only what you need. The Elders and I have prepared a small capsule full of the planet's most historical items. You leave at daybreak. I will be there. As will the Elders and many others. Hopefully, Smedge will join us. Get some rest, son. You're going to need it."

Zot walked away, with a lot on his mind, into a small den where he usually would go to think. He sat down and looked at a picture of a woman standing with him. His wife. "Oh, my dearest," he said to the picture, "I can't believe it has come to this. It's like you knew the end was coming. Still, these last two years have been nothing but heartache without you." He tried to fight back tears. Hours went by, as Zot tried to make sure everything was ready for the final day of this planet. Some of the inhabitants of the planet just accepted this fate as what it was. The end of everything. Others tried to fight back. But really, what was there to fight, when there was no way to stop this oncoming planet?

Zot thought about the last two years, how he and the Elders had tried everything they could to stop this. How that after his wife was gone, he spent every waking second trying to figure out a solution to this problem. From combining their numerous powers, multiple times, in multiple ways, to trying to build a spaceship that could carry everyone to safety. From trying to build a strong enough structure on the planet that might survive the collision, to even praying it all away. Sadly, nothing had worked. These last hours he had seemed to last forever, but also, they were fleeting.

By the picture of his wife, was a necklace. He looked at it and smiled. He picked it up, and thought, "You used to wear this every day, my love. I miss you so much." He cried silently.

He heard a noise at the door of the den. "Father?" Clory said, as he walked into the small room. "I haven't been able to sleep. I have so much on my mind. And I have been thinking."

"We all have, son," Zot said, with tears in his eyes.

"Father, I found a way to save us all. I think we can save everyone!"

"Son," Zot said, "we have tried everything. There is no more time. Here, take this. This is perhaps the most important piece of our planet's history. At least to me and our family."

He handed the necklace to his son. "Is this, mother's necklace?" Clory cried.

"Yes, son. And she would be glad to know you have it now. Cherish it forever." His father cried.

"Father, wait. I have an idea! I know this will work!" Clory said sternly.

"Get some rest, son," Zot said. "We have all accepted this. It's okay for you to accept it too."

"But father…"

"Son. I love you." Zot nodded at his son.

Dejected, Clory left the den. He went to find his brother. Smedge had some plans of his own, however. Clory couldn't find him anywhere. He went back to his father.

"Father, have you seen Smedge?" Clory asked. He walked closer and saw that his father had finally cried himself to sleep.

Feeling uneasy, Clory knew something was wrong. He left their house and went to the first place he thought his brother would go. "I bet he went to talk to the Elders to try and change their minds. Maybe he'll help me with this new plan, though!" Clory thought.

The spaceship they had built, that could carry one passenger safely and successfully away from the colliding planets, was kept in a highly guarded laboratory. Many had tried to steal it away, thinking themselves worthy of being the one that should be saved.

Clory got to the building where the laboratory was, where he knew all the Elders were waiting by the spaceship. For the moment they would send Clory off was merely hours away now.

Walking up to a couple guards, Clory could tell something was already wrong. "Are you guys okay?" he asked. They said nothing. Having this uneasy feeling in his gut, he went running towards the laboratory where the spaceship was. Along the way, he saw guards passed out, some still standing, but they looked like they were zoned out. For nearly five minutes, as he went running through the building, every single guard he saw looked like there was something wrong with them. Like they were being controlled.

"Oh no, brother. No!" Clory went running faster. He stopped just behind his brother, who was standing outside the doors that led to the laboratory where the spaceship was. Smedge looked back at him and growled, "Stay away, brother! This is how it has to be!"

"Smedge, it's not too late! I have an idea!" Clory said, excitedly.

"I don't need your ideas, brother."

The laboratory doors swung open, and the Elders looked at Smedge and Clory.

"Hello, sons of Zot," one of them said.

Before anybody could say anything else, Smedge tried to telepathically control the Elders like he did to the guards. Smedge immediately fell to the ground.

"Smedge," another Elder said, "why are you so angry? One of your family was chosen to carry our entire heritage. Be proud of him."

"NO!" Smedge yelled. "IT SHOULD BE ME! IT WAS SUPPOSED TO BE ME!" he demanded.

Smedge was on the ground, under the Elders' control. Clory walked up to another Elder.

"Sir," he said, "I found a way to save everyone."

"Oh, Clory," the Elder said, "We have tried everything. I'm afraid we must stick to the plan at hand."

"But Elders!" Clory said, looking at all of them. "Look!" He pulled out a piece of paper from one of his pockets and handed it to an Elder. The Elder looked at it.

"Astonishing," the Elder said.

"That's what I thought!" Clory said. "I got the idea when Smedge and I were talking the other day!"

Smedge scowled. "Don't bring me in on this idea, brother, unless I get to survive in this plan of yours!"

"Brother!" Clory exclaimed. "Everyone survives!"

Smedge tried to get up, but he was still under the Elders' control.

"It is intriguing," the Elder said, "but I'm afraid there is no time for all of this." He handed the paper back to Clory. "Go, spend these final hours with your father. He needs you."

The Elders guided them out the doors of the laboratory, releasing Smedge from their control. Clory looked at his brother. "Brother, we have to do this."

Smedge snatched the paper from his brother's hands.

"I figure, instead of sending someone away from the planet, we send them around the colliding planets. As fast as we can. And with the help of the Elders, I think this could work." Clory continued, "In this scenario, everyone lives. But no one remembers. We all get a fresh start, brother."

"Let me get this straight." Smedge sneered. "Your plan to save us all, is to fly around the colliding planets, risking the life of the one in the spaceship, the only one that will carry the planet's legacy. This spaceship, along with the help of the Elders and the people of the planet, will travel so fast, that what will happen?" He couldn't make out what his brother meant on the paper.

"Sorry, brother, once I figured this plan out, I was so excited I guess my blueprints got a little confusing." Clory pointed to the blueprints. "The ship will travel so fast, time itself will move backwards. Forcing the planets away from each other. But, everyone on the planet, and whoever is in the spaceship, will also be sent through time."

"Won't that bring people back to life that are gone? Do you know how time travel works?"

"I am trying to do this while two planets are about to collide. I'm not sure. That might have an effect on how this all works. It's not perfect, but neither is sending me!"

"I agree with that at least," Smedge frowned.

"I also found a planet. It is pretty far away, but after this time traveling trip, I think the ship itself might become more powerful from the energy."

"How do you know anything about planets? The Elders barely know—"

"They know more than you think," Clory interrupted him. "What do you think?"

"It's stupid," Smedge said. "But it's the only way I survive. What is the plan to make this happen?"

"I'm going to go back in there and talk to the Elders again!"

"Fool!" Smedge said. "That won't work."

"Then, you need to cause a commotion out here. I need to do this," Clory said.

Before he could finish the sentence, Smedge slammed on the doors. They opened. "What are you two still doing here?" an Elder asked.

"This." Smedge went running towards the Elder and past him. He went running around the room, screaming, which distracted all the Elders. Before Clory could say or do anything, he knew this was the only chance he would have to carry out his plan. He teleported into the spaceship and started pressing buttons on the controls. He changed the course on the ship to a pattern of ever-increasing speed around the two colliding planets. He then set the destination for the far away planet that the ship would eventually land on. He then looked around and teleported out before anyone could notice.

The Elders were furious with Smedge. "ENOUGH!" they yelled. They threw him out, and he landed by Clory, who had teleported outside the laboratory without anybody noticing.

The Elders slammed the doors. Clory smiled. "That about does it!"

"What makes you think the Elders won't check the coordinates again before they send you off?"

Clory shrugged. "I can't know everything!"

Clory and Smedge slowly walked home. "So, does this mean you and I won't exist for thirty years? If the planet is essentially going back in time, how does this all work?"

"Honestly, brother, I have no idea what to expect," Clory admitted. "We have barely perfected space travel. So, adding time travel, many things could go wrong. Different than I or we expect. Only time will tell, brother."

Clory and Smedge walked into the house and were immediately greeted by their father. "Sons," he said, "I just woke up from this weird dream."

"What happened, father?" Clory asked.

"We tried to send you away," Zot started to cry, "but we were too late! The impact of the colliding planets was greater than we ever anticipated. Your ship blew up! Our entire history was lost forever!"

"That's horrible, father!"

"We must go tell the Elders!" Zot cried.

"Father. Wait." He unfolded the piece of paper he had shown the Elders and Smedge. "Look."

Taken aback, his father looked at the paper, then at Clory, then back at the paper. "This... this is unheard of! Time travel? This is quite brilliant!"

"And best of all? It gives us another chance! It gives us more time to figure it out this next time around, to build a better ship. Father, we just need more time!"

"But son," Zot said, "how will going back in time help us if time just rewinds? We'll need to know sooner what is coming. More time is good. But just more time? Would anything change?"

Clory was saddened for a moment, then realized, "That capsule with the planet's most important history! We add a couple things to it, warning everyone of what is coming!"

"But son," Zot said, "how are you going to keep the capsule out of reach of this time rewind? If time rewinds, then these books might disappear from existence!"

Clory stared at his father. "Couldn't mother stop time?"

Zot looked down. Then back at his son. "Yes."

"You have never spoken of your powers," Clory frowned, "but I know you have them. What are your powers?"

"I... I don't..."

"Father, please, the fate of our history depends on this. The fate of everything."

"I can imitate the powers of those I love," Zot said, quickly.

"So, mother's powers, can you still imitate them?"

"Yes. No. Maybe. I don't know. I just know that when I imitate the powers of the ones I love, they are only a fraction of the powers they are based on. In other words, I'm not nearly as strong as your mother."

"But this could work?" Clory said.

"You'd have to convince the Elders..." Zot said, with a little hope.

"No, we don't." Clory smiled. "I already recalibrated the ship. And father, I think this all can actually work!"

"My dream felt so much like a reality. I think you're right, son. We can't lose everything. I think we all should get some rest. It is going to be a terribly busy day tomorrow," Zot said.

Two hours went by. Zot and his sons showed up to what would be the end of their world. Zot looked at his sons. He wanted to tell the Elders, but the thought of them carrying out the original plan and his son dying, was too much to think of. He wouldn't let that happen.

The Elders looked at Zot, Clory and Smedge. Inhabitants of the planet had gathered all around to watch this historical end.

"Bring the capsule!" an Elder yelled. The capsule with all of the planet's important history was brought forth.

"Hold on!" Zot yelled. He ran up to the capsule, opened it up, and stuck a small, loose-leaf looking book inside of it.

"What is the meaning of this?" an Elder asked.

"A little more history!" Zot smiled.

The capsule closed. They went to load it on to the ship. Clory was nervous. He didn't have much of a plan to make sure this went the way he and his family wanted it to go.

Another Elder said, "Behold, the one that is going to carry our legacy, Clory!" Clory stepped forward and went to step on the ship.

"Wait!" Smedge yelled. "It's all a lie!"

"Smedge," Zot said, "what are you doing?!"

"Neither of you are worthy!" Smedge smiled. "Oh, great Elders. These two were trying to trick you! Look. Look at the ship. It has been recalibrated. It is not on course to where you set it!"

"Smedge!" Clory screamed.

"Oh, great Elders," Smedge said, louder, "I have pretended to go along with my family. I was always going to tell you their plan. I mean, seriously. Time travel? Yes, let's travel around a couple of colliding planets so fast, that we go back in time! That makes sense! And great Elders, the plans didn't stop there! My father, Zot, I assume, was going to sustain a time bubble around that capsule with the planet's most important items. Using a phantom of my mother's powers. That book he threw in there was detailed information about this day and how it would come again! Important discoveries, a bunch of science, blah blah blah! Elders, rewinding time and sending future knowledge back seems impossible. It seems stupid. You know what is best, wise Elders. I did all of this to prove that I am worthy! I should be the one sent! It has been, and always will be, me!"

The Elders stared at Smedge. Looked at Clory, and finally at Zot. After many moments of silence, one of the Elders stepped towards Smedge. "Now that you put it that way, son, we have agreed that this in fact is the best course of action."

"Wait, what?" Smedge was dumbfounded. "Are you serious?! No! I am going on that ship!"

He went running towards the ship.

The Elders stopped him and looked at Zot. "We will carry out this plan. With one modification. Zot, you will enter the space pod."

"What? Why? No," Zot said.

"If Clory or Smedge goes," The Elders continued, "and the time traveled is more than their current age, what will become of the ship if there is no passenger on it?"

Realization came over Zot, Clory and Smedge. Still unacceptable to him, Zot said, "Is there any other way? One of you Elders! You go on the ship! If I go, will I never exist on this planet?"

The thought of this made the Elders rethink everything. They were all having conversations with each other, but no one could hear what they were saying.

"Change of plans again," The Elder said. "No time travel. Not technically. That opens up many sets of problems. This is why we originally dismissed this idea. However, the theory still somewhat stands. We do exactly as you have said, but we shield the planet from the effects of the time travel. We will essentially travel back many years, but this planet and everything on it that happened will have still happened. These many years will not be erased from our planet. However, this comes with many sacrifices. One of them being memory loss. No one will remember any of this. As far back as we go, it will all be forgotten to the mind. Any writings, however, will still exist. All of the planet's history is still written in those historical books. Everything happened. But the knowledge will not be retained in our memories. And that's not the only sacrifice to be made."

Zot looked at the ship, then at the Elders. "We've turned the tables," he said.

"Very smart," the Elder said.

Clory looked at his father. "What does that mean?"

"Everyone on the planet is safe," he said. "Instead of only one being saved, whoever goes on that ship, will be giving up their life."

"On the contrary," another Elder said, "whoever goes on that ship will be starting their life again. Everything they have done here will have mattered. It won't be erased from time. Because everything that happened still happened. But the one that goes would be living another life. Somewhere else. And they may never know of this life."

Clory looked around, uneasy.

Smedge looked around. "I'm not going. I don't want to forget who I am."

Zot stepped forward. "I'll do it."

The Elder smiled. Clory was about to argue with his father, but his father just looked at him, nodded and said, "I love you, Clory. You too, Smedge." He nodded again.

Everything started to shake. "It's now or never!" Zot yelled. He pushed the capsule off the ship. "Our history needs to stay here!" he said.

Clory went running up to his father. He handed the necklace his father had given him, back to his father. "Take mom with you," he said. Zot was about to argue, when Clory looked at him, and said, "I love you." He nodded.

Zot got into the ship. "I hope this works!" he said. The door closed. The roof in the laboratory opened. The ship looked somewhat like a rock. It flew through the roof and was on its course.

The Elders looked at Clory and Smedge. "We will not survive this," they said suddenly. "But this is how it shall be." Shocked, Clory stared at Smedge, who was staring up into the sky.

They could notice the ship getting faster and faster.

"Clory. Smedge. Everyone will forget all these years like we have said. Everyone will forget. But you two will remember. You will use this knowledge to further better our chances of success when the time comes again. Smedge. Use your powers to protect your brother and you from forgetting."

The Elders started concentrating on the shield that would form around the entire planet.

"The amount of time you have until the two planets colliding depends on Zot now. Whatever he does on that ship, will determine everything."

The Elders connected telepathically to Zot and projected his image so Clory and Smedge could see him.

The ship got even faster. Zot looked like he was in pain from the speed the ship was going.

"Elders!" Zot said. "Get ready to protect this planet!" He looked around the ship, and down at his hand. He was still holding his wife's necklace. Holding it to his heart, he yelled, "Fifty-seven years! This ship is about to go back fifty-seven years. That is the most time I can give you without disappearing from existence."

The Elders approved.

"Father, you'll revert back to a baby!" Smedge said.

"It's fine," Zot said, he could hear everything because the Elders were projecting everything back to his ship. "That planet Clory found. I'll land on it. They will find me and raise me. I'll be fine. Maybe I'll find you two again someday! Maybe," he said, hopefully.

"Father!" Clory yelled. "Use mother's powers to stop time around you! Maybe you won't revert back to a baby after all!"

"Son. I appreciate your enthusiasm, but I don't have nearly enough strength to do that. Have no fear, son. I love you." He nodded. "However, I do have enough strength to do this." He held up the necklace and stopped time only around the necklace. "This way, though everything else will revert, this won't leave me. I'll still get to keep your mother with me. Forever." And with that, the Elders lost the connection. The speed of the ship was too much to keep the connection open.

Everything started to shake, it started to get dark as the oncoming planet closed in. As fast as it got dark, however, it became light again. The other planet started moving away from their planet. Extremely fast. The Elders were straining from shielding the entire planet.

The Elders looked at Clory and Smedge. "SMEDGE. NOW!" they yelled.

Smedge put a telepathic force field around his brother and himself. They watched, as everyone else started to look confused, forgetting everything they knew. They saw the Elders start to poof out of existence. And they looked on as everything came to a sudden stop.

"I guess this is it, brother," Smedge said. He let the force field go. "Here we are, fifty-seven years in the past."

"Let's save our planet, brother!"

[Back to the present.]

"Everyone caught up?!" Smedge demanded.

They were all dazed from the memories they just witnessed. Especially Zot.

"I remember two lives now!" Zot cried. "Growing up on this planet and growing up on Quo's planet. I was told by my parents that I was found on a ship. Alone. With nothing but, that necklace!" He looked over at Glor and noticed she was holding the necklace. "I remember being obsessed with space travel for some reason. Working my way up through the ranks. Getting my own ship. Recruiting Quo. Traveling."

"I suppose I shouldn't be surprised you ended up back here, father!"

"But what did you do with all the time I gave you? Haven't you come up with a plan to stop the planets from colliding this time?!" Zot cried.

Smedge growled, "Brother became obsessed moments after we saw the Elders disappear. After everything was finished. After we had 'saved the day!'" He became more furious. "I told him we had time. To relax. It would all be fine. He was so obsessed. I couldn't take it anymore. So, I did things my way. Like I said earlier, I went into hiding. I wrote books trying to persuade everyone to fight The Destroyer!"

Clory screamed. "WE DON'T NEED TO FIGHT A DESTROYER, BROTHER. WE HAVE TO STOP A PLANET FROM COLLIDING WITH OURS!"

"And your plan was becoming incredibly similar to the last one!" Smedge yelled. "About thirteen years ago, you came to me and told me that if this didn't work out, if we didn't find

66

another way, we could do this all over again! I don't want to do this all over again! You had advanced plans. More power this time. We could do the exact same thing without all the Elders! I had heard ENOUGH. That is why I decided to start altering your memories. I didn't need you putting us through more ENDLESS YEARS leading to even MORE ENDLESS YEARS."

"You messed with my memories because you didn't want us to be in the same situation again! Look what you've done, brother! Now we are worse off!"

"No, brother. We are not. I have said this before. This is all your fault, because of your stupid plan. The Destroyer must be destroyed. Brother, I'm sorry, but you are The Destroyer. I had to stop you before you tried another of your stupid plans. Do you understand now?"

Clory stared at his brother.

Smedge yelled again, "Now where were we, troops? My crew is here. My ships are here. All under my control. Ah, yes! I remember now!" He stared at Clory, and yelled, "The Destroyer must be destroyed!"

Chapter 15
The Plan

"Brother!" Clory yelled. "What is the point of destroying me, all of us, and any of this? Once the planets collide, we will all be dead anyways!"

Smedge stared at him. "I have lived many YEARS in your shadow, brother!" He pointed at their father. "Because he and his precious Elders didn't choose ME in the first place! None of this had to happen! None of it! If you had just chosen me, sent me off, I would be out there, off this wretched planet, with our planet's legacy!"

Zot looked at him. "Son! Do you not remember? I had a dream, that your brother took that path, and ended up being destroyed with both planets! If we would have sent you, you too would have died!"

"Why were we basing our entire plan on a DREAM, father?!" Smedge demanded. "I have had more than enough of this! So, I might as well just tell you all!"

"Tell us what?!" Quo interrupted.

"No one is even talking to you, fool!" Smedge sneered. "Why are you so important to father anyways?!"

Quo looked at Zot, then at Smedge. "He was like a father to me." He sighed. "My family was not happy with me when I joined the space program. They stopped talking to me after I had made the decision to leave my planet." He started to tear up. "Zot was a better father to me than my own father. He was there for me more than my own father ever was. My family was always distant from me anyways. But joining the space force was the final nail in that coffin." He looked at Zot. "Thank you."

Zot smiled.

Smedge rolled his eyes, then laughed. "Well, father. Looks like you have failed yet another 'son'!" he said mockingly. "All of the suffering I have been put through, the never ending, unnecessary suffering, will now be upon ALL OF YOU!"

"You're going to die with us," Zot said. "You know that, right?"

"Finally! I can tell you the climax of my entire plan!" Smedge smiled. "See all those escape pods?! Don't forget, they form a huge ship. 'The Boulder', was it called?!"

Smedge pulled a small remote control out of his pocket and pressed a button.

"Your technology was so simple to control!" Smedge said, looking at Zot. "And now, it's all mine!"

All twenty-four rock pods came together, up in the sky, to form the ship, now as a whole.

"Behold, The Boulder!" Smedge laughed. "This is how I get my victory! Father, it looks like you were useful after all! You saved the day!"

"We all won't fit on that ship," Glor said, staring up at it.

"Foolish thought!" Smedge yelled. "As it should have been fifty-seven years ago, in the first place, BEFORE ALL THIS PAIN AND SUFFERING, I, SMEDGE, will get on this ship, ALONE, and fly away to safety."

Clory spoke up, "Brother, that ship can hold so many more people! Why would you do this?!"

"WHY?!" Smedge yelled. "YOU ARE SO BLIND! I WILL CARRY OUR PLANET'S LEGACY TO OTHER WORLDS WITH THIS SHIP. OTHER GALAXIES! I, SMEDGE, WILL BE REMEMBERED!"

Zot frowned and walked towards his son. "Son, it would be a shame if all of that happened. You are not worthy of any of this. Your selfish acts have proven what the Elders and I knew to be true. The legacy of this planet is not safe with you. You love yourself too much."

Upset at his father's disapproval, Smedge backed away, and said, "I already knew how you felt. But it hurts to hear you say it out loud. Goodbye, father. Goodbye, Clory. Goodbye to this entire wretched planet."

"Smedge. It's not too late," Clory said. "Let's figure something else out, brother!"

"Son," Zot said to Smedge, "you may have let us down, but there is always room for forgiveness. Stop all of this. Release everyone from your control. We'll find another way. Smedge. I love you." He nodded at his son.

Smedge just stared at his father for a moment, smiled, and then shook his head. "No. No. I am ashamed to call you my father. You should have chosen me. You should have CHOSEN ME! Let me make myself more clear. You, Clory, and you, father, are both worthy of the name 'The Destroyer'. Your actions have led me to all of this. The Destroyer must be destroyed! Along with EVERYTHING ELSE! Goodbye, traitors!"

Still holding the remote in his hand, Smedge yelled, "Troops, attack these worthless fools!"

He pressed another button on the remote and vanished on to The Boulder, alone.

Captain Zot's crew went running towards Clory, Zot, Quo, and Glor.

From The Boulder, everyone could hear a voice, now broadcasting. Smedge could be heard for miles.

"FROM THE BEGINNING, THIS IS HOW IT SHOULD HAVE BEEN. I, SMEDGE, WILL CARRY THE LEGACY OF THIS PLANET TO OTHER WORLDS. IT IS MY HONOR AND DUTY, TO TELL NO ONE OF ANY OF THIS. THIS PLANET ALONG WITH ITS HISTORY, AND ALL OF YOU, DIES HERE. IT DIES NOW. EVERYTHING DIES. AND I REGRET NOTHING!"

The Boulder's engines got louder, as the ship slowly started to speed off, into the sky. Still under Smedge's control, the thirty-seven crew members started fighting with Clory, his father and his friends. The planet started to get dark. It was time. The shadow of the other planet was coming over their planet, as the time of the planets colliding drew near.

Clory, Zot, Quo, and Glor were helpless, as they tried to fight off the thirty-seven oncoming crew members.

Chapter 16
Gloria

Clory looked at his father, at Quo, and at Glor, who were all trying to fend off these crew members that were still under Smedge's control.

They all heard yelling in the distance. Someone was calling them.

"Clory! Glor!" the voices were calling. "You'll never guess what we found!" Running into view, Clory felt hope as he saw Trolk and Gleck come running towards them.

They stopped, taking in the scene of all these people fighting with their friends.

Quo and Glor saw them standing there. "Trolk! Gleck!" they both said, fighting off the crew members.

Gleck and Trolk looked at each other, then decided to join the fight. They went running into the crowd of people. Clory said to them, "Try not to harm these people! They are under my brother's control!"

Realizing Trolk and Gleck had been gone for a while, Clory thought how confusing that statement must be.

Trolk looked at Clory. "Oh, trust me. Gleck and I are all caught up, Elder," Trolk said with a smile.

Gleck looked at Zot, then at Clory. "Is he really your father?" he asked Clory, fighting off a crew member.

"How could you possibly..."

Gleck interrupted him, "Between the old books we found at the old abandoned building we used to work at, where we met, and the wave of memories that hit us on the way back..."

Trolk smiled, as she pushed away a crew member. "We would have been here a lot sooner, were it not for your brother's interruption. Smedge broadcast those memories pretty far. Half of the planet probably knows about this now!"

Clory was about to speak, but he was interrupted when he was hit hard by a crew member and he fell to the ground.

The Boulder was now out of sight. It had been flying faster and faster away from all of them.

A crew member was standing over Clory, about to kill him. The other crew members had overtaken Trolk, Gleck, Glor and Quo. Everything, in that moment, seemed lost.

Glor looked at the necklace she was still holding on to for dear life. She looked at her friends. Concentrated. And screamed, "CREW MEMBERS, STOP FIGHTING!"

They immediately obeyed, backing away from everyone.

"Don't move!" she yelled.

They all stood there, motionless. Everyone looked at Glor.

Zot stared at Glor, and the necklace. "You remind me of her," he said.

Being the newest member of his crew, Zot didn't know much about her. "How did you do that?" he asked.

"I, I don't know. I just concentrated on what needed to be done," she admitted.

Zot stared in amazement. "Those powers, are so similar to…"

Clory interrupted him, "What planet are you from?"

Quo quickly said, "We found her on a planet about four months ago."

"I didn't belong there," she admitted. "I always felt like my home was somewhere else…"

Zot had a look of realization. He started to remember more memories of his first life.

With all the memories rushing into his head, he fell over, stood back up, and started talking.

"This is so confusing!" he cried. "But I just got flooded with memories from fifty-nine years ago."

"Fifty-nine?" Clory asked. "That's from your first life! How could you remember that?!"

"I'm not sure," Zot admitted. The necklace in Glor's hand started to glow.

"Two years before we stopped the planets from colliding last time… I can't believe this." Zot was in shock. He fell to the ground again. "The last day I saw my wife, she told me she was pregnant." He stood back up. "That was the same day… the same day we got the message from the Elders."

"What are you talking about, father?!" Clory cried.

"The Elders came to us. They knew of the oncoming collision. They had a backup plan… but no one could know about it. No one. Not even my family or the Elders themselves would be able to remember this plan if we agreed to carry it out. They came to my wife and I, Gloria?"

Glor looked at him. "Don't call me that! That's not my name!"

"No, no, not you. Gloria. The name of my wife was Gloria!" He continued, "The Elders said that the oncoming collision could wipe out everything. Everything that our planet was, is, and could be. They wanted a safety net in case everything failed. They wanted... my wife!"

"Mother?!" Clory cried. "Why would you agree to such a sacrifice?! Why did they want mother?!"

"I didn't approve! Knowing just that day that she was pregnant. It wasn't worth the risk! My wife, and future child, were so important to me, but she was also important to the Elders. Your mother was the only one in our entire race that could stop time."

"What happened to mother, father?" Clory cried.

"I think... they wanted to send her away in a small space pod."

"I thought there was only one spaceship created!" Clory yelled.

"It was a prototype. An advanced prototype. The Elders came to us and explained everything. This back up plan would ensure our planet's history would be safe. They didn't know she was pregnant. She had just found out that day... the Elders told us to think about it. Gloria would leave on this prototype ship, and if anything were to go wrong, she could stop time, and find a way out of the problem. I remember the last conversation we had..."

Zot told them the story of that final conversation.

[Fifty-nine years ago.]

Gloria walked into the den, where her husband Zot was sitting. "I think I need to do this," she said.

"But I need you!" Zot said. "Our boys need you! This little one," he put his hand on his wife's stomach, "it will need you, and me. If you leave, what if the baby's life is put in danger? Or your life? I can't lose you."

"And you won't. Because you'll figure this out on time. You'll come and get me and bring me home!"

She hugged her husband and said, "This is how it has to be. I love you." She nodded.

Zot cried. "What will I be allowed to remember?" He cried louder. "How am I going to remember to find you if the Elders wipe this from my memory? From all of our memories?"

She smiled. She took off the necklace that she had worn every day since he met her. "Keep this with you," she said, "to remember me." She winked at him.

"What about our baby?" Zot asked.

"You know I'll protect this baby with everything I am. I'd give up my life for this baby," she said.

Still unsure, he took the necklace and hugged his wife. The two of them went to a laboratory where the Elders were. She told them that she agreed to do this for them.

"After all, two years would fly by," Gloria thought. "Then surely, after we avert this crisis, Zot will find me."

The Elders looked at them. "The following knowledge we are about to give you will be permanently erased from the memories of everyone on this planet, including us, the Elders, upon your wife's departure."

Zot was holding Gloria's necklace. He noticed it starting to glow. He quickly slipped it into his pocket.

"However," the Elders continued, "the memories that will replace these ones will be pleasant. You will remember that your wife is still alive, but she had to leave. We will leave the rest open to interpretation to your own imagination. So you may someday, reunite."

Gloria looked at her husband, then at the Elders. "But I will remember?" she asked.

"You are the only one in the entire galaxy that will remember," they said.

"I will dedicate every second of my being to stopping this collision. And then I will find you," Zot exclaimed.

"It is time," the Elders said. "We must ensure no one tries to stop this from happening. Remember, Gloria, stop time if anything goes wrong. Find a way to survive. The planet's history, the best of it, is carried with you. We have loaded this ship with important books, and food for you for many, many months. We have found a planet, about four months travel from here. You will land there. We have been in contact with the locals. They will welcome you with open arms. You will be safe. Godspeed, Gloria."

Zot ran to his wife. They hugged for a good while. Zot put his hand on his wife's stomach. "Protect the baby at all costs," he whispered to his wife.

Then, Gloria got on the prototype ship. Looking at her husband, she said, "I love you." She nodded.

"I love you." He nodded. He said it again, unknowingly to the Elders, he was talking to his future child. "I love you." He nodded.

The door to the prototype ship closed. The ship zoomed off, through the roof of the laboratory. And the Elders immediately erased this memory from everyone present, including themselves.

Zot found himself standing there, amidst the Elders, with tears in his eyes. He looked at the Elders, who went about their business, and then he went home.

[Back to the present.]

Immediately after Zot finished telling the story, the necklace Glor was holding was now blindingly bright. Out of nowhere, memories rushed into Glor's head. She looked at Zot.

"Dad?!"

Chapter 17
Missing Pieces

Zot stared at her. "This all makes sense now! Your powers were so familiar!"

"My, powers? I, I don't..." Glor fell to the ground.

Clory stared at his father. "I have a sister?!" he said.

Zot looked at Clory, then he stared at Quo, who helped Glor up. He looked at Glor. "Your mother could stop time," he said. "I too have powers..."

"What can you do?" Glor asked him, curiously.

"I can imitate the powers of those I truly love..."

Glor remembered everything she had been through. All the times she had accused The Newcomer, Quo, of having powers, when it was her all along.

"Dad," Glor said, "I think my powers are a combination of you and mom's. I've stopped time, teleported people away..."

Clory's mouth dropped open. "Glor, my sister, you imitated my powers! Even when you didn't know me, you must have somehow loved me, your brother!"

Zot smiled. "My daughter, I am so proud of you and everything you have become."

"The necklace!" she exclaimed. "It was present every time I used my powers!"

With that realization, the necklace started to overheat. Without meaning to, Glor dropped it on the ground. It broke into many pieces. They floated around Glor, who started seeing memories from her mother's perspective.

"No!" she cried.

"What's wrong?" Zot asked.

"It's mother!" she cried. "I can see her on the spaceship!"

"How is that possible?" Clory asked.

"The necklace!" Zot exclaimed.

"But she didn't have the necklace at this point!" Clory realized.

"My son," Zot said, "maybe your mother and I have always been connected to each other... telepathically."

"Smedge's telepath powers!" Clory cried. "You loved him. You must have been subconsciously emulating his powers the whole time! Always connected to mother, telepathically, even though you forgot why she left, you could never truly be fully apart from her!"

"My wife. Clory, your mother's memories must have telepathically transferred into the necklace!" Zot said.

Without meaning to, Glor projected the memories she saw for everyone to see. The memories came rushing, flying by fast.

[Fifty-nine years ago.]
[On the prototype spaceship.]
"My beloved baby," she said, "we'll be alright. Everything will be okay."

[Two months into the journey to the new world.]
Looking more pregnant, Gloria sat there, reading a book out loud to her baby, rubbing her stomach.

[A couple days later.]
Gloria felt the baby kick. She then felt a little sick. The feeling passed quickly.

[One month later.]
She was now remarkably pregnant. "I love you so much," she said to the baby, looking at her stomach. She looked at the viewing screen on the ship. "Only about one more month of this."

She clenched her stomach in pain. "What are you doing in there, my baby?" She ate some food, then felt better.

She picked up another book. "I've already read this four times. Oh well." She sighed, as she ate some more food.

[One month later.]
"Oh, my beautiful baby!" she exclaimed. "It won't be long now! I'll get to officially meet you soon! And we are about to land on this planet. Our new home, for now! I hope you're okay, my love. You haven't been active this last month..." she was worried.

On the screen, she could see the planet she had been headed towards these last four months.

"Gloria," she heard. The voice was coming from the ship. She quickly realized she was finally in communication range with the planet.

"I am here!" she said excitedly. Just then, she felt something in her stomach, a pain she hadn't felt before. "AAAAAHHH!" she cried.

"Gloria. Gloria. You are clear for landing. You need to land the ship! Are you okay?"

She reached for the controls and tried to steer the ship. The pain increased. "I need a doctor!" she cried. "Have a doctor ready to meet me when I land!"

"Will do, Gloria! We have been awaiting your arrival. And we await the knowledge bestowed upon us by the Elders. We are incredibly grateful that we were the chosen planet!"

"Glad to hear that!" Gloria tried to laugh. But she was in too much pain.

As the ship descended on to the planet, Gloria started to lose consciousness.

[Back to the present.]

"MOM!" Glor screamed. She was crying. Zot was crying. Clory was shocked, trying to take everything in.

"Wait, where is mother now?" Clory cried. "When was the last time you saw her?!"

Quo took Glor's hand. "Glor. Are you okay?"

Sobbing, she looked at Quo, and then at Clory and her father. "I am so sorry. I am so... I'm sorry!" She started crying uncontrollably, as the memories continued, for all to see.

[Back to the same memory.]

Gloria came in and out of consciousness, as she still tried to steer the ship to safety.

"What's going on up there?" someone from the planet said. "This ship was built to safely carry one life form for at least six months safely! Nothing should have gone wrong! That's what the Elders told us!"

In a moment of horrifying realization, Gloria whispered, "One life form... how did I not foresee this?" She looked down at her stomach, then started speaking to the landing party.

"Promise me!" she said. "Promise me you'll protect..."

"Protect who?!" someone demanded.

"I'm pregnant! I've been pregnant the whole time. I never told the Elders. I... I never told them."

She remembered what the Elders said. She was to use her powers to stop any complications that might put her in danger. But that might halt the mission.

"Land the ship! Maybe we can save you both!"

Realizing that the mission would still be successful without her, she sighed, and whispered to herself, "All of the planet's history. All of it is on this ship. I only regret not being able to see my husband... my family... ever again. But nothing is too much for my baby's safety."

"This ship was designed for only one life form!" Gloria cried. "I don't want to put this baby in jeopardy any longer. Don't waste time trying to save me. I will not lose my baby to save myself! I will protect her, with my life!"

Just then, under all the stress of everything, Gloria cried, and her water broke.

She could see the ground where she would land now.

"Promise me!" she said. "PROMISE ME!"

"I promise!" she heard a voice say.

"I'm going into labor!" she cried.

"The doctors are waiting for you! They'll be here right when you land!"

She made sure the ship was on course to land, and then took a deep breath.

After two minutes, that felt like hours, the ship landed. The doctors immediately took Gloria to their hospital. Coming in and out of consciousness still, she blinked a couple times, and found herself in the hospital bed, pushing. With all of her strength, she gave everything she had left to make sure the baby was delivered. After nearly twenty minutes, the baby was born.

"Is my baby okay?" she asked, blinking, trying to see her baby.

"She is fine," a doctor said.

"She?" Gloria beamed. "We have a girl!"

She remembered a conversation she had with her husband Zot, before she knew she was pregnant.

"Her name is Glor," she simply said.

The doctor placed Glor in her mother's arms. "I love you, Glor." She nodded at her.

Just then, Gloria felt weaker. "Protect her!" she said.

The doctor took the baby. Glor immediately started to cry.

"It's okay, honey, mommy loves you!" Nodding at her baby, Gloria started to close her eyes. She opened them back up and saw her baby one last time. The baby stared at her mother. Into her eyes. Straight into her mother's eyes.

After a couple moments staring at her newborn baby, Gloria finally closed her eyes.

Someone said, "Quick! Get the stasis pod!"

And with that, Gloria completely lost consciousness.

Chapter 18
Loose-leaf

[Back to the present.]
    "Mom is still alive!" Glor suddenly said.
    As the pieces of the necklace still floated around Glor, she witnessed her own memories. She remembered being a baby. She remembered the two lovely people that adopted her that very day. She remembered how she used to visit her mother's stasis pod every day, until she was four. She then remembered how they had to stop allowing visitors because her mother was getting weaker. She remembered growing up with her adopted parents, but how they didn't talk much about her birth mother, as it caused too much pain for the child. She remembered all the days she went to school on this planet. She remembered all the good days and the bad days. And the overwhelming feeling that she didn't quite belong on that planet was always in the background of her mind.
    She remembered the day she met Quo. Space explorers had landed on their planet. The thought of getting away from it all to just explore was intriguing to Glor. She met Captain Zot that day, not knowing at the time that he was her birth father. Zot himself didn't know that she was his daughter. Once she met them both, she knew she was going to travel with them. She then remembered how, though they were upset, her adopted parents let her go. "She's an adult now," they said. "Maybe after exploring for a few months, she'll come back."
    She remembered saying goodbye to everyone on the planet. Saying goodbye to her family and friends. She remembered everything. The months she spent with Quo on the ship. Getting to know everyone. Making new friends.
    She remembered the day Captain Zot found out the ship was going to crash. And finally, she remembered boarding the escape pod with Quo and taking his hand as their pod came crashing down on to the planet they were currently on, to the exact place they were currently standing.
    "She's alive?!" Zot exclaimed.

"Just barely. In the stasis pod," Glor said. "I have to get to her!"

The planet started shaking violently, and it got darker, as the planets were just an hour away from colliding.

Gleck spoke up quickly, "Trolk and I may have a solution!"

Everyone looked at them.

Quo asked, "What else did you find in the old abandoned building?"

Trolk pulled out a loose-leaf book.

"Where did you find that?!" Clory exclaimed, recognizing it.

Zot stared at it. "That's... that's the book I wrote! That very night, fifty-seven years ago! The one I placed into the capsule at the last moment!"

Trolk smiled. "Captain Zot," she said, "you may have just saved this planet. Forever this time."

Trolk handed the loose-leaf book to Glor. "Go to the last page," she said.

Zot didn't even remember what he had written. Curious, he asked what it said.

Glor read it out loud, "'To my beloved child. If you somehow ever find this, we may have a fighting chance. If I am correct, you should have powers like your mother and me. The combined powers of this entire family, including you, might be enough to save us all.'"

"That's all it says?" Zot said, still not quite remembering.

"No," Glor cried. "Looks like there is one more message on here. But it's hard to read."

Clory asked for the book from his sister, who still had the floating pieces of the necklace around her. She handed it to him.

"I think it's a message from the Elders..." Clory gasped. "The original Elders, from fifty-seven years ago, before they all disappeared."

Zot reached for the book. "I never knew about that. May I see that?"

Immediately when Zot saw it, it was as if the writing itself contained a message directly from the Elders, that Zot understood. "The Elders were prepared for this," he said. "It seems they somehow knew Smedge would always be selfish..."

"What do you mean?" Clory asked.

"Fifty-seven years ago, when we did what we did to the planet... the Elders knew Clory and Smedge would be the only ones to remember. They knew Clory was worthy, but not so much Smedge. This is unbelievable! We still have a chance now!"

"What is it?!" Glor asked.

"Smedge shouldn't be able to leave the planet's orbit!" Zot cried. "The Elders did something to his molecular structure without him knowing! He literally can not survive if he leaves the planet!"

Chapter 19
Descending

"Do the Elders know everything?" Quo asked.

"Sadly, no," Zot said, "or they would have known my wife was pregnant when they sent her off. They couldn't have known. I hope they didn't know…"

Just then, Quo yelled, "EVERYONE LOOK UP!" Coming at them faster than it ascended, The Boulder came crashing down towards them.

"Now we're about to get hit by your own spaceship, then crushed by a planet," Gleck stated. "I really thought this day would have ended better."

From the ship, Smedge started projecting his voice to the crowd that was on the ground. "WHAT HAVE YOU DONE?!" he screamed. "I WAS FREE! I WAS THE CHOSEN ONE!"

The Boulder was now about to crash into them. Glor looked at the ship, and concentrated. "Stop!" she yelled.

The ship stopped just yards before smashing into them. Glor had stopped the ship. However, time was still moving on it, as Smedge started screaming again.

"I DON'T KNOW WHICH ONE OF YOU IS RESPONSIBLE FOR THIS, BUT YOU WILL ALL DIE AT MY HAND!"

Telepathically, he sent a signal that started knocking over the thirty-seven unmoving crew members, until all of them lay on the ground. He then broadcast the signal to Clory, and everyone else.

"YOU WILL ALL DIE!" he demanded.

Clory fell to the ground, along with Zot, Gleck and Trolk. Glor was still standing.

Glor heard the ear-piercing noise but didn't fall to the ground. Imitating his powers back to him, she yelled, "YOU WILL STOP THIS RIGHT NOW, BROTHER!"

Smedge was completely taken aback by what she said, releasing everyone from his telepathic power. Glor could finally release the thirty-seven crew members from her control as well, as they were no longer under Smedge's control either.

"What did you just call me?!" Smedge demanded. "I am not your brother!"

Everyone stood up, and looked at Glor, who was standing there, still surrounded by the pieces of her mother's broken necklace.

The planet shook again, as collision was now only thirty minutes away, if that.

"I AM YOUR SISTER, SMEDGE," she screamed. "AND EVEN THOUGH YOU HAVE BEEN NOTHING BUT SELFISH. I STILL LOVE YOU."

Clory yelled, "I love you, Smedge!"

Finally, Zot, imitating Smedge's powers, telepathically said, "I love you, son." The three family members nodded.

Having nowhere else to go, Smedge just stopped talking. Glor, having the ship under her control still, carefully landed it in front of them all, and she released it from her power.

Smedge opened the door and stepped off the ship. He walked straight up to his father. "I love you too, father." He nodded and hugged his father. As he was hugging him, he whispered in his ear, "Now watch as the one you love more dies."

Catching them off guard, Smedge concentrated all of his telepathic energy on Clory. Lifting him off the ground, he filled Clory's head with so much noise, Clory had no time to fight back.

Glor rushed over to help him, but Smedge put up his hand, stopping her from advancing. He also stopped her before she could use any of her powers against him.

Trolk and Gleck came running towards him, but he stopped them from advancing as well. The thirty-seven crew members started to regain consciousness, and realizing who the bad guy was, they all went running towards Smedge.

He stopped every one of them.

"FINE! IF THIS IS HOW YOU WANT IT TO END, SO BE IT. NO ONE IS MOVING UNTIL WE ARE ALL DEAD. AND THERE IS NOTHING ANYBODY CAN DO OR SAY TO STOP ME. SO SIT TIGHT, EVERYONE!"

Zot walked toward his son, the only one currently not under Smedge's control.

"Don't," Zot said.

Smedge stared at his father. "I will never be anybody's favorite."

He used his telepathic powers to stop his father from advancing.

Knowing he had finally lost, Smedge sighed.

Still telepathically stopping everyone in their tracks, Smedge resolved to just stand there, with everyone, in silence, until everything and everyone was destroyed.

Chapter 20
Savior

Ten minutes went by. Zot and Glor had tried to telepathically talk some sense into Smedge. He completely ignored them.

"It all ends here. No more history. No more life. No more pain."

The planet shook and the ground started to crack around them. One of the crew members nearly fell into the planet below.

Smedge heard a small noise. He looked around to see where it was coming from. It got louder, louder than the planet shaking. Smedge looked up in awe.

A single ship, that he had never seen before, was coming into view.

"Who in the world could THAT be?!" Smedge yelled. "We don't have any other spaceships on this planet!" he growled, as this ship landed next to The Boulder.

The door slowly opened. The planet shook. The ground broke beneath them.

The end was only five minutes away. Smedge was getting tired holding everybody back, including his super powered family, and he was also weak from his descent back to the planet. Whatever had been done to his molecular structure was now catching up with him. He felt dizzy, tired, he just wanted it all to end.

He stared at the ship, then he noticed someone stepping outside. In complete and total shock, he released everyone from his control, as he stared at the woman stepping off the ship.

"Mother?!" Smedge cried.

In awe, everyone stared at her. Gloria. The mother of Clory, Smedge and Glor. The wife of Zot.

"Mother!" Clory said.
"Mom?!" Glor said.
She looked at them and smiled.
"Gloria!" Zot went running towards his wife, but he tripped on the jagged ground. The planet shook and the ground opened up. Zot landed on the edge of the now open ground. He lost his footing as the planet tried to swallow him.

"Father!" Clory said. He went running over, but the ground crumbled in front of him. Panic ensued, as the thirty-seven crew members were all trying to flee from the planet breaking beneath them.

Gloria ran towards her husband. "Take my hand!" she cried. Without hesitating, Zot went to grab her hand. Almost out of his reach, he managed to take his wife's hand. She pulled him to safety.

Smedge growled. "This makes no sense! Where did you even come from, mother?!"

His mother looked at him and smiled. "Son," she said, "come with your family."

"I will not go with a bunch of traitors!" he screamed.

"Smedge," his mother said, pleading with him.

Clory ran to his mother and father, unsure of what was about to happen, but certain he needed to be with his family.

Glor, still surrounded by the pieces of her mother's broken necklace, ran to her family. She called Quo over.

"I have no special powers," Quo said. "I couldn't possibly be any help."

Captain Zot looked directly at him. "Come over here, Quo. You are most definitely part of this family."

Quo obeyed his captain. Trolk and Gleck stared at them.

Looking back at Smedge, Zot said, "Son, come join your family. We all need you. And we all most definitely love you!" They all nodded at him.

Furious, Smedge screamed. "I WILL NEVER FEEL WELCOME IN THIS FAMILY! I WOULD RATHER DIE RIGHT HERE AND RIGHT NOW THAN EVER HAVE TO SEE ANY OF YOU EVER AGAIN!"

Just then, the ground opened up under him. Not expecting this, he grabbed onto the edge at the last second. He looked around, regretfully.

"Help, help! Save me!" he said. Quo went running over to him. "I've got you!" He took Smedge's hand. Quo lifted Smedge out of trouble. Smedge smiled at Quo and immediately pushed him down into the planet.

"No one replaces Smedge!" he growled. He went running towards his family, who all backed up.

Zot cried. "Did you just…"

"Of course I did! He is not family! Now quick, let's get out of here."

Trolk and Gleck went running towards the chasm that had swallowed Quo. They looked down. Seeing his family watching them, in a fit of jealousy, Smedge, by a telepathic burst of energy, knocked Trolk and Gleck into the planet as well.

"NO MORE GAMES!" he yelled. "I HAVE FINALLY MADE UP MY MIND. LET'S GET OUT OF HERE, FAMILY!"

Seeing all the destruction he had just caused, Clory looked his brother straight in the eyes and said, "You are not my family."

Gloria and Zot stared at their sons. They looked over at Glor, who was concentrating on something.

"WHAT IS THE MEANING OF THIS?!" Smedge yelled.

Rising from the chasm, behind Smedge, was Quo, Trolk and Gleck. As they came into view Smedge screamed.

Smedge turned around in anger. "WHY?!"

Glor was still concentrating. With the three of them being under her control, she pulled them over to be with Zot, Gloria, and herself.

Now, standing in front of the mother's ship, was Gloria, Zot, Clory, Gleck, Trolk, and Glor.

Now less than a minute away from collision, everything started crashing and breaking uncontrollably.

"Last chance, son," Zot said. "There is always room for forgiveness. Come join your family. We all love you!" They all nodded, even Clory.

Chapter 21
The Gift

Smedge went running towards his family. He was so lost. He didn't know where to go or how to feel. He just knew one thing. Maybe they were right. Maybe he always had been selfish. He slowed to a walk, unsure if he could possibly be accepted. He couldn't even trust himself at this point. He had turned on everyone so many times. He stopped.

"No, I don't think I better." He looked to the left at a huge break in the ground. He looked at his family, then jumped down into the planet.

Everyone was shocked. But the planets were now colliding, so it was time to act.

They all looked at Gloria, who they hoped had a plan.

She smiled at them. "Of course I have a plan."

She looked up, as many more spaceships appeared in the sky.

"Who, who are they?" Clory asked.

"We'll answer questions later," she said.

Hundreds and hundreds of spaceships filled the dark sky. Big spaceships, small spaceships, so many spaceships.

"Captain," Quo said, "perhaps we should join them."

Gloria looked at her husband and nodded.

Quo took Glor's hand as the entire family went running towards the Boulder. As they were running, Captain Zot quickly told the still panicking crew members to follow them.

Now on the ship, were all thirty-seven crew members, Trolk, Gleck, Clory, Glor, Quo, Gloria, and The Captain himself, Zot.

The ship Gloria came in seemed to take off by itself.

Now safe on The Boulder, they all started to talk, as the planet continued to break around them.

Zot tried to set a course away from the planet, but the ship wouldn't move.

"It's okay," Gloria said to her husband, "we'll be safe. Trust me."

Zot nodded.

"Will everyone on the planet survive, mom?" Glor asked.

"As many as we can carry!" Gloria said.

"We?" Zot asked. "I would love to carry more people on my ship. But for a ship that is supposed to hold no more than thirty people, I think forty-four might be the limit." He smiled at his wife. "Unless you think we can honestly hold more crew members. I wholeheartedly stand with you. Everyone on this planet deserves to live."

"I think forty-four is enough," she smiled. "Our friends will take care of the rest."

"Who are they, anyways?" Gleck asked.

"How did you survive? I thought you were in stasis," Glor said.

"Oh, good," Gloria smiled. "You got my messages! I'm assuming you got all of them then?" She looked at her husband.

Zot smiled. "All of the memories. Yes. How did you transmit them to the necklace?"

"You already know the answer to that." She smiled again. "That was all you, my love. As much as we love each other, you have the power to imitate the powers of anyone you love. Smedge, oh Smedge. Poor, lost Smedge. You used his powers to stay connected to me the whole time. And I knew you would do that. That's why I gave you the necklace."

"Where did you get that necklace anyways?" Glor asked. She still had the broken pieces of it floating around her.

"Go on, guess," she smiled. "I'm sure you can."

Clory's eyes widened. "I think someone finally gets it," Gloria said.

Glor looked at Clory. "What is it?!"

Zot smiled. "No way."

Glor looked at them both and finally realized. "It's always them. That's them right now, isn't it? Saving everybody. Somehow."

Gloria smiled. "Every. Single. Person."

Gleck and Trolk stared at them. "Anybody care to share?" Gleck asked.

Gloria laughed and told them everything. "When I was a baby, I was given a special gift by the Elders."

"The Elders!" Gleck said. Trolk shot him a look.

Gloria continued, "The Elders knew I was special. They knew I was the one that would be able to stop time. So, on the day I was born, my family got a visit from them. Not many people get to see the Elders, let alone get a visit from them, so my family was surprised. The Elders came, told my parents how special I was, and gave them this necklace. My family was told by the Elders, 'Keep this with you at all times, and you'll be safe.'"

"That's amazing!" Zot said. "We have never talked about this!"

Gloria apologized. "I was told not to tell anybody about it until the time was right. The time is right."

"I'm sorry, mom, your necklace is gone. I accidentally broke it," Glor frowned.

"No, you didn't!" she said. She waved her hands around the floating, broken pieces of the necklace, pulled them into her hands, closed her hands, then opened them back up.

Glor looked in her mother's hands. She saw the necklace, fully assembled again.

"How did you…?"

"Once we get to where we're going, I'll answer all your questions."

Looking at the view screen on The Boulder, it was clear that it was now over. The two planets were now seconds away from exploding, killing everything on them.

Glor took Quo's hand. Gloria took Zot's hand. Gleck took Trolk's hand. She shot him another look but held on to his hand. Clory laughed at his family.

Everything went dark. Then, everyone saw a blindingly bright light. A light that was so bright, Quo himself thought this was truly the end of everything.

Chapter 22
Second Chances

The light started to fade. Quo looked around. He was still holding Glor's hand.

"Where are we?" Quo asked.

"Home," Gloria said. "We made it home!"

"I don't understand..." Quo said.

"Let me start explaining," Gloria laughed. "After I left my husband, my family, to go to the other planet, as some of you know, I had complications. It was a long four months alone in that ship."

"You had me with you!" Glor smiled.

"Yes, I did." Gloria smiled back. "Without you, I might have gone insane. I had you there with me, to talk to. I read you books. Sang you songs. I went through good days and bad days. But the real complications started when I was arriving on the planet. From my spaceship, I was talking to one of the locals from this new planet and that's when I finally realized. This ship I spent the last four months on was made to carry only one life form safely. Only one. So, by the time I landed on the planet, I knew I wouldn't survive. I told them to take care of my baby. You, Glor."

Glor looked sad. "I'm sorry to put you through that, mom," she said.

Gloria looked at her daughter and said, "There is no need for you to apologize, my daughter. After you were born, I got to hold you for just a moment. In that moment, I felt forever pass by so quickly. As I became weak, the doctor came and took you from me. But the strangest thing happened."

"What?" Glor asked.

"As they were taking you away, you looked back at me. You looked straight into my eyes. And in that moment, I knew I would see you again. It was such a beautiful moment. One of the last ones I would have for many years. After you left the room that day, they called for a stasis pod. They immediately placed my body in that pod, to keep me safe until they could someday save me. They told me to stop time while I was in the pod, so I did. I was doubly protected. With a stasis pod and my powers to stop time, I was able to survive a lot longer, which is good, because they nearly lost me a couple times. For many years, I felt your presence, even though time was stopped. I know, it sounds crazy. But I did. After about four years, the visits stopped. I didn't understand at first. But three months later, I got a visit from someone. It was unexpected."

"Who was it?" Glor asked.

"Your adopted mother!" Gloria cried. "But that's not the craziest part. I recognized her. I couldn't believe it. It was my mother. Your grandmother. To my knowledge, my mother went missing when I was younger. I never knew why, but I never asked…"

"I was raised by grandma?!" Glor cried.

"Your grandmother, my mother, is an Elder. I never knew it. They never told me. To protect me. Though now it makes sense, why the Elders visited me, why I got the necklace. It was my mother's necklace."

"But why would your mother leave you when you were young?" Glor asked.

"The Elders have been aware of the collision of planets for many generations."

"How many times did we go through the cycle of almost colliding with another planet?!"

"One is too many," she said. "I don't know too much about all that. But my mother was sent to that other planet to see if it would be habitable for us. I stayed on my home planet, raised by my father."

"Where is he now? Is he the man that raised me? Is the man that raised me my grandfather?!"

"Of course," Gloria said. "My father raised me to be the woman I am today. Once I turned twenty-one, he told me that he had to go on a mission. This mission was crucial. I needed to trust him. So I did."

"Was he an Elder too?" Glor asked.

"Your grandfather? An Elder? He has an exceptionally good heart. What do you think?" Gloria asked her daughter.

"He was. I can't believe I was raised by my grandparents! How did they travel between planets?"

"The Elders can do a lot more than they let you believe. We may have had no space travel, per say, but that didn't stop the

Elders from transporting themselves from planet to planet. They are unbelievably strong."

"Wait!" Clory said. "Then when they all 'disappeared' years ago, did they really?"

"I believe every single Elder transported themselves to the same planet they sent me. Now they were sure we could survive here. The locals were significantly advanced in space travel. All-powerful Elders plus space travel equals a surefire way to save our planet."

"What happened when your mother visited you in the stasis pod?" Quo asked.

"Ah, yes. She opened the stasis pod and smiled at me. I was sure I had gone to heaven. To the afterlife. She looked at me and said, 'I am going to heal you. Hang in there.' Many years went by with no visits. She was trying to conserve my energy. After many, many years, she had figured it out. It's funny how a little thing like death could take an all-powerful Elder years to figure out. But I had been through so much in that ship. There wasn't much of me to save. My mother and father both worked endlessly. And that one fateful day finally came. It was the day you left with Quo. They missed you so much."

"How did they save you?" Glor asked.

"Don't get me wrong," Gloria smiled. "They may have saved me after you left, but it was all because of you that I could be saved."

"How?!" Glor asked, excitedly.

"The day you left, you said something that made them think. 'I will see you again,' you said, 'but for the time we are not together, you'll always be in my heart.' 'In my heart,' you said. And my mother knew immediately how to save me. Didn't you ever wonder why they put that little chip by your heart on that day?"

"A precaution. To keep me safe while I traveled through space."

"It was so much more than that." Gloria smiled. "That quick, painless moment in time, is when you saved me. The Elders also inserted a chip by my heart that day. Honey, the two chips were connected!"

"But how…?"

"You didn't even know much, if anything, about your powers, and they were already working! You have the combined powers of your father and me. I wouldn't be surprised if you could imitate anybody's powers, whether you loved them or not. You are a lot stronger than me, I imagine. And you can stop time like your father. You are the most powerful one of our species."

"But why did the Elders leave Smedge and I alone to watch the planet all those years ago?" Clory asked.

"They trusted you. Maybe not Smedge. But they all came to that new planet to get everything ready. Ready to save all of us."

"Have they been on that planet the entire time?!" Clory asked.

Quo was trying to take everything in. "So, to sum everything up, Gloria, that planet the Elders sent you to, is the same planet they went to themselves two years later... and that is also the same planet your own mother and father, or Glor's grandparents, both ended up at when you were younger?"

"Sounds right to me!" Zot laughed.

"Exactly," Gloria continued. "And three days after you left, Glor, the link to our hearts revived me. That link is still connected. It was always connected. Through space. No matter what. I woke up that day, and after a few days of rest, my mother told me everything that had happened up to that day. She told me everything. Those fifty-seven years that all the Elders relocated themselves to that planet, they started the work. They built so many spaceships. All different kinds. You can build a lot of spaceships in fifty-seven years."

"That's amazing," Clory said.

"It's like the Elders knew how everything would play out all along," Quo laughed.

"I don't know about that," Gloria said, "but one of the main things that helped us succeed in this all, was how friendly the locals on the new planet were. They were so welcoming to the thought of another species living with them on their planet."

"So," Gloria was finishing her story, "With the power of all the Elders and the spaceships themselves, and many trial and errors, we perfected traveling many months distance in mere minutes. I was shocked to see how far they had come when they awakened me that day about four months ago."

"So, did our planet explode?" Gleck said.

"I'm afraid so," Gloria admitted. "It was an event that could not be avoided no matter how much time we had, no matter how many tries we got. So, we had to change our plan."

"Wait," Gleck said, finally realizing what was going on. "Where have we landed?!"

The Boulder's door started to open, letting in the outside light. "Welcome to our new home!" Gloria said, beaming. "Here's to second chances!"

Just then, Clory frowned. "Smedge…"

Two Elders walked onto the ship. They were carrying a baby.

"Welcome home, daughter!" a man said, looking at Gloria. He looked at Zot. "Son," he said. "And my grandchildren!" He looked at Clory and Glor.

"We lost Smedge," Clory frowned.

"He was, unbelievably selfish in the end. I don't know what compelled him to jump into the planet. I suppose he was so miserable, he couldn't take it anymore. We told him there was always room for forgiveness. There is always room for second chances," Zot said.

"Funny you should mention that," Gloria's father said. "Look."

He moved aside. And his wife, Gloria's mother, came walking up to Gloria.

"I don't understand," Gloria said. She looked at her husband.

"No way," Zot said.

In a moment of realization, Gloria said the same thing. "No way!"

"When Smedge jumped into the planet," Gloria's mother said, "we immediately tried to save him. But all the time energy from the inside of the planet started to leak out. I guess rewinding time has its consequences. He had fallen deep into the planet. We did everything we could. When we got him on one of our ships, he started getting younger. And younger. And he didn't stop, until he got this young. We were afraid we were about to lose him. And that's when he started crying. Here, daughter," she said to Gloria. "Here is your son, Smedge. Looks like he gets a second chance after all!"

Looking around at all the crew, Quo realized something. "Um, captain? These thirty-seven crew members might not want to stay here."

Zot laughed. "We have a million spaceships at our disposal now! Traveling the galaxy is not an issue on this planet!"

Some of them in fact, did want to stay. Some wanted to leave. As the weeks went by, everyone that wanted to, settled into their new home. The rest left indefinitely to go traveling through space. There was no more danger of colliding planets. Everyone lived happy lives.

Trolk and Gleck decided early on to learn how to fly a spaceship so they could go on adventures. But they would never forget Clory or any of their friends. They always found their way home to their friends. And their friends were now their family.

Quo and Glor eventually got married. They went on many space adventures. And they eventually had children of their own.

Gloria and Zot went on a few space adventures, but mainly stayed on the planet.

The Elders made sure everyone was treated well. And even Clory himself eventually found love.

After many years, Quo looked at his wife Glor, smiled and said, "I wouldn't want to spend my life with anybody else."

She smiled at him. "Quo, I love you." She nodded.

"I love you," Quo said back. He nodded.

They had many more adventures.

And their best days were still ahead of them.

The end. No, that's not true at all. This is only the beginning...

Epilogue

One night, three weeks after they settled on their new home planet, Quo and Clory were talking.

"Hey Quo," Clory said, "remember when we first met?"

"Of course!" Quo said. "What about that day?"

"You mentioned the humans. What do you know of them?"

"I'm honestly not sure what that was all about," Quo admitted. "How do you know about the humans?"

"I have only read about them," Clory said. "One of my home planet's earliest books mentioned them. A simple race. No powers."

Quo shrugged. "I remember something else. I was talking to Glor. I spoke this language. I said, 'Déjà vu'. But Glor knew what I was talking about somehow."

Glor came walking into the room, wearing the necklace that now meant so much to her. After Trolk realized how important it was to their family, she immediately told Glor to keep it. "That is because you told me while we were traveling through space!" Glor laughed.

"But how would I know what it meant?" Quo asked.

"Quo," Clory said, "what planet are you from?"

Quo tried to think, but he couldn't remember.

"Wherever he is from, that's where Captain Zot, our father, landed and was raised his second life, right?" Glor said. "Let's go ask him!"

"He left on a mission to a local planet with Mother!" Clory reminded her.

"Oh yeah," Glor said. "Hey, it's getting late. I'm gonna get some sleep." She left the room.

"Clory, where am I from? Why can't I remember?" Quo asked.

"Get some sleep," Clory advised. "Zot comes back tomorrow. We'll talk to him then."

Quo went to his room. He sat down, thinking about everything. After many minutes of contemplation, Quo finally decided to lie down and rest.

He had trouble falling asleep. For the first time, he was worried about where he had come from. After maybe two hours, he finally drifted off to sleep.

He opened his eyes. He was standing with Captain Zot. "This must be a dream," he thought to himself.

He looked around. Everything looked familiar. "Wait…" he said. "This is the day we left my home planet!"

Excitedly, he looked around for clues as to where he might be from. He saw a bunch of people get on to the captain's ship, The Boulder. He saw people on the ground, watching as everyone boarded the ship for takeoff. Captain Zot faced the crowd. He addressed them.

"Thank you, everyone," he said. "Ever since I was born, I knew I needed to travel through space. To everyone that helped make my dream come true, I thank you."

The crowd clapped.

Zot looked at Quo. "Are you ready?"

"Of course!" Quo said.

He was about to ask Zot what planet they were on, when Zot said something that made him remember everything.

He addressed the crowd one last time. "My fellow humans," he said, "we shall make you proud. Our mission is just this, exploration. And that's what we are going to do. Explore. We're going to make Earth proud!"

Quo stared at everyone, as what he had forgotten was now remembered.

Memories of his life on Earth flashed through his mind. Leading up to a new memory. He did not recognize this memory at all.

"Quo!" a man dressed in a uniform said. "You need to come home. Tell Captain Zot, wherever he is. We are in danger!"

Quo looked around again. "This is so weird," he said.

The man continued, "We are sending you this message, transmitting it to your mind. We hope you receive it. We lost contact with your ship a while ago, as we had discussed might happen before you left. It has taken us many weeks to set up and transmit this message directly to you. Quo. We are under attack. The Earth needs you. These ships appeared in the sky. They told us to beware. They said they were coming back. Quo, come home! We are not sure what you found out there, but you need to come home! Help us!"

Quo sat up quickly, awake from his dream. Awake from the message that he just received. He ran out of his room to find Clory and Glor talking with Captain Zot and Gloria. They had just come back from their mission. Captain Zot looked at Quo.

"Hey, what's wrong?" he asked.

"I just received a message," Quo said frantically. "Captain, what planet are we from?"

"Originally, I'm from the same planet as Clory, remember? But I suppose you meant my second life. A little blue marble in a small galaxy. Wait. What message?"

"From home. They need our help. I'm not sure why or how I forgot about this."

"I'm sorry," Zot cried, "I never knew you forgot about that! I would have told you!"

"Captain. Glor. Gloria. Clory. We have to go save my home planet from oncoming destruction. We have to go back to Earth!"

What if you found yourself stumbling around, dazed and confused, on a strange planet full of aliens with superpowers? What would your first thought be? For The Newcomer, he just wants to know what is going on. He wants to know where he is. How he got there. But he can't even remember his own name.

After a group of aliens, Clory, Trolk, Gleck, and Glor, notice The Newcomer, he must try and figure out exactly who he is. Is he in fact The Destroyer that his new friends are talking about? Or is it someone else in the group? Maybe. But maybe The Destroyer is something else completely...

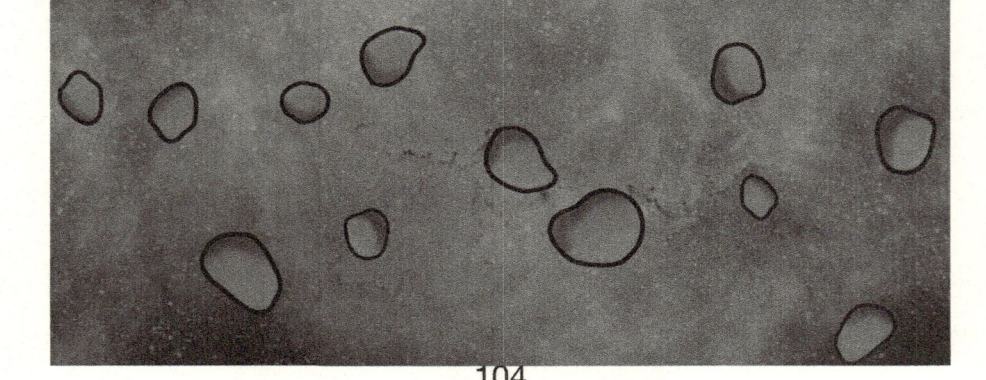

The Elders' Chronicles:

DIVI/SION

Keith Imbody

The Elders' Chronicles: Division

The Elders' Chronicles:
Division
By: Keith Imbody

Copyright © 2020 Keith Imbody

All rights reserved.

This book or any portion thereof

may not be reproduced or used in any manner whatsoever

without the express written permission of the author

except for the use of brief quotations in a book review.

Cover art created by Alecia Witbart

Preface

You would think, after writing book one entirely on my smart phone, that surely I would use a computer to write book two. That is not the case. I decided to write book two on my smart phone as well. And, spoiler alert, I'm writing book three the same way.

Book two took about four days to write. I had three days off from work nearly in a row, so that Friday night after work, I decided it was time to start writing the sequel. I wrote a little bit Friday night, wrote all day Saturday, I was busy on Sunday with church and work, then I wrote all day Monday, and finished up writing by Tuesday afternoon.

If, by chance, you're reading book two first for some reason, I hope you still enjoy the story. You might better understand what is going on if you first read book one. But this is SciFi. You can read the books in whatever order you want!

Keith Anbody

Acknowledgments

To my family:

Once again, my sister created the cover art for this book. She also helped me with the editing and the formatting. Thank you, Alecia.

My parents are usually the first to hear my stories. I read the book to them. This works as one of the first steps in editing. Sometimes, I catch mistakes during this first read through. And they usually suggest edits while we're reading. Thanks, mom and dad.

To the reader:

Maybe you liked book one enough to pick up book two? Or maybe you're reading book two first? Who's to say I didn't write book two first? Okay, I didn't. But hey, I am writing SciFi here, so who really knows? Thanks again for checking out my book! I've said it before, I'll say it again. Without you, the reader, reading wouldn't exist. And I suppose, if reading didn't exist, there would be no reason to write. And if writing didn't exist, what would you read? Okay, that was confusing. Thank you.

The Elders' Chronicles: Division
By: Keith Imbody

Table of Contents
Chapter 1. The Warning
Chapter 2. The Interns
Chapter 3. Follow
Chapter 4. The Satellite
Chapter 5. Setup
Chapter 6. The Roof
Chapter 7. Recovery
Chapter 8. Cam's Trip
Chapter 9. Cam's Admission
Chapter 10. Information
Chapter 11. New Plan
Chapter 12. Dream Thoughts
Chapter 13. Message Sent
Chapter 14. The Battle
Chapter 15. The Planet Taker
Chapter 16. The Call
Chapter 17. Departure and Arrival
Chapter 18. Lies and Truth
Chapter 19. The War
Chapter 20. Survival
Chapter 21. Decision
Chapter 22. Shockwave
Epilogue

Chapter 1
The Warning

"What is that?!" A man with black hair was staring up at the sky, standing outside of his house.

A woman walked slowly towards him from inside the house. She was just shorter than the man. She also had black hair. Both the man and the woman wore glasses. She was staring at the man, as if she didn't notice anything up in the sky.

"Bob," she said, "it's your day off. You have been out here for hours looking at that sky. I know they said the meteor shower would be visible tonight only, but I think you should come back--" the woman finally looked up. "What on Earth?!"

"Spaceships!" Bob yelled. "But I don't recognize these. They are not ours. They are not from Earth at all!"

As Bob and the woman looked up at the sky, more spaceships seemed to appear. Bob looked at the woman. "Carol," he said, "I think we better get to safety."

Before they could move, they heard a voice that seemed to broadcast everywhere that sound could be heard.

"Humans of Earth," the voice said, "you must prepare yourselves for the fight that is coming your way. You must be ready. You need to know the truth, before it's too late."

"What are they talking about?" Carol asked Bob.

"I'm not too sure..." Bob's thoughts wandered, as the voice continued.

"We will return, when the time is right. Fair warning, humans. Be ready. Beware. Don't squander your time. Be. Ready."

The spaceships, one by one, disappeared from the sky. Bob looked at Carol, and they both darted towards a car. It was a beautiful, blue convertible car. Bob jumped in the driver's seat, as Carol quickly buckled up in the passenger seat. They both knew where they needed to go.

Bob worked for Earth's space program. It had been quiet for a while. All of Earth's projects were either just completed, in progress but waiting for results, or beginning shortly. Carol worked alongside Bob. That's how they met. That's where they spent many, many years together. That's where they fell in love.

Bob was in charge of the space exploration division. Organizing teams, plotting out missions, he even built some of Earth's finest ships.

Carol saw Bob all of the time at work. She was in charge of her own division. She tracked the skies for unidentified flying objects, aliens, and anything else that showed up in space.

"How did we miss this?" Carol frantically said, as Bob started the car and drove fast towards their place of work.

"I don't know!" Bob cried. "It has been eerily quiet around here these past few days. The crew of our newest ship 'The Wanderer' left yesterday. And three teams just got back within this last week. We still have that one ship out searching the skies, but we lost contact with them yesterday."

"Should we be concerned about that?" Carol asked, as Bob had to slow down for a red light. "They have traveled so far."

"That's the best part," Bob said. "The wonder of what they are going to find. The hope of finding new species out there in space. The thought alone makes you think!"

"The thought alone makes you think?" Carol laughed. She then looked at Bob. "Good thing you're not a writer!"

Bob laughed. The light turned green, and he continued driving.

"Oh well, that dream had to move aside for this new dream," Bob said. "Leader of space exploration. Besides, I may not be a writer, but I think the wedding vows were pretty good."

Carol laughed, "Yes. I will admit that! I didn't expect them to be so corny, but I married you anyways!"

Bob laughed and quoted the vows that he said to his wife, Carol, on their wedding day.

"'You were searching through space when I was here all along. I was leading teams, planning other people's lives, and building the ships that would change their lives, when the best change in my life was meeting you. We didn't always see eye to eye. Some thought we might break up. They said we should take some space. But I told them that we didn't need space. Space needed us!'"

Carol smiled, but her smile quickly faded. "What about our friends on that ship we lost contact with yesterday? Our friends from 'The Boulder'? They need to come home. I think whatever those aliens were talking about, whatever fight is coming, I think we might need to bring everyone home for this one."

"I agree with you. But I'm pretty sure my boss would not be happy with me if I canceled everything and brought everyone home. Even after what just happened."

"True," Carol sighed.

"But if it makes you feel better, I'll find a way to transmit a signal to our friends from 'The Boulder'. I'll work day and night until we figure all of this out."

They pulled into a parking lot and parked their convertible.

"Let's go see what the admiral has to say about this."

They both got out of the car and started to walk towards the building.

"Bob!" Carol yelled. "Watch out!"

Chapter 2
The Interns

Bob and Carol jumped out of the way, as a mechanical drone creature almost hit them.

"Is that ours?" Carol asked.

"No," Bob said, "that is most definitely not from Earth."

The drone looped back around and stopped in front of Bob. It froze for a moment, then flew towards Carol. After another moment, the drone zoomed away.

"That, was weird," Carol said.

"And that's coming from people who work with space travel!" Bob laughed, trying to relieve some of the stress.

"Let's go find your boss," Carol said.

They were almost to the building, when they heard a buzzing sound. They looked around but saw nothing.

"So, just so we're clear, neither of us know what is going on?" Bob asked.

Carol shook her head. "Of course not!"

As the buzzing got louder, Bob and Carol kept looking to see if they could find where the noise was coming from.

"Let's just find the admiral," Carol said.

They walked up the stairs leading to the building. Bob went to open the door.

"Why is it locked? Where is everyone?" Bob was confused, but he thought he heard a noise on the other side of the door.

"Hello?" Bob said.

"I think it's Bob!" someone from the inside said. "Is that you, Bob?"

Someone else from inside spoke up, "What if it's an alien pretending to be Bob? Today is Bob's day off! Why would he be here?"

"It could have something to do with the alien visitors that told us to be ready. Bob is in charge of space exploration!"

"But who is in charge when space comes exploring Earth?!"

"Why are we even having this conversation? We were told to wait inside and lock the door until the admiral comes back. There are a bunch of workers in here with us, we are on the front lines. The first line of defense."

"The admiral said he would be back in five minutes. He said not to let anybody in no matter what! It's been seven minutes! What if they got to him?!"

"Who? The aliens? They left!"

"For now. But they are coming back!"

"Guys, it's me, Bob, and my wife Carol!" He turned to Carol, and said, "I think those are the new interns. They have only been with us for four days. They picked a crazy time to intern."

Someone walked up behind Bob and Carol. They both turned around to see the admiral walking towards them.

"Bob!" he said. "I thought I'd see you here."

"Where were you, admiral?" Bob asked.

"The answer might be above your pay grade!" The admiral laughed.

He walked by Bob and Carol and unlocked the front door to the big building.

"Come on in, guys," the admiral motioned for Bob and Carol to follow him. "Thank you for holding down the fort for me," he said, as he looked at the two interns.

The admiral was a strongly built, middle-aged man. He had blonde hair and looked like he worked out every day. He had a mustache and a beard that looked like it took at least two years to grow. His name was Noah.

The two interns watched as everyone entered the building.

The first intern, the one that had initially spoken, was a shorter man. He wasn't fat, but he also wasn't thin. He was bald, by choice. His name was David.

The other intern, the one that suggested that an alien might be pretending to be Bob, was skinny. He had dark brown hair that came down to his shoulders. He had a tattoo of a spaceship on his left arm and a tattoo of an alien on his right arm. He was obsessed with space, aliens, and everything involving them. He believed many conspiracy theories and even created some of his own. His name was Cam. Short for Camouflage. Needless to say, his parents were trying to be original. He looked at all of them and said, "Admiral, is it done?"

The admiral laughed.

Bob was curious. "You told David and Cam but you can't tell me?!" he said jokingly, with a tad of seriousness.

"Cam is just being Cam!" Admiral Noah said, winking at Bob.

"Anyways," Carol broke the tension, "what do you think we are dealing with, admiral?"

"Aliens!" Cam said.

Admiral Noah stared at Cam, then looked at Bob. "Bob, we have to talk. Let's go to my office."

Carol started to follow, but the admiral stopped her.

Bob spoke up for his wife, "Admiral, with respect, please let her come with us."

Hesitantly, the admiral agreed. Cam started to follow them. Without planning it, Bob, Carol, and the admiral said, in unison, "No!"

They all laughed. David laughed. Cam, however, did not find it amusing.

"Stay here, you two," the admiral ordered. "Watch the door."

Cam sat back down. "'Watch the door!'" he said, mockingly.

"Excuse me?!" the admiral said.

"Sorry, sir," Cam said, sincerely.

Bob, Carol, and Admiral Noah walked to his office. Bob and Carol sat down. The admiral closed the door. He walked over towards his desk and sat across from them.

"Bob. Carol. We have to talk about our one missing ship. I know we expected this to happen. We expected to lose communication. But for it to happen immediately followed by a day like today? I'm not sure it's a coincidence." He had a serious look on his face. "What was the last message you received from our ship, 'The Boulder'?"

Chapter 3
Follow

"The last message that we received from 'The Boulder' was nothing out of the ordinary," Bob said. "Captain Zot gave us the weekly update. As you know, sir, the crew has picked up new passengers along the way. One of the newest crew members, Glor, was still getting along with the crew. Especially with Quo."

Carol looked at the admiral. "Why do you think losing contact with them has something to do with this invasion, or warning, that we got today?"

Admiral Noah just smiled and said, "I've been in this program long enough to know when something isn't right."

"What are we going to do?" Bob asked.

"Can you find a way to send a message to them?" Admiral Noah asked.

"I can try," Bob said, unsure, "but it might take a little while."

"Then you should get to work on it right away!" Admiral Noah advised.

"Sir, it's his day off," Carol laughed.

"No, this is important," Bob said. "I'll get to work on it right away."

"Maybe they found something that can help us out in our current situation," the admiral said. "Is there anything else out of the ordinary, besides the obvious events of the day, that you two have noticed?"

"Yes," Carol said, "we almost forgot! There was this drone creature outside."

"You saw them too?" Admiral Noah asked.

"Yes, I think it was looking for something," Bob said.

"Or someone," Admiral Noah seemed concerned.

"Then, after it flew away, Carol and I heard this buzzing sound. It got louder, but we couldn't see anything."

"More drones," Admiral Noah sighed.

"Sir, what do you know?" asked Carol.

"Too much. Not enough. Oh well. You should get to work on a way to send our crew that message!" Admiral Noah smiled and simply said, "Dismissed."

Bob and Carol stood up and left the office.

"I think we should ask the interns for their help," Bob suggested, as they walked back towards the front door of the building.

Now back in the first room by the door, Bob looked around.

"Where are the interns?" he asked.

"Maybe they left for the day?" Carol guessed.

"Admiral Noah told them to stay here. Why would they disobey a direct order?"

They heard a noise outside. Carol went running towards the door and opened it. Looking outside, she yelled, "Bob, I found them!"

David was annoyed. "I told him we had to stay inside!"

Cam spoke up, "I heard it. I know it's out here. I heard the buzzing!"

"He's gone crazy," David said. "Crazier than normal."

"No, there was a buzzing noise earlier," Bob said to David.

David sighed. "You're all crazy."

Just then, Cam started running away from the building. "There it is!"

"Where is he going?!" David asked, still annoyed.

"Maybe we should follow him!" Carol suggested.

Reluctantly, David started to follow Cam.

Bob and Carol followed the interns, not knowing where any of them would end up.

Cam stopped suddenly, as a drone creature came from high in the sky and slowly descended towards him. It was now hovering in front of him.

"What is the extra buzzing noise?" David asked as everyone caught up to Cam. "If that one is making that noise--"

He stopped talking, as three more drones came towards them from the sky.

"Okay," David said. "Four of them, and four of us."

"There are way more than four," Cam said. "More like four hundred."

"What?" Carol stared at Cam. "Cam, are you okay?"

"Four hundred?" Bob became anxious. "Yeah, we have to get our crew back here immediately."

The drones stopped for a second, as if they were listening. They then zoomed upwards towards the sky.

Cam stared up as they all left. He looked back at everyone. "Maybe more."

"What are they?" Bob asked Cam. "Do you know?"

"They look partly mechanical and partly organic. Maybe a hybrid. They shouldn't have done that."

"They shouldn't have done what?" Bob asked.

"Fifty-seven," Cam said.

"Cam, you're not making sense again!" David said.

"The collision is happening three weeks from now. But you'll be fine."

"What is he talking about?" Bob asked.

"Send the message to him," Cam said. "But first he has to wake up!" Cam fell to the ground.

"Is he okay?" Bob asked.

"He's been doing this a lot," David admitted. "Maybe he shouldn't have joined this internship."

"Let's bring him back to the admiral. Maybe he'll have some answers."

David and Bob carried Cam, as Carol ran ahead to tell the admiral what had just taken place.

Carol and the admiral were waiting outside when the guys finally caught up.

"Is he okay?" the admiral asked. "What was he saying? Something about a collision? Who does he want you to send the message to?"

"I'm not sure," Bob said.

They carefully placed Cam on the ground below the steps. He started to wake up.

"Where am I?" he asked.

"You did it again," David said. "You started talking nonsense."

"It sounds like some of it made sense," the admiral admitted. "Cam, I think you should get some rest. Admiral's orders."

"I'll make sure he gets home," David said.

"Feel better," Carol said, as David and Cam walked away. "Where exactly does he live?"

"A nearby apartment complex," Bob said. "They are interns. Our space program is helping them pay their rent while they are helping us. Speaking of help, Admiral, I think once Cam is feeling better, he and David should help us figure out a way to contact Captain Zot and the crew."

"Excellent idea!" the admiral said. "I've got lots of work to do, and so do you!"

The admiral walked up the stairs and went inside the building and straight to his office.

"Well," Bob said to Carol, "guess we better get to work!"

Chapter 4
The Satellite

Over the next week, Bob and Carol worked endlessly on a way to transmit a signal to Captain Zot and the crew. There were many different places in this building where one could work. Carol had her own office, which was more like a small laboratory. This lab was full of computers and telescopes. Bob had many different rooms where he would work. He had a quiet office similar to Admiral Noah's where he would plot out missions with the data he was given. He had another room that was perhaps the biggest laboratory in the building. This is where he helped build the spaceships that Earth calls their own. And he had a few other areas where he would help organize teams and train them for their missions.

After a week with basically no results, Bob started to wonder if they were wasting time.

"This is hopeless," Bob said.

Carol sighed but tried to reassure Bob. "Hey," she said, "why haven't we heard from the interns all week?"

"That is a good question," Bob said. "But after Cam had that weird episode, I wanted to give him some space before asking them to help."

The admiral walked into the room. Tonight, they were in Carol's small laboratory. They changed rooms daily in hopes of getting inspired by changing their surroundings. "Any progress?" the admiral asked.

"No, sir," Carol admitted.

"Well, I think the interns are finally ready to help!" Admiral Noah said, as David and Cam walked into the room.

"Cam, are you okay?" Carol asked.

"Oh yeah," Cam said, "never felt better!"

"I'll leave you four to it." Admiral Noah left the room.

"So, what are we doing?" Cam asked.

"We have to send a message across space to one of our ships, but they are out of communications range," Bob said.

"Didn't Cam mention sending a message to someone?" David asked.

Bob looked at Cam, who seemed to be concentrating on his thoughts. "Cam, what's up?"

After nearly twenty seconds of silence, Cam looked at Bob and said, "Have you tried boosting the power through every computer in this building, using that satellite dish over there?" He pointed to a lone satellite dish that was in a glass case in the corner of Carol's lab.

Though a somewhat simple solution, Carol looked at Bob. "Should we try that?"

Bob didn't like the idea. "I don't know why, but I don't think that will work. Carol, where did we get the satellite dish?"

"Oh that one was floating through space. We managed to get it safely to Earth about two weeks ago. I haven't had much time to study it this week, but what I've learned from it last week is minimal."

"So we don't even know where it's from."

"Try it," a voice said. Apparently, the admiral had stepped back into the doorway while no one was looking.

"Are you sure, sir?" Bob asked.

"What's the worst that could happen?" the admiral said.

"Well," Bob said, "I don't know. What if it calls more of those drones to Earth? We haven't seen a single one for nearly a week."

"And what if it sends the message that needs to be sent to our crew?" the admiral asked.

"What if it does both?" Cam said.

"No matter," the admiral said, "for a week we've had no progress. Let's try this."

Immediately, the five of them got to work on connecting all the computers and getting the satellite ready.

"I suppose we should put this on the roof of the building, so it can broadcast the signal further," Bob said.

David laughed at him. "I don't think that'll make much of a difference. If it's on the ground, or on the roof."

"No, it might," the admiral said. "It may only seem like a few stories of difference from the ground to the roof. Though that doesn't seem like a lot of space, it might make all the difference."

This plan took two days to completely set up. Bob and Carol had to make sure everything was perfect. After calibrating and connecting all the computers, the last step was to put the satellite on the roof of the building. They carefully removed it from the glass case and brought it outside.

"I'm not going up there," David said.

"I'll do it!" Cam said, excitedly.

"Oh no," the admiral said, "I think Bob's got this one!"

Bob laughed uneasily. "Yes sir," he said.

There was an elevator on the side of the building that brought Bob straight up to the roof. This building was five stories high. Once at the top, Bob went straight to work. He started to attach the satellite to the roof, when he heard a buzzing sound.

"Oh no. No, no, no. Not this. Not now."

To Bob's horror, a lone drone creature came flying straight towards him.

Chapter 5
Setup

Whoosh! The drone went right by Bob but quickly looped back around.

"What do you want?!" Bob asked.

The drone came back around and landed in front of the satellite. It looked as if it were staring directly at the satellite. It zoomed around Bob and the satellite multiple times and eventually flew back up into the sky.

Bob reached into his pocket and pulled out his cell phone to call down to his colleagues. He dialed his wife's number.

"Why isn't she answering?" he thought. He slipped the phone back into his pocket.

Even though he knew he'd regret it, he went to the edge of the building to look down and see if his colleagues were still there.

"Oh no!" Bob screamed.

He saw nearly ten more drones near the ground, as his colleagues stood there, unmoving, while the drones hovered around them.

"Why aren't they moving?!" Bob said, nervously.

Forgetting about the satellite, Bob rushed to the elevator and tried to get back down. The elevator wouldn't work.

"Maybe there is electrical interference from the drones?" Bob said to himself.

"Or maybe it's the satellite," a voice said.

"Hello?" Bob said. "Who's there?"

"It's Cam!" the voice said.

"Cam, where are you?" Bob asked, confused.

"On the ground!" Cam said.

"Cam, are you guys okay? Cam? Cam?"

Bob heard no reply. He walked off the elevator back towards the satellite on the roof. "I really don't like this," he said. He finished attaching the satellite to the roof and was startled by his phone ringing. It was his wife.

"Bob? Bob, are you okay?" Carol said.

"Yeah, I'm fine. But there was a drone up here."

"They were down here too. We tried to stand still so they wouldn't harm us. There were so many of them."

"Carol, did Cam move?"

"No, he stood still the whole time. Why?"

"I heard his voice. I don't know how."

"That's strange," Carol said.

"Is the admiral sure about this?"

Bob heard Carol ask the admiral. The admiral took the phone to speak with him. "Obviously, we're doing something right. Over a week without a single drone. Then they come back right now?"

"What if they want this satellite?" Bob asked. "Maybe that's what they wanted the whole time. They did start to appear after we acquired it."

"I've thought about that. But Earth needs this. We'll give it back after we've sent the message. Turn on the switch and head back down," the admiral said. He hung up the phone.

"But... the elevator is broken," Bob said to himself. He flipped a switch on the satellite and walked towards the elevator. "Maybe it will work now?"

Bob walked onto the elevator, and closed his eyes, as he pressed the down button. He breathed a sigh of relief as the elevator slowly went down to the ground. He stepped out to see everyone waiting for him.

"It's done?" David asked, trying to be funny.

"Yes," Bob said. He looked at Cam. "Cam, do you remember talking to me?"

"Of course!" Cam said. "We were talking earlier today!"

"No, I mean, when I was on the roof."

"I, don't know what you're talking about," Cam said. He seemed upset.

Admiral Noah broke the silence. "Let's send them a message!"

They all walked inside the building, to Carol's laboratory.

"How long will this message take to reach them?" Bob asked.

"It might be instantaneous. If it even works. Maybe a week or two?" Carol guessed.

The admiral was ready. He had a microphone. They were going to record him and then immediately send the message. Everyone was quiet, as they pressed record.

"Captain Zot," the admiral began, "we are trying to send you this message to let you know to come home as soon as you can. We've been advised by--"

Sparks started flying uncontrollably. The microphone that the admiral was holding heated up and electrocuted him. He fell to the ground.

"Turn it off!" Carol yelled.

"I'm trying!" Bob said, "but it won't stop recording! I knew this was a bad idea!"

The computers started to make a loud beeping noise. The lights started flickering. Then, there was what sounded like a big explosion on the roof, immediately followed by everything turning off. The computers shut down and the lights went out. Everything in the building went dark.

Chapter 6
The Roof

"Admiral, are you okay?" Bob asked.

The admiral stirred, and slowly opened his eyes. "Did it work?" he laughed.

"Sir, are you alright?" Carol asked.

"I'm fine! That's not the first time I've been electrocuted, and it probably won't be the last!" He stood up. "We better clean this up. This might take a while."

"How are we going to send a message now?" Bob sighed. "I knew this was a bad idea."

"Bob," the admiral said, "it's alright. We'll figure this out."

"I think there was an explosion on the roof," Carol said. "Should we be concerned?"

The admiral rushed outside, followed by everyone else.

"Is it gone?" David asked, looking up.

Bob went running towards the elevator, as did the admiral. "You all wait here," he said to Carol, David and Cam.

Bob and Admiral Noah tried to use the elevator, but it wouldn't work. "Oh yeah. We drained the power," Bob said.

"Get the ladder!" the admiral said.

Bob walked off the elevator and went towards the back of the building. He went to a locked door that was attached to the building. He unlocked and opened it. There were tools and things they might need in a crisis. He located the ladder. He walked back towards the admiral.

"Sir, this ladder only reaches the third story. How are we going to get to the roof?"

"It's gone," Cam said.

The admiral looked at him.

"The satellite is gone," Cam said.

"How do you know?" the admiral asked.

"We have to fix the building," Cam said.

The admiral looked up towards the roof, then back at Cam. "Are you sure it's gone?" he asked.

"All I know is, twelve days until the collision. Wake up, Quo! Wake up!"

They all stared at him. He smiled at them.

"Anyways," Carol said, "I still think we should make sure the structure of the roof is safe."

Bob looked at the admiral. "Can we use the suction cups instead of the ladder?"

"Good thought," the admiral said, "but use the ladder first. Then climb the remaining two stories with the suction cups."

"Oh, I'm not sure I'm strong enough to climb--"

Bob was interrupted by his wife. "I'll do it."

The admiral looked at both of them. "Why don't you both go up there? A double check on structural integrity is never a bad thing."

Hesitantly, Bob agreed. They set up the ladder, and they each got a pair of suction cups, and a backpack to carry them in.

"Wait until Bob reaches the roof. Once he makes sure it's okay, follow him," the admiral advised.

Bob stepped onto the ladder. He couldn't tell if he was shaking, or if it was the ladder, but he shook the thought and climbed. Once he reached the top of the ladder, he looked back down and regretted that immediately. He took a deep breath and reached for his suction cups. He continued ascending the building. With each move, he had to suppress the feeling that he was going to fall. He had to be brave.

He finally reached the top of the building and climbed up onto the roof. He didn't see any damage. But the satellite was gone. There were some burn marks left where the satellite once was. He called his wife on her cell phone. "It's safe," he said, "but the satellite is gone."

Carol started to climb the building. She was a little more confident than Bob, but that was because she took classes on rock climbing. This, however, was a bit different.

Carol reached the roof, and Bob helped her up. They both examined the roof. There were no cracks in it, and the only noticeable difference was the missing satellite and the scorch marks left behind.

They both walked around, surveying everything, making sure it was safe. After nearly an hour of double and triple checking everything, they started back to the ground. Carol went first. There were a couple of times she thought she might fall, but she made it to the ladder and climbed down safely.

Bob started to climb down. He heard a voice. "Wait, Bob, not yet." Confused, Bob ignored the voice. "Bob, go back onto the roof! Now!"

"Cam?!" Bob said. "Is that you?!"

No answer.

Bob decided to obey the voice, so he quickly jumped back onto the roof. Just then, he heard a loud noise. His phone rang.

"Hello?" he said, answering the call.

"Bob? Bob?! Are you okay?" It was Carol.

"Yeah, I'm fine," Bob said. "What's going on?"

"Sparks came from the windows of the building. They became stronger and reached the ladder itself. The entire ladder just lit up. If you were on it, or ever scaling down the wall above it, you would have fallen! What made you go back?"

"I keep hearing a voice," Bob admitted to his wife. "It sounds like Cam. It was Cam."

"Cam didn't say anything," Carol said. "We didn't hear him say anything."

"One problem at a time, I suppose," Bob said. "I need to get down from here! I'm glad you made it to the ground safely."

"I told the admiral that the roof itself is fine. It's safe. But it's going to take time to get this building running again. Time I'm not sure we have."

"Once I get down there, we'll all get to work fixing up the building," Bob said. "If the sparks have stopped, ask the admiral if we should remove the ladder from the building. I'll scale the wall all the way to the ground."

"I thought you hated those suction cups."

"I hate getting electrocuted and falling to the ground more," Bob laughed. "Maybe wait a little while. We don't need anybody else getting electrocuted."

While still on the phone, Carol talked to the admiral. Bob overheard them.

"I think we should wait at least thirty minutes to make sure there are no more sparks coming from the building," Carol said to the admiral.

"I think we should wait an hour," the admiral said.

All Bob could think was, "Oh great, I'm stuck on this roof for another hour?" He thought about scaling down the building before they removed the ladder, or even on another side of the building, but he then imagined getting hit with electricity and falling to the ground, so the hour wait finally seemed reasonable.

"Do you want to stay on the phone while we wait?" Carol asked.

"No, I'm going to use this time up here to think. We'll need more ideas once we get the building back to one hundred percent."

They ended their call. Bob looked around. How had life become so complicated this quickly? Left with his own thoughts, Bob sat down in silence, waiting for time to pass by.

Chapter 7
Recovery

Bob looked around. Twenty minutes had already gone by. He stood up and started walking around the roof. He noticed a small piece of metal in the far corner. He thought about picking it up but then thought better of it. It looked a little familiar, though. He stared at it for another moment.

"That looks like a piece of the satellite," Bob thought.

Staring at it wasn't doing anything, so reluctantly, Bob picked it up. It was about the size of a small coin. He heard a slight buzzing noise that was so faint, it was almost inaudible.

"What are you?" Bob said. The piece of metal started to heat up, so Bob quickly dropped it. It started to glow red from overheating, then vanished, leaving a small char mark on the roof.

Bob called Carol. "Carol, how's it going down there?"

"There has been no sign of electricity for over twenty minutes. How's it going up there?"

"I think a piece of the satellite was left behind."

"That's awesome!" Carol said. "Maybe it will help us figure out what to do next."

"Unfortunately," Bob said, "it disappeared in a similar way as the satellite, I think."

"How so?" Carol asked.

"It heated up, turned red, then disappeared, leaving a char mark on the roof."

"Similar technology?" Carol guessed. "Maybe it was left behind when the satellite itself disappeared?"

"More questions," Bob said. "Oh well, there is nothing else up here. I suppose all I can do for now is wait."

"We'll see you soon," Carol said. The call ended.

Bob was trying to clear his head. This all had to be connected, somehow. The warning, the drones, the satellite, this small metal piece of, whatever it was. Then there was Cam. Cam seemed to be talking about the passengers of 'The Boulder' as if somehow, he knew what was going on.

Bob must have been lost in his thoughts for over forty minutes. The sound of his phone ringing startled him. He answered it.

"It's time to come down! It's safe. There has been almost no sign of any electricity for over an hour. We already managed to get the ladder down," Carol said.

Bob was ready. He went to pick up his suction cups, which he had left in the middle of the roof. He jumped back, however. There was another small, metal object by the suction cups.

"What?" Bob thought.

He looked all around the roof. He saw many more of them just sitting there, scattered around the roof.

"Okay, those were not here before," he said.

He closed his eyes, shook his head, and opened his eyes back up. They were all gone. "I am going crazy," Bob thought.

He picked up his suction cups and started his descent. He was more concerned about what these round metal objects might be than he was afraid of climbing down, which actually helped him move faster.

Once he finally reached the ground, Carol hugged him. He looked around. Everyone was still there, David, Cam, and even the admiral himself.

"So, you know that round metal thing I mentioned that I saw? I saw a bunch more after we hung up the phone. But I'm not sure if I saw them, really," Bob said, confused.

"What do you mean?" Carol said.

"I'm not sure if they were really there or not," Bob admitted. "Anyways," he looked at the admiral, "could we please get to work on fixing this place up? We still have to send out that message!"

"He's still not awake!" Cam yelled.

"Cam, it's alright," Bob said. "It'll be okay."

Still wondering what was up with Cam, Bob knew that he and the team needed to focus on fixing everything in the building.

The act of fixing everything and getting it back to the way it was took about a week and a half. Throughout this time, Bob randomly saw the round pieces of metal. Whenever he saw them, he tried to point them out to Carol, but it was as if they weren't actually there.

David and Cam were extremely helpful. The admiral had many more workers helping out with this project, as the damage was significant. With everyone working day and night, the reconstruction went fairly quickly.

It did seem like Cam was counting down to something important, as every couple of days he mentioned some sort of collision and how many days until it happened. But with no way to contact the crew of 'The Boulder', all they could do was keep moving forward until they could send a message.

The day had finally arrived. The building was back to running at nearly one hundred percent.

"Everyone, go home and get some rest," the admiral said to David, Cam, Bob, Carol, and all the workers that helped get everything back to normal. "Tomorrow, we'll find a way to send a message!"

Though everyone wanted to keep working, everyone knew the importance of rest, so they all started to head home.

In the parking lot, Bob and Carol were talking to David and Cam before going home. They were trying to think of some new ideas on how to send the message, one final brainstorm before they split up.

Cam looked around and started shaking. "Collision is tomorrow. We have to send a message. If Quo doesn't wake up, if Quo doesn't remember his name, everyone could die."

"What are you talking about, Cam? What is this collision?"

"I don't know," Cam said, "but we have to help Quo!" He started to feel dizzy.

"You need rest," Carol said. "Quo will be okay. You'll be okay. Go home. Get some rest. We'll figure this out tomorrow." Carol smiled, as David and Cam walked home to their apartments.

"Do you think he's okay?" Bob asked.

"Who? Cam, or Quo?" Carol said.

"Both," Bob said, unsure of their future. "Why am I seeing things that aren't there?"

"We all need rest," Carol said. "We've been working too much. Maybe tomorrow, after we all get some rest, we'll all be in our right minds."

Bob nodded.

Carol and Bob got into their car and drove home.

Chapter 8
Cam's Trip

The next day, everyone felt much better. The building was back to one hundred percent, and everyone showed up refreshed.

Bob and Carol pulled up and parked their car. When they got out, they saw David and Cam walking towards the building. The admiral was already there too. He was in his office. Many other workers were inside, brainstorming.

Bob went running towards David and Cam, Carol following behind.

"Cam, do you feel better?" Bob asked.

"He woke up," Cam said. "He finally woke up."

"That's good!" Bob said. "Right?"

"No!" Cam said. "He needs to remember his name!"

"He will," Carol said. "Quo is a smart man, he's got this!"

"Why does he call himself The Newcomer? He has to remember his name now!" Cam started to frantically twitch. "I could ask you the same thing!" he said.

"What?" Bob said.

"Maybe you should find out who you are before you find out who I am!" Cam said. "Do you want to know who you are?"

"Cam, who are you talking to?" David asked.

"Isn't that easy?" Cam said. "Just remember!"

"Cam?" Carol said. "Cam, come back to us!"

"Have you?" Cam said. He fell to the ground.

"Cam? Cam?! Who was he talking to?" Bob asked.

"He kept saying that this Quo fellow needed to remember his name. Who is Quo?" David asked. "Does Cam even know him? He's never met him!"

"Are you saying he was talking to Quo?!" Bob asked. "Is that possible? David, how exactly do you know Cam?"

"We went to school together," David said. "I've known him for nearly five years now."

The four of them were still outside near the steps to the building. Admiral Noah opened the front door. Seeing Cam on the ground, he ran down the stairs. "What happened?"

"I think he thought he was talking to Quo," Bob said.

"Remarkable," the admiral said. "That gives me an idea! But we have to get Cam's permission."

"You don't think he was actually talking to Quo?" Carol said.

"We deal with space travel," the admiral said. "Science fiction is becoming science fact before our very eyes."

"This is outrageous!" David said. "Cam is possibly going insane and you want to use him to reach that crew?"

"It is my duty to protect Earth," Admiral Noah said, sternly. "And I would never do anything without Cam's permission. Let's get him inside."

Bob and Admiral Noah picked up Cam and brought him inside, propping him up on a chair in the admiral's office. Carol and David waited in the first room of the building, still trying to think up any new ideas on how to send the message.

Bob and the admiral sat there, in silence, as they waited for Cam to wake up.

After an hour, Cam started to stir.

"Cam?" Admiral Noah said.

"Cam, it's us," Bob said.

"Remember. Remember," Cam said.

"Is he still talking to Quo?" Bob asked. "Cam, who are you talking to?"

"REMEMBER!" Cam yelled.

"Admiral, what do we do?" Bob asked.

"I'm not sure," the admiral admitted.

"Should we splash water on him?" Bob suggested.

"I'm not sure that is a good idea," the admiral said.

"REMEMBER! REMEMBER! REMEMBER! REMEMBER!" Cam screamed, it nearly shook the room.

"Cam," Bob said, "wake up!"

The admiral stood up. He was about to call for Carol and David to see if that would calm Cam down. Before he could reach the door, Bob called to the admiral. "Sir, what is happening?"

The admiral looked back. He walked back towards Cam.

"Is his body disappearing?" Bob asked.

They both stared at Cam as his body started to fade.

"He's still here, but it's like he's trying to be somewhere else," the admiral said. "There is no way. Our crew is so far away. There is no way he's trying to move himself across space that far."

"Admiral," Bob said, "isn't Cam a human?"

Before he could answer, Cam started to speak.

"Why don't you remember?" Cam asked. "You need to remember!" he said, pleading. "Please!"

After he had spoken those words, Cam's body reappeared fully. "Now he'll remember his name," Cam said.

"Cam, where were you?" the admiral asked.

Cam smiled, and said, "He will be The Newcomer no more. Quo is about to remember his name, thanks to me. I just saw him and Glor."

"Cam, have you ever met them before? How do you know it's them?" Bob asked.

"He knows," the admiral said.

"Admiral, with respect, please tell me what is going on!"

"Alright," Admiral Noah said, "I'll tell you everything. Bob, what do you know of the Elders?"

Chapter 9
Cam's Admission

"There isn't much information on the Elders," Bob said. "But what I do know is that the Elders are powerful beings. Legend says that they are watching over everything. Legend says that they have been around since nearly the beginning of time. They are spread out across the galaxies and the universe."

"I'm glad you know that much," the admiral said.

"Is Cam an Elder?" Bob asked.

"Bob, have you ever heard of the Seniors?"

"The people that play bingo on Sunday nights at the old church building?"

"Bob, come on now," the admiral said. "In context with this conversation. Have you ever heard of the Seniors?"

"I can't say I have, sir," Bob said. "Who are they?"

"Where do I begin?" the admiral said.

Cam spoke up, "I'm tired," he said. "I'm so tired of hiding. Admiral, may I?"

The admiral nodded.

"My name is Camouflage. Cam for short. I've been on this planet for over five years now. Trying to blend in. That's why I got these tattoos. That's why I grew my hair out. You humans are very interesting creatures."

"Wait a minute," Bob said. "So you're not human?"

"Not at all," Cam admitted.

"Does David know? Aren't you guys friends?" Bob asked.

"Yes, we are," Cam said, "but no, he doesn't know. Everyone can not know."

"Cam, are you an Elder?"

"Yes," Cam said, "but we were about to talk about the Seniors."

"Who are they?" Bob asked.

"The Seniors are all Elders," the admiral said.

"But not all the Elders are Seniors," Cam admitted.

"Wait, are you a Senior, Cam?" Bob asked.

"So the Seniors say they are higher than the Elders," Cam continued, "they just want to make sure the Elders are doing the right thing. The Elders, however, don't agree with the higher ranking the Seniors have bestowed upon themselves."

"Then, who is the higher ranking?" Bob asked.

"Neither," the admiral said. "Okay. Don't freak out."

"Whenever someone says 'don't freak out', why does everyone start to freak out?" Bob asked.

"What we are about to tell you can not leave this room," Cam said. "We don't want to jeopardize our mission."

"But what about my wife? Can she know?"

Cam looked at the admiral.

The admiral shook his head. "The fewer people that know, the better. Though, for some reason, I don't think Bob will listen to us otherwise. You may tell your wife. But no one else. Especially not David."

"Okay," Bob agreed.

The admiral looked around and sighed. "Bob, I am not a human."

Bob gasped.

Cam smiled. "Oh, it gets better," he said.

Bob stood up, feeling uneasy. "Does our government know?"

"What do you think?" Admiral Noah asked. Without giving Bob the chance to answer, he continued talking, "Bob, I'm an Elder. I have been stationed on Earth for nearly ten years. I was sent here to make sure everything goes as planned."

"What do you mean by that?" Bob asked.

"Other alien species don't like you guys," Cam said. "They just don't."

"My main mission is to prevent the human race from becoming extinct," Admiral Noah said.

"Yes, humans are thinly spread across the universe," Cam admitted, "but there are very few humans out there compared to the billions that live here on Earth."

"Is something coming for Earth?" Bob asked.

"When is there not?" the admiral laughed. "If it's not aliens, it's meteors, conspiracies, or plagues. Honestly, I'm not sure how you've survived this long." He smiled, as if he was trying to lighten the situation, then continued, "Because you're resilient, that's how."

"What's coming for Earth this time?" Bob asked.

"Not yet," Cam said. "Don't you want to know what I am?"

"What are you?" Bob asked.

"Whatever I want to be," Cam said. He transformed his body to look like Admiral Noah, then he took the form of Bob himself.

"Shapeshifter?" Bob asked.

"Not just," Cam said. He flew off the ground towards the ceiling, then slowly lowered back to the ground.

"Wait, were you actually talking to Quo earlier?"

"I was trying to," Cam said. "I think he might have seen me. Or maybe a projection of me."

"Cam, admiral, why are you telling me this now?"

"Because. You have to know the truth," Cam said.

Admiral Noah looked at Cam, who shapeshifted back to his familiar form.

"Bob, as the Elder in charge of Earth, I want you to know, I agree with what Cam stands for. It's time for the other Seniors and Elders to quit these juvenile shenanigans."

Cam looked at Bob, and said, "Bob, I'm not just an Elder. I'm a Senior."

Chapter 10
Information

"Cam, you're a Senior, and admiral, you're an Elder?" Bob was trying to understand everything.

"But we are both Elders," Cam said. "I come from the ones that call themselves Seniors. But I don't think myself to be better than the other Elders."

"Nor do I," Admiral Noah said.

"Admiral, do you have powers too?" Bob asked.

"I'm an Elder!" the admiral said. "Yes." He smiled.

"So why can't you two protect us from what's coming?" Bob asked.

"Bob, don't you understand what's coming yet?" Cam asked.

"No," he admitted.

"The Elders and the Seniors--I hate when I have to group us like this," Cam sighed. "All of the Elders are about to have an all-out war with each other. For millennia, the Elders themselves have disagreed with each other. Some want to think they are better than others. Don't get me wrong. Some of the Seniors and some of the Elders feel this way. There is good and bad on both sides. I wish we were all on the same side."

"So, what exactly is coming to Earth?"

The admiral sighed. "All of the Elders," he said.

"Why would they bring their war to us? We are just humans!"

"I think we've filled your head with enough information today," Cam said. "We still need to send out that message to Quo and the crew. Though, I guess at this point, they'll receive the message after the collision."

"What is this collision you keep mentioning?" Bob asked.

"That's a story for another day," Cam smiled.

"Why does it seem like your power is limited? I thought the Elders were more powerful," Bob said.

"The combination of your yellow sun and the amount of gravity on this planet are some of the reasons," Cam said. "But that doesn't just hinder us. We can also use it to our advantage."

"How so?" Bob asked.

"It makes it easier for us to hide here," Cam admitted. "They can't detect us while we remain on Earth, as long as we keep the use of our powers to a minimum."

"That's surprisingly convenient," Bob laughed. "But admiral, they know you're here?"

"They sent me here. Yes, they know I'm here. I fear they know Cam is here, but they haven't said anything for five years. I meet with them regularly to update them on everything. But I haven't told them about Cam."

"To be clear, admiral, you're not a Senior?" Bob asked.

"No," the admiral said.

"So, even with your combined powers, we can't send a signal to the crew of 'The Boulder'?"

"I'm afraid not," Cam said. "If we did that, the Elders would know for sure that there were two of us here. Though, as the admiral said, I too fear they already know."

"I want the crew to come back too," Bob admitted, "but how are a few dozen humans going to make a difference in the war?"

"First off," the admiral said, "one human can change history. For the worse, but hopefully, for the better. But that's not why that crew needs to come back. According to Captain Zot, they have picked up some new passengers from a few different species. The more help we get, the better chance we have of stopping this."

There was a knock at the door. The admiral yelled, "Come in!"

Carol opened the door. "Hey, how's it going in here? Is Cam okay? David was also starting to worry."

"Everything is fine," Bob said. "I think."

"Sounds convincing," Carol said.

"Any new ideas on how we might send that message?" Bob asked.

"Unfortunately, no."

"Okay. We'll be finished in five minutes." Bob smiled at his wife, who left the room and closed the door. "One more question," he said. "Who exactly was it that visited us three weeks ago? Who gave us the warning? Did you recognize any of them? Were they even Elders at all?"

Cam looked troubled. "That's the scary part," he said. "That's why we decided to tell you about all of this. That's why we have to send out that message as soon as we can."

The admiral looked at Cam, then at Bob. "Neither of us have any idea who that was. Whether it was Seniors, Elders, or a third party, all I know is this: we must heed their warning. And we must be ready."

"Thank you for trusting me with this information," Bob said. "I guess we all better get back to work on sending that message. I'll have an idea by the end of the day."

"Thank you, Bob. Dismissed," the admiral said, smiling.

Bob walked out of the room. Cam followed behind. Carol and David saw them coming, and the four of them immediately started discussing any new ideas that came to mind.

Chapter 11
New Plan

After many hours of speculation, Bob asked if he could talk with his wife alone for a few minutes. Cam understood why Bob needed to talk to her, so he and David waited in the main room as Carol and Bob went to her lab. Bob sat down in a chair and advised his wife to do the same. She sat down. She knew he was about to tell her something important.

"Before you tell me," Carol said, "let me guess. Cam isn't human."

"You've got that right," Bob agreed. "You can't tell anybody what I'm about to tell you, especially not David. That's what they told me."

Bob told his wife everything the admiral and Cam told him, that Admiral Noah was an Elder, and that Cam was not only an Elder, but a Senior.

"And these Seniors," Carol said, "built their entire status upon thinking they were, better than the Elders?"

"I'm not sure how it all started," Bob said. "But not all Seniors feel they are better than the rest of the Elders. There is good and bad on both sides. That's how I understand it."

"And who was it that visited us in those spaceships three weeks ago?" Carol asked.

"That's the most interesting part. They have no idea," Bob said.

Carol was pondering everything. "Let me get this straight. The sun and the gravity of our planet obstruct their powers from working fully? But if they use their powers, both of them, the Elders will know there are two of them on Earth. Do you really think the Elders don't already know?"

"I, and they, fear that they do," Bob said.

"Then why don't we just use the two of them to send the message?" Carol asked.

"I don't think they liked the idea," Bob said. "I'm not sure why, but I guess there's still a small chance the Elders don't know?"

"So they can use their powers a little bit?"

"I think so," Bob said. "Hey, that gives me an idea! Let's go find everyone!"

Bob went to get up and he noticed something. He looked over towards the glass case where the satellite once was. "Carol, do you see that?!"

"No, I don't see anything!" she said. "Is it the round metal things again?"

"They are everywhere!" Bob cried. He walked towards them. "Are they real?" he asked Carol.

Carol walked over to the glass case. "Be careful!" Bob said, as she put her hand on the glass case.

"Move your hand, there is one on you now!" Bob said, frantically.

Carol shook her hand violently, though she saw nothing. The metal piece went flying towards Bob's face! He went to move out of the way, when it turned red and disappeared just before hitting him. He saw a small puff of smoke where it once was. He looked back at the glass case. They were all gone. He ran over to it.

"You didn't see any of that?" Bob cried.

"I seriously didn't," Carol said. "I'm sorry!"

Bob stared at the glass case. Concerned, he looked at his wife. "I'm going to open it again," he said. "We haven't opened this thing since we took the satellite out of it."

"That glass case is from Earth, though," Carol said.

"But what we kept inside of it was not. On the count of three. One, two, three!"

Bob quickly opened the case. Nothing happened.

"Do you see anything?" Carol asked.

"No," Bob said, "no I don't." Still worried, Bob shrugged his shoulders and said, "One problem at a time, I guess." He closed the glass case. "Now, about the idea I had."

"You sure you're okay?" Carol asked.

"I'm fine," Bob said. "What if, instead of trying to send this message instantly, we use lower power. Some of the Elders' power, and a little of the computer power. We don't want a repeat of that roof day we had nearly two weeks ago."

Carol laughed. "Did you just say 'that roof day'?"

"Yes," Bob said, "I was trying to be funny! That roof day. That rough day."

"Oh, I got the joke," Carol smiled. "I think that is the best plan I've heard all day. So, it might take a little while for the message to reach them? Are we talking hours or days?"

"That depends on how much power Cam and Admiral Noah are willing to give us. Two or three weeks, maybe a month tops? Let's go tell them our idea!"

"Do we have that kind of time?" Carol asked.

"I'm not sure we even have a choice," Bob said. "Let's see what they think!"

Carol nodded and they both left the lab. They went straight to the admiral's office. They knocked on his door.

"Hello, sir?" Bob said, "We have an idea! This one might work! Admiral?"

The door was ajar. Bob pushed it open and they walked into the office. "Where did the admiral go?" he asked.

"Okay, now I see them!" Carol cried.

"See what?"

"Those round metal things! They are all over the admiral's office!"

"Carol? Don't be alarmed. But I don't see them this time!"

Chapter 12
Dream Thoughts

The admiral came walking towards his office. Bob turned around and saw him. "Admiral," Bob cried, "what do you see in your office?"

"I see Carol. Why does she look so frightened?" he asked.

Carol saw many of the metal pieces, but none of them were turning red or disappearing as Bob had described. She went over to one and picked it up.

"Be careful!" Bob said.

She held the piece of metal and looked closely at it. "Oh my," she said. "I think it's alive!"

"How could you know that?" Bob asked.

"What are you two talking about?" the admiral said. He couldn't see anything either.

"I don't know," Carol said, "but I think it needs our help!"

The metal that she was holding started to heat up and turn red. At the last second, she let go of it. It disappeared in a puff of smoke before reaching the ground. Carol looked back up, and she couldn't see any of them anymore.

"What did I just witness?" the admiral said. "Is that what you were talking about when you came down from the roof?"

"I've been seeing these small metal round things," Bob admitted. "No one else could see them. For nearly two weeks now. But for the first time, Carol saw them just now and I couldn't see them anymore."

"Quite interesting," the admiral said. "What do you think they are?" He looked at Bob, then at Carol.

Still slightly shocked, Carol regained her composure and simply said, "One problem at a time, sir. Bob and I have thought of something. A way to transmit a message. It might take some time. I'm not sure we have much time before those aliens come back, but it is worth a try!"

"What's your idea?" the admiral asked them.

"We use a small bit of your Elder powers. You and Cam's. Enough from each of you to not cause you pain, as Bob told me the sun and gravity hinder your powers, but not too much, so the Elders won't detect both of you."

"It's still risky," Bob said, "but with your power combined, constrained, but combined, we use some power from the computers as well. Not as much as last time, though I think the problem was the satellite. So, admiral, what do you think?"

"I think it's a crazy plan," the admiral admitted, "but we are running out of options. Let me go get Cam."

He left and came back moments later with Cam.

"Where's David?" Bob asked.

"Thinking," Cam said, "in case this crazy plan doesn't work."

"One problem at a time, Cam," the admiral smiled.

"So, how exactly are we doing this?" Carol asked. "How do you send a message to someone across space? Some of these sentences I'm saying today sound like something from a dream!"

"A dream!" Bob said, quickly. "Carol, you're a genius!"

"What did I say?"

"Cam. Admiral. Can you send this message to them through a dream?"

"Not to all of them," Cam said. "That would use too much of our power."

"What about to one of them?" Bob asked. "Cam, you said earlier we had to send the message to 'him'. Why did you say that?"

"I... don't know," Cam said. "I thought I was just playing the part of crazy Cam."

"You've been talking about how Quo needs to wake up and how he needs our help. Is that who you think we should send the message to?" Bob asked.

"I think that might actually work," Cam said.

"Do you know what the crew is going through right now?"

"Somehow," he said, "I've known the entire time. Like now, I know they are all safe on their new planet. They relocated there after the collision, with the help of the Elders. They are going to stay there. Some of the crew are coming back. But not Quo. He still doesn't remember everything."

"How do you know that?" Bob asked

"I don't know," Cam said.

"Wait," Carol said, "why would Quo stay on another planet that was not his home?"

"Why would Captain Zot not come back?" Bob asked.

"He found what he was looking for," Cam said. "He didn't even know he was looking. He found his wife, Gloria. And Quo is happy with Glor."

"Zot doesn't have a wife," Bob said.

The admiral listened to everything. He was trying to understand all that was being said, but he was a little lost.

"Cam, I think you know more than me about all of this," Admiral Noah admitted.

"I do," Cam said. "I haven't even mentioned Clory, Trolk, or Gleck."

"Is he even speaking English right now?" Carol asked.

"Can we please send the message?" Cam said, concerned. "Set up the computers. Get everything ready. Quo still has to remember where he came from. He isn't even thinking about it. We must remind him somehow. We'll project this message into his mind like a dream."

Thirty minutes later, they had some computers set up.

They had moved from the admiral's office to Carol's laboratory. Admiral Noah and Cam were ready. Ready to remind Quo where he came from. It was time to remind Quo of Earth.

Chapter 13
Message Sent

"Who's going to speak to Quo?" Bob asked. "Maybe the admiral? Someone Quo would recognize."

The admiral looked at Bob. "You," he said. "You trained him. He saw you more times than he saw me. But Bob, you should wear the uniform you wore the day he left. That might help him remember."

"I think I have an extra outfit in my office," Bob said. "But sir, are you sure it should be me?"

"It should be you," Cam agreed.

Bob went to his office and changed. He came back wearing the same uniform he was wearing the day Quo, Captain Zot, and the entire crew left.

"Cam, when you were talking to Quo the other day, the day your body started to fade, you were talking with him instantaneously, right? Like a space phone call?"

"Yes," Cam said, "but I can not do that again. I nearly killed myself."

"We're going to have a time lag here, right?" Bob asked. "According to my calculations, it will be at least three weeks before he even receives the message. How are we going to know if he receives it?"

"One problem at a time," Cam laughed. "Now before we send the message, I'm going to send a thought towards them. A thought that will get them thinking."

Bob looked at Carol and smiled. "See? I could have been more than just a writer. I could have been an Elder!"

Cam continued, "I'll send this thought to his friend. Just a thought about humans and Earth. His friend will then start the conversation that will lead Quo to this message. Hopefully, talking about this will trigger Quo's memory about Earth. Are you ready to send the message?"

Bob stood there, in his uniform, ready. The computers were connected, the admiral and Cam looked at each other, stared at Bob, and said, "Now!"

"Quo!" Bob said. "You need to come home. Tell Captain Zot, wherever he is. We are in danger!" He stopped for a moment, then continued, "We are sending you this message, transmitting it to your mind. We hope you receive it. We lost contact with your ship a while ago, as we had discussed might happen before you left. It has taken us many weeks to set up and transmit this message directly to you. Quo. We are under attack. The Earth needs you. These ships appeared in the sky. They told us to beware. They said they were coming back. Quo, come home! We are not sure what you found out there, but you need to come home! Help us!"

The admiral and Cam stopped transmitting.

"That should be good enough, right?" Bob asked.

"All we can do is hope, and wait," Cam said.

"In the meantime," the admiral said, "maybe you should talk to Cam about the round metal things you two saw?"

Cam looked at them.

"We don't know much more than that," Carol said. "Bob and I have seen them, but when I saw them, he didn't, and before that, he saw them and I didn't."

"Round metal things? Give them a name," Cam laughed. "It has to be tiring to always say, 'round metal things' every time you tell this story."

"They looked like they were the same metal as the satellite," Bob said.

"So they are basically just unidentified metal objects? How about UMOs?" Cam suggested.

"Why are we naming them?" Bob laughed.

"Because we have about three weeks until Quo gets the message, if he even receives it. I just hope the Earth is still standing by then." Cam frowned.

"Are you all kidding me?" David stood in the doorway of Carol's office. "I should have known. You are all insane."

"David," Cam said, "how long have you been standing there?"

"Long enough," David said.

"Uh oh," Carol said.

"I better go talk to him," Cam sighed.

"No need to talk! I know everything now!" David said.

Everyone was sure David had figured out that Cam and Admiral Noah weren't humans. The more people that found out, the more complicated it was going to get.

Bob was about to speak, but David interrupted, "I thought we were all a team. You figured out a way to send a message and you left me out? I am part of the team! I want to help! Apparently, I fell asleep. I just woke up like two minutes ago."

"Wait, you didn't see us sending the message?" Cam asked.

"I walked into the doorway and you were all talking about 'round metal things'?"

"UMOs," Cam said.

"I also overheard you say Quo wouldn't receive the message for three weeks? What are we going to do for three weeks?"

Bob started to hear a slight buzzing sound. He looked up. "Guys?" Bob said.

"We'll just have to wait it out," Cam said.

Carol heard a buzzing noise too. She looked up and saw what Bob saw. "Hey guys?"

"Three weeks of waiting! That sounds like so much fun. Why did we intern here again?" David asked.

The admiral looked up. As the buzzing noise became a little louder, he also heard it. "That's not good."

David and Cam were so busy arguing, they didn't even notice anything.

"We became interns so we could learn about space!" Cam said.

"David! Cam! Do you hear that?! Look up!" Bob said.

They finally looked up at the ceiling, as the buzzing noise intensified. The ceiling was covered with a bunch of the round metal things. Everyone looked around, then at the ground. They saw more of them appearing. They were on the walls. They were everywhere.

"Look at all of them!" Bob said. "Everyone can see them this time, right?"

"Yes," Carol said.

"And I can hear them!" the admiral said.

"What are they?" David asked.

"That's a lot of UMOs," Cam said.

Everyone looked at him, then back at the UMOs, as they seemed to take over the entire laboratory.

Chapter 14
The Battle

"What are we going to do?" Bob said, as the UMOs started moving towards them.

"Wait!" Carol said. "Do you hear that?"

"The buzzing? Yes," Cam said.

"No," Carol said. "I think they're trying to tell us something."

The admiral looked at her.

"You guys," Carol said, "I think they're saying a word. Over and over."

"What word?" Cam asked.

"It sounds like, 'Searching… searching… searching…', you don't hear it?"

"Wait a minute," Bob said, concentrating. "They are saying that! But, how?"

"I told you I thought they were alive," Carol said.

The admiral, David, and Cam finally heard what Carol heard. Just then, some of them started turning red and heating up. They started disappearing, leaving scorch marks everywhere, one by one, until there was only one left on the ground in front of them.

It moved across the floor like a bug. It climbed up to the ceiling, then down the wall, eventually ending up on the glass box where Carol kept the satellite.

"It's looking for the satellite?" Bob asked.

"Look!" Cam said. Inside the closed glass box, was another UMO. "I think it's searching for that one!"

Cam rushed over and opened the box before consulting anybody.

"Cam!" the admiral yelled.

The UMO inside the box moved out of it and was now sitting next to the other one. The buzzing noise was now nearly inaudible. The two UMOs both heated up, turned red, and vanished in a puff of smoke.

"Okay," Admiral Noah said. "What was that?"

The buzzing sound started to come back, louder. Through a small window in Carol's laboratory, Bob noticed something outside. A drone had come down from the sky and was hovering at the window.

Cam walked up to the window and opened it.

"What are you doing?!" Carol said.

"What are you?" Cam said to the drone.

In a deep robotic voice, the drone spoke, "A form of communication."

Taken aback, Bob walked towards the drone. "What do you want?"

"The satellite is ours," the drone said. "Where is the satellite?"

"It's gone," Admiral Noah said. "Who sent you?"

"Where is the satellite?" it asked again.

"It exploded," Carol said. "It was on the roof."

"It is not gone," the drone said. "It is still here. It is tricking you."

"What is tricking us?" Cam asked.

"Where is the satellite?"

The buzzing noise started to return, as UMOs appeared in Carol's office again. The drone somehow noticed them.

"UMOs and a drone?!" Bob said.

The drone flew in through the window. More flew in behind it. The room was now filled with drones and UMOs.

The drones looped around the room, scanning everything, as the UMOs scattered around everywhere. Just then, the drones started shooting at the UMOs.

"Are they enemies?" Bob asked.

"The satellite has been located," the drone said.

The UMOs seemed to be fighting back. They climbed the walls and jumped onto the drones, turning red and heating up.

"Is that a defense mechanism?" Carol asked.

As the battle between the drones and the UMOs continued, everyone tried to keep out of the line of fire. Eight UMOs had managed to attack one drone at the same time, as all eight heated up and turned red, exploding. The drone fell to the ground, now inactive.

When the other drones noticed this, they quickly flew out the window. The UMOs followed them outside, climbing the wall and also exiting through the window.

Everyone rushed towards the window to look outside. The drones seemed frightened as they went straight up towards the sky.

"I think the UMOs won," Cam laughed. "The drones are going home!"

"Do they live in the sky?" Bob asked. "What is up there?"

Carol gasped. Everyone watched, as the UMOs started to raise themselves off the ground.

"They can fly?!" Bob said.

The UMOs gained speed as they chased after the drones. All of them, the drones and the UMOs, were now out of sight, except for the damaged drone inside Carol's lab.

"Well," the admiral said, "at least they have taken there fight elsewhere."

Everyone turned back inside. Carol looked at the inactive drone that was still on the ground.

"We're in a laboratory," Carol said. "I guess we should check this out."

Cam rushed over to the drone and picked it up. "Are you okay?" he said to it.

Bob walked towards the drone and examined it. "That is remarkable," he said. He took it from Cam and admired the detail of it. It was black and had some metal components. Some components were made from something else. "What is this part made of?"

"It's organic," Cam said.

As they stared at the drone, it sparked, and Bob unintentionally threw it on the floor. The drone sparked again, then it seemed to wake up. It didn't have enough strength to move but it began to speak to them.

"The satellite has been located," it said.

"The satellite exploded, leaving char marks on our roof," the admiral said.

"No," the drone said. "They are tricking you."

"Who is tricking us?" Bob said.

"The satellite," the drone said, "the satellite has been… located." The drone seemed to turn off, then back on. "They attacked us. They attacked us first. We didn't start this. They did."

"Who did? The UMOs?" Carol asked.

"They want to destroy us. They want to destroy all of us. Don't trust them." The drone started to spark more.

"Don't trust who?" Carol asked. "The UMOs?"

"Watch the skies," the drone said. "Watch the skies. You must prepare yourself for the fight that is coming your way. You must be ready. You need to know the truth."

"That sounds hauntingly familiar," Bob said.

"That's what the aliens said to Earth! The warning!" Carol said.

The drone continued, "Beware. Don't squander your time. Be. Ready. For I fear, it is already too late."

"Already too late?" David said. He had been silently freaking out the entire time. "I truthfully just wanted extra credit when I joined this internship! I didn't expect any of this. I was supposed to learn from this, not defend the world against aliens, drones, UMOs, and whatever tomorrow may bring!"

The drone started to regain its mobility. It got itself off the ground, hovered for a moment, and began to speak. "We aren't the enemy," the drone said. "This fight goes deeper than you could imagine. Don't trust them. No matter what they tell you. We aren't the enemy!"

The drone flew towards the window and stopped for a moment. "They're coming," it said. "They're coming back!" It flew out the window and towards the sky, disappearing.

Everyone went towards the window and looked outside.

"They're coming back?" Bob said.

"Who, the UMOs?" David asked.

"The aliens that warned us," Carol guessed.

Cam stared outside, wide-eyed. "All of them."

Everyone watched, as spaceships appeared in the sky, one by one. There were too many to count. Or so they thought.

"Fifty-seven," Cam said.

"Again with the fifty-seven?" Bob asked Cam.

"Look!" Cam said.

Hundreds of drones came from the sky.

"That's a lot of drones!" Carol said.

"Four hundred," Cam observed. "Maybe more."

"Okay," Bob said, "you're officially freaking me out."

"Don't trust them," the admiral said, thinking out loud.

Bob stared out the window. "Is this it? Is this what we were warned of? Quo most likely hasn't received the message yet. If he gets the message in three weeks, there might not be any of Earth left to save."

"Should we go outside?" the admiral asked Cam.

"You'll die!" David said. He still had no idea they were Elders.

"No we won't!" Cam said.

"Why, because you're an alien, Cam?" David asked.

Everyone turned to look at David.

"Oh come on!" David said. "It was a joke!"

Carol looked back out the window. "Oh no!"

Bob looked and saw what she saw. "Of course! Why wouldn't they show up too?!"

Admiral Noah, David, and Cam looked outside.

Everyone saw them. The UMOs were coming from every direction.

"And how many UMOs are there?" Bob asked Cam, jokingly.

"Thousands," Cam said, seriously.

Something was about to happen. No one knew quite what though.

As everyone stared at the many spaceships, hundreds of drones, and thousands of UMOs that filled Earth's sky, Bob looked at his friends then back outside. Trying to be funny, he simply said, "One problem at a time?"

The drones started shooting. Some of their shots were hitting the building.

"Watch out!" Carol exclaimed, as one of the shots hit near the window.

The UMOs started retaliating by flying towards the drones and landing on them. They started to turn red. As the chaos continued, Bob noticed the spaceships weren't doing anything.

"Why aren't they helping?" Bob wondered.

Drones started to fall out of the sky. UMOs were shot down and fell to the ground. As the shots continued, the spaceships started to move closer to Earth.

"Why aren't they stopping them?" Carol asked. "These spaceships told us to be ready. What if this is what we were supposed to be ready for? I don't think we're ready."

Shots came through the window. "Watch out!" Cam yelled. Someone fell to the ground. Bob turned to see David, holding his chest, near his heart. He screamed in pain.

"David!" Bob shouted.

They all went running towards David. He moved his hand to see the wound. He had been hit badly.

"David!" Cam cried. "Don't give up. The team needs you!"

Coughing, David said, "Why? Why do any of you need me? Bob and Carol are used to this kind of thing. Cam, you and the admiral aren't even human!"

"We are," Cam said.

"Why lie to me now?" David cried. "I'm dying!"

Admiral Noah looked at Cam, then at David. "You're not dying!" the admiral said. "Admiral's orders!"

"If only it worked like that," David said, coughing still. He blinked a few times, then closed his eyes. He opened them back up. "I lied to you."

"What?" Cam asked.

"Earlier, when I said I had been sleeping. I saw when you were sending the message. I saw everything. You're not human. The admiral is not human. Just tell me the truth!"

"Okay!" Cam said.

"No, Cam, don't!" Admiral Noah advised.

"I have to tell him!" Cam said. "The admiral is an Elder. I'm an Elder too!"

"Cam, wait, something isn't right," Bob said. "The firing has stopped!"

"I just wanted an extra college credit," David said sadly. He closed his eyes.

Not paying attention to anything but his dying friend, Cam simply said, "I'm not just an Elder. I'm a Senior!"

David opened his eyes. He looked down at his wound. Everyone watched as the wound healed itself.

"Admission!" David said. "ADMISSION!"

David disappeared from their sight, as if he was transported away.

Everyone looked outside. The UMOs all turned red and exploded. The drones disappeared into the sky, leaving only the spaceships outside.

"Humans of Earth," a voice that was loud and clear said, "you have been warned. Today's battle is only a glimpse of what is coming. Beware. You still have time. You must be ready."

"Is that the alien spaceships?" Bob asked.

"Yes," Cam said.

"Where did David go?" Carol asked.

Bob noticed something outside. Among all the other spaceships, was one spaceship that didn't look like any of the others.

"Is that their spaceship too?" Bob asked.

The voice continued, "They're coming. All of them." The voice stopped talking for a moment, as the spaceships came even closer to Earth. All of them came towards Earth, except the one that looked different.

"That one isn't theirs," Cam said. "The one leaving, it has David!"

Cam went running towards the window and yelled to the spaceships. "Look! Look over there!" He pointed as the other spaceship was now out of view.

The many spaceships didn't move, as if they knew what was going on.

"Cam!" the voice said. "They didn't take your friend. He chose to go with them. He chose his destiny. Now you all must choose yours."

"Who are you?!" Cam demanded.

"Beware!" the voice said.

Bob spoke up, "How much time do we have? What is coming for us?"

"The biggest war that has ever come to Earth," the voice said. "So be ready."

"What are those drones? Where did they come from? Why were they fighting with the UMOs?" Carol asked.

"Consider the events of today as another warning of what is to come," the voice said. "This battle is over. Now you must be ready for the war!"

The spaceships all disappeared, leaving Admiral Noah, Cam, Bob, and Carol in silence.

Chapter 15
The Planet Taker

It was silent for only a minute. Someone had to break the silence. Someone had to say what they were all thinking about.

"It almost feels like this was all a set up for someone to get information," Bob said. "Once Cam admitted that the admiral was an Elder and he himself was a Senior, it's like David got what he wanted."

"He was never really dying, was he?" Carol said. "We all saw him heal himself."

"Who is David, really?" Bob asked.

"None of this makes sense," Cam said.

"He was a human," the admiral said. "That's what Cam told me."

"David said he has known Cam for nearly five years. They went to school together. Cam, is that true?" Bob asked.

"Yes," Cam said. "We have been friends for five years. And admiral, I thought he was human."

"Obviously, we're missing something," Bob said. "How are we supposed to get ready for the war that is coming?"

"The aliens said that David chose to go with that other spaceship," Carol said. "Was that spaceship not with them? Was it not part of their warning? And why did the spaceships all just sit there while the drones and the UMOs were fighting?"

"They said David chose his destiny," Cam said. "But we still don't even know who any of them are!"

Admiral Noah was troubled. "I recognized the spaceship."

"What?" Cam asked.

"I recognized the spaceship. The one that looked different than the rest. The one that was leaving Earth."

"How so?" Cam asked. "That's probably the one that David was on."

"That was an Elder spaceship," the admiral admitted.

"So, David is an Elder too?" Cam asked.

"Not necessarily," the admiral said. "But I would guess he is at least working with them."

"Oh great!" Cam said. "One of the only friends I've ever had on this Earth now has vital information about you, admiral, and about me. Oh no."

"What's wrong?" Bob asked.

"They found me," Cam said. "If that was an Elder ship, and that's where David went, the Elders know I'm here now. They know there is a Senior hiding out on Earth."

"I'm sorry," the admiral said.

"It's my own fault! You were trying to stop me from telling him! I thought he was dying!" Cam said, upset.

"So, now what do we do?" Bob asked. "The Elders were already headed this way for an all-out war. Admiral. Cam. You never answered the question I asked before. Why are the Elders bringing their war to Earth?"

Cam sighed. "Bob," he said. "Near the beginning of time itself, after the Earth was formed, the humans were visited by someone."

The admiral felt uneasy. "I guess we have to tell you now," he said.

Cam continued, "An alien spaceship came to the Earth and asked the humans for help. The alien was running from someone. He wanted to hide out here, with the humans."

"Okay," Bob said. "What species was this alien?"

"No one knows," Cam admitted. "But that's not the point."

"He was running from the Elders," the admiral added.

"Running from the Elders? The Elders are good, aren't they?" Carol asked.

"As is true for any species, there are some good and some bad," Cam said.

"Why was he running from them?" Bob asked.

"He had stolen something from the Elders," the admiral said. "Technology."

"What sort of technology?" Bob asked.

"A weapon," Cam said.

"It's always a weapon," Bob said, disapprovingly. "What kind of weapon?"

"The Planet Taker," Cam said.

"Okay, just from the name, I don't like the sound of that," Carol said.

"He hid it," Cam continued.

"What do you mean?" Bob asked.

"He hid the weapon on Earth, so the Elders couldn't find it," Cam said.

"Why couldn't the Elders find their own technology on Earth?" Carol asked.

"You already know the answer," Admiral Noah said.

"The planet's yellow sun and gravity obstruct our powers. The weapon too is undetectable here," Cam said.

"Wait, is the weapon still on Earth after all these years?!" Bob said.

"The Elders think so," said the admiral.

"And… the Seniors believe it is too," Cam admitted.

"You're telling me that right now, somewhere on this Earth, there is a weapon called 'The Planet Taker'? I'm going to ask a stupid question here. What does The Planet Taker do?"

"I think you can figure that out," Cam said. "But it can only be used once."

"Why would the Elders ever create such a weapon?" Bob asked, angrily.

"We told you the Seniors have existed for nearly as long as the Elders," Cam said. "After the first generation of Elders, there was already division among them. The weapon was created to wipe out the opposition."

"And who created it? The Elders or the Seniors?"

"No one knows," Cam said.

"And you don't know who stole the weapon?" Carol asked.

"Again, we have no idea," the admiral said.

"So, let me see if I understand this," Bob said. "The Elders are all coming, including the Seniors, to fight over a weapon that is supposedly somewhere on Earth. A weapon that could destroy Earth itself. An alien spaceship came to Earth thousands of years ago with an unknown passenger who somehow stole this weapon from the all-powerful Elders. They hid this weapon from them somewhere on Earth. And the winner gets, what, the weapon? Why didn't they just make another one? That is not a suggestion. It's a question."

"Bob," the admiral said, "the weapon is made from the remains of our original home planet. It's one of a kind."

"The Elders' home planet exploded?" Bob said. "Why?!"

"No one knows," Cam said. "The Elders blame the Seniors, the Seniors blame the Elders. It's a good thing we're a strong species. They sensed it coming and all escaped."

"How could this division among the Elders become so strong?" Bob asked. "You blame each other for the destruction of your own home planet?"

"Wait," Carol said. "I'm starting to get this strange feeling…"

"What is it, Carol?" Bob asked.

"Someone hid a weapon on Earth. They supposedly came in a spaceship and hid a weapon somewhere. Undetectable to the Elders. And our government never found the weapon?"

The admiral was deep in thought. "The drone said, 'Don't trust them.' What if it was talking about the aliens that gave us the warning?"

"How did I miss this?" Cam said. "How else could a weapon hide on a planet for thousands of years? I can't believe I missed this." Cam began to shake.

"Cam?" Bob said.

"And we don't know who they are. We don't know who they are!"

"Cam!" Admiral Noah yelled. "What is it?"

"The Elders are all coming to Earth to fight for a weapon that is no longer here," Cam said.

"What do you mean?!" the admiral demanded.

"Admiral, I think the weapon is in the hands of those spaceships that warned us. The spaceship that looked different was actually theirs."

"You don't think…"

Cam interrupted the admiral, "They weren't just warning us. They were here to make sure they got what they came here for! We had the weapon with us all along! It was David! David is The Planet Taker!"

Chapter 16
The Call

"But who would even know about the weapon?" Bob asked.

"A lot of alien species know of its existence. And a lot of them could use it," Cam said, upset. "How could I not see that my best friend was The Planet Taker?"

"It's not your fault," the admiral said.

"Wait," Bob said, "they told us to be ready for the war. Are we sure they're the bad guys?"

"No," Cam said, "but they have a very powerful weapon now."

"What exactly does The Planet Taker do? How does it take the planet?"

"I don't know!" Cam yelled. "My head! My head hurts so much!" He fell to the ground. "Fifty-seven days from the first warning. They will arrive fifty-seven days from then."

"Fifty-seven days? Who? The Elders? Or these other aliens?" Carol asked.

"The other aliens already came back," Bob said. "I think he's talking about the Elders."

"Fifty-seven days would be about eight weeks," Carol said.

"Eight weeks and one day to be exact," Cam said. He passed out.

"It's only been three weeks," Bob said. "What are we supposed to do for the time remaining?"

"Be ready," Carol suggested.

"I can't just sit here and do nothing," Bob said.

"We'll do the opposite," the admiral said. "Carol, scan the skies for those drones. They might actually be on our side. I'm not sure about the UMOs or even the aliens themselves, but we should do an extra thorough scan. Look for anything strange. Even if it seems mostly normal. Investigate every detail."

"Got it," Carol said.

"Bob," the admiral said, "organize a new team of recruits. I didn't want to do this, but we're taking a ship up there to see what is going on. We'll fly around the moon and nearby planets. If there are any cloaked ships, or anything out of the ordinary, we will find them. We will question them. And we will figure this out."

"Sir, what are you going to do?" Bob asked.

"I'm going to have a much needed conversation with the Elders. Once Cam wakes up, I think we have to tell them who he is. This is no longer an Elder against Elder war. Someone else is involved and I plan on finding out who. Dismissed."

Carol looked at Bob, then back at the admiral. After such a busy day, the admiral didn't even realize they were still in Carol's laboratory.

"Well, I'll see myself out," the admiral said. "Call me when Cam wakes up!"

The admiral went to his own office to think.

Bob and Carol were still in shock, but Carol went straight to work. Bob started thinking about the team he was going to put together.

"Carol," he said, "I think we should be the ones to go into space."

"Oh, I've never been to space," Carol said.

"Carol, we don't need space. Space needs us."

Carol stared at her husband. "Okay," she said.

Bob walked to the admiral's office. He heard crying. He carefully peeked into the office without the admiral seeing him.

"This division has gone too far!" the admiral said. He was on the phone with someone. "No, sir, I don't think that's true! They aren't the enemy. They never have been."

Bob couldn't hear the other half of the conversation, but he listened to what he could hear.

"They aren't! It isn't them! There is someone else involved now! How do I know it's not the Seniors? I... can't say."

Carol came running towards Bob. "Cam woke up. He's coming to speak to the admiral."

Cam walked up behind and straight past Bob and Carol. He went into the admiral's office and took the phone.

"Hello? Who am I speaking with?" Cam asked.

The admiral noticed Bob and Carol, and he dried his eyes. He looked at Cam.

Cam spoke into the phone again, "Well, you may be a very important Elder, high in power, you may know a lot, but I have something to tell you. You're not going to believe this."

The admiral reached for the phone. He pressed a button so everyone could hear the other half of the conversation.

"We already know," the Elder said over the phone.

"You told them?" Cam asked the admiral.

"No, he didn't," the Elder said. "David did."

"You have David?" Cam said, surprised.

Bob walked into the room. "Sir," he said to the Elder on the phone, "was your spaceship just on Earth?"

"Who is this?" the Elder asked.

"Bob," he said.

"Yes, we were," the Elder said. "We were taking what was rightfully ours. After so many years, I can't believe we finally found it."

"Why did you create him?" Cam said. "He's The Planet Taker, isn't he?"

"Cam. I don't personally blame you for not knowing. Oh, Camouflage. Thank you for leading us to the weapon."

"I did no such thing!" Cam cried.

"Not intentionally, no," the Elder said. "It was thanks to all of our friends."

"What?" Cam asked.

"The aliens that gave you the warning. They are on our side. Well, maybe not your side, Senior."

"How do you know?!"

"Let's just say, ever since you've been on Earth we've been tracking you."

"I had no idea, I swear," the admiral said.

"No, he didn't know," the Elder admitted, "but he sure helped us out! Sure, it's tough to track an Elder on planet Earth. But it isn't if you search slowly for years. We listened in on conversations. Noah, how did you not know your office was bugged?"

They heard a small buzzing sound. A UMO came crawling out from inside the ceiling.

"The UMOs are a creation of the Elders?!"

The Elder laughed. "Yes, we overheard when you named them. I must admit, Cam, UMO is a pretty interesting name for it. Every time you saw one, or didn't, we were listening! Oh, the conversations you had in this office. Thank you, Bob, for needing to know their secrets. We found out a lot that day."

"Are the drones yours too?" Bob asked.

"We have no idea who those belong to," the Elder admitted. "Not that that matters. We have what is ours now. We have what we've been searching for."

"Are you the bad guys?" Carol asked.

"No!" the Elder said. "The bad guys are the ones who blew up our home planet! Cam's people."

"My people are your people!" Cam yelled. "We are all Elders. We are all the same!"

"I agree with him," the admiral said.

"Yes," the Elder said. "We are aware of where you stand on the issue. Noah, thank you for your service. We hereby relieve you of your duties."

"As admiral?!" he asked.

"As Elder." The phone call ended.

Chapter 17
Departure and Arrival

"Can he do that?" Bob asked.

"Technically, no," the admiral said. "I'm still an Elder. Just not to them."

"How many of them are like that?" Carol asked. "He was so upset."

"A lot of them," the admiral said. "But it's on both sides. There are some Seniors that are just as upset. They blame each other for the planet exploding."

"But not all of them are like this?" Carol asked.

"No," the admiral said. "Many of them have moved on to more important things. The destruction of our planet was a tragedy. But fighting each other, living in the past, that won't change anything. Some Elders have, in fact, moved on."

"What if we found out who really blew up your planet?" Bob asked.

"That's a dangerous road to go down," the admiral said. "It might help, but how would you find proof from something that happened thousands of years ago? Besides, some of the Elders had that same thought. Now look at them. They are at war."

"Sadly, we're all at war," Cam said. "Even if we don't want to be. They are still all our people."

"So the Elders have David. What is our next move?" Bob asked. "Are they even coming to Earth anymore? They have what they wanted. There is no need for this war to happen on Earth."

"I wish that were true," Cam said. "But I fear they'll still battle it out here."

"Why?" Carol asked.

"I'm not sure yet," Cam said. "Just, look outside."

Everyone went running out of the admiral's office and straight towards the front door of the building. They opened the door and looked up. They saw four spaceships. They were different than any spaceships they had seen so far. One of the ships landed on the ground, right in front of the building. The door opened and a woman stepped out.

She walked towards Cam and said, "Come with us."

"Who are you?" he asked.

"We don't have much time. They'll notice we're here."

"I don't know who you are," Cam said.

"My name is not important."

"Are you Elders?"

"My species is not important."

"I can't just go with you blindly," Cam said.

A drone came flying out of the ship behind her. "Trust her," the drone said in its robotic voice.

"Are these your creations?" the admiral asked.

"Yes," the woman said. "You must come with us too, Admiral Noah."

"What?" Admiral Noah was confused. "I can't just leave here…"

"We must keep you safe," the woman said. "Please, come with us."

The admiral looked at Bob, then at Carol and Cam. "Cam?"

"We have to go with her," Cam said. "Just in case they decide to come back."

Bob looked at them. "Admiral, what are we supposed to do without you?"

"Bob, I hereby make you interim admiral. Watch everything while we are gone. We will make this right. This division has got to end."

The woman smiled. "The division will end. One way or another."

"What does that mean?" Bob asked.

"Come, we must be going," the woman said. She went back to the ship, followed by the drone. Cam and the admiral looked at Bob and Carol.

"Hold down the fort," the admiral said. "I trust this woman and I don't know why. Hold off on sending any teams out into the skies, Bob. Carol, watch the sky. And if the crew of 'The Boulder' receives our message, well, I'm sure you'll know what to do when the time is right."

Cam looked towards the sky. "I don't feel safe on Earth anymore," he said. He looked back at Bob and Carol. "And neither does the admiral. We have to stop the division."

Admiral Noah and Cam entered the ship. The four spaceships took off into the sky.

Bob looked at his wife and said, "Carol, I have no idea where to go from here."

"There is nowhere to go," Carol said. "The admiral said not to send any teams. All we can do is watch the sky, and just wait. I don't like this, Bob."

"I guess waiting isn't so bad," he said. "It gives Quo and the crew the time to receive the message. Quick, we better start waiting!" Bob smiled at his wife.

"You'd still be a terrible writer," she smiled.

The next three weeks were quiet. They were extremely quiet. No alien ships, no more UMOs, no more drones. Nothing out of the ordinary. Carol watched the sky every day. Bob trained new teams for any future missions. They still wanted to be ready. Just in case. They were trying to get ready for anything. For whatever might come next.

After the three weeks of silence, something finally happened. Bob and Carol were in her lab, talking about everyday life, when they heard a noise outside.

"What was that?" Carol asked Bob.

Bob looked out the window. He couldn't see anything. They walked towards the front door of the building. He opened the door to see five people standing outside.

"Message received!" someone said. He walked closer to Bob and Carol.

"Quo!" Bob exclaimed.

"We got your message!" Quo said.

"Captain Zot!" Bob said.

"This is my wife, Gloria," Captain Zot said.

"You have a wife?" Bob asked.

"I was surprised when I found out too!" Captain Zot laughed.

"Who is that?" Bob asked.

"That's Glor!" Quo said.

"She's our daughter," Captain Zot added.

"Hello," Glor said. "It's nice to meet you."

"You have a daughter too?!" Bob asked. "How is that possible? You haven't been gone that long!"

"Oh, I'm not sure you'd believe us," Gloria said. "But maybe we should go inside and exchange stories. We received your message, and we're here to help."

"How did you get here so fast though?"

"I, for one, am an Elder," Gloria smiled. "We all transported across space. From our current home planet, straight to Earth. We have a teleporter in our family as well. Clory, come meet our friend Bob!"

Clory walked up to him and smiled. "I'm not sure what danger awaits Earth, but I am happy to help defend something that means so much to my friends."

"Nice necklace!" Carol said to Glor.

"Thank you," Glor said. "It is very important to my family and especially to me." Glor looked at her mother and they both smiled. "This necklace is one of our most important pieces of history."

"Are you all Elders?" Bob asked.

"No," Captain Zot said, "not technically."

"But that doesn't matter!" Gloria added.

Quo looked at Bob and Carol, and said, "Bob, thank you for sending me that message. Clory and I were talking earlier that day and he just randomly started thinking about the first conversation we had."

"That wasn't random," Bob smiled. He looked at Carol. "I guess even just the thought that Cam sent to Quo's friend worked. It got them talking."

"Who's Cam?" Captain Zot asked.

"Let's all go inside," Carol said. "We have a lot to talk about."

Chapter 18
Lies and Truth

They all went to Carol's laboratory and began to talk. Quo told them of everything he had been through. From the moment he woke up to the moment he received the message.

"How did you send the message?" Quo asked.

"Cam and Admiral Noah sent it to you," Bob said. "Cam was worried about you, Quo."

"Who is Cam?" Quo asked.

"He was talking to you directly a few weeks ago," Bob said.

"I've never met him," Quo said.

"He was trying to get you to remember your name," Bob replied.

"That was him?!" Quo was shocked. "Glor, remember that?!"

Glor remembered. "He was the voice in the forest! I heard him too! We saw a humanoid figure."

"Is Cam an Elder?" Quo asked. "How else could he have done that?"

"Yes, he is," Bob said.

"Admiral Noah is an Elder too," Carol added.

Captain Zot was shocked. "The admiral is an Elder?! Wow."

"Where are they now?" Quo asked.

"They left about three weeks ago," Bob said. "We don't know who they left with, but they didn't feel safe on Earth anymore."

"Why not?" Gloria asked.

"Ever since the Elders found out the truth about Cam, they were pretty mean," Bob said.

"The Elders? Mean? That doesn't sound like them," Gloria said. "What truth?"

Bob hesitated, but then decided he could trust Gloria. "He's a Senior."

"What?" Gloria said.

"What's a Senior?" Quo asked.

"Not only that, but the Elders have been spying on us for years," Bob said.

"That doesn't sound like them at all," Gloria replied.

"They were using their technology against us," Bob said. "The UMOs. They are little round metal things that apparently can listen in on our conversations."

Gloria was puzzled. "What are you talking about?"

"Gloria, you're an Elder, are you telling me you have never heard of the Seniors?"

"Oh, I've heard of them," Gloria said. "I just didn't think there were any of them around anymore. I thought that title was forgotten about when the fighting ended hundreds of years ago."

"Hundreds of... wait a minute," Bob realized. "How did you transport all the way to Earth? Aren't your powers obscured from the yellow sun and gravity?"

"Bob, where did you get all this information?" Clory asked. "That's not true at all."

"Cam and Admiral Noah told me. Wait, Gloria, is it true that the Elders original home planet exploded? And the Seniors and the Elders were fighting because of that?"

"Yes," Gloria said, "that much is true. But I don't think I trust this Cam or this Admiral Noah. Their information seems off."

"What about the weapon?" Carol said.

"What weapon?" Gloria asked.

"The weapon made from the pieces of your original home planet."

"I've heard about it," Gloria said, "but it's almost ancient history at this point."

"Legend said it was on Earth somewhere," Bob said. "That's what Cam and the admiral said."

"Mom," Glor said to Gloria, "someone has been spreading hate through the galaxies. The Elders worked together to end this problem hundreds of years ago. They forgave each other. They learned from their mistakes. They stopped blaming each other. The explosion was no one's fault. It just happened."

Gloria looked at her daughter, then at Bob. "What else did they tell you? Tell us everything."

Bob and Carol caught everyone up on their side of the story. They told them in detail about the original warning Earth had received six weeks earlier. They told them about the drones. They told them about the satellite, about that day on the roof, and the first time Bob saw the UMOs. They talked about how the aliens had returned, how the drones and the UMOs were battling each other, and how there was a spaceship that seemed out of place that day. They talked about when David got shot but how he healed himself after gaining the information he was looking for. They told them about the phone call and how the Elder had told the admiral he was no longer an Elder. They told them about the day those four spaceships came to Earth and how a woman came out of the ship with one of the drones. They talked about how the admiral and Cam just left, how it seemed out of the blue but how they understood their choice. And finally, they told them they believed that David was the weapon.

"You really think David is the weapon?" Gloria asked.

"Yes," Bob said, "but I don't know what is true anymore."

"If they truly put all of this behind them, how did it resurface?" Carol asked.

"Sadly," Gloria said, "hate has its way of resurfacing."

Clory looked around. "If someone has the weapon, shouldn't we be afraid for the galaxy, or the universe?"

Gloria sighed. "Not a day goes by that I'm not worried about that."

"How do we fight this? How do we stop this? What are we even fighting?" Clory said.

Quo looked up at the ceiling. "What is that?" he asked.

Bob looked up as a UMO quickly went back into the ceiling. "Oh no," he said. "They were listening again!"

Bob and Quo both looked out the window. The spaceships that had warned Earth started to appear in the sky again. Other spaceships appeared, similar to the one that took David. Even more spaceships appeared.

"Those are Elders' spaceships!" Gloria cried. "What is happening? What have they done?"

"I think you guys got here just in time," Bob said. "We were told to be ready. I hope we're ready."

They all walked out of Carol's laboratory and exited out the front of the building. The sky was filled with many different kinds of spaceships.

"Those look like the Elders' ships that saved us from the collision," Quo said.

"And those look like Elders' ships too," Gloria said, noticing more spaceships. "How many of them knew about this? What is this, a rebellion? We were past this!"

"Good," a voice from the sky said. "It's here! That took a lot of work. A lot of years. But man, oh man, was it worth the time!"

Glor noticed that her necklace started to glow. "Mom?" she said.

Clory looked up towards the ships. "WHAT DO YOU WANT?!" he screamed.

"Oh, please!" the voice said. It sounded so familiar. Someone transported from a ship to the ground. It was David.

"The weapon!" Bob said.

"I'm not the weapon!" David said. "You guys truly will believe anything! It's hilarious."

Two more bodies transported from the ships to the ground. It was Cam and Admiral Noah.

"Cam! Admiral!" Bob said. "I'm so glad you're okay!"

Cam laughed. "That took forever! But we had to make it convincing."

Captain Zot looked at the admiral. "Admiral Noah, are you okay?"

"Never been better," he said. "I finally see the truth. I'm finally on the right side!"

"And what side is that?" Clory asked.

"The winning one!" the admiral said.

Glor's necklace became brighter. It started to heat up, so she took it off her neck. "Mom?" she said. "What is happening?"

Gloria looked at her daughter and then realized. "The weapon!" she said. "Glor, give me the necklace!"

Glor threw the necklace to her mother, who was about to catch it.

"Oh no, no, no!" Cam said. He put up his hand and stopped the necklace midair before Gloria could catch it. He then started to pull the necklace towards him telekinetically.

Quo looked at Bob, as they both realized. They said at the same time, "The necklace is the weapon!"

Chapter 19
The War

"Cam!" Bob yelled.

"What?" Cam said, as the necklace came towards him.

"Is that why we had to send the message to Quo and the crew?" Bob asked. "You somehow found out that Glor's necklace was the weapon, so you had this elaborate plan to get the necklace to Earth? I don't understand! Was anything you said true?"

"Yes," Cam said. "The Elders were the ones that blew up our planet. The Elders will pay!"

Cam was struggling. Glor, who recently found out that she had the combined powers of her parents, was using her powers to stop time around the necklace.

Bob looked up and saw more spaceships coming. "This is it," he said to Carol. "I don't know whose side anybody is on anymore, but this is what the warning was about all along. Are we ready?"

Carol looked at Bob, then at Quo, Clory, Captain Zot, Gloria, and Glor. "Because they're here," she said, "I think we are ready."

Everyone started transporting from the many ships to the ground. Two, four, eight, until there were a dozen, no, three dozen of them now on the ground. Everyone looked around, as a voice began to talk. It was the same voice that came to Earth and gave them the warning.

"Humans of Earth," it said, "welcome, to the war."

Some of the bodies that had transported down were Elders. Some were other species. One final body transported down. He walked straight up to the admiral.

"Hello, Admiral," he said.

"That's the Elder that was on the phone with him that day! The one that relieved him of his duties as Elder!" Bob said.

"How could you know that?" Quo asked.

"The voice," Bob said. "It's definitely him."

The Elder turned to look at Bob. "Bob? Is that you?" he said. "Allow me to introduce myself."

"I know who you are!" Bob said.

"Good," he said. "That makes this more satisfying."

He looked at the necklace still floating in midair. He saw Glor and Cam both struggling to hold their powers against one another.

"By the way," he said, "my name is Erysichton. But you can call me Ery for short."

"Okay, Ery," Bob said, "why are you doing this?"

"Isn't it obvious? The hatred that these Seniors have bestowed among us has got to end. The hatred must be destroyed. So I say, we kill them all."

"How do you not hear yourself? That. That right there is hatred!" Bob cried.

Another Elder stepped forward. She had transported down among the three dozen bodies moments ago.

"Erysichton!" she said. "My name is Clotilda. I am speaking on behalf of the Seniors."

Ery looked at Clotilda. "I don't care what you have to say!"

"I'm glad you feel that way," Clotilda said. "Because I was just going to say, you better be ready to die! You do know the Seniors have been picking up many allies along the way, making us superior."

"Oh, Clotilda. You have nothing compared to what we, the Elders have."

"I never liked the Elders," Clotilda said.

Bob overheard and yelled, "YOU ARE THE ELDERS! ALL SENIORS ARE ELDERS!"

Clotilda laughed. "No, they don't deserve the title. After they blew up our home planet, we started watching them throughout history. The Seniors are better. The Seniors would never do what the Elders have done."

Ery looked at her. "You know that to be a lie! It was the Seniors who blew up our home planet!"

A voice from the sky could be heard again. The same voice that warned Earth over a month ago. "SOLDIERS, DEPLOY!"

Hundreds more individuals transported to the ground. Some Seniors, some Elders, and some allies both sides had picked up along the way.

Cam and Glor were still struggling, holding the necklace in midair.

Ery turned back to the admiral. "Oh, are you finally on our side now?" he snapped his fingers in front of the admiral's face. The admiral didn't even blink. "Good. It worked. Good work, Cam. I'm glad you finally made him see the truth."

Bob looked at Captain Zot. "He's under their control! That means the admiral isn't actually a traitor!"

Gloria looked directly at Admiral Noah. "Do I know you?" she said.

All-out war was inevitable now. There were so many different species. Some were blue and green. Some had superpowers, some didn't.

Ery looked out towards the crowd and yelled, "ATTACK!"

Clotilda looked on, as Ery himself went running towards the crowd. Thinking she was better than him, she too went running towards the crowd to fight. It wasn't pretty. Elder against Senior still meant Elder against Elder. They fought each other for nearly a minute, when Bob looked at Quo and said, "Quo, how do we stop this?"

"I have no idea," Quo said. He looked at Gloria, as she stared at the fighting.

"We were past this," Gloria said. "It doesn't make sense. How are there so many of them full of hatred?"

Glor, still struggling to use her powers, looked at her mom. "Mom," she said. "Something doesn't feel right."

Gloria felt it too. There was something wrong about all of this.

The fighting among the crowd continued, as even more bodies transported to the ground. Some were fighting using their powers, some were using hand-to-hand combat.

Though there was all of this hatred and chaos, a woman simply walked out of the crowd towards Cam. She kept walking towards Bob, Carol, Quo, and their friends.

"That's the woman that took Cam and the admiral!" Bob said. "The one that was trying to keep them safe!"

She stopped just in front of the floating necklace. Before anybody could react, she grabbed the necklace and transported away. Cam disappeared as well as the admiral. A lone spaceship quickly flew into the sky out of view.

Glor was taken aback when all this happened, but she, being as strong as she is, just stood there, in shock. She stared at her mother. "Mom, it was all a setup!" She began to cry.

The fighting continued and became more dangerous as more of them started to use their powers against each other.

Gloria started to realize what had just happened. Bob looked at her, he finally realized.

"I'm going to be sick," Glor said.

"EVERYONE STOP FIGHTING!" Gloria said, in a loud voice that echoed through the crowd. They all stopped, but for a moment, to listen.

"Do you not realize what has just happened?" Gloria asked. "Are you so angry with each other that you haven't even noticed? Your hatred has blinded you all! Look! What you are fighting for, this necklace, this weapon that you all want so badly, is gone!"

Ery and Clotilda walked out of the crowd.

"You have tricked us!" Ery said to Clotilda. "It was all a trick so you could have the weapon!"

"I did no such thing!" Clotilda said, sternly. "I have more pride than that. I am a Senior. I wouldn't use such trickery. This is something your people would do, Elder!"

"ENOUGH!" Gloria yelled. "You are both Elders! Seniors are Elders! And the title of Seniors hasn't even been around for hundreds of years! We put this behind us!"

Clotilda stared at Gloria. "For fifty-seven years now we have been growing in numbers. The Seniors have risen back to the top! We are superior!"

Ery laughed. "Yes, all eight of you!"

Clotilda stared at him. "You know full well there are many more than eight!"

Bob looked around at everything. He stepped forward and asked, "When did the hate return?"

"What?" Clotilda didn't understand the question.

Bob said again, "When did the hate return? If the Elders truly put this behind them hundreds of years ago, when did the hate return?"

The voice from the sky began to speak. Again, it was the same voice that not only originally warned Earth, it was also the same voice of the aliens that Ery had earlier admitted to being on the same side as the Elders while he was on the phone with the admiral.

"This is precious," the voice laughed. "And it all took only fifty-seven years to build back up! Hate spreads so quickly. We brought back in fifty-seven years, what had been forgotten for nearly five hundred years!"

"Who are you?!" Bob demanded. "You sent the warning to Earth. You warned us to be ready!"

"And you weren't!" the voice said, mockingly. "You really want to know who I am? Are you sure your little minds want to see who defeated you all?"

Bob started to recognize the voice. "Is that...?"

"I'll project my image. Our image for you all to see. But we are far away now. No way you'll ever catch or even find us!"

The image was projected. The voice of the one that had warned Earth was now known to all.

"That's the woman who came to Earth and supposedly took Admiral Noah and Cam to safety!" Bob said. "The same woman that just took the necklace and the admiral and Cam now! But, when you took them the first time, you were in a different spaceship!"

She laughed. "Shapeshifting. It's a cool talent. Especially when you learn how to modify that power to work in other ways!"

Ery was furious. "You said you were on our side!" he said.

"That's the funny thing about sides," she said. "You and the Seniors should've been on the same side all along. Glad I could put that wedge of division back between you! All so I could get what I wanted for my agenda!"

Bob stared at the image, as two more images were projected. It was Cam and the admiral.

Cam smiled at them. "Hello!" he said.

"Cam," Bob said, "when did you start working with this, this woman?"

"When did I start?" Cam laughed. "I've always been faithful to this woman. She is, in fact, my wife! Say hello, Enyo!"

"Cam, are you even an Elder?" Bob asked.

"I'm whatever I want to be! I'm a shapeshifter! I'm of the same species as my wife!" He shapeshifted to look like her. "I'm an Elder!" He shapeshifted to look like an Elder. "I'm a Senior!" He didn't shapeshift at all, to prove a point that the Elders and Seniors were always the same.

His wife laughed at this.

"Camouflage!" he laughed. "Honestly!"

The crowd looked on, realizing it was their war, this very war that was being mocked by Cam and his wife, Enyo.

"Oh, and by the way," Cam continued, "the admiral is safe. For now. We just need him for a little bit longer."

The admiral wasn't saying anything.

"He's currently under our control," Enyo said.

"Who are you two?" Bob demanded. "Why do you want the necklace?"

The communication started to cut out. It came back. "Why," Cam said, "we're just two simple shapeshifters who want to see justice prevail!"

"There were many ships that warned Earth!" Bob said.

"Four ships that came to get the admiral and Cam. Are you telling me this was all orchestrated by you two alone? No one else? Explain the other ships!"

"Why?!" Enyo laughed. "It would just be a projection of what already happened!"

Cam laughed at his wife.

"Just a projection?" Bob thought. He spoke, "How are we even supposed to know what is real anymore?!"

Enyo and Cam smiled. "We're real!" they both said.

"What are you going to do?!" Gloria said, nervously.

"Oh, never mind that," Enyo said.

Cam laughed. "Oh come on, let's tell them!"

Enyo smiled. "Alright. Remember how your planet exploded all those years ago? Time to make history!" She laughed.

They flickered out of sight, then came back. "One more thing!" Cam said. "Remember how you thought David was the weapon? Well, obviously he is not THE weapon. But he is A weapon!" He looked at Enyo. "I think he grew up to be the weapon we always wanted him to be!"

"Our beautiful weapon!" Enyo said. "Ah yes. Time to give you one final warning! Humans of Earth, Elders, every other species that took part in our lovely master plan. So, so sorry. You were not ready. And I'm afraid it's too late. You, just like the Elders' home planet, will no longer exist. It was nice working with you all. Enjoy your lives! All three minutes of what's left of them!"

Enyo pressed a button, and the projection disappeared.

David wandered out of the crowd. He had been fighting with everyone once the chaos had begun.

"Oh no," David said. "I guess I was wrong! I guess I am a weapon! Thank you, mother and father!" He looked up towards the sky, then he walked towards Bob and stopped. He looked at Clory and Captain Zot. He looked at Glor and Gloria. He stared at Quo, Carol, and finally at Bob. "The end," he said.

Chapter 20
Survival

David looked around, expecting destruction. He was shocked when he didn't see death everywhere.

"What is the meaning of this?" David growled.

Everyone was staring at David. The Elders, the ones that called themselves Seniors, and every other species that was on the ground. Anybody that was left in the ships above were looking out. Everyone was concentrating. Everyone was using their powers to stop David.

Gloria smiled. "There are a few things that will bring everyone together quicker than hatred can," she said to everyone. "One of them is love. Love is the most powerful emotion there ever has been, and ever will be."

"This isn't love, though," Glor said to her mom.

"No," Gloria replied. "But it'll do for now. Until we can all heal from this. We are stronger when we come together. We'll learn to love each other again. We'll put this behind us. It will take time. It will take so much effort from everyone involved. But we will regain the unity that we once had."

Bob looked at David, then at Gloria. "What is it that saved us today?"

Gloria smiled. "Survival!"

No one wanted to die. No one wanted it to end like this. Some of them felt guilty about everything. Some of the crowd didn't know what to feel. They didn't know where they stood. All everyone knew was one thing. They all wanted to survive.

With everyone concentrating their powers on David, he started to glow. Glor looked straight at him and yelled, "Stop!"

And there he stood, frozen in time.

"I don't feel safe with him here!" Ery said. "What if he goes off another day? We must destroy him!"

"There is always another way," Gloria said. "We'll take him with us, put him somewhere he can never harm anybody!"

"What if he goes off on another planet?" Clotilda said. "Destroy him!"

"No," Ery said. "I'll destroy him! I'm the superior Elder!" Clotilda became furious.

"Are you two kidding me?!" Bob said. "After all of this, you still consider yourselves better than each other?!"

Gloria looked at Bob, then at Clotilda and Ery. "You two," she said, "haven't you learned anything?"

"Yes," Ery said. "I learned something from Cam and Enyo. If you catch everyone off guard, you get what you want."

He rushed towards David and put a force field around him, so David wouldn't destroy anything but himself.

"I will destroy him!" Clotilda said, angrily. She jumped at Ery, making him lose control of the force field, and landing herself and Ery on David.

"No!" Ery cried. "I already set him off!"

Just milliseconds before the explosion that would have wiped out half of Earth, something had to be done. The crowd realized that they were all about to die. Everyone simultaneously tried to use their powers to restore the force field around David, but Ery and Clotilda were just too close. It was too late for anyone to do anything.

Glor looked over and was about to stop time again, when David looked directly at her and stopped her.

BOOM!

Everyone looked at the ground. Where David, Clotilda, and Ery once were, was now a pile of ash.

"Are they gone?" Glor cried. "I tried to stop time, I tried to save them!"

Gloria rushed to her daughter and hugged her. "I'm sorry, sweetie," she said. "I guess some people truly never learn from their mistakes."

Now that the war was over, everyone in the crowd just looked around at each other. Some of them were embarrassed by everything that happened. Some of them were somber. Some of them had no emotion. But most of them were now lost.

Gloria noticed everyone just standing there in shock, so she walked towards the crowd and began to speak. "Everyone," Gloria began, "I know you all come from different backgrounds. Different places. But I would like to offer a place of refuge for anybody that would like to come with me."

Glor looked at her mom and smiled, as her mother continued talking.

"The Elders have recently found themselves a new home planet. We share this with another species. They are friendly. We all get along. If anybody would like to join us, just let me know."

The crowd started to stir, as one by one they transported back to their spaceships. Every single one of them left, until there were only two standing where the crowd was, and only one spaceship left in the sky.

"Thank you," one of them said. "Thank you for helping us realize how wrong this division was. I hope to once again rid our species of this. We'll work towards it." The two of them transported to their ship and left.

Now left outside was only Clory, Quo, Gloria, Captain Zot, Glor, Carol, and Bob.

It was silent. Glor looked at her mom. "Not a single one of them accepted your offer," she said.

"I suppose they need to think about everything that just happened. I'm sure we'll see some of them again. Hopefully fighting the good fight. Spreading love, not hate. Because love always prevails in the end."

Glor smiled at her mom, then walked towards Quo.

"We did it," she said, still smiling. "We saved Earth."

Quo smiled, but he felt uneasy. "I think we have another problem now though," he said, as his smile faded. "We have to go stop them from blowing up the Elders' home planet in the past."

Clory was troubled. "I'm not sure we can," he said. "What if, by stopping them, we change history too much? What if we end up being the ones that cause the explosion?"

"But they still need to be stopped," Gloria said. "We don't want them roaming free. I don't think the Elders would want that either."

The seven of them looked around. Then, they looked at Gloria.

"We're going to need a spaceship," she said.

Chapter 21
Decision

It took less than an hour for Bob to have a spaceship ready for everyone. They were all about to board the ship.

"But the admiral said not to send any teams," Carol said.

"The admiral isn't thinking straight," Bob said. "I don't know how long he has been under the control of Cam and Enyo. But I'm thinking it's been nearly the five years that Cam has been here."

Carol nodded.

The seven passengers stood by the ship.

Bob looked at Zot. "Captain," he said, "could you please pilot this ship?"

Captain Zot smiled. "It would be my pleasure."

"I haven't had a chance to name this one yet," Bob said. "Any suggestions?"

"Revision!" Glor said. "You should call it Revision!"

"Why?" Gloria asked, curiously.

"Aren't we going to save the original home planet of the Elders from exploding? That's an epic revision!"

"I don't know what we'll end up doing," Gloria admitted. "We just have to stop them!"

"Decision!" Captain Zot exclaimed. "We are not sure what to expect, but we have decided to go anyways!"

"I love it!" Gloria said.

"Then everyone," Bob said, "all aboard our new ship, 'Decision'. It has been decided!"

Everyone walked inside and sat down on the bridge of the ship for takeoff.

"So, how are we supposed to find them?" Bob asked.

"Now that is the easy part," Gloria said. "That necklace is important to my family. To my people. I can easily track it."

"Are they traveling back in time?" Bob asked. "The destruction of your planet was so long ago. How can they time travel?"

"I don't know much about them," Gloria admitted, "but I know how we're going to time travel."

Glor looked at her mom. She had been practicing using her powers for the last three weeks. The three weeks since the collision. On the new home planet, Glor had started to learn a new trick. It took a lot of concentration and the help of her family.

Gloria herself had powers. She could stop time. Captain Zot also had powers. He could imitate the powers of those he loved. Clory could teleport. And Glor had the combined powers of her parents. She had stopped time and imitated others' powers on multiple occasions. She was stronger than both of her parents.

"What's the plan?" Bob asked.

"First," Captain Zot said, looking at his wife, "do you know when they went?"

"I don't know exactly," she admitted. "I think we'll find them."

Captain Zot pressed some buttons on the control panel in front of him. "Ready?" he asked everyone.

Bob looked at Quo. "How are we going to time travel?"

Quo motioned towards Glor. Glor was concentrating on something. "She is putting some sort of force field around the entire ship," Quo explained. Gloria was also concentrating. "She's helping Glor with the force field."

"Gloria and Glor's powers allow them to stop time," Quo continued. "They have been finding other ways to use their powers. They have found a way to not only stop time, but if they work together, they can actually rewind time. Moving us back through time itself."

He then looked over at Clory and then at the captain. "Clory can teleport," Quo said. "Captain Zot can imitate the powers of those he loves. And Glor can help out with that too. With three of them rewinding time and three of them that can use the teleportation powers, we have time travel!"

"Woah!" Bob was amazed. "Wait, they're going to teleport the entire ship to where it needs to be after rewinding time?! That's awesome!"

Quo smiled. "Add to that the connection that necklace has with their family."

"That's an awesome family," Carol said.

"One of us isn't even here," Clory said, sadly. "My brother, Smedge. He is at home with his grandparents. He was very selfish."

"Yeah," Bob said, "Quo mentioned that earlier when he talked about the collision."

"Smedge is a baby again," Captain Zot said. "Jumping into a planet full of time energy has its consequences, I suppose."

"Time energy?" Carol asked. "Interesting."

Before she could ask any more questions, Glor yelled, "NOW!"

Gloria tried to telepathically lock onto the necklace, as Clory, Captain Zot and Glor teleported the ship. The ship appeared in the middle of space. Quo looked out the window. He saw a planet.

"It is so beautiful!" Gloria gasped. "There it is! I've only seen it in pictures!"

Glor looked out at the planet, in awe.

Everyone was admiring the wonder of this planet. They had, in fact, found the home planet of the Elders before it had been destroyed.

The ship shook. "Someone is shooting at us!" Captain Zot said. "Guess who?"

Everyone looked as a familiar ship came into view.

It was Cam and Enyo's ship. It was time to stop them. Whoever these shapeshifters were, wherever they came from, that didn't matter.

No one knew how this might change history. But they had to save the admiral. They had to stop Cam and Enyo if they could.

"I have so many questions about everything!" Quo admitted.

Bob smiled, as everyone was now at the ready for whatever came next. He simply said, "One problem at a time, Quo! One problem at a time!"

Cam and Enyo's ship came closer to their ship. It stopped. The ship was hailing them. Captain Zot pressed a button and Cam and Enyo could be seen on the main viewing screen.

"It's about time!" Enyo said, laughing.

Cam looked at everyone on the ship and smiled. He held up the necklace. "Come and get it!" he said. He ended the transmission.

Cam and Enyo's ship went flying past them, towards the planet.

Captain Zot looked at everyone. "I should probably say something important here," he admitted.

"You might want to make a decision!" Bob said, jokingly. "The name of the ship? It's, oh, never mind."

Quo laughed.

Carol smiled at Bob.

Captain Zot laughed and said, "Okay, Bob, I guess the 'Decision' has been made for us!"

Bob found that hysterical, as he helped build this ship.

The captain smiled, as he steered the ship towards Enyo and Cam's ship and towards the planet itself. No one knew what was to come. But somehow, they were all ready for it.

Chapter 22
Shockwave

Enyo and Cam started firing back towards the 'Decision'. The ship started to shake.

"We have eighty percent shields," Captain Zot said, as they held their course.

"We better go faster if we want to catch them!" Glor suggested.

Captain Zot listened to his daughter's advice. He gained on the other ship, but just as he caught up, Cam and Enyo's ship zoomed around them, and was now flying away from the planet.

"What are they doing?!" Gloria asked.

Enyo and Cam hailed their ship again.

"What?!" Captain Zot said, answering the call.

"Why are you spreading so much hatred and chaos?!" Glor demanded.

Cam looked at his wife and smiled. "Chaos? Hatred? Me?"

Enyo laughed. "You do know that 'Chaos' is the name of our ship, right?"

"I'm so glad you found me," Cam said, staring at his wife. "Anyways," he continued, "I suppose it's time to deploy the weapon!"

Cam held up the necklace, which was glowing brighter than Glor had ever seen.

"No," Glor said, "don't!"

The 'Chaos' flew around causing confusion and mayhem. Captain Zot tried to match their course, but it was hopeless.

Cam and Enyo were still on the main screen of 'Decision', as they never ended the last call.

"Cam!" Bob said. "What is your fight with these people?!"

"My fight is the same as my wife's," Cam said. "The Elders are not all good. Some of them have been known to take over planets. And to rule them as their own."

Glor looked at her mom. "No," Gloria said. "The planet that we're currently living on, we had permission to relocate there."

"Well," Enyo said, "I'm glad you gave them a choice. My people were never so lucky."

"The Elders are not evil!" Gloria defended. "If, by chance, there is a small group of them that have taken your planet, I'm sorry!"

"Oh," Enyo said, "your apology makes everything better! My people have a home now! Oh wait, they don't. Once those Elders took over, they gave us spaceships to find new homes. They pretended to be friendly at first."

Glor looked at her mom again. "No," Gloria said. "That's not what is happening on our new home world!" she reassured her daughter.

"That's what we thought," Enyo said. "No matter. I'm just simply returning the favor. It'll all be over soon. As they say, the past is in the future!"

"Where is the admiral?" Captain Zot asked.

"Sleeping," Cam said.

"Why do you have him?!" the captain demanded.

"The more Elders that watch, the happier I will be!" Enyo said.

"Oh, honey," Cam said, "can I tell them now? Please?!"

"Not yet," Enyo said. "First, let's destroy this planet!"

The 'Chaos' zoomed away from the 'Decision' so fast, the ship itself was out of sight. They were still connected on-screen by the hail call, however, as Enyo and Cam themselves were still visible on the ship's viewscreen.

"So," Cam said, "how should we use this weapon?"

"Well," Enyo said. It sounded like they had rehearsed this conversation. "The Planet Taker can be used in many unthinkable ways. I was thinking, oh this would be so sweet." She whispered to her husband.

"Yes, yes!" Cam laughed. "I love the idea."

The planet already looked empty. The Elders already sensed the danger. It was too great to face, so they all had left the planet.

"See?" Enyo said. "We aren't all that bad! We aren't killing anybody! They're gone! Though what we are about to do will alarm you, oh so much."

Captain Zot noticed the ship near the surface of the planet. He started to fly towards it, when Glor stopped him. "No!" she cried. "It's too late!"

The captain stopped the ship. On the viewscreen, Cam held up the necklace one last time. It was glowing with a blinding brightness. "How did you not accidentally set this off?" Cam asked Glor. "Oh, right," he said. "I'm smarter than you are!"

"Not yet!" Enyo said. "Wait for the perfect moment!"

Cam waited a moment, then left the view of the screen. Captain Zot saw him. He was just a dot on the surface of the planet. A dot with a blinding weapon, which was somehow activated.

"How did you activate this weapon?!" Gloria demanded.

"Oh, you know," Enyo smiled. "It would take an awful lot of energy," she said. "If, perhaps, an entire family used all of their powers across thousands of years of time and across space, maybe that could charge up a weapon! Oops, did I just reveal who the bad guy truly is?!"

Glor cried. "What? What?!"

"Oh my word," Gloria said. "It was always us."

"It gets so much better though," Enyo laughed. "You don't even realize! You filled this necklace with so much power! The love alone that has always surrounded it was a good addition of power. But charge a necklace with time travel power, guess what we can do?!"

"Oh no," Clory said. "No. No, you can't. That is impossible!"

Cam had left the necklace on the planet. "It's time!" he laughed.

"Mom, should I stop time around the necklace? Clory can teleport it and--"

"Yes, more energy!" Enyo laughed. "It will make the collision even better!"

"What?" Captain Zot cried.

"Well," Enyo said, "time to get away from here!"

The 'Chaos' sped away from the planet as fast as it could. "Captain Zot!" Quo said. "We have to get out of here!"

They followed Cam and Enyo's ship away from the planet, as the planet completely disappeared.

The impact of a planet moving through time and space is devastating. It knocked both ships off course, causing great damage everywhere.

"Captain!" Quo cried. "Are we okay?"

"No," Captain Zot admitted.

"I can't believe what they just did," Gloria said. "I don't think the Elders will believe it. I almost don't believe it myself!"

Bob looked around. He made sure Carol was okay, then looked at everyone else. "What did they do?! Where did the planet go?!"

The video link was disconnected, but they still had an audio connection with 'Chaos'.

"You never wondered?!" Cam growled. "No one ever talked about the second planet in the collision. I guess we don't have to wonder anymore!" he laughed.

Quo looked at everyone. Then at Bob, who was a little confused.

"The entire time!" Gloria cried. "It was us the entire time!"

"Mom?" Glor cried. "Mom!"

Enyo and Cam could be heard laughing. "Just in case anybody is behind," Cam sneered, and continued in a mocking voice, "the other planet that caused the collision on Clory's home world was the Elders' original home world! You had to relocate an entire species because your first home planet was colliding with your new home planet! Oh, this is so hilarious!"

Captain Zot was furious. He used what power they had left to shoot at 'Chaos'. Just when he shot at them, Glor noticed something. "SHOCKWAVE!" she yelled.

From where the planet once was, a shockwave came rushing towards them.

"Now, why did you hit our ship?!" Cam asked. "Did we do something wrong?!"

The shockwave came closer. The captain fired one more shot at 'Chaos'. It was about to explode. They heard Cam and Enyo ruffling around for something.

All at once, the shockwave reached the 'Decision', the 'Chaos' exploded, and they heard a noise on their own ship.

Everyone braced for impact. They closed their eyes as time shifted around them. They opened their eyes, and in shock and horror, Cam and Enyo were standing in the middle of the bridge with the admiral. Cam and Enyo each had a small device in their hands. Cam was holding onto Admiral Noah's arm. He let go of it.

"Teleportation," Cam laughed. "Some are born with it, and some," he looked at his wife, "some are smart enough to create it ourselves." He smiled. "I even brought the admiral! You're welcome."

Bob, Carol, Quo, Glor, Gloria, Clory, and Captain Zot stood opposite Cam and Enyo. Admiral Noah was on the ground, unconscious. They were all now left on a ship with almost no power, unsure of where they were. Unsure of when they were.

All ten of them were now stranded in time and space. Out of the windows, they could see nothing but space all around. There was nowhere to go.

Epilogue

"That's enough for one day," Cam looked at everyone. "Surely, there's nothing left to tell!" He looked at Enyo. "Now? Can I tell them now?!"

Enyo smiled. "Sure! I don't think we have anything else to do!"

"I'm sure you know the admiral has been under my control. For years. Now, how does that sound familiar? Anybody want to guess?"

Captain Zot stared at Cam.

"I feel I have been around time energy all my life! The past, the future, what is time anyways?! Oh, I'm going to enjoy this."

Gloria looked at him. "Wait," she said, looking closely at him.

"I am a shapeshifter," Cam said. "I was lost. Wandering. But this beautiful creature found me. She found me when I was at my lowest point. Okay, maybe not my lowest point, but she found me!"

Enyo smiled. "I'm glad I could share my shapeshifting powers with you. Science fiction is becoming science fact! The good old admiral said that, didn't he?" Enyo laughed. "Admiral! Wake up! We want to see your face!"

"Now," Cam continued, "how could I have known so much about the collision? Anyone? Quo? Would you like a chance to guess? No? Okay, maybe I'll just tell you!"

The admiral started to stir. "Where am I?" he said, confused.

"Get up!" Enyo demanded. "Go stand on that side with your friends. Bob and Carol miss you!"

Still confused, the admiral obeyed. He got up and walked over to Bob. "What's happening?"

"What's happening? WHAT'S HAPPENING?! Enyo, do you hear this?" Cam laughed.

"Go on," Enyo said. "Tell them!"

"Would you like to see my original form? Would you like to see the original form of the man who beat you? Who outsmarted you? Who defeated all of you?"

Everyone stood there, in shock, as Cam waited for an answer.

"No one wants to guess?! It's a shame. Oh well, it's time to tell you all who I am!"

They all watched, in horror, as Cam slowly shapeshifted into his original form. His original body. "NOW EVERYONE WILL REMEMBER ME! HELLO, FAMILY! DID YOU MISS ME? NOW EVERYONE WILL REMEMBER MY NAME. THE NAME, OF SMEDGE!"

The second book in The Elders' Chronicles series begins on planet Earth. Bob and Carol work for Earth's space program. After receiving a mysterious warning from alien spaceships, they must decide how to react on behalf of the entire planet. Who is warning Earth? What are they warning Earth about?

Two mysterious interns have recently joined the space program. One of them starts talking nonsensically about a collision. What is he talking about?

While trying to understand what is going on, Bob learns about a small group of Elders that disagree with the majority. They call themselves Seniors. For millennia, there has been quarreling. There has been animosity among them. There has been division.

Something is coming for Earth. They must be ready. They must learn the truth, before it's too late...

The Elders' Chronicles:

REVISION

Keith Imbody

The Elders' Chronicles: Revision

The Elders' Chronicles:
Revision
By: Keith Imbody

Copyright © 2020 Keith Imbody

All rights reserved.

This book or any portion thereof

may not be reproduced or used in any manner whatsoever

without the express written permission of the author

except for the use of brief quotations in a book review.

Cover art created by Alecia Witbart

Preface

Revision. What does that word mean? To revise something is to change it. No one likes change, do they? But sometimes, it seems like the only thing that doesn't change is the fact that everything changes.

Typed up entirely on my smart phone once again, the third book in The Elders' Chronicles series is over thirty-six thousand words that brings change to the character's lives.

Revision is change. Change is constant. But somehow, something that is constant doesn't change. Makes you think, doesn't it?

Combining the word count of Revision with the first two books in the series, Collision and Division, these three novellas total about eighty-five thousand words now. That's the size of a regular novel. And that was kind of a goal to reach. And with time, I've finally reached it.

Collision. Division. Revision. Three books, one story. The Elders' Chronicles.

Keith Anbody

Acknowledgments:

To my family:

My sister, mom, and dad have helped me throughout this entire journey. My sister created the cover for me once again and she formatted the book. My parents have supported me, offering editing help along the way. Thanks Alecia, mom, and dad!

To the reader:

Book three. Here we are. I've written three books... that's cool, I suppose. But you, reader, are back once again, to read the next book in this collection of stories. Thank you.

The Elders' Chronicles: Revision
By: Keith Imbody

Table of Contents
Prologue
Chapter 1: Time Shift
Chapter 2: Impossible Decision
Chapter 3: The Third Choice
Chapter 4: Carol
Chapter 5: Bob
Chapter 6: Noah
Chapter 7: Clory
Chapter 8: Trolk and Gleck
Chapter 9: Gloria and Zot
Chapter 10: Glor
Chapter 11: The Portal
Chapter 12: Return
Chapter 13: Enyo's Realization
Chapter 14: One More Story
Chapter 15: Smedge Versus Smedge
Chapter 16: Nova Shines
Chapter 17: Rebirth
Chapter 18: Burnout
Chapter 19: After Talk
Chapter 20: The Funeral
Chapter 21: Fifty-Seven
Chapter 22: The Final War
Epilogue

Prologue

"I can't believe we are piloting a spaceship!" A woman with green hair smiled. "We just finished our training two days ago. I'm nervous, Gleck!"

Gleck, the other passenger on this spaceship, looked at the woman. "Trolk," Gleck said, "if the Elders have faith in us, if they believe we are capable of flying this small spaceship alone, I think we can trust ourselves!"

"Good point," Trolk agreed. "It's so exciting! We have no idea what we are going to find out here! We could find anything!"

Gleck laughed. His laugh was quite obnoxious. It sounded like a hyena and a crow, if that sound was even possible. "I do miss our friends."

Trolk frowned. "It is so quiet without them."

"I wonder what they decided to do after settling on our new planet."

"Who knows," Trolk said. "I'm sure we'll see them soon. It's only been about a week since that devastating event."

"Collision," Gleck sighed.

Trolk and Gleck had been through a lot with their friends. Some of their friends had powers. They, in fact, came from a planet where everybody had powers. Sadly, that planet had recently collided with another. Everyone made it safely to a new home, however. So, though two planets colliding was ultimately bad news, everyone surviving was good.

Trolk could fly and Gleck could turn invisible.

Just then, after a minute of silence, the ship started beeping.

"What does that mean?" Gleck asked.

"Someone has sent a signal," Trolk said, as she stared at the viewscreen of the ship. "it's coming from over there!"

Trolk and Gleck both knew how to pilot this ship. It was a small vessel. This was the first time the two of them had been piloting on their own. Over the last week, they had rigorous training. They had gone on a huge ship with hundreds, a tiny space shuttle with just five, and a few other ships. Each day that week they had training on a new vessel. Today was the day. The day they would take a small ship out and go exploring. They had enough supplies for two months on their spacecraft. They were told by the Elders that they could come back that day or stay exploring for weeks.

Trolk steered the ship to the right.

"I don't see anything!" Gleck admitted.

Trolk rolled her eyes at Gleck. "It's a signal, Gleck! They could be transmitting from far away! We just have to follow it!"

They followed the signal for five minutes. They saw nothing but continued to blindly follow.

After another five minutes, Gleck thought he saw something. "Trolk, look!"

Trolk was staring straight ahead. "At what?" she asked. She then saw what he saw. "Another ship!"

They were about to hail the other ship, but before they could, it was gone.

"Did they just disappear?" Gleck gasped.

"I think so," Trolk said, staring at where the ship once was. "I suppose we have seen and will see stranger occurrences than that!"

"What should we do?" Gleck asked.

"Not much we can do," Trolk admitted. "We'll wait here for a little while, we'll document what happened today, and eventually, we'll bring all the information we have collected back to the Elders!"

They waited for twenty minutes. Nothing changed. There was no one there.

"Guess we can move on!" Gleck yelled, breaking the silence.

"Wait," Trolk said, as the ship started to pick up a signal again.

"Is that coming from behind us now?" Gleck asked.

"I think it is," Trolk said.

They turned the ship around and started flying towards the signal again. They flew around aimlessly for hours trying to find this signal. But whenever they got close to it, it was as if the signal changed locations.

"I don't like this, Trolk," Gleck said.

"It is alarming," Trolk admitted.

"Should we head home and tell the Elders what we found now?" Gleck asked.

"Maybe," Trolk was hesitant. "But we don't have much information. If we go home now to ask for help, the Elders might think we aren't ready for space travel."

"Good point," Gleck agreed.

"The signal is gone now," Trolk said. "Maybe we should try to forget about it for now, until it shows up again?"

"Good idea," Gleck admitted.

They traveled around for a while before the signal came back. An entire week went by. During that week, they had collected tons of information from nearby stars and planets. They had even picked up a strange piece of rock. They had no idea where it came from. It was just floating through space. But there was something about it. They transported this rock to the ship and kept it with them.

In that week alone, Gleck and Trolk had enough adventures to fill a book. They almost forgot about the wandering signal. Until it came back.

"Hey, Trolk!" Gleck yelled. "The signal!"

Trolk walked over to him, as he steered the ship towards the signal. As they followed it, they started talking about the adventures they already had. Until the other ship, the same exact ship that they saw a week earlier, came into view.

"There it is!" Gleck exclaimed.

Trolk quickly pressed a button to hail them, but there was no answer. Then, the ship disappeared.

"Who are these people?!" Trolk demanded.

The ship popped back into existence. They were being hailed. Gleck quickly hit a button to answer. There was no image, only audio. And the audio was distorted.

"Don't quit… weak… stabilize… need…"

"What does that mean?" Gleck asked.

"Gleck, I want to know what that means too… but that voice… Gleck, that voice! Listen!"

The message repeated but was now a bit clearer. "Don't quit trying to find… signal is weak… trying to stabilize… we need your ship!"

"Was that… me?!" Gleck cried. "That was me! How…?"

The ship disappeared again.

"This just got more interesting!" Trolk cried.

"Now should we head home and tell the Elders?" Gleck asked.

"Yes," Trolk said. But then she thought about it. "They said don't quit trying, though. Should we wait a little longer to see before we tell them?"

"Maybe… it did sound like me on the other ship. But that was clearly not our ship. That ship seemed drained. They didn't have much power."

"Do you think it was us from another dimension?" Gleck asked.

Trolk rolled her eyes at him. "Another dimension? Really?"

Gleck shrugged. "Then, should we just keep exploring and wait a little more time before heading back home?"

"If we don't have this figured out in one week, we'll head home."

Gleck agreed.

Their mission of exploration continued, and in the next week, they had many more adventures. They even landed on a planet and met a new species. Though they had so many adventures, at the same time, the week flew by. They did encounter the signal multiple times along the way, but they only saw the other ship again once. Other than trying to trace the signal and that one sighting of the ship, they had collected no more information on the matter.

"Two full weeks of exploration," Trolk smiled. "This is what I was born to do!"

Gleck agreed. "I guess it's time to head home!"

Before Trolk could answer, the ship they had been trying to follow appeared directly in front of them. If they had been any closer, the ship might have appeared over their ship, which could have been disastrous. That might have destroyed both ships.

"Gleck?" Trolk said. "I think they are stable. I think we finally get to see who is on the ship! We finally get to figure this out!"

"Good," Gleck sighed, "because I want to know how there is another Gleck out there!"

Trolk smiled. "One Gleck is more than enough," she said to her friend.

Gleck laughed. "What is our next move?"

Trolk looked at the ship, then at Gleck. "I guess we should hail--"

Before she finished her sentence, their ship was being hailed.

"I know our next move now!" Gleck said. He looked at Trolk. "Whatever is about to happen, Trolk, these last two weeks have been the best of my life."

Trolk rolled her eyes again, then smiled. "Okay, Gleck. It has been pretty awesome."

They both turned to the viewscreen. Since the ship was now stable, the video link was sure to work. They were about to solve this mystery.

Trolk took Gleck's hand, and together, they hit a button on the console to answer the hail call.

Chapter 1
Time Shift

The Elders. Unbelievably powerful creatures that watch over the universe. They had survived the destruction of their home planet. Twice. The collision of two planets, their original home planet, and their new home planet, caused them to relocate again, to yet another planet.

Quo and Bob, two humans from Earth, found themselves involved with these powerful beings.

Quo and Bob had been through a lot. They had two separate adventures that somehow intertwined. Now, here they stood, on a spaceship with no power.

Standing beside them, were their friends. Zot, who was the captain of the ship, his wife, Gloria, who was an Elder, and two of their three children, Clory and Glor. The four of them had powers.

Also with them, was Bob's boss, Admiral Noah, who was an Elder.

And last but not least, Bob's wife, Carol.

Standing opposite the group, was a woman named Enyo. She was a shapeshifter, and the wife of someone who called himself Camouflage. Cam for short. He also had the powers of shapeshifting, among other powers that he and Enyo bestowed upon themselves using science. And he had just revealed his true form to everyone.

He revealed himself to be Smedge. The third child of Zot and Gloria. Everyone was shocked, as the Smedge they knew, in the present, had previously jumped into one of the colliding planets before it exploded. He was saved by the Elders, but not before he reverted to a baby. The energy from the planets and the time travel used to try and stop the collision caused this.

So, everyone was shocked, as Cam shapeshifted into his original form. Smedge. They stared at him. No one said anything for nearly a minute. Finally, someone spoke.

"Are you serious?!" Clory said to his brother. "You just caused so much destruction. And for what?!"

Smedge looked at Clory. "Oh, relax, brother! I was just having some fun! No one was harmed! Everyone is okay!"

"Smedge," Clory cried, "how can you say that? We are all stranded in the middle of nowhere! We were hit with a shockwave that must've come through time itself! We have no idea where we are! We have no clue when we are!"

"Brother!" Smedge scolded him. "There is no need to be so selfish!"

Clory became furious. Glor put her hand on her brother's shoulder.

"Don't let him get to you, Clory," she said.

"That is big talk coming from someone who just caused the collision of two planets. Thanks again for all your powers, sister!" Smedge laughed.

Glor stared at him.

Captain Zot stepped forward. "Son, how could you do this?"

"You too are so blind! I bet Gloria knows more than she tells you. I found out so much. The Elders are actually pretty selfish, you know."

Zot looked at his wife, Gloria, and she shook her head. "I don't know what he is talking about."

Smedge shook his head in disgust. "I always have to spell EVERYTHING out for all of you! I'll give you one last chance to come clean, mother, then I'm telling them."

Everyone looked at Gloria, who was honestly lost.

Smedge sighed. "Clory," he said, "what species are you?"

"I'm... not sure of the name of our species."

"And that never concerned you?" Smedge growled. "You just don't have a name for your species. Somehow, that's just how it is supposed to be. Who cares? You come from a no-named species that live on the same planet as the Elders."

Gloria looked at Smedge. "What did you find out?"

"You're an Elder," Smedge said to Gloria. "You know your species. Well? What species is your husband?"

She stared at Zot, who felt uneasy.

"Smedge," Zot said, "what species are you? You're the same species as Clory, Glor, your mother, and me. What did you find out?"

"So," Smedge began, "you know how we just blew up the Elders' home planet and our own home planet as a family?"

Glor's eyes became angry and sad at the same time. Gloria took her daughter's hand and whispered, "It's okay, sweetie."

"No it's not!" Smedge yelled. "Either you knew this whole time, mother, or the Elders knew and hid it from you! It is everything but okay!"

The ship jolted, as time seemed to shift around them.

"Aftershock from the shockwave," Smedge laughed. "Looks like this ship is traveling through time uncontrollably. I wonder what, or who, we'll meet along the way!"

Time shifted around the ship a few more times, then the mayhem seemed to stop.

"Clory!" Smedge demanded. "What species are you?! What species are we?!"

Clory yelled at his brother, "Enough of the games, Smedge! Just tell us what you know! Now!"

"I like the anger!" Smedge laughed. He looked at his wife, Enyo, and said, "Maybe he will become like me someday after all!"

Clory glared at him. "I will never become like you."

Smedge shrugged. "Calm down, brother! I'll tell you. I'll tell everyone here! But, I think someone is following us!"

Everyone peered out the window to see a small ship. Smedge, who also had the powers of a telepath, quickly invaded the thoughts of the passengers on the other ship.

"Yes!" Smedge laughed. "This is so much better now! Enyo, our plan just got a thousand times better!" He whispered to his wife.

The ship outside disappeared, as time shifted around them again.

"Look!" Quo cried. "There's the ship again!"

Time shifted three more times. The ship outside showed up two out of the three times during these time jumps.

"Who's following us?!" Bob's wife Carol asked.

"I have no idea!" Bob said.

"Friends," Smedge said, "I think you're going to be so happy to see these two." He laughed.

Time shifted, and now there was no one and nothing outside.

"I might as well tell you what species you are before those two interrupt us again!" Smedge sneered.

Captain Zot stared at his son. "Smedge!" he demanded. "Tell us!"

"Father," Smedge said, "don't tell me what to do. You never liked me. You always liked Clory more."

"That is not true!" Gloria defended Zot.

Zot nodded in agreement with his wife. "We love all of our children the same," he said.

"You'll finally love me more now," Smedge hissed. "It just took me a while to find out how our species became weaker. But it all makes sense now."

"What do you mean by that?" Gloria asked.

"Mother," Smedge cried, "our species is the same. It makes sense. You thought because you, as an Elder, married father, Captain Zot, whatever species he was, you thought, 'Maybe that's why my children have only one power.' That makes sense. Well, other than Glor. You must have thought she just got the powers from your side of the family. But you never questioned this planet where everyone had superpowers. Most everyone only had one power each at this point. So, how could this be?"

"Are you saying we are all Elders?" Clory cried.

"Oh, you thought that was a rank?" Smedge hissed. "but why were the new Elders weaker than the previous generation?"

Gloria stared at her son. It all made sense, but no one ever really thought about it before.

"I think it had something to do with that necklace," Bob said.

"Bob! You are smart!" Smedge laughed. "Because, remember, that necklace was filled with so much energy. Including the time-traveling energy from mother locking onto the necklace, and you, my lovely family, following it through time. That and any other energy the necklace could siphon. I think the love alone among our family somehow charged it. And my anger. And with all this energy, I suppose the necklace just didn't know how to not siphon energy!"

Clory looked at Smedge. "Are you saying that every single one of us on that planet was an Elder?"

"A weaker Elder, I suppose," Smedge said. "Well, I'm strong again. I have many powers, thanks to my lovely wife and science!"

Gloria shuddered. "They... we... are all Elders..."

"What's the matter, mother? Are you upset that your parents kept secrets from you?"

"I just don't understand why they wouldn't say anything." Gloria cried.

"Maybe they think they are BETTER than the ones with only one or two powers? The word Seniors comes to mind!" Smedge laughed.

"No!" Glor cried. "The Elders are not full of hatred! None of them—none of us think we are better than another!"

"Easy to say," Smedge growled, "coming from the most powerful creature our species has." He looked at Gloria. "Yes, mother, I'm sure in the past you have referred to us, me, Clory and Glor, as your species, because we would have been at least half Elder. But guess what? We are all one hundred percent Elder! You're welcome, family! Now you know!"

"So, even Gleck and Trolk are Elders," Quo said quietly.

"What was that, Quo?" Smedge scowled. "You want to see Gleck and Trolk? Okay!"

Smedge whispered to his wife and the two of them shapeshifted to look like Gleck and Trolk.

"You've never even met Trolk!" Clory cried, looking at Enyo. "How--?"

"Hello?! Shapeshifting telepath here!" Smedge, who now looked like Gleck, said. "She knows because I know! Oh look, a time shift is coming! Ready, Trolk?!" Smedge said, looking at Enyo.

Time shifted around them as Smedge reached for the controls. "I'm sending that ship a message! They should find us again in three… two… one…"

"There they are!" Quo cried. "Who is on that ship?!"

Smedge hit a button, sending an audio-only message to the ship.

"Don't quit trying to find us! Our signal is weak. We are trying to stabilize, and we need your ship!" Smedge said, in Gleck's voice.

Time shifted yet again.

"That should keep them guessing," Smedge laughed. "I bet they'll be on the lookout now!"

"Who?!" Clory demanded.

"Oh, you know," Smedge smiled, still in the form of Gleck. "Me."

Enyo laughed.

Gloria was still in shock. "I can't believe that necklace has caused so much trouble."

Glor frowned. "Mom, is that necklace really the reason the new generations of our species is weakening? One power each…"

"I crash-landed on a planet full of Elders," Quo said, in amazement. "They weren't just aliens with superpowers. They were all Elders."

"But why would the Elders make it seem like they were Elders, and everyone else on your planet was not?" Smedge yelled. "They think they are better than you. Better than me. Not anymore. My revenge is coming. And it's time everyone knew the truth."

"What are you going to do, brother?" Clory cried.

"We'll see! The only thing I'm sure of, is, here they come! And just to get you thinking, you know that other species that welcomed you with open arms on your, what, third home planet now? Who's to say they aren't Elders too?"

A ship appeared directly in front of them. It was a small vessel. The one that had been following them.

"Okay," Smedge said to his wife, "hail them! This is gonna be epic!"

They hailed the other ship. Two familiar faces were now on the viewscreen.
It was the real Trolk and Gleck.

Chapter 2
Impossible Decision

"Hello, friends!" Smedge said, still in the form of Gleck. Enyo still looked like Trolk.

"Is that, us?!" The real Gleck said over the viewscreen.

"Of course it is!" The real Trolk said. "Who else would it be?!"

They noticed their friends behind the imposters.

"Clory!" Gleck exclaimed. "And... everyone else! What's up?" He whispered to Trolk, "I don't know them." He was talking about Admiral Noah, Bob, and Carol.

"They are all our friends!" Smedge said.

Clory sighed. "It's not you, Trolk. Or you, Gleck. They are shapeshifters."

"You ruin all the fun, brother!" Smedge said.

"Okay, I know it has been a while since we have seen you," Gleck said, "but there is no way Clory is my brother. Right?"

Trolk rolled her eyes.

"Why do you always roll your eyes at me?!" Gleck asked.

"Hey!" Smedge said. "Where did you get that ship? Where are we? When are we?"

"When are we?" Gleck laughed. "It's the present. Like it always is."

"It is not always the present," Smedge growled. "Do you not know who I am?!"

Gleck shrugged. "You look like Gleck to me!"

This made Smedge furious.

"Gleck!" Trolk realized. "I think that's... there is no way..."

"Yes, it is me!" Smedge scowled.

"Smedge?" Trolk asked. "How?"

"Smedge?!" Gleck was shocked.

"Enough!" Enyo demanded. "Smedge, shouldn't we execute the next part of our plan?"

"Hold on," Smedge said. "Trolk, Gleck, how long ago was the collision?"

Trolk didn't answer.

"About three weeks ago?" Gleck guessed.

"Gleck!" Trolk scolded him.

"Yes!" Smedge smiled. "Clory, look! It's your friends, in the present! This is right after you chased us through time, I imagine... though I'm sure Trolk and Gleck have no idea yet."

"What are you talking about, Smedge?!" Trolk demanded. It felt weird to yell at Smedge, as he was still in the form of Gleck. "And please, change back to your original form!"

Smedge obeyed. "It's more satisfactory to tell you the good news looking like myself anyways."

"What good news?" Gleck asked.

Clory began to speak, "Wait, Smedge, let us--"

"Silence, brother!" he demanded. "I will tell them! Go on, Enyo, change back to your original form too."

She shapeshifted to her own form.

"Now," Smedge continued, "Trolk, Gleck, my two best friends, what species are you?"

Trolk looked at Gleck, who was confused.

"We are from the planet... our species is called..." Gleck didn't know. "Trolk, why don't I know?"

"I don't know either, Gleck!" Trolk cried.

"You don't know?!" Smedge gasped. "But surely you know by now who caused the collision!"

"Who caused the... Smedge, you're not making sense!" Trolk yelled at him. She noticed someone crying. "Glor? Are you okay?" she asked.

"No!" Glor cried. "I don't know how any of this happened!"

"Someone, please!" Trolk demanded. "Tell me what is going on!" She got closer to the viewscreen as if she noticed something. "Glor, where is your necklace?"

Glor cried louder.

Smedge shook his head. "Not the time, Trolk."

"Enough, Smedge!" Gloria demanded. "This has gone on long enough! Stop this!"

Smedge looked back at his mother, then slowly walked away from the viewscreen. "You tell them," he sneered.

Gloria walked towards the viewscreen. "Trolk, Gleck, we have so much to tell you."

Enyo walked over towards Smedge. They started whispering to each other.

Captain Zot and Clory walked towards the viewscreen. "Trolk, Gleck," Clory cried, "We are all Elders."

"What do you mean?" Gleck asked.

Trolk just stared at the screen.

"We, everyone on the planet, we are all Elders," Clory repeated.

"How is that so?" Trolk asked. "I thought the Elders were--"

"A rank?!" Smedge growled from behind Clory. "No, we are all Elders. Some just aren't as important as others."

"But," Clory continued, "we all have limited powers, most of us only have one power each, as opposed to previous generations that seem to have multiple powers."

"I want more than one power!" Gleck smiled. "But why do we only have one then?"

"The collision of planets, the weapon, the necklace, it was so powerful…" Clory looked away from his friends in shame.

Glor got the courage to walk up to the viewscreen. "Trolk?" she said, with a tear in her eye. "The necklace that was given to you for your birthday… you let me keep it after the collision because you saw how important it was to me… it was a family heirloom. It was given to you by Clory, and my father, Captain Zot, gave it to Clory and Gleck that day to give to you. And before that, it was my mom, Gloria's necklace. And even before that, it belonged to her parents."

"I'm glad you have it then," Trolk smiled at her friend. "But Glor, where is it?"

"Trolk," Glor cried, "It was a weapon. A weapon created by the remains of our original home planet."

Smedge laughed in the background.

"Enough, Smedge!" Captain Zot demanded.

"So, if we are all Elders, why were we unaware of this?" Trolk asked.

Glor wiped away tears and continued her story. "Trolk, Gleck, after you two went off exploring, we received a message from them." She pointed at Bob, Carol, and the admiral. "They told Quo and the rest of us to come home. It was Quo's home planet, Earth. They needed our help. Long story short, there was a fight for the weapon. That necklace."

Gloria walked over to hug her daughter.

Glor composed herself and continued, "Smedge and his wife, Enyo--"

Gleck interrupted her. "Smedge got married? That is rather sudden."

Trolk shot him a look and asked Glor to continue.

"Smedge and Enyo got the necklace. They took it right out of the crowd that was at war. And they left with it. They used it to cause the collision!" Glor's eyes filled with tears again, as she finished her story. "They went back in time to cause the collision. They sent the original home planet of the Elders at the planet we were all on at the time. They sent our original home planet at our new home planet! And that stupid necklace is the reason newer generations of Elders are weaker. It was siphoning power from everything for who knows how many years!"

"I like this story better when I tell it," Smedge sighed.

Trolk and Gleck stared in shock. They didn't know what to say.

Smedge broke the silence, "Okay, that's enough storytime!"

They pressed a button on their wrists and appeared on the other ship with Trolk and Gleck. They quickly put the small teleportation devices on Trolk and Gleck before anybody could react. They pressed a button on them and backed away, as Trolk and Gleck appeared with their friends on their ship.

Enyo pressed a button on the control panel of Trolk and Gleck's ship, as did Smedge.

"There!" Smedge said. "Now, no one can teleport on or off your—I mean my ship!" He looked at Enyo. "Well played, right? Distract them with a story, and boom, the ship is ours!"

Enyo stared directly at everyone on the other ship. "You call that ship 'Decision', right? Well, it's time for you to make a decision."

Smedge stared directly at his family and everyone else through the viewscreen. "The choice is yours."

"What choice?!" Clory yelled.

"The necklace isn't going to create itself!" Smedge laughed.

Clory looked back at his friends, then at Smedge. "No," he said.

"No?" Smedge asked. "You don't want to fly through time on your ship that is already popping through time anyways, and gather pieces of our exploded home planet to create the necklace? Well, I'm not going to do it. I don't think I could live with myself if I created the weapon that caused the destruction of our home planet. Twice." He smiled.

Glor looked at her mom. "No," she said. "Absolutely not."

Gloria frowned. "It was one thing to cause this collision by accident. But to purposefully create the weapon that caused it? No!" She walked over to the viewscreen.

"All of you," Smedge said. "Be sure of your choice. You either have to create the weapon that caused the collision and weakened our species, or, don't create the weapon. But, I wonder, what would that do to time? To us? If the planets never collided, would we still all live on our original home planet? Would we all be more powerful? There would be, in fact, no necklace to siphon our powers."

Quo looked at Bob. "Wait, what about us?"

"You?!" Smedge cried. "Oh, I suppose if the planets never collided, the Elders would have had no reason to send father, Captain Zot as you call him, away from the colliding planets. He then never lands on Earth, doesn't inspire Quo to go traveling through space… his influence is never on Earth at all! Which means, oh no…" Smedge laughed.

Glor went running towards Quo. "If we don't create the necklace, we don't ever meet…"

Quo frowned.

"I suppose the admiral might never show up on Earth either?" Bob asked.

"Maybe! Maybe not," Smedge growled. "That's why my wife and I have decided this decision is too important for little old us to make. Besides, we have some news to tell the Elders, you know, in case you choose to keep the present the way it is. Sounds like you lose either way! Glad I'm not choosing!"

"What are you going to tell the Elders?!" Gloria cried.

Smedge shapeshifted to look like Gleck again and Enyo changed her form to look like Trolk.

"You know," Smedge said, using not only Gleck's form but also his voice, "that Trolk and I are done exploring. That we found nothing of importance. That everyone from our home planet is an Elder… that Clory, Quo, and his friends caused the collision… but don't worry! You can stop all of that if you don't create the necklace! But, then Quo, Bob, and Carol will poof back to Earth! They won't remember anything. You won't remember anything… I wonder what I'll be like in this new reality. Oh well! Time is wasting, and your ship is about to shift through time again! Make a decision, friends! Time is running out!"

Smedge ended the call, as he and Enyo, in the form of Trolk and Gleck, headed back towards the planet where the Elders were all currently living.

Glor looked at Quo and cried.

Bob was sitting next to his wife, holding her hand.

Everyone looked at Gloria and Captain Zot for direction.

They had to make a decision. But no one wanted to. No one could. So everyone just sat there, as time shifted around them once more.

Chapter 3
The Third Choice

As time shifted around them, Quo broke the silence. "On one hand, my life would be so incomplete without Glor. But on the other hand, the fate of your entire species is in question."

Bob looked at Quo, then at Gloria. "If the Elders are becoming weaker as the generations go on, does that mean you'll eventually have no powers?"

Gloria frowned. "I don't know. I always wondered why I only had one power, but I figured it was something having to do with me. I didn't realize it was a genetic mutation affecting our entire species."

"Before today, we didn't know that everyone with only one power was also an Elder," Clory said, sadly.

"That is alarming," Bob said. "Why would the Elders keep that from you?"

Gloria started to cry. "I don't understand any of this."

"How do we make the right choice?" Quo asked.

Carol looked at Bob, Gloria, then at Quo. "I think this needs to be a decision the Elders make," she said, somberly.

"No," Glor cried. "I won't choose! Either I never meet Quo, or my entire species is doomed because we create a weapon?! I WON'T CHOOSE!" The ship began to shake, as time continued to shift around them.

"Glor, I'm sorry," Quo cried.

"This is all wrong!" Glor screamed.

"I don't like this!" Gloria said to her husband. "How could Smedge cause this much pain in our family?!"

Captain Zot looked at his wife and hugged her. "I don't know. I'm sorry."

Admiral Noah, who had been silent for quite some time, finally offered some advice. "We can't create the weapon that could destroy our species... but changing history might be dangerous. Who knows what would change if we choose not to

251

create the necklace and lose all the memories we have now? However, maybe there's a third option."

Glor dried her eyes.

Quo looked over at the admiral and said, "What are you thinking?"

"Gloria. Zot. I'm not sure if this is possible, but what if we decided not to create the necklace, but before the universe changes around us to create a new timeline, we put a force field around the ten of us? That way, we don't have to create such destruction, but we'll live in a timeline where we have all of the memories from now."

"I honestly don't know what that would do," Gloria admitted. "Would we replace the copies of us in that timeline or would there be two of each of us?"

The admiral thought for a second, then said, "I think we would replace the us that would exist in the alternate timeline. I'm not sure, but that would mean everyone else around us would be different. We might not know anybody that we know now. The ten of us would be alone in a brand-new timeline."

"This… this is crazy," Quo cried.

Gleck was trying to understand everything. "Smedge is pretending to be me. If we create this new timeline, would that stop him and Enyo from doing whatever they are doing?"

"If we create the new timeline?" Trolk cried. "This is a huge decision. But what will come of our families if we do this? Some of us might not even exist! This is too much."

"You'll remember everything," Captain Zot replied. "It will be up to you, up to us to keep our memories of this past life alive. But I'm not sure what will happen if we try to explain ourselves to them…"

"So, in this new reality, the ten of us have to keep a secret from the rest of the universe?"

"Maybe," Captain Zot guessed. "Or maybe we should tell them. Maybe something good can come from this."

Quo looked around the ship, then out the window. "Is time still shifting around us?" he asked.

Captain Zot walked to the window. "Looks like it," he said.

Just then, everything outside started to slow down, as the ship finally landed somewhere in time.

Captain Zot quickly noticed something out the windows. They were now surrounded by many ships.

"Where are we?!" Captain Zot cried. "We don't have any control over this ship. Steering it is impossible!"

"Captain!" Quo yelled. "We are being hailed!"

The captain pressed a button to answer the call, and an unfamiliar face was now on the viewscreen.

"Are you here to help us?" the unfamiliar face said. He was an old man, with short white hair. He was wearing an old raggedy robe. "We have been waiting for help. Please, help us."

"We would be happy to help if we could," Gloria said.

"Good," the creature said. "We are the last of our kind. There are only fifty-seven of us left. We became weaker and weaker… our species used to be so great."

Knowing the answer to this question, Gloria asked, "And what species are you?"

"The Elders," the frail old man said, gasping for breath. "We used to be so strong. We used to watch over the universe. We used to…"

He started coughing. Another Elder walked up behind him.

"Please," she said, "you must help us. Our species will never survive." She had long silver hair and looked like she was older than the man. "We are all powerless. Our great, great, great ancestors had powers. They were lucky to even have one power. As time went by, our entire species just became weaker and weaker. Some say it was because of the collision of planets."

"Who told you that?" Gloria cried.

"The great Smedge," she admitted. "He and his wife told all of us to pass the story through time. Through generations. And that a way to revive our species would show up someday."

"I am so sick of Smedge and his games!" Clory yelled. "Does he not realize how selfish he is?!"

"Smedge isn't selfish," the Elder said. "He offered us hope. Though he has been gone for many, many years, we have hope because of him."

"How long has Smedge been gone?" Clory asked.

"Nearly one hundred years," the Elder said.

"You said generations!" Captain Zot interrupted. "How many generations can there be in one hundred years?!"

"We are so weak," the first Elder cried. "We are only twenty-one years old. All of us."

More elders could now be seen on the viewscreen. "Help us! Help us! Help us!" they all chanted.

Time shifted around their ship again.

"That was spooky," Gleck admitted. "So, is that a vote for creating the necklace?"

"I thought Smedge went back to the planet as us," Trolk wondered.

"His ego got the better of him, I suppose," Clory sighed. "I'm sure he and Enyo just decided to shapeshift back to their original form."

"But wouldn't the Elders have recognized Smedge?" Quo interrupted. "None of this is making sense."

Time stopped shifting around the ship. They were in front of a glorious planet. A familiar planet. Clory gasped.

They saw their home planet. The second one. The one that Clory was from.

"No!" Quo cried. "Look!"

Headed straight towards their second home planet, was the Elders' original home planet.

"We do not want to be here when the planets collide!" Quo cried.

Bob and Carol stared on. "This is it? This is where the planets collide?" Bob asked.

Gloria looked closely at everything. "The eye of the storm," she said.

"Mom, what are you talking about?!" Glor cried.

"This is where everything goes wrong. This right here."

The planets collided directly in front of them.

The pieces of each planet flew closer to them, as the impact and shockwave rushed towards them. They witnessed pieces disappear from the sky, scattering across all of time and space.

"There is no way we are surviving this!" Bob cried.

The same shockwave that had originally propelled their ship, the 'Decision', through time, had finally come full circle.

"What's going to happen when this shockwave hits us?!" Bob asked.

"Nothing," Glor said. "Everything. We are either about to be completely destroyed, or maybe we'll end up where we started."

"Something seems off about all of this!" Quo cried. "Are we missing something?"

"If we end up where we started, we might be stranded there, forever!" Bob shouted.

"Are we seeing this through, or making a decision now?!" Gleck cried.

The ship started to break up. "We can't see this through," Captain Zot cried. "It's decision time!"

"If we choose to make the necklace, we may die right here." Trolk sighed. "Our species will die out. It seems only bad comes from the necklace! I'm not sure creating it is even an option anymore! We could've tried to teleport off the ship to a safer place before we ended up here. But now, we may have waited too long to make that choice. Even if we decided right now to make the necklace, how are we going to survive this impact?"

"Should we try the admiral's idea?" Gleck asked. "The one where the ten of us replace ourselves in a new timeline?"

The admiral looked at Zot and Gloria.

The ship started to crumble as the shockwave from the colliding planets was seconds away.

"Fine!" Glor said. "I feel like I was being selfish. Of course I want to save our species, but it never felt right if I didn't meet Quo. Mom, will the admiral's plan work?"

"I have no idea," Gloria admitted. "Guess we'll find out. Are we in agreement? None of us will create this weapon. We will not create the necklace. Even if we survive this impact, we will not create this necklace!"

Captain Zot looked at his wife and nodded. "Okay! We aren't creating the necklace!"

Bob, Carol, Admiral Noah, Gleck, Trolk, Glor, and Clory agreed.

Quo looked at Glor. "We'll be okay."

He held her hand.

"Okay," Captain Zot said as the bridge of the ship began to crumble around them. "Admiral, put up a force field around us. Glor, Gloria, hold time around us. As everything changes, we should remain unchanged. Our memories, our thoughts, will all be safe. And finally, since I don't know how this will work, Clory, you, me, and Glor will all use your power to teleport us to the nearest planet. It's now or never!"

With a force field around the ten of them and the unified decision that none of them would ever create the necklace even if they survived the impact of the shockwave, everything started to change around them. Time seemed to shift backwards to just before the planets collided. The original home planet of the Elders disappeared, returning to its original location, unharmed. Their second home planet remained in the sky.

The ship completely crumbled until there was only a small platform that the ten of them were standing on.

"I feel dizzy!" Glor cried.

"I can't do this!" Captain Zot exclaimed.

Gloria felt nauseous. "This isn't going to work!" she cried.

"It's too late!" the admiral cried.

"There is no way all of us are going to survive this!" Glor yelled. "I think the new timeline is rejecting us!"

"Ten displaced bodies is too much…" Captain Zot realized. "I think only one of us can physically go if we want this to fully work!"

"But if only one of us goes, what good is any of this?!" Carol cried.

"Whoever goes must reunite us," Zot said. "Remind us all of who we were. Who we are! And from there, we'll move forward!"

"Quo!" Glor cried. "You have to be the one. You'll find me. Find everyone. Please!"

Gloria nodded at her daughter.

256

Gleck started glowing. He pulled a rock out of his coat pocket.

"Where did you get that?!" Gloria asked.

"Gleck, I told you not to carry it!" Trolk scolded him. "We don't know what it--"

Gloria interrupted her. "Gleck, you may have just made Quo's job much easier!" She reached for the rock. "I don't know where you found this, but this is a piece of our planet. And though everything is changing, we have unknowingly stopped time around it too. Quo. Take this. Somehow, it will help you to help us remember!"

Quo took the rock. "But how am I going to know what to do?! I have to remember everything for everybody and save everyone?!"

"Ironic, isn't it, Newcomer?" Clory winked at him.

"I'm not ready!" Quo said.

"We all believe you can do this!" Bob said.

"We'll send you back to Earth. Back to your own house. Quo, everything will be different. Everything. So be careful," Captain Zot advised. "Your friends might think they're your enemies, your enemies might think they're your friends…"

"And this rock will help?" Quo asked.

"Yes!" Gloria cried. "I'm transferring our memories into it now. Just find us all, gain our trust, and everything else should fall into place. Good luck, Quo!"

"Find me and Carol first!" Bob cried. "Hopefully in whatever world we're creating, we have an easier way to contact the Elders!"

"What if I fail?" Quo cried.

"Quo," Glor said, "I love you." She nodded.

Everything Quo knew disappeared around him. Everything went dark.

Quo opened his eyes and found himself lying in his own bed at his own house on Earth. He looked over at a nightstand. The rock was there.

Quo rubbed his eyes and honestly, somehow, he felt well-rested. He sat up. He hadn't been to his home for a while, as he had settled on the Elders' third home planet with them.

He stood up, picked up the rock, and headed to the front door. He was ready. He had come a long way from being The Newcomer, who crash-landed on the Elders' second home planet and had forgotten all of his memories. Now, he had everyone's memories with him. And if he could find everyone, he was going to be the reason everyone remembered.

Chapter 4
Carol

Quo grabbed a light jacket and put the rock in the jacket pocket. He turned the doorknob not knowing what to expect outside. So far, everything looked the same.

"Okay," Quo thought, "first things first I have to find Bob and Carol. That should be the easiest task. They should both be at the building where they work."

Quo knew exactly where this building was, as he used to go there every day in his original timeline to train with Bob.

It took him about fifteen minutes to walk to the building. On the way, he looked around, trying to notice any differences in this new timeline. The only thing he noticed is that it was eerily quiet. But maybe it was just a quiet day.

Just as the building was in his sight, someone from across the street yelled to him.

"Hey, Quo!" they said.

Quo looked. He didn't recognize them at all.

"Hello!" he said.

He must have had friends on this timeline that he never met on his own timeline.

The man started to walk towards Quo.

"Have you figured it out yet?" the man asked.

Quo looked confused.

"Quo, it's me! Adam!" Adam said as he finally reached Quo. "I'm telling you, you need glasses! Have you figured it out yet?!"

"I don't know what you're talking about!" Quo cried.

Adam's face became serious. He stared at Quo, then he burst out laughing. "Quo, did you get tickets to the game?! The game that has been sold out for weeks? You said last night you were going to find a way! We were going to double date, remember? Me and my wife, and you and the blind date I was going to set you up with!"

Quo was taken aback. He forgot that in this timeline, Glor wasn't his girlfriend.

"Oh, I am so sorry," Quo said. "I have something more important to do. I am really sorry."

Adam shook his head. "Quo. Why are you so afraid of commitment? I promise it's a good thing!"

"It's not that," Quo admitted, "I just have something more important to do!"

"Can I help you?!" Adam asked. "As your best friend, I'm pretty sure it's my duty to help you! I'll call my wife. We'll double date some other day!"

"I don't think it's a good idea for you to help me," Quo admitted.

"Quo!" Adam exclaimed. "I am your best friend! Please, let me help you!"

Hesitantly, Quo agreed. "Okay, I'm trying to find some friends. First, I need to speak to Bob and Carol. They work in that building."

"Quo," Adam said, "are you okay?"

"What do you mean?" Quo asked.

"That building has been abandoned for years," Adam admitted.

"What?!" Quo cried.

He went running towards the building and up the stairs. He tried to open the door. After it didn't budge, Quo looked back towards Adam.

"Where is our space exploration building?!" he cried.

"Space exploration?!" Adam exclaimed. "You know for a fact that all space exploration was terminated due to the order of the Elders three years ago!"

Quo shuddered. "What? What are you talking about?!"

"Quo, are you okay? You've been acting weird!" Adam cried.

"I need to find my friends!" Quo screamed. "What do you mean the Elders have stopped all space exploration?!"

"They are doing what is best for us!" Adam admitted. "The universe is a scary place, and they just want to keep us safe!"

"No, no, no, no!" Quo cried. "What have we done?! How am I going to find any of my friends now?!"

"I'm right here!" Adam yelled. "Quo, maybe you should go see a doctor!"

Quo frantically ran down the stairs of the building. He looked around, and for just a moment, he lost all hope.

"I have nowhere to begin," Quo admitted. "How am I supposed to save them now?"

He took the rock out of the jacket pocket and looked at it.

"What is that?" Adam asked. "I've never seen that before!"

"It was supposed to help me and my friends…" Quo said somberly, as he put the rock back in his jacket. "But I'm not sure I'm going to find them now."

"Quo," Adam said, "tell me what is going on! I want to help!"

Before Quo could answer, a woman came walking towards the building. Quo noticed her. She had a small purse. He was about to move out of the way when he finally realized, "Carol?!"

The woman jumped. "Hello?" she said. "How do you know my name?"

Adam looked at Quo and then at Carol.

"Is she one of your friends?" Adam asked.

"No!" Carol exclaimed. "I have never met this man in my life!"

"Carol," Quo cried, "you have no reason to believe me, but… I don't know how to say this. Where is Bob?"

"Bob?" Carol asked. "I don't personally know anybody named Bob."

Quo's eyes widened. "Aren't you married to Bob?!"

Carol stared at Quo. "You have no idea who I am. Why on Earth do you think I am married to this Bob?!"

"Because, you… because I thought… you met while working for Earth's space exploration, and…" Quo finally understood. "You never met Bob because you didn't work in space exploration…"

"Not that this is your business, but I did work in space exploration. Until the Elders terminated that division. I even worked in this building years ago. But I never worked with any Bob. Not that I remember. In fact, the only Bob I know of at all is an author."

She reached into her purse and pulled out a book. She handed it to Quo.

Quo read the cover. "'We Don't Need Space. Space Needs Us.'"

"I love the title," Carol said. "He is my favorite author. I wish I could meet him. I don't know why, there is just something about him."

Quo turned the book over and exclaimed, "Bob! That's him!"

Carol snatched the book back. "You think I'm married to him?!"

"You were!" Quo cried.

Carol was intrigued. "Okay," she said.

"My name is Quo by the way," he said.

"Hello, Quo," Carol said.

"I'm Adam!" Adam said.

Carol laughed. "Hello, Adam."

Quo looked at Carol. "I'm sorry," he said. "I didn't mean to scare you. I'm truly just trying to find my friends."

Carol looked closely at Quo. "And you think I'm your friend?" she asked.

"Yes," Quo admitted.

"Quo," Carol said, "your jacket is glowing."

Quo pulled out the rock from his jacket pocket. It was, in fact, glowing.

"Can I see that?" Carol asked.

Quo handed her the rock. She stared at it. She now had the rock in one hand and Bob's book in her other hand.

"This looks like it's from another planet," she admitted.

"It's from another timeline," Quo stated.

"Another timeline?" Carol thought.

The rock began to glow even brighter as she began to remember.

"The thought alone makes you think," she said. "We don't need space, space needs us! Bob!" she cried. "Quo, it worked?!"

Adam stared at them. "What is happening here?"

"I remember everything!" Carol exclaimed. "We have to find Bob!"

Chapter 5
Bob

Quo smiled. "This actually might work!" he said, excitedly. "But how are we supposed to find Bob?"

"I can't believe he became a writer!" Carol exclaimed.

"I can't believe you had his book..." Quo said. "Yes, I can. You two were meant to be together, no matter what timeline we are in!"

Adam stared at Quo. "Why do you keep talking about alternate timelines?" he asked. "I don't think the Elders would approve of such talk."

"Oh no," Carol cried. "Quo, I remember everything from both timelines. The Elders came to Earth many years ago. I think they believe they are trying to help. But they have halted all space exploration as they think it is dangerous for us humans."

"One problem at a time," Quo smiled. "We have to find Bob! Are you coming with us, Adam?"

"I am your best friend!" he said.

Carol whispered to Quo, "You have no idea who that is, do you?"

Quo shook his head. "Traveling to an alternate timeline is confusing."

"Do you trust him?" Carol asked, still whispering.

"I'm not sure yet," Quo admitted.

"So," Adam said, "how are we going to find Bob?!"

"He is doing a book signing in a city twenty miles away today," Carol admitted. "I never had the courage to actually go and meet him in this timeline... but I do know his book signing schedule."

"Anybody want to take a trip?" Quo asked. "Looks like we are going to a book signing!"

Carol squealed in excitement. "I feel like I haven't seen him in forever!"

"It's time to remind Bob who he is!" Quo said.

"I guess I'll come," Adam said. "Let me just call my wife."

As Adam called his wife on his cell phone, Quo whispered to Carol, "He is my best friend in this timeline but I'm not sure I trust him. I guess he can come. Do you think it's okay?"

"I don't know," Carol admitted, "but I'm not sure we have a choice. We'll just have to be careful around him."

Adam had finished talking to his wife. "Are we ready?" he asked.

"Yes!" Quo exclaimed.

"My car is just down this way," Carol said. "I parked it over there so I could just walk by this building. I just had to see the old building I used to work at… I didn't know why, but now it all makes sense…"

The three of them walked away from the abandoned building towards Carol's car.

In the other timeline, Carol and Bob had a blue convertible.

As they walked up to her car, Carol said, "It's not as nice as the car Bob and I have, but I suppose it will do for now."

This car could seat five people. It was dark green. Carol sat in the driver's seat, Quo jumped in the passenger's seat, and Adam sat in the back.

"You know exactly where this book signing is?" Quo asked Carol.

"I am his biggest fan," Carol admitted. "And his wife."

"That's a yes," Quo laughed.

The twenty-minute ride was mostly silent. Carol and Quo feared they had already said too much in front of Adam, and Adam didn't know what to say to his best friend or Carol.

Adam finally broke the silence in an attempt to be humorous. "Are we there yet?" he laughed.

Carol looked at Adam through the front mirror of the car. She shook her head. "He thinks he is hilarious," she said, smiling.

Quo shrugged. "It was a little funny," he admitted. "But, honestly, are we almost there?"

Carol rolled her eyes and laughed. "Yes," she said. "That building right there. I'm actually nervous. I can't wait to see him!"

She pulled into a parking spot. The parking lot was packed.

"Wow," Quo exclaimed. "Bob is extremely popular!"

"He is one of the best-selling authors in our state," Carol said.

"Good for him!" Quo said.

They got out of the car and walked into the building.

"That line right there," Quo realized. "The one that comes almost to the door here. That's the line to meet Bob?!"

Carol was proud. "That's my Bob! I can't believe I'm actually this nervous to meet my husband!"

They all stood in the line. Time moved slowly, as they got closer to meeting Bob. Some people were taking photos with Bob. Some just shook his hand. They didn't have a book for him to sign. There were copies to buy, but not everyone could afford them.

Now, there were only two people in front of them. The first person got Bob's signature, snapped a photo with him, and quickly walked away. The last person in line before them now walked up to Bob.

"Hello, Bob," he said. "You have inspired me to become a writer. I have been reading your work for years. I don't have any money to buy one of your books right now, as I've spent all I have trying to make it in this industry. Do you have any tips on how to get noticed? I brought one of my works with me and would be honored if you could read it."

Bob smiled at him. There was another man standing near Bob. He had an earpiece in and looked like he was talking to someone.

Carol noticed him. "That must be Bob's manager," she said.

"Excuse me," the manager walked over towards Bob and the man talking to him. "No solicitation other than that of Bob's writings."

"I am so sorry, sir," the man said.

"Buy a book, or move along," the manager demanded.

"I can't afford one," the man frowned.

Bob looked at his manager disapprovingly, then at the man. He was about to offer the man a free copy, when the manager sternly stared at Bob and said, "No. Not again. We are here to make money, not friends."

The man was about to walk away, when Carol walked up next to him and said, "I'll buy you a book."

"Oh, thank you so much!" the man said. "I have been wanting to read this new book for months!"

"It is his best work yet," Carol smiled. She handed Bob the money for the book.

"Who should I make this out to?" Bob asked the man.

"James," the man said. "Thank you so much, Bob. Thank you, ma'am!"

"To James," Bob said, as he wrote a message on the inside front cover of the book. "Some people think writers are a dime a dozen, but I think each writer is priceless. Everyone has their own voice. Everyone has stories to tell. Use your voice. Tell your stories. Don't ever give up."

The man was so excited. "Thank you so much!" he said again, looking at Carol and Bob.

"Hey," Bob said, "don't thank me, thank this generous woman. And James, who knows, maybe there is an alternate timeline where you're the famous one and I'm not known at all!" He winked at James.

James nodded at Bob and thanked Carol again. He walked away excitedly.

"Hello," Bob said to Carol. "That was the nicest thing I've seen in a while. Thank you so much for doing that."

"It was my pleasure," Carol smiled at Bob.

They stared at each other for a moment.

Quo broke the silence. "Bob, why did you make that joke about an alternate timeline?"

"Sir," he said, "I am a Science Fiction writer! I love the thought of time travel, alternate timelines, multiple universes, and everything having to do with them!"

Quo looked at Carol, then at Bob. "Even in this timeline, with the restriction on space exploration, you found a way to do what you love. You're still exploring space. Through books."

"I'm not quite sure what you're talking about," Bob admitted, "but yes, I am doing what I love. I was going to explore space for real. But the day I was scheduled to start my job, the building I was going to work at ceased operations. And soon after, space exploration itself became a thing of the past."

"Why is that?" Quo thought out loud.

"The Elders just want to keep us safe," Bob said. "They said writing books about space exploration was okay because it was better than actually exploring space and getting killed out there."

Carol looked at Bob's manager, who started to look annoyed.

"I think he wants us to move along," Quo said to Carol. "You might want to tell him."

"Tell me what?" Bob asked.

"You love science fiction," Carol said, "but…" she looked at Quo, Adam, the manager, then back at Bob. "Science fiction is becoming science fact before our very eyes."

"That sounds familiar," Bob laughed. "Why does that sound familiar?"

"Bob," Carol continued, "my name is Carol. I am your wife."

Quo stared at Carol. "That's one way to get him to remember," he laughed.

"I don't have a wife!" Bob cried. "What are you talking about?"

"Bob," Carol said, "I am your wife."

Bob looked back at his manager, who started to come towards him and Carol.

"Carol, I don't think this is going to work!" Quo cried.

Carol looked around frantically as the manager and a couple of guards were about to come and escort her, Quo, and Adam out of the building.

Bob stood up. "I do love science fiction," he said to Carol. "But I don't think anybody would choose to marry me in any timeline."

He was about to walk away. Something had upset him.

Carol began to cry. "Bob!" she said. She had an idea. It might not work, but it was all she had left. "You were searching through space when I was here all along," she said. "I was leading teams, planning other people's lives, and building the ships that would change their lives, when the best change in my life was meeting you."

Bob turned back towards Carol. He put his hand out to stop his manager and security from escorting them away.

The rock in Quo's jacket began to glow. He took it out and handed it to Carol.

Now holding the glowing rock, Carol continued, as everyone in the building stared at them. "We didn't always see eye to eye. Some thought we might break up. They said we should take some space."

"What are you quoting?" Quo asked Carol.

She looked at Quo, and whispered, "Bob's marriage vows to me."

She held the rock out for Bob to take. Fascinated by everything, he took the glowing rock, as his wife finished reciting the vows.

"But I told them that we didn't need space. Space needed us!"

Bob looked at the rock, then at Carol. With those final words she recited, his memories came rushing back to him.

"Carol?!" he cried. He hugged his wife. "I am so sorry!"

Bob's manager stared at everything in shock. He spoke to someone on his earpiece, and said in a loud voice, "The show is over! Everyone go home."

Security helped clear the building fast, until only Quo, Adam, Carol, Bob, and Bob's manager were left.

"Bob," his manager said, "this isn't going to work anymore. You always try to give away free copies of your book. I'm sorry. It is good to be generous, but we can't afford the kind of generosity you have. We have tried to work with you over the years. But whatever this is, this stunt you just pulled, we feel it might be in your best interest to step back from our company for a bit. Call us in a week, or maybe give yourself a month. Think about everything. If we hear back from you, we'll know you finally see things our way and can renew the contract. If we don't hear back, we'll assume you have moved on."

Bob nodded at his manager, who shook his head and walked out of the building.

"Sorry about that," Bob said. "He is a good person. He tries. They have treated me well at that company."

"You're a writer!" Carol exclaimed.

"I suppose I am," Bob smiled. "But I suppose now it's time to give up that dream. Let's go save our friends!"

Adam looked at the three of them. "You guys really know each other somehow?"

Bob smiled. "Science fiction is becoming science fact. Hello, my name is Bob."

"I'm Adam. It is nice to meet you."

"How do you know him?" Bob asked.

"My best friend in this timeline," Quo admitted. "So, who do we have the best chance of finding next?"

"Gloria, Captain Zot, Clory, Trolk, Gleck, and Glor will be found on the same planet," Bob guessed. "Do you think Admiral Noah is still on Earth?"

"Admiral Noah?" Adam asked. "I know a guy named Noah."

"You do?!" Quo gasped.

"Yes," Adam admitted. "Noah is my father-in-law!"

Chapter 6
Noah

"What are the odds that this Noah is the Noah we are looking for?" Quo asked.

Adam shrugged. "I don't know, but if you want to meet him, I could have him come over for a meal tonight."

Quo looked at Bob and Carol. "I guess we might as well meet this Noah!"

Adam called his wife and asked her to invite her parents over. This one seemed simple. If this was, in fact, the Noah they needed to find, what could go wrong?

"I guess we'll all have to pile in my car for the ride back to Adam's house!" Carol said.

They all walked outside to Carol's car.

"Where is our car?" Bob asked. "Where is our blue convertible?"

"We don't have that in this timeline!" Carol said.

"Oh yeah," Bob sighed.

They all got into the car. This time, Bob sat in the passenger seat. Carol drove. Adam and Quo sat in the back.

"They're expecting us in about ninety minutes," Adam said. "I live about five minutes from the abandoned building. Since we are nearly thirty minutes from my house right now, that gives us about an hour to wait. Unless you want to show up early. I don't think they would mind."

"I just want everyone to remember," Quo admitted.

"What exactly is going on?" Adam asked. "You can trust me."

Quo looked at Bob and Carol. Then, he looked at Adam.

"I wish I could tell you," Quo said, "but I don't know if it's a good idea."

Carol sighed, then said, "Quo, if he is going to be with us much longer, helping us out, maybe we should just tell him what is going on. Especially if his father-in-law is our Noah."

Bob agreed with Carol. "Quo, if he is your best friend, maybe you should trust him. I'm sure you have good taste in friends no matter what timeline we're in."

Still unsure, Quo began to explain everything to Adam. Bob and Carol also helped tell the story. They talked for nearly an hour, just sitting in the car.

Adam was not as shocked as they thought he would be.

"My father-in-law sometimes talks about science fiction. He is definitely knowledgeable on the subject."

"That's good to hear," Carol said.

"Is that rock really from the other timeline?" Adam asked.

Quo nodded.

"That is so cool!" Adam exclaimed. "Though, I guess you yourself are from the alternate timeline, right?"

"I am," Quo admitted. "My friends, though technically from this timeline, are sort of from the other timeline too. They have their memories from both timelines."

"How does that feel?" Adam asked.

"A bit weird," Bob said, "but now I have memories of being a successful writer and the leader of space exploration. So, it is kind of cool!"

Carol smiled. "As long as we are together," she said to Bob, "I don't care how many memories we remember."

Bob nodded.

"And who am I to you in this other timeline?" Adam asked.

Quo looked away. "I don't know you in my timeline."

"Oh well," Adam said, "you know me now! That's all that matters, right?" He smiled.

Quo looked back at him and smiled. "I suppose so."

"Well," Adam said, "I think we can go straight to my house now! It's been about an hour, and we have a twenty-five minute drive ahead of us. I'm sure my wife's parents are already there now. They only live a block away from us."

Carol started the car, and they began their drive to Adam's house. On the way there, they continued to talk about everything that had happened and what might happen after everyone remembers.

"I guess we'll all settle in on this new timeline," Quo sighed. "I've seen good and bad changes so far. I do wonder why the Elders don't want us traveling through space, though."

"I think they honestly just want to protect us," Adam admitted.

Bob agreed. "Now having both sets of memories, from what I can remember from this timeline, the Elders just want to keep us safe."

"Yeah," Carol said, "though it doesn't make much sense. In our timeline, we travel through space. We, as humans, learn more from exploring. So there is something off here."

"One problem at a time," Bob smiled. "I guess our next task is to meet Noah!"

After a few more minutes of talking, they finally arrived at the abandoned building. From there, Adam directed Carol to his house. They parked the car and walked up to the doorway.

Adam opened the door. "Hello?" he said. "We have arrived!"

A woman met him at the door. "Hello, Adam!" she said. She hugged him

"Hello, Quo!" Adam's wife said. She looked at Bob and Carol.

"This is Bob and Carol," Adam said. "They are friends of Quo. Bob and Carol, and Quo, this is my wife, Nova."

"Quo knows who I am!" Nova said.

"Well," Adam hesitated, "we might need to talk."

"That sounds ominous!" Nova laughed.

"Are your parents here yet?" Adam asked.

"Of course!" Nova said. "They are just waiting for us in the dining room. Dinner is nearly ready."

"I must say," Carol interrupted, "you got a meal together rather quickly!"

"She's the best cook you'll ever meet," Adam said.

"I try," Nova said, humbly.

"All those years of cooking school definitely paid off," Adam smiled.

Nova laughed, then brought everyone to the dining room.

Not knowing what to expect, Quo, Bob, and Carol were almost excited to see Admiral Noah again. However, there was only a woman sitting in the dining room.

"Where's dad?" Nova asked.

"He stepped outside," Nova's mother said.

Nova looked at her mom, then back towards Adam and everyone else.

"This is Bob and Carol," Nova said. "You know Quo. Guys, this is my mom, Veronica."

"Nice to meet you," Veronica said. She stood up. "I'll go get Noah."

She walked outside. After a minute, she walked back in by herself.

"Noah doesn't feel well," Veronica said, frantically. "I don't know what is wrong with him!"

She motioned for everyone to follow her.

As they all ran outside, they quickly recognized Noah.

"Admiral!" Bob exclaimed. "It's you!"

"Admiral?" Veronica asked. "Noah is not an admiral."

Carol sighed. "Everything is changed," she said.

"But at least this is our Noah," Quo replied.

"What do you mean by that?" Veronica said.

Noah looked around at everyone. "Veronica," he said, "I feel so dizzy!"

Bob and Carol went running towards Noah. Standing on either side of him, they each took one of his hands.

"Admiral Noah," Bob said, "please remember."

"Bob and I remembered," Carol said.

"If we humans can remember," Bob continued, "surely an Elder can remember!"

"Excuse me?!" Veronica cried.

Nova stared at them. "My father is not an Elder. He is a human just like my mom. Just like me."

"How is that possible?" Quo asked. "If he was an Elder in my timeline, how in the world could he be a human in this new timeline?"

274

Noah looked at Quo. "Alternate timelines are real?" he asked.

"Sir," Quo said, "they are! I come from another timeline. Bob, Carol, and I have found you to help you remember who you are!"

"Who am I?" Noah asked.

Quo reached into his jacket and showed Noah the rock. "On my timeline, you are Bob and Carol's boss. You were sent to Earth to keep the humans safe. You were under the control of someone else for a while, but you finally just got to be yourself. Remember," Quo cried.

"I don't like this," Veronica admitted.

"Wait," Nova cried, "I think this is helping him!"

"Under their control..." Noah cried. "I will no longer be under their control!"

The rock started to glow immediately. Noah reached for it.

"The Elders have been controlling me," he cried. "Wait, I remember something else."

As the rock continued to glow, memories flew through Noah's head as he remembered everything from the other timeline.

"Quo!" he cried. He handed the rock back to Quo. "You found me!"

"We found you," Quo smiled, as he put the rock away and stepped back towards Bob and Carol.

"The Elders... what have they done? Oh no..."

"What happened?" Quo asked.

"They had me under their control on this timeline!" Noah cried. "They made me believe I was a human."

"For what purpose?" Carol asked.

"I'm not quite sure," Noah admitted. "My parents..."

"What about your parents?" Bob asked.

"My parents didn't want me," Noah said, sadly. "My parents didn't want me so they dropped me off on Earth with a nice family of humans... and they had me under the thought that I was a human this entire time!" Noah began to cry.

Veronica wanted to console her husband, but she too was frightened. "Where is this all coming from?!"

Noah cleared his throat. He looked at Carol, Bob, and Quo, who all nodded at him.

"Let's go inside," Noah said.

They all sat down at the dining room table. Before anybody could eat, they had to have this conversation.

Noah began. He told Veronica, Nova, and Adam of his life in the original timeline, and why Bob and Carol had called him Admiral. He then talked about his life in this new timeline. He told Bob, Carol, and Quo how he met Veronica. He told them about their daughter Nova and how they were lucky to have a son-in-law as amazing as Adam.

"I guess, in some ways, this timeline is better than the last one!" Noah finished. "I never found love until we changed everything."

Veronica knew how much Noah loved science fiction. Since everyone already knew of the Elders and how powerful they were, what they just heard somehow seemed believable.

"What does that make me?" Nova asked. "Am I half human and half Elder?"

"I guess so," Veronica said. "But whatever that means, we love you the same, if not more. I'm sorry, Noah, this all startled me at first. But you're still you. The man I fell in love with."

Noah smiled. "Are you okay, Nova?" he asked his daughter.

"I think so," Nova sighed.

"So, you all came from this alternate timeline where basically, it sounds like there was almost no escape from the chaos," Veronica said. "I am glad I found you, Noah."

Nova stood up. "Who's ready to eat?" she asked.

Everyone ate and enjoyed Nova's cooking.

"This is the best food I've had on any timeline!" Bob smiled.

Carol laughed.

"So, what is our next move?" Noah asked.

Quo sighed. "Do you have your powers?" he asked.

"I might," Noah said.

276

"Since space travel is prohibited," Quo said, "I think the only way we have a chance of finding the rest of our friends is by teleporting there."

"You don't mean…"

"Noah, can you teleport all of us across space to the Elders' original home planet?"

Chapter 7
Clory

"I think I should be able to," Noah guessed. "But I'm not sure how my powers work in this timeline."

"If anything," Quo said, "you are stronger than you used to be. Without the necklace ever being created, there is nothing to siphon the power of the Elders. Though you were stronger than some already, chances are you might be even stronger here!"

Noah looked at his family, then at his friends. "Does everybody want to go on this mission?" he asked.

Veronica nodded.

Nova was quiet.

"Are you okay, honey?" Veronica asked.

"Yeah," Nova said. "I'm sorry, it's just a lot to take in. Yes, I want to go on this mission. Of course I want to help dad and his friends."

"And Quo is my best friend," Adam reassured his wife. "If this is important to him, this is important to all of us."

Nova smiled at her husband. "Okay," she agreed, "I'm ready to help."

"I guess we're doing this!" Noah exclaimed. "Is everybody ready?"

Everyone was ready. Noah began to concentrate. He thought of the Elders' original home planet.

"I'm not sure where exactly we'll end up on the planet," Noah admitted. "Truthfully, I've never been to our original home planet. It's a good thing I know where it is. Though maybe that doesn't even matter. I'm going home. We are all going to the planet my species originated on. And we're landing there... now!"

Everyone closed their eyes as their surroundings changed. They opened them up and were in the middle of what looked like a marketplace.

"This is interesting!" Quo admitted. He walked towards someone. They stared at him.

"Human?" an Elder said, walking towards Quo.

"Is that a bad sign?" Quo asked.

Just as the words left his mouth, every Elder in the marketplace stopped what they were doing and stared at the seven of them.

"Humans!" someone else screamed as they slowly walked closer to them.

"Humans?!" another cried, hesitantly walking up to Bob and Carol.

"I think the Elders are shocked to see us," Bob laughed.

"How did you get here?!" another Elder asked.

"Elder!" the first Elder to speak said, pointing at Noah.

"Okay, they can detect our species," Noah said. "Maybe it's a good thing."

"What am I?" Nova said, as she walked towards the first Elder.

The Elder stared at her but said nothing.

"Of course," Nova sighed.

"You are Nova," Adam said. "I personally don't care what species they classify you as. You are my wife and I love you."

Nova smiled.

The Elders stared for another moment, then they slowly walked away from them.

"Where are they all going?" Bob asked. "Are they afraid of humans in this timeline?"

They all heard a loud noise.

"That sounds like a signal," Noah said. "I think they are calling for their leader."

Someone came walking towards them. He was wearing an elaborate cloak with the hood over his head. He had two Elders on either side of him and three Elders behind him.

"He must be important," Quo guessed. "No way. There is no way that is him. Is that…?!"

"Who?!" Veronica cried.

"Oh no," Bob exclaimed.

The man walked up to them and smiled. "Welcome to my planet. You are all welcome. Humans. Elder." He stared at Nova. "I've never met a creature that was both human and Elder. No matter, welcome, everyone!"

He took the hood off to reveal himself.

It was Smedge.

"Smedge, are you everywhere?!" Quo cried.

Confused, Smedge looked around. "No," he said, "I'm just right here."

"What selfish trouble have you gotten yourself into this time?!" Quo asked.

"Quo," Bob whispered, "alternate timeline. This could be a completely different Smedge."

"Is there more than one of me?" Smedge asked. "I'm truly only aware of myself."

"This is weird," Carol admitted.

"I bet he knows where Clory and the rest of his family are, though!" Bob exclaimed.

"Friends," Smedge said, "it would be my honor to introduce you to my family. I see you have come with an Elder. You must be good people if a fellow Elder has agreed to bring you to our home planet. Come, follow me."

The Elders from the marketplace watched as the seven new arrivals followed Smedge and company out of view.

"I wonder where he is taking us," Quo whispered to Bob.

"Hopefully he is taking us to Clory," Bob replied.

Carol looked back towards Bob and Quo. "Can we trust this Smedge?" she whispered.

"I don't care how nice he seems," Noah admitted. "He's going to have to prove himself before anybody can trust him."

Quo, Bob, and Carol agreed. They all followed Smedge for what seemed like forever. Finally, they came upon a mansion.

"Your family," Quo asked Smedge, "are they all living here with you?"

"I wish!" Smedge cried. "Some of the Elders wanted to go exploring space. Everyone loves our home planet, but some of them wanted a change of scenery. Three groups left in different directions months ago. One of the groups settled on a brand-new planet. It was uninhabited, so they claimed the planet as a second home planet for the Elders. The second group just found a nice planet last week. Though it was already inhabited, the local people welcomed them with open arms. And finally, the last group is still out there, searching. I think sometimes, whether we be humans or Elders, we find ourselves searching and searching with no answers... it's not that the answers aren't there, it's just that we become so obsessed with the thought of searching, we start to fear what it would be like if there was nothing left to search for. So we ignore the answers we were originally looking for just to continue searching. If that makes sense."

Quo was dumbfounded. He didn't think Smedge could say something so eloquent and unselfish. "Maybe he is different," Quo thought.

They walked inside the mansion.

"Clory!" Smedge yelled. "We have company! Clory?"

A guard came up to Smedge and whispered to him.

"Oh my," Smedge cried. "It seems Clory has stepped away."

"What do you mean?" Bob asked.

"I was just told that..." Smedge hesitated. "I'm sorry, I should be able to trust you. I'm just nervous."

"Nervous about what?" Quo asked.

"Could you please help?" Smedge cried. "Clory hasn't been himself lately. Something has been upsetting him and I don't know what is wrong!"

"Where is he?!" Quo demanded.

"He's about to leave the planet!" Smedge cried. "He is the only family I have on this planet."

"Where is the rest of your family?!" Quo asked.

"They were in charge of one of those three groups I mentioned."

"Which one?" Carol asked.

"The one that is still searching," Smedge sighed. "Sometimes, they seem so lost."

Quo couldn't believe what he was hearing. It was as if everyone was coming undone in their family.

"We'll help you!" Quo exclaimed. "Take us to Clory."

Smedge nodded. "I'm humbled that you care so much to help a family you don't even know," he said. He had tears in his eyes. He threw off his cloak so he could run fast. "I don't need you to follow me, guards," Smedge said to the Elders that always followed him. "I think I already trust these people."

Quo smiled at Smedge. Everything seemed different, but maybe it was okay.

"Follow!" Smedge yelled as he went running.

The seven of them ran behind him. They ran through the mansion.

"I didn't expect to get such a workout today," Bob said, as he tried to keep up.

"Oh come on," Carol laughed. "You're the leader of space exploration and a writer. Maybe there's another timeline where you're an athlete!"

Bob laughed.

"This way!" Smedge shouted as he turned the corner.

They all ran out a back door of the mansion and through a beautiful garden. There were flowers Quo had never seen before. Some fruit that Bob didn't recognize, everything about what they saw was so beautiful.

They kept running. Quo looked at Adam and smiled. "Are we there yet?"

Adam laughed as they all continued to run.

"Here he is!" Smedge cried.

They all saw Clory walking onto a spaceship. It looked like he was ready to leave.

"I don't know where he is going," Smedge held back tears. "I need him." He looked at his brother and shouted, "Clory, I need you!"

"Clory!" Quo yelled. "It's us! Don't go on that spaceship! Your friends and family need you!"

Clory turned around. He recognized his brother, but he didn't recognize anybody else.

Quo went running towards Clory.

"Who are you?!" Clory cried.

Everyone walked up behind Quo.

"We are your friends, Clory," Quo said. "Just give us time to explain before you decide to leave."

Clory looked at Smedge who had tears in his eyes. "Okay," he said. "I'll give you five minutes."

Chapter 8
Trolk and Gleck

"What are you running from?" Carol asked Clory.

"I'm not running from anything," Clory admitted. "I just need to find out what's out there. Why are these all-powerful beings flying through space in spaceships when we can teleport from planet to planet? I want to understand. I have to understand why."

Quo looked at Smedge, then back at Clory. "Clory, do you recognize the names Trolk and Gleck?"

Clory looked towards the spaceship. "Why?" he asked.

"Because they are your friends."

"Yes, they are," Clory said. "But how do you know?"

"Alternate timeline," Quo blurted out. He thought being blunt would help Clory remember. But it did the opposite.

"You're crazy," Clory sighed, "and your five minutes are up." He walked towards the ship, then turned back. "Trolk and Gleck are on this ship with me. If you want to come, you are all welcome. Even you, Smedge."

Clory walked onto the ship.

Smedge looked around. He wanted to go but he also wanted to stay and help watch over the Elders on the planet. However, Clory was his family, so he decided to go with him.

"The guards will watch over everything while we are gone," Smedge said. "I just sent them a telepathic message. Are you all coming?"

They all followed Smedge onto the ship.

Everyone boarded the ship. There were many crew members. Quo immediately started looking for Gleck and Trolk.

The seven of them tried to stay together, but they quickly got lost among the crowd of passengers.

"This is your captain speaking," someone yelled. "It is my honor to announce that this ship is ready for takeoff!"

"I know that voice!" Quo exclaimed.

He went running towards the captain and realized who it was just as he saw her.

"Trolk!" Quo exclaimed.

Trolk stared at him.

"Hello, sir," Trolk said. "Please refer to me as Captain Trolk!" She smiled.

Quo was taken aback. "I'm sorry, Captain Trolk!" he said. "Where is Gleck?"

"Our pilot Gleck is about to bring this ship into space."

"Should I sit down somewhere while the ship takes off?" Quo asked.

"Well," Trolk said, "this ship was designed by a group of Elders and currently residing on it are dozens of Elders… and some humans?" she looked at Quo. "There's no need for safety precautions. You can stand or sit. Besides, we're already in space."

Quo found a window and looked out. He couldn't believe his eyes.

Captain Trolk smiled at Quo. "And what is your name? I have never seen you before. You're somewhat of a newcomer, I imagine."

Quo laughed to himself. "Trolk," he said.

"Captain Trolk!" she stated.

"Right. Sorry. Captain Trolk. My name is Quo. Could you please bring me to meet Gleck?"

"Do you know him?" she asked.

"Yes," he said. "but he doesn't know me yet."

"Intriguing," Trolk said. "Follow me."

On the way to meet Gleck, Bob and Carol caught up with Quo and Trolk.

"Where is Noah?" Quo asked.

"I'm not sure," Bob said. "He was with Veronica, Nova, and Adam."

"And Smedge?"

"I don't know where he went. He probably went to talk to Clory."

"Why didn't Clory remember like everyone else?" Quo asked.

"If I had to guess," Carol said, "he wasn't ready to listen."

Trolk turned back to everyone. "Oh, are we all meeting Gleck now?" she asked.

"If that's okay," Carol said.

Trolk had a serious look on her face as if she were about to deny their request. She then turned back and walked towards a door. "Well, come on! Gleck is right this way!" she said.

The door opened automatically, and they all walked onto the bridge of the ship.

"Gleck!" Quo exclaimed.

Gleck turned around to see the group standing there.

"Captain Trolk!" Gleck said. "I see you have brought some visitors!"

"They wanted to meet you," Trolk laughed. "I still don't know why!"

"Hey!" Gleck laughed.

He hit a couple of buttons on a console and stood up. "Auto navigation controls are enabled. You have my attention. How can I help you?"

Bob and Carol looked at Quo.

"Gleck," Quo began, "and Captain Trolk, I don't know how to say this…"

Bob whispered to Quo. "Don't start with alternate timeline this time," he laughed.

Quo smiled, then tried to continue, but was at a loss for words.

Trolk and Gleck were interested. They wanted to hear what they had to say.

"You're a writer, Bob, say something smart!" Carol smiled.

"I don't know Trolk and Gleck like Quo does!" Bob whispered.

Gleck and Trolk overheard him.

"What do you mean by that?" Trolk asked. "I have never met this Quo in my life."

"I don't recognize him either," Gleck admitted.

"I'm just a newcomer to them," Quo sighed.

"Newcomer?" Gleck thought.

"Trolk called me that," Quo admitted. "Though that was my nickname in our original timeline."

"Our original... timeline?" Trolk exclaimed.

"The necklace!" Quo remembered. "Trolk, do you remember the necklace? The one that was given to you at your birthday party?"

"I, I don't think I know what you're talking about."

"And Gleck, you were there when Clory was given the necklace to give to Trolk! Remember?"

Quo pulled the rock out of his coat pocket as it began to glow.

"This is from an alternate timeline," Quo said.

"Quo!" Bob yelled. "That didn't work last time! Clory thinks you're crazy because of that talk!"

"Can I see that?" Gleck asked.

He took the rock and stared at it.

"Trolk?" he said.

"Captain Trolk!" she demanded, as she also stared at the rock.

"I think I'm starting to remember something!" Gleck admitted. "Captain Trolk, do you remember searching through an old abandoned building with me?"

"We found that loose-leaf notebook!" Trolk cried. She took the rock and started to remember more.

"Trolk and Gleck," Quo said, "on our timeline, you were traveling through space, exploring. Gleck, you were the one that found that rock! You helped make my job easier. I don't know how I would've done any of this if we hadn't put our memories in that rock!"

Right when Quo said that, all of Trolk and Gleck's memories from their original timeline returned to them.

"Whoa!" Gleck exclaimed. "Trolk, I helped save the day!"

Trolk smiled at him. "Captain Trolk!" she said.

"Don't be alarmed," Quo said, "but Smedge is on this ship."

"What?!" Trolk cried. "Why is he here?!"

"In this timeline," Quo said, "I don't believe it myself, but Smedge is good."

"Smedge is good?!" Gleck exclaimed.

"We were all just as shocked as you!" Quo said.

"Clory is really upset in this timeline," Gleck admitted. "I think we might need to find out what is bothering him."

"You don't already know?" Quo asked. "I just thought because you were friends in this timeline, you might know what's wrong."

"Sometimes, being a friend means just being there with your friend, even when he doesn't want to talk about it," Gleck said. "He always gets upset around this time every year. I want to ask why, but I don't think he wants to talk about it."

"Okay," Quo sighed. "Maybe if we all go talk to him, we can help him remember. If he remembers, maybe he'll feel comfortable enough to tell us what's bothering him in this timeline."

"Good idea," Gleck agreed.

"Hey Gleck," Trolk said nervously, "look out the window!"

Gleck ran over to the controls and put the rock down by them. "How did this happen?!" he cried. "The controls were on auto navigation!"

He pressed some buttons and tried to manually control the ship.

Quo looked out the window to see another spaceship. They were headed right towards this spaceship. And the controls weren't allowing Gleck to change course.

Chapter 9
Gloria and Zot

"We are being hailed!" Gleck cried.

Trolk ran over and pressed a button. "Hello!" she said. "This is Captain Trolk! Our ship is out of control and we don't know how to--" She looked and finally realized who was on the other side of the viewscreen. "Captain Zot? Gloria?!"

"Apologies," Captain Zot said. "We lost control of our ship for a moment there."

"So did we," Gleck admitted. "We don't know why."

Quo whispered to Bob, as he noticed the rock faintly glowing, still sitting near Gleck's control panel. "I wonder if the loss of control has anything to do with all of the extra memories we are bringing to this new timeline."

Bob sighed. "You don't think the timeline is going to try to reject us again, do you?"

"I hope not," Quo said. "we still have a few more people to return memories to."

"Excuse me," Quo heard someone say. It was Captain Zot over the viewscreen.

"Captain Zot, sir!" Quo smiled. "How have you been?"

"Do I know you?" Captain Zot asked.

"Yes. No. Sir, permission to board your ship? Better yet, can you come to our ship?"

"I don't think that's a good idea," Captain Zot said. "Our ships just almost crashed into each other. And I think it might have something to do with that rock."

"Why do you think that, sir?" Bob asked.

"Because it looks like something from another timeline!" Captain Zot said.

"Don't mind him," Gloria said over the viewscreen. "I'm sorry. The reason we almost crashed might have had something to do with the rock, but it just as easily could have been a malfunction on either or both of our ships."

Quo smiled at Gloria. He wanted to ask if Glor was with them, but before he could, Clory and Smedge came running onto the bridge. Clory was carrying what looked like a notebook.

"Mother, father!" Clory cried. "I need to talk to you."

"He's upset again," Smedge sighed, "and I wish he would tell me why. I think it has something to do with that journal!"

Gloria gasped, and she began to cry.

"What is it?!" Smedge cried. "I feel like everyone knows something that I don't know!"

Captain Zot put his hands over his face and began to cry.

"I'm sorry, Clory. I'm sorry, Smedge," Captain Zot said.

Quo began to get nervous. "Why is everyone upset? What is going on?! Gloria. Zot. Where's Glor?!"

When she heard the name, Gloria began to cry uncontrollably. Captain Zot hugged his wife, then looked at Quo.

"How do you know her name?!" he cried.

"How do I know her name?!" Quo exclaimed. "How do I know the name of the one and only love of my life?! I'm sorry! This whole mission was definitely to save your species, yes, but I only agreed to this crazy plan because this seemed like the only way Glor and I were actually going to survive together!"

The rock started to glow brighter.

"The alternative was to create a necklace that Smedge would use to send the Elders' home planet flying through time at the Elders' second home planet, causing a collision that would explode the two planets through time, and slowly drain all of the Elders of their powers until you all died off, weak and frail! We were not creating that necklace."

The entire room was lit up by the glow of the rock.

"Another option was to not create the necklace and let the timeline reset around us! But if we did that, we would have never met! So Admiral Noah gave us the idea of the plan we are currently carrying out! I would go around and find everyone and remind them of their lives from the original timeline!"

Quo pointed to the rock.

"That rock, which Gleck found floating through space, is a piece of our exploded planet from that timeline. It carries all of our memories and shouldn't even exist in this timeline! So, I will ask again! Where, is, Glor?!"

Clory gasped, as he walked towards the rock. Everything Quo said sounded so familiar. He looked at his parents, then at the rock.

"I remember!" Clory cried. "Quo, I'm so sorry! Oh no."

Gloria was still crying. Captain Zot was staring at the rock.

"Gloria," Captain Zot cried. "Do you remember?!"

"Yes," she said. She opened her eyes and stared directly at Quo.

"Quo," she said, "it didn't work."

"What do you mean it didn't work?!" Quo cried.

Smedge was confused. "Who is Glor?"

"How does Smedge not know Glor?!" Quo cried. "How does he not know his own sister?!"

Smedge's eyes widened.

Clory walked over to his brother and handed him the notebook. He opened it to a page in the middle.

"I'm sorry you found out that way, Clory," Gloria cried. "Your father and I didn't think we should tell you and Smedge. It was so depressing for us."

"We've failed," Captain Zot cried.

Clory looked at his parents. "I found this notebook eight years ago," he cried. "I wanted to talk to you about this so much. But I figured there was a reason you didn't tell us. That's why I have been so upset. That's why I get so upset this time every year."

Smedge had tears in his eyes. He handed the notebook to Quo.

"Quo," Gloria said, "that's my journal. I thought I lost it about eight years ago. I guess that's when Clory found it. Quo, before you read that, look at me. Look at me, Quo."

With tears in his eyes, Quo looked at Gloria.

"This isn't right," Captain Zot said.

He called for someone over an intercom, and five crew members came onto the bridge of their ship.

"Watch this ship," Captain Zot said to one of them. "In fact, I'm making you the captain. My family needs me, and this is what you've been training for. I'm going to transfer to that ship."

The crew members nodded and immediately took action.

Captain Zot and Gloria teleported to Captain Trolk's ship and both ran over to Clory and Smedge. Though they now remembered everything, and how evil Smedge was in the other timeline, they just as much remembered how good Smedge was in this timeline.

The hail call ended, and the other ship slowly flew away.

Quo couldn't bring himself to read the journal entry. He could already guess what happened. He handed the journal to Gloria.

"Quo," she cried, "I'm sorry!"

"What happened?" Quo cried. "Why did it happen?!"

"I was four months pregnant," Gloria began, "Zot and I had just found out that day. We had gone to the doctor. Everything was fine. We went back for checkups regularly. Every week. We didn't run into complications until months later."

Smedge cried. "Was this the year Clory and I were off world training with the Elders?"

Clory sighed. "Of course it was. The one time we weren't allowed contact with our family. And in those eight months we weren't around, the most devastating thing happened to our family."

Gloria continued, "I'm sorry, sons," she said, "and Quo, I am sorry. We found out when I was about seven months pregnant. That was when the complications began. We couldn't understand how this could happen to someone as powerful as Elders, but Quo, it happened. I wrote about it in my journal, but other than the doctor, Zot, and myself, this wasn't something we talked about with anybody. Glor was stillborn at seven months and twenty-three days."

"Why did this happen?!" Quo demanded. "WHY WOULD WE GO THROUGH ALL OF THIS JUST TO FIND OUT WE HAVE FAILED?! I DON'T WANT TO BE IN THIS TIMELINE ANYMORE!" Quo was furious, but his anger quickly turned to sadness. "Gloria, why?"

"I only just figured it out now," Gloria cried. "With my memories from the first timeline. Remember, I went on that mission for the Elders just after I found out I was pregnant. I went on that ship, knowing I had a baby with me. We thought the Elders didn't know," she began to cry. "They sent me on that mission knowing I was pregnant. We thought it was a bad thing that the ship I traveled in for months only sustained one life form, all along the Elders knew that was the only way my baby would survive! That ship sustained my baby's life. Something the Elders didn't figure out in time or even think of in this timeline."

"What do you mean?" Quo asked.

"They must have known I would miscarry along the way. So, they used me for their mission. Yes, maybe they needed someone like me to do the mission anyways, but now I know the Elders did everything to protect my baby." She looked at Zot. "We honestly tried to hide my pregnancy from them. We thought they didn't know."

"But they put you in danger," Clory cried. "You were in a stasis pod for years!"

"And as a mother, I would have done the same thing for any of my children even if it meant I only had a one percent chance of survival. The Elders saved my baby in our original timeline. And now, here we are, stuck in this one."

Quo felt dizzy because of the news that he would never see Glor again. "I don't want to do any of this without her."

Smedge looked at everyone. "My heart hurts," he cried. "I'm sorry, family."

"Can we change it back?" Quo asked. "Please? I would do anything to change it back… I would even… create the necklace."

Gloria stared at him, then at Zot. "We couldn't do that, could we?"

"Save our daughter? Why not?" Captain Zot asked. "Other than the fact that it might cause the destruction of our own species…"

"Everything comes to an end," Smedge said. "What if it was their time to end? What if it was time for the Elders to end? I don't want the destruction of our species, but if we can save my sister, I say, let's try this."

"Are we really going to try to create the necklace?" Quo asked. "How would that even work? All we have is that rock.

Other than that, we don't have any other pieces of our exploded planet. And if we create the necklace in this timeline, would that bring back our old timeline?"

"I don't know what we are supposed to do," Captain Zot admitted, "but I think we have to involve everyone that made the trip from the original timeline in this decision."

"Fine!" Quo cried. "But I can't see why any of us would choose this timeline over the original one. I miss Glor so much."

Just then, Noah, Veronica, Adam, and Nova came to the door of the bridge.

"There you are!" Noah exclaimed. "What did we miss?"

Chapter 10
Glor

"Admiral Noah?" Captain Zot said.

"Who are they?" Clory asked, noticing Adam, Veronica, and Nova.

"This is my wife, Veronica," Noah said. "And this is our son-in-law, Adam!"

"I'm Quo's best friend," Adam stated. "In this timeline, at least! Right, Quo?"

Quo stared at him and started to realize that Noah might not agree to go back to the old timeline. He had a family. A wife.

"And this," Noah said, "this is my daughter, Nova."

"Hello, everyone," Nova said. "It is nice to meet you."

Quo thought to himself, "He has a daughter too? I can't ask him to give this up." His heart began to ache with the horrifying realization of never seeing Glor again.

"Why does everyone look so sad?" Nova asked. "Was it something we said?"

Noah looked around. "Hey, where's Glor?"

Gloria wanted to answer the question, but the words weren't coming. Her heart was broken, and all she could do was cry.

Quo burst into tears.

Captain Zot took a deep breath and simply said, "We failed."

"What do you mean?!" Noah asked.

"She didn't survive in this timeline," Captain Zot said, sadly. He too was fighting back tears.

"Oh my," Noah cried. "I am so sorry!"

"Hey," Nova exclaimed, "is that the same rock that brought back dad's memories? Why is it so bright?"

The rock continued to increase in brightness.

"What are we supposed to do now?!" Quo cried. "Everything was supposed to be okay!"

The room began to shake.

"Everyone was supposed to remember!" Quo yelled. "Here we are, nine out of the ten of us remembered... but it all seems meaningless now! Glor, I'm sorry!"

"Quo," Clory said, "I've been dealing with this loss for eight years. I have both sets of memories, so I know how much Glor meant to you. She meant so much to my family and me, and the fact that she is gone hurts. It hurts twice as much as it did before I got my memories from the original timeline."

"The original timeline," Quo cried. "I can't even ask everyone to go back to the original timeline now! Noah has a family! Smedge is good!"

Smedge looked at Quo. "Wait, what am I like in the original timeline?"

"And this is all nothing without Glor!" Quo cried.

The rock was near the edge of the control panel now, as the room shaking had moved it.

"Quo," Gloria cried, "I am so sorry. Having two sets of memories... one where she survives and one where she doesn't... and being in the timeline where my baby doesn't exist, that hurts my heart."

Quo frowned. He stepped towards the glowing rock. "Glor, I love you." He nodded.

"Quo, I love you," someone said.

Everyone looked around.

"Did you hear that?" Quo asked.

"Yes, we did," Gloria exclaimed. "Where did that come from? The rock?"

Gloria and Captain Zot stepped towards the rock.

"Quo, I love you!" someone said again.

Gleck and Trolk stared at the rock. Clory walked towards it. Bob, Carol, Noah, and Smedge were also looking at the rock.

Veronica, Adam, and Nova looked at everybody, then at the rock.

The room was still shaking. The rock, still brightly glowing, finally reached the edge of the control panel. Quo picked it up so it wouldn't fall.

"Glor, can you hear me?" he asked.

There was no answer.

Quo looked at everyone.

"I don't understand," he cried.

The rock began to heat up, but Quo didn't want to let go of it.

"Ouch!" Quo exclaimed. "The rock is heating up!"

"You might want to put it down then," Bob suggested.

Quo was about to put the rock back, but he accidentally dropped it.

Everyone watched as the rock fell to the ground. It broke into many pieces. The pieces floated in the air.

"This looks familiar," Quo remembered. He looked at Clory. "Do you remember? Before the planets collided in the original timeline. The necklace fell to the ground and broke, and the broken pieces floated around Glor."

"I remember that!" Clory smiled. "She remembered some of mother's memories because of that, and even some of her own!"

"The pieces were floating around her when Gleck and I gave that loose-leaf book to you!" Trolk said. "The one we found at the old abandoned building!"

"Oh yeah!" Gleck exclaimed.

"They were still present when we found out Gloria was still alive in the stasis pod!" Captain Zot cried.

"And when Glor revealed herself to be the sister of Smedge!" Clory laughed.

For the first time in a while, Gloria smiled. It was a true smile. "When I landed on the planet and stepped off that ship, that was one of the first things I noticed. I noticed those broken pieces of the necklace floating around her."

"She thought the necklace was broken but you fixed it!" Quo found himself smiling.

"I love you, Quo," everyone heard someone say again.

The pieces of the rock were still floating in midair. What looked almost like a hologram began to appear.

A faint hologram that looked like a woman could now be seen, with the pieces of the rock floating around it.

"I have nowhere to go," a voice said. It was clearly coming from the floating pieces of rock and this hologram. And it was clearly Glor's voice. "Where am I? Quo, it's dark. Help me."

Quo began to choke back tears again. "Glor? Is that you?"

"Quo, everyone remembered! We did it! Where am I?"

"Glor," Gloria cried.

"Mom?" Glor's voice could be heard saying, "It's dark! Where am I? Why can't I see?"

"Glor, we failed," Clory sighed.

"Is that Glor?" Nova asked.

"Hello? Who's speaking? I don't recognize that voice."

"My name is Nova," she said. "I am the daughter of Veronica and Noah."

"Admiral Noah?"

"Yes," Nova said. "And this is my husband, Adam."

"It's nice to meet you… if I could meet you… wait a minute…"

"Are you okay, honey?" Captain Zot asked.

"I have no idea. I think it's time for me to go."

"No!" Quo pleaded. "I need you. Please, Glor, we have to find a way…"

"I can't take away someone else's joy to receive my own."

"What do you mean?" Quo cried.

"She means me," Nova said. "I don't exist at all in the other timeline. My father is an admiral. He never found love. He exists in the other timeline. My mom exists in the other timeline though she never met and married my dad. And Adam still exists in the other timeline. I'm not supposed to exist… it's like the universe traded out Glor's life, for mine…"

"That's not true," Glor said. "Nova, this isn't your fault. This isn't anybody's fault."

"Glor?" Smedge cried.

"Smedge?!"

"It's okay, Glor," Gleck stated, "Smedge is good in this timeline."

"I would have loved to see that."

"Why does everyone keep saying how good I am in this timeline?!" Smedge asked. "What, was I a horrible creature in this original timeline?"

"Worse," Quo exclaimed.

"I'm sorry," Smedge said.

"I never thought I would hear Smedge say those words," Glor admitted.

"Glor, I want to go back to the original timeline," Quo cried. "Maybe we can still create the necklace."

"Would going back to the original timeline and creating the necklace before coming to this timeline be what is best for everyone here and now?" Glor asked. "No, you can't do that."

"Why do you say that?!" Quo cried.

"I won't allow anybody to take away someone else's joy for my own."

"What if we create the necklace in this timeline?" Quo asked.

"No," Glor said.

"Is there a way to save you?!" Gloria cried. "We all miss you so much!"

"The only way you might be able to save me is to enter back into the original timeline in the present. I would not advise that."

"Why not?!" Quo cried.

"I'm not sure how I know this, but Smedge and Enyo have taken over the third home planet of the Elders."

"The original timeline still exists?!" Quo asked.

"Not for long," Glor sighed. "Smedge and Enyo have found a way to allow more powerful Elders from the alternate timeline you are on into our original timeline. They are destroying everything!"

"That's not possible!" Quo yelled. "This timeline rejected the ten of us! That is why we have this problem to begin with!"

"Our timeline was around for thousands of more years than the new timeline we created. It is stronger. But not for long. Oh, it all makes sense now."

"What does?" Quo asked.

"I see both timelines. What happened on them. What is happening on them. After the Clory and Smedge in the new timeline left our home planet, the home planet of the Elders, there was no one watching over it anymore…"

"The Elders are powerful," Clory said. "Why would Smedge or I watching over the planet make any difference?"

"They couldn't execute this plan until you left the planet… the paradox of two Smedges on the same planet was one hundred percent rejected in this new timeline… and Clory, though he was upset, would not have allowed the Elders to go along with this…"

"Why did the Elders go along with this?!" Gloria cried. "They aren't bad!"

"They are not all bad," Glor said somberly, "But they are more powerful." She looked at Clory. "After Smedge and Enyo took over the Elders' third home planet in the original timeline, they somehow, with the help of some from the planet they conquered, traveled back in time to the collision of our first two home planets. They were waiting there. They knew that was where time was weakest. And they had somehow figured out that's where we all last were. They used that moment in time, the exact moment we changed timelines, to go through to this new timeline themselves… they showed up on the Elders' home planet and quickly recruited as many as would join their cause and are now back in the original timeline. There are hundreds of beings in the first timeline now that shouldn't be there…"

"How?!"

"These Elders are much stronger as you know! They are using their powers against the timeline itself to stay alive!"

"Why would anybody agree to help Smedge and Enyo?!"

"Fear. Power. I'm sure Smedge and Enyo knew exactly what to say."

"Wait," Quo cried, "this timeline rejected all of us coming through physically! How did Smedge and Enyo manage to do what we couldn't?!"

"They are too strong," Glor cried. "The new timeline fought against the original Smedge, but he and Enyo fought back until they got their way."

"What do we do?!" Gloria cried.

"If you choose to fight for the original timeline, be careful."

"Can both timelines exist?" Clory asked.

"Not forever," Glor said. "Whatever you choose, try to keep everyone in mind. You mean well, Quo, and I miss you too. But make sure the choice is made for the right reason. And you must all agree. It is time for me to go for now. I am tired."

"Glor," Quo cried.

"Quo, I love you."

The hologram disappeared. The pieces continued to float in midair.

"Gloria," Captain Zot said, "can you put the rock back together?"

Gloria went over and waved her hands over the pieces of rock. She pulled them all into her hands and closed them. She opened them back up to reveal the rock, back to normal. She handed it to Quo.

"Are her memories still in there?" Quo asked. "Is Glor still in here?"

"I think so," Gloria said.

"So, what do we do now?" Bob asked.

"Why is this Smedge so evil?" Smedge asked. "And who is Enyo?"

"How did Glor know all of what she told us?" Carol said.

Nova stared at everyone. She wanted to run off the bridge of the ship and be alone somewhere, but she knew that wouldn't help. She cleared her throat.

"If you go to the other timeline, can I come with you?"

"Of course!" Quo said. "Right?"

Noah sighed. "If we all go back to the original timeline, physically, there would be copies of us. If the timeline even allowed us to exist, no one is to say how long until we run into complications because of this. We don't even have a way to get there if we wanted to."

"Didn't you hear what Glor said?" Nova asked. "The Elders are using their powers against the timeline itself! You said that rock is from the original timeline, right?"

"Yes," Quo said, curiously.

"That might actually work!" Clory cried.

"That's what I thought," Nova smiled. "What if you all focus on the old timeline, using the rock, and use all of your powers to create a rift in time? Sort of like a doorway from this timeline back to the original one."

"But we don't know how this will impact everyone," Quo cried. "Especially you!"

"And Glor was right," Gloria admitted. "We have to do this for the right reasons. We can't throw everything from this timeline away now just to save her. She said she won't allow anybody to take away someone else's joy for her own."

Noah looked at Veronica, Adam, and Nova.

"No one is taking anybody else's joy away," Nova stated. She looked at her family. "I want to help. I choose to help."

Adam stepped forward. "I stand with my wife. I choose to help."

Veronica smiled. She wasn't sure how she felt until Nova looked directly at her.

"Trust me, mom," Nova said. "It will be alright."

Veronica stepped towards Nova and Adam. "I stand with my family."

Noah beamed. He walked towards his family and nodded. He was amazed at how selfless his little family was. "Are we doing this?" he asked everyone else.

Bob and Carol smiled.

Clory, Trolk, and Gleck nodded.

Gloria and Zot were elated.

"I'm coming too," Smedge exclaimed.

"Can he?" Quo asked.

"The new timeline is weaker," Gloria said. "That's why it couldn't contain both Smedges, I suppose."

"The first timeline is still stronger than this one for now," Captain Zot said. "I think it should be okay if Smedge joins us."

Quo smiled. "Thank you, everyone. We'll find a way to save everybody." He looked at Nova. "Everybody."

Everyone was in agreement. They weren't sure how this was going to work, or if it would. But they all stood ready, as Quo held out the rock.

Quo smiled. "Okay, everyone, let's save Glor. And everybody!"

Chapter 11
The Portal

Everyone stared at the rock and thought about the original timeline. They weren't sure if this would work, but they had to try.

Nothing was happening.

"What are we doing wrong?" Quo cried. "I thought this was going to work!"

"Maybe we don't have enough power to get through to the other timeline," Gloria sighed.

"If this doesn't work, are we stuck here forever without Glor?" Quo asked.

Bob shook his head. "No, Quo. We'll find a way."

"This was supposed to work," Quo frowned.

"Give me the rock," Nova demanded.

"Honey?" Veronica said. "What are you thinking?"

"Does she have powers?" Bob asked Noah.

"No," he said. "she's human."

"Half human," Carol said.

Noah stared straight ahead.

"But if she has powers," Bob wondered out loud, "would they be weaker than yours, Noah? Since, I'm sorry to say this, humans are weaker than Elders."

"I'm honestly not sure," Gloria interrupted. "Glor had powers like Zot and me, but she was stronger than both of us. She had more than one power."

"Had?" Quo cried. "You mean has! She's still alive! We'll save her!"

"Please!" Nova shouted. "Let me see the rock!"

Quo handed her the rock. She began to concentrate. The rock began to glow. As Nova stared at the rock, she said, "Now, everyone, think about the original timeline!"

They all obeyed. Adam was staring at his wife and Veronica marveled at what was happening.

A small portal seemed to be opening in front of everybody. This portal gained in size and strength until it was big enough for someone to step through.

"Now," Nova cried, "I'll go through last, so I can keep this open for everybody!"

"I'm waiting with you," Adam said.

"I'll go first!" Smedge exclaimed. "I want to make sure it is safe for you all. If there is anything waiting for us on the other side, I'll lead the charge!"

"Everybody be alert!" Gloria suggested. "Anything could be waiting for us on the other side!"

Nova's eyes started to glow.

"We were on our ship, the 'Decision', when this all started," Gleck guessed. "Maybe we'll go back to that?"

"That ship exploded!" Trolk yelled. "I think it's gone! All that was left was a platform floating in space!"

"I'm not sure what is on the other side," Nova stated, as she was still concentrating on holding the portal open.

Smedge stepped towards the portal. "Ready?" he asked.

Everyone nodded.

Smedge slowly stepped through the portal and was now out of sight.

Captain Zot and Gloria walked up to the portal. They looked back towards everyone.

"Thank you so much," Gloria said to Nova. "We'll see you on the other side."

Captain Zot smiled at Nova, then at his wife.

"Thank you, everyone," Clory said, holding back tears.

Clory ran after his parents, and the three of them were now out of sight.

Trolk and Gleck walked towards the portal.

"Trolk, I'm actually scared," Gleck admitted.

"I am too, Gleck," she cried.

She took his hand and they walked through the portal.

Noah stepped forward. Veronica followed him.

"Make sure she gets through," Noah said to Adam.

"Nova, we love you."

"We'll see you in a minute," Veronica said. "I love you, Nova."

Noah took a deep breath, as he stepped through the portal, followed by his wife.

"Well," Bob said, looking at Carol, "are we ready?"

"No," Carol admitted, "but that's alright. I don't think anybody could be ready for this. No amount of time could prepare someone for what we have gone through, and what we are about to go through."

"We don't need time," Bob smiled. "Time needs us."

Carol laughed.

Nova smiled at them.

Carol took Bob's hand. They were about to step through.

Bob looked back at everyone and smiled. "Thank you for finding us, Quo."

Quo nodded.

Bob and Carol walked through.

Adam, Nova, and Quo were the only ones left now.

"Okay, Quo," Nova said, "your turn!"

"You're coming too, right?" Quo asked.

She said nothing.

"Nova?" Quo asked.

"How am I supposed to go through if I'm the one holding the portal open?"

Adam stared at her. "We aren't going through, are we?"

Nova frowned. "I'm sorry, Adam," she said. "You can go through, though."

"No!" Adam exclaimed.

Quo stared at the portal, then at Nova and Adam.

"Glor said she wouldn't allow anybody to take away someone else's joy for her own," Quo cried.

He looked around, then had a thought.

"Give me the rock back," he demanded.

"You're a human," Nova said, "what makes you think you can hold this portal open?"

"Glor," he said.

He held his hand out for the rock. Hesitantly, Nova handed the rock to him.

"How are you going to get through?" Adam asked.

"Somehow," Quo said, not knowing the answer. "This is right. No one can be left behind."

Quo was standing there, trying to contain the power and the energy coming from the rock.

"Quo, you don't remember this timeline at all," Adam began, "but we were the best of friends. Thank you for trusting me. Thank you for allowing me into your life. All of the memories I have of us are real to me. I admire the love and dedication you have shown to those close to you in this timeline and your original timeline. I am so glad to call you my best friend. I only hope that someday, I can be half the friend to you that you have been to me. Thank you, Quo."

Quo smiled.

"Quo," Nova said, "everything Adam just said is true. You have always been there for him. For us. Thank you."

"It will be my honor to get to know you two more," Quo said. "Thank you for all your help as well."

Nova nodded.

"You'll see her again, Quo," Nova smiled. "You deserve to."

Quo nodded. "Once I step through, I'll know she's alive, right? She'll be somewhere on our original timeline. We just have to find her!"

Nova didn't say anything.

"Adam!" she cried. "He has them! He has all of them! We have to go now!"

Nova took Adam's hand and bolted through the portal. Frantically, Quo looked around as he was now alone.

"Glor," he said out loud, "I love you!"

The rock split into two. Both pieces began to glow.

"Leave one piece here," Quo heard Glor say. "That should keep the portal open long enough for you to cross through. It will close permanently after that. Take the other piece with you. It contains my memories. We'll figure the rest out later."

"What do you mean?!" Quo cried. "Aren't you still alive in the original timeline?"

"Quo, you must go now! Your friends are in trouble!"

Quo left a piece of the rock on the floor. He stared at it, as it somehow held the portal open by itself. He then stared at the other piece. He put it in his coat pocket. The portal began to weaken.

"Quo!" Glor cried. "Hurry, before it's too late!"

Quo ran towards the portal and jumped through, just as it was about to disappear. The portal closed behind him.

Chapter 12
Return

Quo's eyes were closed as he traveled through the portal. He wasn't sure if he should open them, but he finally just decided to.

What he saw was beautiful. It was a cross between space and the ocean. That was all he could see no matter where he looked.

After what seemed like an eternity, Quo finally reached the other side of the portal. Since he went running through, he lost his footing on the other side. He tripped and fell, as he landed back in the original timeline.

The first thing he saw when he stood up was his friends, all standing in a group. Even the Smedge from the new timeline was standing with them.

"Oh, good! We all made it safely!" Quo cried.

He started to walk towards his friends, but they looked nervous.

Clory shook his head. "Quo, be careful! We aren't--"

"SILENCE!" someone yelled, interrupting Clory.

In horror, Quo whipped around to see Smedge. The original Smedge, Enyo, and many other beings.

"Quo!" Smedge hissed. "Thank you SO MUCH for catering to my every whim!"

"What are you talking about?!" Quo demanded.

"Oh come now!" Smedge scowled. "It was because of you that the final phase of my plan worked. Everything I have done. EVERYTHING I HAVE EVER DONE HAS BROUGHT ME TO THIS! It's a shame, though. It's a shame what had to be lost along the way."

"Smedge! We are back in the original timeline now! Nothing is going to be lost!"

"Oh no!" Enyo growled. "He doesn't know yet!" She smiled and began to laugh.

"Quo, you incompetent fool," Smedge smirked. "I have orchestrated EVERYTHING to go MY WAY! Do you think I didn't have a little fun along the way?"

Gloria began to cry.

"Gloria, what's wrong?" Quo asked.

"Hey. HEY!" Smedge hissed. "This is my time to shine! I want to shine brightly too! Quo, aren't you going to ask about my friends?"

"I know about them!" Quo shouted. "Those are Elders from the alternate timeline!"

"Who told you?!" Smedge growled.

"I also know that you took over the Elders' third home planet. The one they settled on after the collision." Quo began to shout louder, "The collision that you caused!"

"How could I have caused it? You never created the necklace! But, then again… maybe I recruited someone else to create the necklace."

He backed up towards the Elders from the alternate timeline.

"Why didn't you just create the necklace yourself?!" Quo screamed. "Why did someone else have to create it for you?!"

"It was all part of my plan!" Smedge smiled. "All part of our plan!" he said as he looked at Enyo. "If I created the necklace, how would I have created that alternate timeline? I needed you to choose not to create it, so I could finally be victorious! Then, once my friends came through to this timeline, I had them create the necklace! After they created it, I had them bring it where it needed to be to complete its journey in this timeline. Besides, I told you. I couldn't live with myself if I created such a weapon."

"Why would the Elders ever listen to you?!" Quo demanded.

"Quo, Quo, Quo!" Smedge said, mockingly. "You have no imagination! Once I finally got through to the other timeline, I was welcomed by the Elders! It seems they already knew me!"

The other Smedge yelled, "They knew me!"

"Silence!" the original Smedge yelled. "That is the one thing I didn't see coming. I can't believe such a meaningless version of me exists. But even that worked in my favor! Once I got through to the other timeline, they welcomed me with open arms. They told me everything I wanted to know. I learned a lot about the Elders on this alternate timeline. For instance, Quo, would you like to know why they didn't allow the humans to travel through space?"

"They were trying to keep everyone safe!" Bob yelled.

"Be quiet, fool!" Smedge growled.

"What Bob said is true," Quo stated.

"No, it's not!" Smedge screamed. "The real reason humans weren't allowed to leave Earth is way better than that stupid excuse anyways."

"What is it, Smedge?!" Quo demanded.

"The Elders were afraid!" Smedge said. "If the humans left Earth, they would grow as a species. They would become smarter. They might not need the protection of the Elders if that were to happen. They just wanted to be needed! But there was one more reason…"

"What?!" Quo shouted.

Smedge walked over to Quo's friends.

"Guess!" Smedge laughed. "The Elders told me about the fear they had when you all appeared out of nowhere on their planet."

"They knew our species was human," Quo said. "And they knew Noah was an Elder."

"And what did they say about Nova?" Smedge smiled.

"What about her?!" Quo yelled.

"She is the other reason," Smedge stated. "She is the reason space exploration was forbidden!"

"I am half human, half Elder," Nova said. "The Elders were trying to prevent that from ever happening. They are afraid of me. But they didn't even know I existed."

"I WANTED TO TELL THEM!" Smedge screamed. "No matter."

"How did the Elders not know she existed? They were more powerful in that timeline!"

"They had no clue she was on Earth," someone said.

It was one of the Elders from the alternate timeline. He had stepped forward towards Smedge.

"Great Smedge, may I explain?" the elder asked.

"Of course!" he agreed.

"We still have no idea how an Elder got on planet Earth. The halt on space exploration wasn't just to keep the humans out of space. We, as Elders, were also forbidden from going to planet Earth for the same reason. All of us Elders were afraid of this amalgamation occurring." He pointed to Nova and continued talking. "If Elders and humans were allowed to dwell on the same planet together, or even allowed to go near each other, if they fell in love and had offspring together, that might jeopardize the Elders' species. That might slowly weaken them over time."

"All of that fear was over selfishness?!" Quo cried. "You were that much afraid of humans that you made up a story that you were protecting us?!"

"It wasn't my choice alone!" the Elder screamed. "It was a choice made by all of us. Humans are dangerous. And the thought of human DNA forever altering the DNA of the Elders is unthinkable!"

Bob looked at Carol. She knew exactly what he was thinking. The Elder had just basically said, "The thought is unthinkable." That was definitely something Bob would say.

Carol stared at Bob, smiled, and said, "Now isn't the time, Bob. But yes, I heard what he said."

Bob smiled at his wife.

"So the Elders had no idea she was on Earth," Quo said.

"There was no reason to think it!" the Elder said. "There was no reason to even look! Planet Earth was contained. No humans leaving Earth, no Elders going to Earth. How did you get there?" the Elder asked Noah.

"It's none of your business!" Noah said.

"ANSWER HIM!" Smedge yelled.

"My parents didn't want me!" Noah cried.

"Oh, how pathetic! Your parents didn't want you." Smedge walked towards Gloria and Zot. "It must be awful to know deep in your heart that your parents don't want you. But I know the feeling."

Gloria was still crying.

Zot stared at Smedge. "That is not true."

"So, who were your parents?" Smedge asked, now looking at Noah.

"I... don't remember," he said.

"And maybe you're better off that way," Smedge said, as he stared at his parents once more. "Enough about Noah, and his problems. Maybe what he believes is true, maybe an Elder just planted him there and changed his memories... we may never know. But that doesn't matter, as that timeline is now irrelevant! The Elders in that timeline were more than happy to help me with my cause. Especially after I told them about you, Quo."

"What about me?!"

"You still don't know?! Go on, Quo, ask yourself! Where is she?!"

"Glor?! Glor and the other eight of my friends are somewhere in this original timeline!"

"Do you not remember how you got to the new timeline?!" Smedge growled. "Your ship basically blew up!"

"We were all standing on what was left of our ship! I physically left, but I only assume when the timeline went back to the way it used to be, that they used their powers to protect themselves from space, and they probably teleported far away from there. I'm sure they are on their way here now."

"I'm sure they are not," Smedge said.

"You're wrong!" Quo shouted. "My friends are strong. Glor is one of the strongest, if not the strongest one of all!"

"Yes, I suppose she was," Smedge said.

Quo stared at him. "What did you do, Smedge?!"

"I didn't do anything!" Smedge laughed. "I was just cleaning up your mess. We didn't need two copies of all of you, the good guys. It took a lot of power to follow you through to that other timeline. I needed any extra power I could get. Even if it meant the original copies of you all were turned into that power. And besides, once I told my friends about you and your girlfriend, well, you already know where they stand on a human and Elder relationship. Whatever chance they had of survival, has been destroyed. When my friends and I came back from the alternate timeline, we blew up the rest of your ship, along with anything and anyone on it. It is gone. They are all gone. Forever."

The rock in Quo's coat began to heat up.

"SMEDGE, ALL YOU HAVE EVER DONE IS EVIL. I AM SO SICK OF YOU AND YOUR SELFISH WAYS," Quo cried. "She is your sister!"

"She was my sister," Smedge stated. "And I am not selfish!" he said, shocked. "I was thinking of our species when I let all these Elders come with me. Now, with the necklace created, our species was still doomed. Not anymore! With all of these stronger Elders, now our species has a better chance of surviving many more millennia! You're welcome, family."

"How long do you think all of these Elders can survive out of their timeline?!" Quo screamed. "You think our timeline is going to just accept all these extra bodies?!"

"If that's the way you feel," Smedge said, "you should be thanking me for destroying your friends. I'm sure the timeline will accept all of you as the originals now. And these Elders may be stronger than any Elders have ever been in this timeline! They can survive as long as they want!"

"Maybe they can," Quo said. "But how dare you take away life and try to say that what you and Enyo have done was somehow good."

"Quo, you shouldn't be acting so selfish. Glor's sacrifice has saved our species. And you need to think of the bigger picture here. Glor is gone. Forever. Move. On."

The rock in Quo's coat pocket heated its way through the coat and landed on the ground, now broken in pieces.

"What is that?!" Smedge screamed.

The pieces began to float in midair.

Everyone watched, staring in awe, as a hologram began to appear among the floating pieces of rock.

Chapter 13
Enyo's Realization

"WHAT IS THE MEANING OF THIS?!" Smedge screamed.

"Doesn't it look familiar, Smedge?" Quo smiled. "Don't you remember before the planets collided? Glor had broken pieces of the necklace floating around her. I'm sure you noticed. I suppose you never found out what they were, since you jumped into the planet. But I suppose you never really cared. You never care about anybody but yourself."

The hologram was clearer in this timeline. It actually looked like Glor.

"Glor?!" Smedge cried. "How?!"

"Smedge!" Glor shouted. "Why have you done all of this?! What is your endgame?!"

"The same it has always been!" Smedge sneered. "I want to be remembered!"

The Smedge from the alternate timeline was staring, wide-eyed, at everything. "That's it?!" he cried. "The reason I am so evil in this timeline is because I want to be remembered?! That's unbelievable!"

Glor looked over at everyone. "Good. You all made it."

Bob smiled at Glor. "Glor," he said, "even the Smedge from the alternate timeline thinks this Smedge is over the top. He is literally so selfish, he can't believe himself!"

Carol stared at Bob. She couldn't help but laugh.

Glor laughed. "Smedge is making it sound like the only Elders to come through to this timeline were evil. I don't even think Smedge knows what's coming."

"What are you talking about now?!" Smedge hissed.

"Sure, some of the Elders you let through were angry, scared, and just as selfish as you. But not all of them were." Glor looked at her family and friends. Then she looked at Quo. "It seems I misspoke earlier. At first, I, too, thought that Smedge only allowed Elders through that agreed with his plan. But even he thought that. That thought, however, is wrong." She looked at Smedge. "As hundreds of Elders came through with you, you just assumed they all came to help you with your evil plan. A selfish move, brother. Some of them just wanted a new life. Some of them did not come here for you. They must have liked the thought of a brand-new timeline, our original timeline. Smedge, you let just as much if not more good through to our timeline. Thank you."

Gloria and Captain Zot smiled at their daughter.

Smedge screamed in anger.

Enyo had heard enough. "Smedge darling," she said, "have you forgotten the other reason we have done all of this? Remember, the Elders took over my home planet, sending my entire species away on spaceships!"

"You know that isn't true!" Gloria cried. "The Elders wouldn't--"

"HE WAS ONE OF THEM!" Enyo cried, interrupting Gloria.

Everyone turned to see one of the Elders from the alternate timeline.

"He was one of the Elders that took over my planet!" Enyo screamed. She went running towards him.

"Stop!" he yelled. "I can explain!"

"You have fifty-seven seconds," Enyo said, halting.

"Hundreds of Elders have moved to a new timeline. We had to find a home."

"So you thought you could take mine?!" Enyo screamed. "This was many, many years ago anyways! You're trying to tell me that you Elders have been in this timeline that long?!"

"We had to spread ourselves out through time so we could be sure this timeline wouldn't reject us!" the Elder cried. "No matter how strong we are, we still wanted to improve our chances! A ninety-nine percent chance of survival is always better than an eighty-nine percent chance! We did all we could!"

"And why did you send my people away?!" Enyo yelled.

"Your people chose to leave! They had to!" the Elder cried. "When my small group found your planet, we asked if we could stay. We wanted to live there with your species! At first, your species rejected us. But just when we were about to leave, we overheard someone talking about how your species had to relocate someday because the atmosphere of your planet was changing. Your scientists found out first. The environment was becoming unlivable for your species. Sure, you had many years left before it became too dangerous, but we promised, if you let us live on your planet with you, we would help you build ships. We would save your species."

"What?" Enyo said, shocked. "I always thought you took over my planet..."

"Some people started groups to twist the truth," the Elder admitted. "Even though the atmosphere was going to kill them, some of your species disagreed with the choice to leave. They wanted to stay. We, along with your species, helped get them safely to spaceships, as the last of your species escaped the harmful atmosphere before it was too late. They stayed as long as they could to help. And we finally got every one of your species off the planet before it caused any of you lasting damage. I'm sorry you thought otherwise."

Glor smiled, as she could tell Enyo's heart began to soften.

"ENOUGH!" Smedge yelled. "Back to me!"

Enyo looked at him. The realization was too much for her.

"I thought the Elders were all evil," she cried. "Do you know where my species are now?"

The Elder she had been talking to smiled. "All across the galaxy," he said. "They eventually found a new home planet. Would you like me to take you to it?"

"Yes!" Enyo exclaimed.

"No!" Smedge growled. "You can't leave me!"

Enyo stared at Smedge.

"Come with me," Enyo said. "Come with us."

"And how would that benefit me?!" Smedge shouted.

"I have found my people!" Enyo smiled. "I must go to them! Come, Smedge, we can start a life with them!"

"YOU DON'T UNDERSTAND!" Smedge screamed at the top of his lungs. "I NEED TO BE REMEMBERED! I NEED TO BE NEEDED! I NEED YOU WITH ME! STAY HERE, AS

WE FINISH THIS FAMILY SQUABBLE, ONCE AND FOR ALL!"

"Smedge!" Enyo pleaded. "Come with me. Maybe you'll feel better among my people."

She went to take his hand.

He pulled away.

"Fine. Go," Smedge said. "After I am done dealing with this, maybe I'll join you."

Enyo grabbed Smedge's hand and pulled him towards her.

"Just come with me," she demanded. "NOW!"

"NO!" Smedge hissed. "You go! I don't know you like I thought. Get out of my life, Enyo!"

Shocked, Enyo's eyes filled with tears. She walked towards the Elder that was going to bring her home.

"Let's go," she said. She looked back at Smedge, then at Quo's friends, she glanced at the hologram of Glor, and finally, she stared at Quo.

"I finally see it now," Enyo said. "He is too selfish. It's always been about him. I am so sorry."

She and the Elder disappeared.

Glor smiled. "Look at that. Even Enyo turned good."

"I HAVE HAD ENOUGH!" Smedge screamed.

Glor stared at him. "Change," she said.

"What?!" Smedge demanded.

"Change before it's too late," Glor said. "I forgive you for everything. You are my brother. You need to change. And I think this is truly your last chance. This is it. Smedge. Change! Change now, or you'll never find your way!"

"Change!" Gloria cried.

"Come on, son," Captain Zot cried.

Smedge looked at everyone. "I have taken over the third home planet of the Elders! I have become so strong, with the technology my wife and I have created, that I conquered our entire home planet! I will never change. I choose, right now, to forever be, this Smedge!"

"That's unfortunate," Gloria frowned.

"Smedge," Quo said, curiously, "how did you manage to take over the entire planet anyways?"

"One more story," Smedge sneered, "about my greatness. Then, this all ends."

Chapter 14
One More Story

Glor stared at him. "You honestly can't see it, can you?" she said.

"I thought you wanted to hear my story!" Smedge yelled.

"He can't," the other Smedge said. "He can't see how selfish he is. But I can."

"Be quiet, Smedge!" Smedge said to the alternate version of himself. "You shouldn't even exist. I'll take care of you first. But before I do, here is how I took over the Elders' third home planet. It is a good story. I showed up to the planet as Gleck, and Enyo was Trolk. We landed our ship and asked to talk to Gloria's parents, my grandparents. In the form of Gleck and Trolk, we told them that we hadn't found much on our mission. But what we did find out was crucial. We told them that you had chased Enyo and me through time. We told them that it was because of all of those shenanigans, and because of the necklace itself, that we found all of your lifeless bodies floating through space. And just for fun, we told them that you were the ones that created the necklace."

"Why did they believe you?!" Quo cried.

"Why would Gleck and Trolk lie?" Smedge asked. "I guess they scanned the universe for any sign of you. But as you know, you were all either just at the point of the timeline where the collision happened, being destroyed, or in the case of you, Quo, physically out of our timeline. They believed us because you all were gone. I outsmarted them! I outsmarted all of them! In that moment of weakness, that moment of sadness where they thought all hope was lost, I gained the upper hand. I gained control of everyone on that planet! And now, I will finally be remembered! I win!"

"How?" Glor asked.

"How what?!" Smedge demanded.

"How did you and Enyo, by yourselves, take over the entire planet?"

"After we gained the upper hand, we changed into our original forms. We told the Elders what we knew about our species. That everyone on the second home planet with one superpower was also an Elder. The Elders have been hiding that information. And we threatened to tell everyone else if they didn't do what we said!"

"So they did what you said?" Glor asked.

"Of course!" Smedge hissed. "They don't want that secret getting out, now do they?"

Glor shook her head. "I can see everything now, Smedge. The Elders made a decision as a species not to use that name anymore after they started to weaken. It wasn't necessarily a secret to be uncovered. Gloria, my mom, was one of the last to be called Elder. But it was a decision made by them. By the oldest Elders."

Bob whispered to Carol, "The oldest Elders? They should call them the Elder Elders."

Carol stared at him.

Clory started to laugh.

They all looked back towards Smedge and Glor.

"So what was our species supposed to be called?!" Smedge cried. "They were ashamed of us for only having one power! Sounds like they have the same complex as the Seniors, who thought they were better than the Elders. Looks like the apple doesn't fall far from the tree!"

Gleck was thinking. He was trying to understand everything. "What about the future?" he asked. "When the ship went to the future and we saw those old creatures. They called themselves Elders!"

Glor thought for a moment. But she had no answer.

Someone came walking towards Smedge from the crowd of Elders.

"Maybe because we finally had realized we made a big mistake," the Elder said.

"Dad!" Gloria cried.

"Grandpa," Glor said. "Hello."

"Hello, Glor," he said. "Gloria." He nodded. "Before all of this nonsense with the timeline, and even before Smedge and

Enyo came to tell everyone the big secret, we had decided to bring back the name Elders to all future generations."

Glor smiled. "Why?" she asked.

"We had a visit from two interesting characters," he said.

"Who were they?!" Quo asked.

"Apparently," Glor's grandfather said, "they were just two Elders that had just witnessed a war on Earth between Seniors and Elders over the necklace."

Another Elder stepped out from the crowd. It was Glor's grandmother. Gloria's mother. The wife of the Elder they had been talking to.

"Gloria," she said, "they said you gave an amazing speech. They said you offered everyone a home on our new planet, but everyone slowly left until only those two remained."

"They said you helped them realize how wrong the division was," Glor's grandfather said, "and they hoped to once again rid our species of it." He looked at his family and their friends. He looked at all of the Elders that had gathered there. He looked at the hologram of his granddaughter, Glor. And finally, he looked at the original Smedge. "When they came to us with this information, my wife and I, and all of the Elders, realized the mistake we had made. And we are sorry, everyone. From now on, every one of our species will proudly be called Elder!"

"No!" Smedge demanded. "You were all under my control! I had won!"

"That's enough, Smedge," his grandfather said. "We were never under your control."

Smedge scowled. "You are a LIAR! How else would I have conquered the entire planet, grandfather?!"

"We let you," he said. "We saw you coming. We all knew it was you. We were aware of the situation with the necklace, and that are species was weakening. And letting you and even everyone on the planet believe that we were conquered was in our best interest. We let you think you were in control. Bringing Elders from the other timeline was a good idea."

"YOU USED ME?!" Smedge screamed. "NO! I AM THE SMARTER ONE! I AM THE BETTER ONE!"

"No," Glor said, looking at all of her family. "Smedge, you lost. Again."

"Well, sister," Smedge growled. "At least I am still alive."

Quo stared at Smedge, then started to cry.

"You weak fool!" Smedge laughed. "Now, it is time to end this!" he stared at the other Smedge. "You are me, aren't you?" he asked. "Kill Bob, and I'll let you live."

The Smedge from the alternate timeline just stared at him. He shook his head in disbelief.

"That was your one chance!" Smedge screamed. "You know what? I know how to get you all to listen to me."

He walked past Glor and straight up to the other Smedge and the crowd of Quo's friends.

Telepathically, Smedge lifted Nova off the ground.

"It would be a shame, if she died," Smedge shouted. "The only half human and half Elder that I know of. I'm sure there are more somewhere out there. But this is the only one that will ever come from that other timeline. I'm sure it's destroyed by now." He stared at Adam, then at Noah. "Come on! Stop me! Save your wife, Adam! Save your daughter, Noah! Don't be shocked at what I know at this point, people. I know everything!"

He raised Nova higher into the air.

"I have so many powers now! Enyo and I have given me just as many powers as the strongest Elder. Some of the powers are given to me with scientific gadgets. Some of the powers we have injected directly into my body! YOU HAVE NO IDEA OF MY POWER!"

Adam stared at his wife, who was floating in midair. Smedge raised her higher and higher.

"No one make any sudden moves, or I'll kill her on the spot!"

Everyone stared in horror. They wanted to help, but they knew Smedge was crazy, and he would actually kill her if he wanted to.

"Please, let her go!" Adam cried.

"Let her go?!" Smedge scowled. "From this height? Okay, if you insist!"

Smedge let her go. She went flying towards the ground. Noah used his power to catch her and safely land her on the ground. Nova went running to Adam.

"Smedge, stop!" Glor screamed.

"You know what?" Smedge bellowed. "I am done with you, Glor! I am done with this family. I AM DONE!"

In an effort to destroy everything, Smedge began to release all of his powers at once.

"COME AT ME, EVERYONE! I AM SICK OF YOU ALL! AND NOW, I WILL DESTROY EVERY SINGLE ONE OF YOU."

Chapter 15
Smedge Versus Smedge

Chaos started to ensue everywhere. There were some Elders there that were actually on the same side as Smedge. They were at the ready to fight with him. Smedge continued unleashing all of his power. He was using his original telepathic powers to lift people off the ground, sending false memories to confuse them, making them hallucinate, sending out sonic blasts from his fists, creating fireballs with one hand, and creating and using ice as a weapon with his other hand.

Bob stared at Smedge as he dodged everything.

"He has a lot more powers than I ever imagined would be possible," Clory admitted, as he dodged a chunk of ice that was flung towards him.

"Fire AND ice?" Bob exclaimed. "He is honestly so confused. I think he could fight against himself and still lose!"

Glor seemed to be safe from everything as a hologram, as the fire and ice went straight through her. She looked on, as Smedge unleashed more power.

"EVEN ENYO WILL PAY!" Smedge shouted. "I thought she was my friend. She was my wife! But she too, like the rest of you, turned on me. YOU ALL TURNED ON ME. You all truly hate me. I finally see the truth. None of you ever loved me."

The Smedge from the other timeline ran up to Smedge with confidence. He had heard enough. And it was time he said his piece.

"You have no idea the pain you have caused to my family!" he cried.

"I know exactly how much pain I have caused," Smedge growled. "I am only trying to make them see how they made me feel! How they always make me feel! Insignificant!"

"Insignificant?!" the Smedge from the other timeline cried. "All this family has shown you is nothing but compassion! Look at me, Smedge! Maybe you'll believe these words if they come from you! Look at me! You are selfish! You have been given more second chances than anybody I have ever known! You only think of yourself! You need to wake up, Smedge, because I think your time is coming to an end. Change, before it is too late!"

As the original Smedge now had his eyes focused on the other Smedge, he was still causing mayhem all around them.

Clory, Captain Zot, Gloria, Noah, Trolk, and Gleck were trying to protect Bob, Carol, Quo, Veronica, Adam, and Nova from the fireballs and ice that Smedge was throwing all around, and from the Elders that were chaotically fighting with each other.

Glor's grandparents were trying to fight off everything that came their way.

Elders were fighting with each other all around the two Smedges.

Glor looked on, but she didn't feel like much help, as she was just a hologram with broken pieces of the rock all around her.

"Call this off, Smedge!" she demanded.

Smedge looked over at her. "No! I won't stop until this is all over!"

As Smedge was looking over at Glor, the Smedge from the alternate timeline used his powers to lift him off the ground, momentarily disrupting some of the chaos.

Smedge quickly looked back at his other self and screamed, "HOW DARE YOU!"

He used his own powers to fight against the Smedge from the alternate timeline. He landed on the ground and grabbed the shoulders of this other Smedge.

"Don't disrupt the chaos!" he shouted. "Everyone is thinking about me! Everyone is remembering me! IT IS ALL ABOUT ME!"

The Smedge from the alternate timeline was sick and tired of this selfish version of himself. He stared into his eyes. "You disgust me. I can't believe such a selfish version of me exists. I really hoped you would change, but you don't want to change, do you? You love thinking about yourself. I'm surprised you even found love. You didn't deserve Enyo. The only reason you ever loved her, was so you could look into the eyes of someone that loved you more than yourself." He shook his head.

Selfish Smedge stared back and tilted his head. "You know what?" he asked.

"What?"

Selfish Smedge put his left hand on the other Smedge's face, and his right hand near the other Smedge's heart. He formed ice in his left hand that quickly fused to his enemy's face and formed a fireball directly on top of his heart, bursting his chest into flames.

Glor noticed, and screamed, "NO!"

It was too late.

Everyone and everything stopped fighting as Glor's voice echoed through the crowd.

They all saw the original Smedge standing over the one from the alternate timeline. He was on the ground, unmoving, with a frozen face, and a burnt body.

"DOES ANYBODY ELSE WANT TO FIGHT ME?!" he yelled.

"I do," someone said.

Smedge whipped around to see who spoke.

"WHO SAID THAT?!" he demanded.

"I did!"

Smedge finally located his next challenger. She walked toward him.

It was Nova.

She was sick of the arguing. Sick of the destruction. Done with the death. And completely ready to stand up for everyone.

Everyone, however, was shocked, as she slowly walked up to Smedge.

"You are no match for me, you half-Elder!"

"Prove yourself!" she demanded.

"Excuse me?!"

"You and me. Half-Elder from an alternate timeline, against a full-blooded Elder. No one helps. Just me, against you."

Smedge looked around. "Okay, but they can't help you either, especially not her!" He pointed to Glor.

"Are you sure, Nova?" Adam asked.

Noah was nervous, but he said nothing.

"Yes, I am," Nova said. "And if Smedge agrees to fight me, one-on-one, I will do my best to make you all proud."

Smedge laughed. "I just took down a full-blooded Elder from your timeline. Nova, please. Do yourself a favor, don't be a hero."

"Hey, everyone, Smedge is too afraid to accept my invitation because he is afraid of losing to me!"

"Silence!" he hissed. "We'll fight. Right now. I gave you a chance to back down. I accept your challenge, Nova."

Nova smiled. She looked at her friends and family and nodded. "I'll be okay," she said.

"Nova, be careful!" Glor advised. "Please."

Nova nodded, looked at Smedge, and said, "This. Ends. Now."

Chapter 16
Nova Shines

Nova stared at Smedge.

"I'll let you throw the first punch," Smedge laughed.

"I don't need your charity," Nova smiled, "but I'll take it."

She swung at Smedge, who caught her hand. He let it go.

Smedge yawned. "On second thought, go ahead and help her if you want. Maybe she'll last an entire minute."

"It takes sixty seconds to reheat a dish of frozen macaroni in the microwave," Nova stated.

Smedge stared at her.

Bob laughed.

Carol stared at him. "Why is that funny?"

"I usually cook our leftover macaroni in the microwave for ninety seconds," Bob said. "It usually burns my mouth. Now I know why."

Carol shook her head and looked back at Nova and Smedge.

"Why is that relevant?!" Smedge demanded.

Nova stared at him. "I'm a chef," she said. "And though I don't recommend using a microwave, sometimes you just have to."

Glor was trying to understand why Nova was talking about the microwave. "Nova, are you okay?" she asked.

"I'm fine," Nova admitted.

She swung at Smedge again. He caught her fist.

"Any more cooking tips before I destroy you?" he asked.

"I might want to know how to cook a roast."

"That depends on the kind of roast," Nova admitted.

Smedge shook his head. "Enough of these games."

He telepathically threw her at her father.

"Catch!" he growled.

Noah caught his daughter.

"I knew a half-Elder wouldn't even be a challenge," Smedge sighed. "I sure wish someone would actually challenge me."

"Smedge," Nova said, now standing on her own two feet, "did you know that chicken has to be cooked to a temperature of one hundred sixty degrees, but fish can be cooked at a temperature as low as one hundred forty-five degrees?"

"Oh no," Smedge cried, "you're actually boring me to death! Quick, tell me your favorite spice so I can die in peace."

"Cinnamon," Adam said. "Her favorite spice is cinnamon!"

Nova smiled at Adam. She looked at Smedge. "What is your favorite spice?"

Smedge threw his hands up in the air. "What is happening?!"

"Personally, I like nutmeg," Carol shouted.

Bob looked at Carol, then at Nova and Smedge. "Thyme is my favorite spice, no matter what thyme-line we are in!"

Nova laughed. "Thyme is an herb, Bob!"

Bob shrugged. "I'm not a chef."

Glor laughed at everything that was happening.

"Enough!" Smedge demanded. "Fight me, or move aside!"

"One more question," Nova said, walking back to face Smedge.

"WHAT?!" Smedge growled.

"What is your favorite thing to eat with Thanksgiving dinner? Other than the turkey, of course. I love mashed potatoes, but I think I love applesauce just a bit more."

Smedge smacked Nova across the face, sending her flying towards Noah again.

She stood back up, unharmed.

"You didn't answer my question, Smedge," Nova yelled.

"Because your questions make no sense!" Smedge sneered. "I think you are trying to distract me. I don't know why, but I don't like it. And I'm done with this. I'm done with you."

He went running towards Nova, fire in one hand, ice in the other. She jumped out of the way.

"You know, Smedge, you remind me of this turkey I cooked once," she said. "It seemed that no matter how long I cooked it, it was never done."

Smedge growled in anger.

"So I finally realized, I must be doing something wrong," Nova said. "It must be my fault that this turkey isn't cooking. Maybe I was just a bad chef."

"ENOUGH WITH THE FOOD METAPHORS!" Smedge screamed.

Smedge went running towards her again.

"I finally realized the truth, though," Nova stated. "I wasn't a bad chef. It wasn't my fault. My oven was broken. And I couldn't believe how long it took me to figure that out. It was embarrassing, actually."

She moved out of the way as Smedge was about to hit her.

"I finally realized something about you, Smedge."

"I don't care!" Smedge shouted. "Fight me!"

"Smedge, your family has tried to fix you for too long. They have put so much work into the hope that someday you might change. Some people, maybe they can change, maybe they can't, who's to know? My point for all this food talk, the point of everything we just went through, was not for you. It was for them." She pointed at Smedge's family, then looked back at Smedge. "You can't change because you don't want to. You don't want to change at all. You are an egotistical maniac, and you like it."

"What is your point?!" Smedge sneered.

"Gloria, Zot, Clory, everyone, I am so sorry, but this isn't your fault. You aren't necessarily a bad chef if you can't get the turkey to cook. Maybe the oven is just broken. And you aren't bad people if you can't get Smedge to change. You're not even bad family members. Or bad friends. If he doesn't want to change, he won't change. No matter what."

Gloria and Zot were amazed at the point Nova was trying to make.

"Smedge, you're a broken oven," Nova said to him, "and I think it's time your family stopped trying to cook the turkey."

Gleck whispered to Trolk, "Is cooking the turkey a metaphor for changing Smedge's behavior?"

Trolk shot him a look. "Yes, Gleck," she smiled.

"So the family and friends are the chefs, right?"

"Gleck, I'll explain it to you another time!" She whispered.

Glor's eyes widened. "Don't do it!" she yelled.

Everyone looked at Glor in confusion.

Smedge mustered all of his power and charged at Nova. She tried to move out of the way, but she was too late.

Both of Smedge's hands were heating up with fire. He threw it at Nova, and she began to burst into flames.

"Nova!" Adam cried.

"Don't come near her or I'll end her life right now!" Smedge warned Adam.

"Noah, save her!" Veronica cried.

Smedge created more and more fire and threw it at Nova, who was now on the ground in flames. He started to walk away from her and created one more fireball. He tossed it behind him. It landed on Nova, who was now on the ground, in flames, unmoving.

Adam was in tears. He ran over to his wife. "Dad! Mom! She's dead!" he cried. "She doesn't have a pulse anymore!"

Veronica was livid.

Noah was about to kill Smedge for what he had just done.

"We could do this all day," Smedge laughed. "I could kill you all one at a time until I'm the only one left. Anybody up for that?"

"You are a broken oven," Gloria realized. "You have had so many chances to change. We have tried to help you. And what has it done? Caused more chaos than before. We are done hoping you will change, Smedge. We give up on you." She shook her head.

"We give up on you," Captain Zot agreed. "This was never our fault. This is all about you. Just like you wanted. But we are done, Smedge."

Clory shook his head. "To think, you murdered the one good chance you ever had at being good. The good version of you. I'm done with you too, Smedge."

Smedge looked at everyone. "Whatever. That doesn't even bother me."

"Smedge," Glor called him. "You wasted your last chance. Now it's too late. I... I am done with you too." She had tears in her eyes.

"Don't you see, family?! I don't care! I don't care about your feelings. I don't care about any of you!"

"Oh, they see it," Quo said. "We all see it. You're a lost cause, Smedge."

Smedge was furious. "I never liked you, Quo."

He went running towards Quo and created a sharp spear with ice. He was about to drive it through Quo's heart. He was moments away from killing him when he heard someone call him.

"Smedge," the voice said.

"Who said that?!" Smedge demanded.

Glor looked around. She finally realized who it was. "No way!" she exclaimed.

"Smedge," the voice said again. "Thank you."

Smedge looked around in anger. "SHOW YOURSELF!" he yelled.

Smedge finally located the voice. He laughed as he saw Nova standing up. A body that he had just burnt to a crisp was walking towards him.

"Have you come back for another round?" he asked.

"Yes, please," Nova said. "Like I said, I don't recommend using the microwave..." the char marks all over her body disappeared. She looked like herself again. "Sometimes, you just have to. Thanks for the charge, Smedge."

Her body lit up. It was so bright, that no one could see for twenty seconds.

"Smedge," she shouted, "your time is up."

She put her hands on his shoulders and he fell to the ground in pain.

"No!" he cried. "Stop!"

She left her hands on his shoulders, as Smedge became weaker and weaker, she continued to light up.

"Please," Smedge cried. "I'll change! I promise!" He looked at his family. "Help me, family. Mother? Father?"

They just stared at him.

"Clory?! Anybody? Quo, I was joking. It was a joke! Help me! Help me…"

Nova stared into his eyes. "Smedge! No more will you hurt the people I love. No more will you hurt anybody!"

"It was all a joke! I was just having fun! Give me another chance! One more chance! Please!"

Nova shook her head. "Sorry, Smedge. You had multiple chances. Eventually, for everyone, those chances run out. Time runs out. Your time is up."

She continued to hold onto Smedge's shoulders. It seemed as though she was taking all of his powers away. The power he was born with and the power he and Enyo had created.

"I want another chance!" Smedge demanded. "How is everyone going to remember me?!"

"They'll remember you, Smedge," Nova stated. "As a cautionary tale." She looked at everyone. "EVERYONE LOOK UPON SMEDGE!" she shouted. "DO NOT EVER LET YOURSELF GET THIS FAR GONE!"

"I'm not too far gone," Smedge whimpered, "I need help. Someone, help me. I'll change! I swear it! I will be good!"

Nova sighed.

Glor looked around and frowned. "Goodbye, Smedge," she cried. "I'm sorry you couldn't change."

Gloria and Zot began to cry at their daughter's words.

Nova still had her hands on Smedge, as his skin started to become old and wrinkly.

"Family," he cried. "I'm sorry! Change… I promise… I'll do anything if you save me… remember my name… remember the name… of Smedge."

As Nova finished draining all the power from his body, his skin and bones turned to dust.

Smedge's family looked on. They knew the right thing was done. They knew it had to be done. But their hearts still hurt. They still cried tears for Smedge. He was family. But he was too far gone. It was too late for Smedge. And this was truly how he met his end.

Glor wiped away tears and looked at Nova. "Thank you for saving us from him," she cried. "We finally realize the truth now. He was never going to change. And that isn't our fault."

Gloria, Captain Zot, and Clory, though they all had tears in their eyes, nodded at what Glor said.

Nova's brightness began to fade away. She took a deep breath and looked at everyone.

The Elders had never seen anybody do that before.

Adam stared at his wife. She looked at him and cried.

"Nova, are you okay?" he asked.

The final glow around Nova's body faded away. She ran to her husband and hugged him. Her mother and father hugged both of them.

"I'm not okay," Nova cried. "That was awful. But it had to be done."

Everyone stood around, with tears in their eyes. They all had questions. But those had to wait. Nova needed a minute to be with her family. She needed a minute to process what just happened. So, everyone waited in silence.

Chapter 17
Rebirth

After a while, Nova finally found the courage to speak.

"Everyone," she cried, "I'm sorry you all had to see that."

Glor's grandparents walked up to Nova.

"Nova," Glor's grandfather said, "I have never seen such power before."

Another Elder from the alternate timeline stepped forward.

"Sir," he said to Glor's grandfather, "I am sorry I joined Smedge in his quest. I was wrong. Please, find it in your heart to forgive me."

He nodded. "We have a lot to figure out," he admitted. "Some joined Smedge in fear. But some joined him because they agreed with him. They wanted destruction. And there is no place for such evil on the planet we call home."

Glor's grandmother nodded. "The Elders have a lot of healing to do from all of this. There are new Elders from the alternate timeline sprinkled throughout time. And every one of them deserves to be called what they are. Elders. And the newer generation of Elders, that inhabited our second home planet, with only one power, also deserve to be called Elders. Never again will we take away the name Elder from any one of our species. That, as we finally realized, was wrong."

"Sorry we followed Smedge," another said.

The crowd erupted in one big apology. Everyone saw how nasty Smedge was until the end, and the thought of any of their lives ending like that made everyone rethink their allegiance.

Glor's grandparents looked at the crowd of Elders. The entire crowd stood there, ready to be lead. The two of them turned towards their daughter, Gloria.

"Smedge is still a baby in the present," Glor's grandfather admitted.

"Well, all we can do," Gloria sighed, "is love him. Be there for him."

Captain Zot frowned. "Even knowing he becomes what he becomes, he is still our son."

Clory had tears in his eyes. "I still want to have hope that he changes this time around, but we all know he won't."

Gloria hugged her son. "It's alright, Clory."

Glor looked around at everyone. She was glad that the evil was gone. The destruction was over. She wanted to smile, but she couldn't shake the sad feeling that she could never hug her family again. As a hologram, she wasn't going to feel anything ever again.

She looked at Quo, who walked towards her.

"We'll figure out a way to save you," Quo said, reassuringly, somehow knowing how Glor felt.

Nova walked over towards Quo and Glor. "I think I can help with that." Nova began to glow again. "I'll be right back."

Everyone stared at Nova, as she disappeared from their sight.

"Where is she going?" Quo asked.

"I don't know," Glor admitted, "but, I… I am starting to feel different…"

"What do you mean?" Quo asked. "Is it a good different?"

"I'm not sure," Glor cried. "Nova?"

Everything began to shake. The lights flickered. Everyone looked around for something to happen.

Gloria and Captain Zot were hopeful.

Captain Zot looked at his wife. "Did Nova find a way…"

Gloria interrupted him. "Is she saving Glor?!"

"How could she even do that?!" Bob asked.

"Who cares!" Carol cried. "Come on, Nova!"

Even Glor's grandparents were unaware of what was about to happen.

Everyone, as one big family, was rooting for Nova to save Glor.

"Glor?" Quo said. "Are you alright?"

Just then, two bodies started to reappear among everyone. It looked like they were struggling to reappear. It looked like one of them was carrying the other.

"Everyone!" Gloria cried. "Focus your powers on them. Whatever your power is! Just focus it towards them! Help pull them through!"

Captain Zot smiled at his wife. "You heard her!" he shouted. "Elders from the alternate timeline, we could really use your help! Use your advanced powers to help bring them home! Everyone else, help where you can! Hope with us! Pray for us! Glor is coming home! We can do this!"

Bob, Carol, Veronica, Adam, and Quo couldn't help but feel helpless.

"You're here," Gloria smiled at the five of them. "You're rooting for her. Having friends to come back to might be more important, more powerful than you think." She concentrated all her power to help Nova and Glor return home. She looked at Quo. "Quo, she loves you. She's coming back to spend her life with you. You're the reason she is fighting so hard right now."

Quo smiled. "Glor," he shouted, "I love you!" He nodded.

A burst of energy came from the two figures, as they finally appeared fully in front of everyone.

The hologram of Glor saw Nova and noticed that she was holding the actual body of Glor herself. Nova carefully placed the body down. Without hesitation, the hologram disappeared among the floating pieces of the broken rock, and the floating pieces of broken rock rushed towards Glor's actual body. They swirled around her, lifting her off the ground. Glor's lifeless body seemed to regain consciousness and life, as the memories returned to their original owner.

Quickly realizing she was floating in midair, Glor slowly lowered herself to the ground, landing in front of Quo.

"We finally did it!" Glor cried as she hugged Quo. She ran over to hug her friends and family. "The plan worked! And we are all okay!" Glor turned to thank Nova. "Nova!" she exclaimed. "Thank you so…"

Everyone turned from looking at this miracle of Glor's rebirth, to see Nova, struggling to stand.

"Nova!" Glor cried. She ran over to Nova and caught her as she fell.

Adam frantically ran over to his wife and took her hand. "Nova!" he cried. "Stay with us!"

Nova smiled at Glor. "I am so glad I saved you," she coughed. "I feared this was going to happen anyways."

"What are you talking about?!" Glor cried.

"I don't have much time left," Nova admitted, "but I would like to spend the time I have left explaining what just happened. I want to explain why everything looks so bad for me right now. I want to explain why it's okay." She looked at Adam. "I owe it to you all to explain why I'm dying."

Chapter 18
Burnout

"Nova," Adam pleaded, "I need you."

"Adam," she cried, "I love you so much. Thank you for always treating me with respect and kindness."

Adam tried to hold back tears. "I have hope!" he cried. "You'll be okay."

"I wish that were true," Nova coughed. "Let me explain." She looked at Quo and his friends. "I went back to the exact moment the ten of you came to my timeline," she said.

"Smedge said he destroyed our ship, destroying all of our original bodies!" Bob frowned.

"Yes, he did," Nova admitted. "And for that, I am so sorry."

"What happened?" Carol asked. "You went there, just now?"

"Yes," Nova cried. She coughed. "I told you all, I didn't recommend using a microwave… but sometimes you have to. I had to. After Smedge attacked me with fire, that is when I knew everything was going to be okay. Sounds funny, doesn't it? I am half human and half Elder. There isn't much about someone like me in any history books."

"That doesn't matter," Adam said. "I love you no matter what."

Veronica was crying.

"Mom," Nova said, "don't cry! It'll all be alright!"

Noah smiled at his daughter's reassuring words. "We all love you, Nova."

"I love you all," Nova smiled. "After I was lifeless on the ground, I felt the power flowing through me. I can't quite explain how or why this happened, but it happened. I stood up to fight Smedge. With the boost of energy I received from the fire, I found the strength to take on Smedge."

"You won that one," Bob smiled.

"It was still tough," Nova admitted. "No matter how evil someone is, no matter how bad they are, ending someone's life is never okay. But he was out of control. I'm not even sure he was capable of anything but evil at that point. I had to do something before he killed anybody else. I had to save my friends. I had to stop Smedge. And it hurt my heart to no end to find out that was the only way."

"He was truly never going to change," Gloria sighed.

"I put my hands on Smedge and slowly drained all of his power. I drained all of his energy."

"Would that include any traces of time energy that followed Smedge throughout his life?" Quo asked.

"I would guess so, yes," Nova said. "All the power he and Enyo had created and injected into his body, any power he was born with, and everything else he encountered that gave him strength. I drained all of it."

"That is a lot of power!" Gleck exclaimed.

"Way too much," Trolk sighed.

"It was way too much," Nova coughed. "After I defeated him, I thought I would be able to survive if I somehow unleashed this power. With that thought fresh in my mind, Quo said that we would find a way to save Glor. Immediately, I had an idea. With all this power now coursing through me, I saw more than I have ever seen in my entire life. I saw wars, famine, violence, hate, and death throughout time."

"That's horrible!" Quo cried.

"It was," Nova said. "But I also saw peace, goodness, forgiveness, joy, hope, life, and love. So much love. That was so beautiful. I saw the entire universe right before my eyes. I saw all your thoughts too. Your memories. And that's when I saw the moment the ten of you left this timeline to come to mine. It was in that moment, I knew what to do. I knew that whether I survived this mission or not, I could use this power to save someone. To save Glor."

"Thank you, Nova," Glor smiled.

Nova smiled back and began to cough again.

"Are you okay, honey?" Veronica asked.

Nova smiled at her mom. "Yes, mom, I think I am." She looked at Glor. "It was a close call," she said.

"What do you mean?" Glor asked.

"I had to time it perfectly. If I took you too soon, I might have disrupted the transfer of your thoughts into the rock. If I took you too late, your body would have been damaged, if not completely gone. I used as much power as I could to try and time everything perfectly. And I am so glad it worked. I appeared on the ship, well, there wasn't much of the ship left, and that's when I ran into some trouble."

"What happened?!" Gleck exclaimed.

"Smedge had shown up. He was using the power from you guys sending Quo to an alternate timeline. And just as quickly, he and his followers began to destroy what was left of the ship. Smedge didn't even notice me, as he was busy carrying out his evil plan, he was so focused on himself. I felt so much power drain from me, just by being there at that moment, but I still had way too much power coursing through me. The universe and even the timeline itself were fighting against Glor and I returning. So I unleashed more of my power. As the two planets collided in front of us, I felt every ounce of power leave my body. But it still wasn't quite enough. Whatever you all did back here surely helped. We all saved Glor. Thank you, everyone."

"I can never repay you for the gift you have given me," Glor smiled at Nova.

"Yes, you can," Nova admitted. "Live a full life. Love. Spread kindness, and above all, name one of your children after me." Nova smiled, as she was joking.

Glor laughed and nodded.

"I feel dizzy," Nova sighed. "I guess, I guess this is pretty much it for me. But don't cry, everyone. Don't cry, mom and dad. Adam, don't cry. I defeated so much evil today. I brought back so much love. And I am happy. I will miss everyone. Adam, it'll be okay."

"No it won't!" Adam cried. "Can't we save you? Isn't there something we can do?" He looked at the Elders.

"They know nothing about me," Nova coughed. "Half human, half Elder. It's funny, really. I was strong enough to defeat an Elder. I was strong enough, with the help of everyone here, to save an Elder. But I am not strong enough, even with everyone else's help, to save myself. But that's okay. I have peace. I have everyone I love with me."

"Just heal yourself!" Bob suggested. "Why wouldn't that work? You are half Elder!"

"Bob," Nova smiled, "I am going to miss your wit. I read a couple of your books in our timeline, you know. You are an amazing writer."

Bob smiled.

"But unfortunately," Nova frowned, "that idea didn't work. I tried it. My DNA is so confused with Elder and human mixed in. I just can't seem to heal myself. Besides, I am so weak after the trip back. Perhaps any power I might have had from being half Elder was drained along with all of the power I had from Smedge."

"What if we put you in a stasis pod like mom?" Glor asked. "Mom survived, I bet you can too!"

Nova smiled at Glor. "It's too late, Glor. I see the end coming for me right now. I am so tired." She sighed. "My death was inevitable, you know. I would have died anyways from taking on all that power. It was my honor to use it to save someone. Thank you, Glor, for letting me save someone."

"Wait, what if I stop time around you?" Glor cried. "With more time…"

"Glor," Nova interrupted her, "I am at peace."

She looked around at everyone, as her mom and dad embraced her. Adam was still holding her hand. His family pulled him in for a hug.

"Adam, I love you," Nova said.

"I love you, too," Adam cried.

"When you tell this story," Nova whispered, "make sure you call me… Supernova."

Nova smiled, then closed her eyes.

Chapter 19
After Talk

After nearly an hour of silence, Bob looked around with tears in his eyes. A thought had popped into his head, and he was shocked that no one else had asked it. But he wasn't sure if now would be the right time to ask.

He looked at Carol and whispered, "Where are we?"

"What?" Carol asked. "What are you talking about, Bob?"

"This clearly isn't Earth, where we all are. Back when we all came through that portal, it brought us straight to Smedge and all his shenanigans, all his evil, everything that brought us to this sad moment in time. But, where exactly are we?"

Quo heard them talking.

"Bob," he said, "I'm sorry no one told you. Most of us recognized this place immediately because we have all been here before. I forgot that you haven't ever been here."

He looked at Adam and Veronica, who, being from the alternate timeline, wouldn't know where they were either.

Quo stood up in front of his friends, and said, "Everyone, welcome to what we have called the third home planet of the Elders. This is where a lot of us have decided to settle down." He looked at Glor. "This is where a lot of us have chosen to be. After going back to Earth to save it, I realized that I will always call it my home, but I also call this beautiful place my home. But wherever she is," he pointed at Glor, "I am home. And I owe everything to Nova for doing what she did." He looked at Adam and Veronica. "Nova was one in a million. She was an amazing person. And I am glad to have known her. She was selfless, and the best cook in any timeline."

Adam, Veronica, and Noah smiled.

Glor's grandfather began to speak, "After Smedge believed he had conquered this planet, the third home planet of the Elders, as you know, he and some of the Elders went back in time to infiltrate the other timeline. After many Elders came back through with Smedge to our timeline, some spread themselves out through the galaxies, and some of them came back here with Smedge. Apparently, he thought a good place for his final showdown, the final part of his plan, whatever that even was, he thought the best place for this was on the planet he supposedly conquered. Good thing he was never fully in control."

He looked at his wife, Glor's grandmother. She smiled.

Quo nodded at them and smiled.

Gloria looked over at Noah and his family, who were still huddled around Nova's lifeless body. "Adam, Veronica," Gloria said, "you are more than welcome to stay here on this planet with us, but if you want to go back to Earth, that is completely understandable."

"Isn't there already an Adam and a Veronica on Earth in this timeline?" Adam asked. "I want to stay here with Quo. He is my best friend. And I hope you stay with us, mom," he said, as he looked at his mother-in-law, Veronica.

Noah smiled at his family. "Wherever you want to go," he said to Veronica, "I'm sure the Elders will be okay if I don't go back to Earth."

Glor's grandfather nodded. "Noah, you and your family are welcome anywhere in the galaxies."

Quo looked around, then had a thought. "Hey," he said to everyone, "if these are all your bodies from the other timeline, those of you that previously only had one power, Clory, Trolk, Gleck, Captain Zot, Gloria, are you still more powerful now since those bodies are from the other timeline?"

Gleck looked around, then tried to fly. He rose off the ground. "I could not do that before!" he marveled.

"I guess I can try to turn invisible," Trolk said.

She tried and succeeded.

"Hey, that was my power!" Gleck exclaimed.

Clory smiled, and he tried to send a thought telepathically to Quo. "Can you hear me, Quo?"

"Yes, I can," Quo said, out loud. Everyone looked at him. "Clory sent me a telepathic message. Trolk turned invisible, Gleck can fly, I would guess it is safe to say that you all are, in fact, more powerful than you once were."

"That is so amazing," Bob cried. "But, I still don't have powers, huh?"

Carol shook her head and stared at him. "You are a space explorer and a writer!"

"But my books aren't famous in this timeline," Bob said. "I haven't even written them yet!"

Carol pulled out a copy of Bob's book, 'We Don't Need Space, Space Needs Us', from her purse.

"Maybe this will help," she smiled.

Bob gasped and took the book.

"I'm going to be famous in this timeline too?!" he asked.

He then thought for a moment and remembered the interaction with his manager and the man who couldn't afford one of his books.

"On second thought," Bob said, "maybe I'll self-publish. I think writing is more of a hobby for me than a profession. The people are more important to me than the money, and I'm not sure any publishing agencies on Earth will agree with me. But I suppose it wouldn't hurt to keep an open mind."

"So, we are going back to Earth?" Carol asked.

"Isn't that where all of our friends are?" Bob said.

He looked around and quickly realized. Many of their friends were right here on this planet.

"Carol!" Bob exclaimed, "Are you suggesting…?"

"Only if you want to," Carol smiled.

Bob looked around, excitedly. "Quo, do you mind if Carol and I hang out on this planet with you for a little while?!"

"It would be my honor to show you around, though I haven't been here too long myself, you know. I was distracted by having to get back to Earth to save my home planet from danger."

Adam smiled at Quo, but his smile quickly faded, as he realized Nova was still no longer with him.

"It hurts," he said. "It hurts knowing I will never see her again. I don't want to say goodbye."

Veronica hugged her son-in-law. "I don't want to either," she admitted, "but, at least she was peaceful. And happy." She started to cry, as she embraced Noah as well.

"If everyone is okay with it, I think we should have a service for Nova on this planet. We can bury her here as well, if that is acceptable."

"Are you sure we shouldn't bury her on Earth?" Veronica asked. "She was born there..."

Adam frowned. "Not in this timeline," he said. "I don't know. For some reason, I feel we really need to put her body to rest on this planet. I don't know why. I can't explain it. But, if it's okay with you," he looked at Veronica, "I think this is the right choice."

Veronica realized that Earth itself was probably a lot different than the Earth in their timeline. So that planet was almost as foreign to Nova as this one. This planet, however, was where Nova defeated a great evil, and saved an amazing person.

"Okay," Veronica agreed. "We'll have a funeral here, and bury Nova on this planet."

Quo looked at Glor's grandparents. "Is that okay with the locals?" he asked. "The ones that welcomed everyone with open arms on this planet... who are they, anyways?"

"Quo," Glor's grandmother sighed, "I think we have had enough stories for now. Let's just say that the locals on this planet are extremely compassionate, extraordinarily kind, and just plain welcoming... besides, I'm not sure they are ready to reveal to the universe who they truly are..."

"That sounds ominous," Gleck exclaimed.

Quo nodded. "So they don't mind if Nova is buried here?"

"I would go as far as to say," Glor's grandfather paused, and scratched his chin, "I'm pretty sure they would insist. They want us to feel like this is our home, because, as they have said, it is our home. It is the third home planet of the Elders!"

"And they don't mind that we call it that?" Trolk asked.

"They have actually started calling it that themselves," Glor's grandmother said.

"Then it's settled," Noah sighed. "We will hold the funeral service for Nova, my beautiful daughter, on this very planet."

Adam sighed. "Nova, I miss you so much," he cried, as he looked at Nova's body. "I wish there was a way you could come back."

Veronica hugged Adam again. "I'm not alright either," she cried.

Noah embraced his family.

Quo and Glor walked over to Adam and hugged him.

One by one, all of Adam's new friends came over to him.

Trolk, Gleck, Bob, Carol, Captain Zot, Gloria, and Clory joined in on this group hug, as Gloria called her parents over to join them.

They slowly walked over and joined everyone.

The amount of love that Adam felt made his heart feel okay for a moment. Just for a moment. He still missed Nova, as did everyone else.

Adam sighed, and cried silently.

"I will always be here for you," Quo said to Adam. "So will Glor and everyone else here. If you ever need anything, or just to talk, call us. Call me. I am happy to call you my best friend."

Adam forced a small smile. "Thank you, Quo. That means so much to me."

Chapter 20
The Funeral

As the days went by, everyone tried to settle somewhat comfortably on the planet, but they also were trying to make the necessary preparations for Nova's funeral.

The days were hard, and the nights were worse for Adam. He would usually call on his family and friends, but some nights he just cried himself to sleep. He let the pain consume him. He let himself hurt. He needed to feel the pain.

Though everyone was sure Nova had passed away, at the advisement of some of the Elders, they refrigerated the body to wait and make sure she was dead. Since she was half human and half Elder, some of them held hope that she might still somehow come back to life.

Adam clung to that hope, and some days, it was all that could keep him from completely breaking down.

There were a few times that Adam, Noah, and Veronica just visited Nova's body. Just to make sure she hadn't by some small chance come back to life. Just in case.

The length of refrigeration was debated among everyone, and every time the day of the funeral was closer, Adam would push for moving it back. The Elders, his family, and his friends were making the accommodations for him, but nearly two months had now gone by, and Adam called for another delay.

"Adam," Quo sighed. "She's not coming back. We have to let her rest. We have to bury her body."

"Why can't we leave her refrigerated indefinitely? Just in case..."

"Adam," Veronica said somberly. "Please. We have to bury my daughter. This hurts me as much as it hurts you. We have waited so you could be ready. Adam. This pains me to say, but please, be ready."

Adam cried. "Why won't she come back to us?!"

Glor looked at Quo, then at Adam. "I am so sorry," she said. "I truly am."

Adam wiped tears from his eyes. "I know you are," he said. "Thank you." He looked at Quo. "Thank you both for being here for me." He sighed. He choked back tears, as he said, "We have to put Nova to rest now, don't we?"

Adam was as ready as he would ever be. Everyone was planning on having the funeral in two days. And those two days, for Adam, were nothing but pain.

The day of Nova's funeral finally came. It had now been nearly two months since she defeated Smedge. Almost two months since she had saved Glor. And everyone was now gathered together for the service.

It was a beautiful service. Quo and his friends learned a lot about Nova that they didn't previously know. Everyone knew how much she loved cooking, though.

Everyone that had spent even five minutes with her had something nice to say. Noah, Veronica, and Adam had so many stories. And they told many of them to everyone.

The time had finally come to bury the body. This was the worst part for Adam. But with his family and friends by his side, he managed to get through it. He managed to get through all of it.

The body was now buried. Many more hours had gone by. Everyone had gone home, except for Quo, Glor, Bob, Carol, and Adam.

"We'll visit her as often as you need," Quo said. "As often as you want."

"Every day," Adam cried.

Glor nodded.

"I can't believe she's been gone for two months already," Quo sighed.

"Fifty-seven days to be exact," Adam replied.

"What did you just say?" Quo asked.

Glor stared at Adam, then at Quo. "Why has that number been following us around?!"

"It has come up quite a bit," Quo wondered out loud.

"You guys noticed that too?" Bob asked.

"What does that number mean to you?" Quo asked.

"Cam, I mean, Smedge said it a lot, as Cam, the shapeshifter," Bob said.

"Though, the reason Smedge may have been so obsessed with that number in the first place could be because fifty-seven years was how long Captain Zot decided to rewind time," Glor guessed. "Clory and Smedge were supposed to use those years to come up with a plan to stop the collision. Though, I think relocation to this planet was always the goal, no matter what Clory and Smedge did with those fifty-seven years."

"What are you talking about?" Adam asked.

Quo was trying to do the math. "Are you sure it has been exactly fifty-seven days since we lost her?"

"Exactly," Adam said. "Not a second goes by that I don't miss her."

Quo looked at Glor. "It's as if the number fifty-seven has been following us."

"But why would it…"

Glor was interrupted as the ground beneath them began to rumble. Everyone looked around frantically, as the rumbling stopped.

"That was weird," Quo admitted. "Maybe--"

Quo was interrupted as a bright white beam of light shot from the ground.

"Okay, maybe we should have waited a little longer before burial," Bob cried.

The ground where they had just buried Nova began to cave in. Not wanting to be too close, Adam still tried to look and make sure the body was still there.

"Where is her body?!" Adam demanded.

Carol walked closer to look. The body was gone. "How deep was she buried?!" Carol asked.

"That doesn't matter much," Adam cried. "The ground where she was laid goes down at least fifty feet now!"

Quo's eyes widened. "Fifty-seven feet!"

"Why?!" Adam shouted. "What is the meaning of any of this?!"

"Is the body all the way down there?" Carol asked.

"I don't know," Quo admitted. "I have no idea what is going on."

"The story of my life," Bob stated.

Everyone quickly turned when they heard a rustling noise nearby.

"Hello?!" Adam cried.

"There is someone there!" Quo shouted.

Slowly, out of the shadows, a familiar woman came walking straight towards them.

Adam's eyes widened when he saw who it was. He couldn't believe it. How was this possible?!

The five of them, at the same time, shouted, "Nova?!"

Chapter 21
Fifty-Seven

"Who is Nova?" the woman asked.

"What?" Adam was dumbfounded.

"We have to call the Elders," Bob cried. "And Nova's parents! And... everyone."

"I am Nova?" Nova cried. "My memories are a bit scrambled..."

"Nova, are you alright?" Adam asked.

"I am not sure," Nova cried. "Why is the number fifty-seven in my head?"

"Smedge was obsessed with that number, apparently," Adam said.

"Smedge... he is my father?"

"Gross!" Bob exclaimed. "Smedge is the one you defeated!"

"I defeated him," Nova stated. "And I am married to..."

"Me!" Adam exclaimed.

"You saved me," Glor smiled. "You brought me back from being destroyed. The power you had absorbed, you thought it was going to kill you anyways, so you used it to save someone. To save me."

"I saved you!" Nova said. "I think I remember! I went back to... to the collision... when you changed the timeline... I pulled you out of there... that was when I, when we almost lost."

"Yes, and with the help of our friends, both of us made it back."

"Fifty-seven!" Nova shouted.

"Oh no," Bob sighed, "now she's obsessed with fifty-seven!"

"Why would she be obsessed with fifty-seven?" Quo thought.

"I have a message for you all," Nova said.

"What is happening?!" Adam shouted.

"From what I can understand," Nova said, "the human side of me died."

"But you were actually dead!" Adam cried. "All of you. Not just the human side. The Elder side was dead too. You had no heartbeat. No pulse."

"I don't have those anymore," Nova admitted. "I don't think I need those."

"You don't have... a heartbeat?!"

"I don't have a heart," Nova sighed. "Oh yeah, this was the plan. The human side of me... the Elder side of me... yes, all of me died! Even I believed I had died. I couldn't even let myself remember. We couldn't even try to save me because we didn't know I could be saved yet."

"Nova, please explain!" Adam said, through tears.

"I am not Nova," she sighed. "I am the excess power that left Nova before she brought Glor back. I was the backup plan she could not tell anybody about. And I have returned to this body to deliver hope."

"Is my Nova alive somewhere in this universe?" Adam asked.

"Nova made a copy of herself. She sent that copy back with Glor. That copy was sent back without the knowledge that it was a copy. She thought she was the original. And that copy is the Nova that died."

"Where is my Nova?!"

"That's why I am here. I am not Nova. But I am the path to finding her!"

Adam truly felt hope for the first time.

"Where is she?!" Adam cried.

"Fifty-seven days after death," Nova said, "that is how long it took for her to send the excess power across time and space to this body. She is becoming weaker with every second. You must rescue her. She didn't want to trick you all. She had to make sure Glor made it back safely. She made a copy of herself to guide Glor back to you. That copy had trouble coming back, but you all helped her with your powers. But Nova couldn't break free herself."

"Where can we find her?!" Quo shouted.

"She is everywhere. And nowhere. No. Wait, there she is!"

"Where?!" Bob shouted.

"She never made it back! She is stuck at the time of collision! Help her!" Nova had a serious look on her face. "Adam, it's me. It's Nova. Please, be careful. This place is so dangerous. I don't know if it's worth the risk to come and save me."

"It is worth it!" Adam cried.

"Nova, you saved me!" Glor smiled. "We will save you!"

"Glor! It is so good to see you. You must only bring those that are willing. Do not force anybody. This point in time is so weak. The timeline was split here, the collision happened here, and Smedge himself was here. No, he IS here!"

"Wait," Bob cried, "we have to go back there again?!"

"This is it," Nova cried. "I had to send that copy of me to die. That was still me, what I would have said, it was a copy of me. But the final war is happening now in the past. The future, your future, could change. Smedge has noticed me! He somehow knows... he knows I defeated him! He's revising his plans with Enyo... they... they are trying to open multiple rifts to alternate realities! No, this isn't good! They are using the breach between timelines and all of the power to open multiple timelin--"

Someone appeared next to Nova. Somehow, someway, and to everyone's horror, it was Smedge. "Okay. I have had ENOUGH of ALL OF THIS! I will unleash everyone and EVERYTHING until EVERY REALITY is DEAD! I will NOT be defeated by this... by this thing! Your past is changing, my friends, and this time, I have the knowledge. COME AND FIGHT ME! All of me."

He disappeared.

Nova, frightened at what she saw, cried to her friends. "There are so many of him... he has opened many possible timelines! There are so many Smedges!"

"How... how many?!" Quo cried.

"Fifty-seven!" Nova shouted.

She disappeared.

"Now!" Quo cried. "We must assemble everyone NOW!"

Within ten minutes, they had managed to assemble everyone that had been at the funeral. They even called on the other species that welcomed them to their planet.

"Everything is in danger!" Quo cried. "Smedge has built an army of himself by the collision. Nova is stuck there. And I think reality itself is in question!"

"Won't our timeline change if Smedge doesn't do the same thing he did the first time?" Bob asked.

"Maybe," Gloria cried, "if time and space weren't so fragile at that point. It sounds like he has somehow accessed multiple timelines, realities, just to get his way. I am so sorry, everyone."

"We have to defeat him!" Adam cried. "All of him."

"But if we defeat him in the past," Quo said, "before Nova, what would that do to our timeline? Nova would never sacrifice herself. She would never save Glor. We could make things worse!"

"But I have to save her!" Adam cried. "Besides, it's too late. Smedge knows now, so if we do nothing, that might be worse too!"

"Friends!" someone spoke up, "This has gone too far."

Everyone looked to see one of the local aliens, the ones that had welcomed the Elders with open arms.

"I speak for every one of my species. This is it," the alien said. "Everyone, are you ready?"

Everyone looked around. Even the Elders were confused. They weren't sure what would come next.

"THE FINAL WAR IS UPON US!" the alien shouted. "ARE YOU ALL READY?!"

Everyone nodded, even though they weren't ever going to be ready for this.

He told everyone to use their powers to transport everyone who was willing to the collision point.

The Elders, the ones that had stayed on this planet in the present, some from the original timeline, and some from the alternate timeline, concentrated their powers on themselves and everyone.

"We have no spaceship," Bob cried. "How are we going to fight in space?!"

Quo shook his head. "This is beyond my comprehension. I don't understand any of it. But," he looked at Glor, "I'm sure we'll all be safe."

Bob and Carol were nervous. But they knew that they, too, would be protected.

Their surroundings began to change, as all of them somehow were about to be in space, opposite Smedge and his army, for what would truly be, the final war.

Chapter 22
The Final War

Quo closed his eyes. He had no idea how he would help, but he was ready.

As everyone appeared in space, the Elders created a force field so everyone would be able to breathe. And to everyone's shock, they created a force field underneath them all, as if there was ground beneath them.

The planets had already collided. Smedge had already destroyed the other bodies. And Nova had already gotten Glor out of there. But now, Glor, and everyone, were back. For one final time.

"Well, well, well!" Smedge hissed. "Look who is back! Look at all my friends! There's me, me, me, and, hey everyone, have you met me?!"

"I don't know how you are doing this, Smedge, but it ends now!"

"I heard," Smedge growled, "that I was defeated by one called Nova. WHERE IS SHE?!"

"She died!" Adam shouted. "Because YOU are so selfish, that to kill you, she had to absorb all of your power, killing herself as well!"

"Good!" Smedge laughed. "Though, Adam, don't lie to me! She's here somewhere, and you know it!"

The other Smedges all laughed.

"That is disturbing," Bob shivered.

"OKAY!" Gloria shouted. "THIS IS IT! EVERYONE, BRING HIM DOWN!"

"Mother!" Smedge gasped. "I knew you never loved me."

"Enough!" Glor demanded. "Smedge, you're too far gone!"

"Yeah!" Bob shouted. "You're a broken oven!"

This phrase threw Smedge off guard. Everyone noticed and took the opportunity. They rushed towards all of the Smedges.

It wasn't pretty. As everyone fought, there were rifts in time opening and closing. The good and bad were fighting in the air and on the makeshift ground. It was as if some enemies were coming and going, jumping between timelines.

"You know what would be absolutely the best?" Smedge laughed. He looked at Enyo, who was still with him at this point in time. "I'll kill Adam now! Maybe that will bring Nova out!"

Smedge landed on the makeshift ground and went running towards Adam, who had no defense. Everyone else was fighting off the other Smedges.

Smedge was about to reach for Adam when out of nowhere, a burst of light shot him in the face.

"How did you do that, Adam?!" Smedge growled.

"It wasn't Adam," a familiar voice said. "And this time, there will be NO TIME FOR TALK! ELDERS, FOCUS YOUR POWERS ON CLOSING UP THE RIFTS IN TIME! I'LL DEAL WITH SMEDGE!"

"Nova!" Glor smiled, as she heard her friend's voice.

The rifts were all over the sky, but the Elders immediately began pushing the Smedges back through and closing them.

"It won't be that easy to defeat ME!" Smedge screamed.

"I'm not going to defeat you now," Nova could be heard screaming. "I'm going to defeat you fifty-seven days ago, in the future!"

Light engulfed Smedge and he began to become confused. Light shot towards Enyo and everyone else that was there the first time around.

"They will all forget this!" Nova screamed. "Everything must happen the way it happened. And we will all be okay! EVERYONE WILL BE OKAY!"

Light blinded everyone that was there. The rifts to the other timelines that Smedge had caused started sucking everything belonging to them back through them, as they closed back up.

Nova sent Smedge, Enyo, and everyone that was with him the first time around, back to the correct time, and towards the third home planet of the Elders, to carry out their evil plan, to capture all of Quo's friends, and finally, to be defeated by her. Everything was back on track to happen the way it was supposed to.

All the rifts were now gone, except for one. The one to the alternate timeline Quo had traveled to. The one Nova and Veronica were from.

"Some of us are staying in this timeline from that timeline," Nova said. "Close that rift now! No one has to go back through that one!"

The Elders went to close the rift, as Adam was sucked towards it.

"No!" Nova could be heard yelling, as Adam was sucked through the rift.

It closed.

Nova, who had only been heard up to this point, screamed, "I DID NOT DO ALL OF THIS JUST TO LOSE YOU!"

The light shot towards where the rift was, and the rift began to open back up. The light went through.

Glor looked around, as Adam and Nova weren't coming back through.

"Let me help her!" she cried. "I can help her!"

Before anybody could answer her, Glor went through the rift. Quo's eyes widened in terror, but he trusted Glor.

Minutes went by. The rift was still there, but there was no sign of Glor, Nova, or Adam.

Everything around them began to shake.

"Time is about to collapse!" Gloria cried. "If that happens, everything we have ever done will have been for nothing!"

Rifts began to open back up, as it seemed that everything around them was about to explode.

Everything. Time. Space.

"But this couldn't be right!" Quo thought. "If we all die here, how does the future happen?! How does anything happen? How?!"

Quo looked at everyone around him, and back at the sky, as reality itself seemed to be at an end.

"They must be lost!" Gloria cried. "Maybe they can't find the way back to us!"

"I have an idea!" Quo cried. "Bob!"

"Yeah?" Bob asked.

"Give me your book!"

Confused, Bob looked at Carol. "Carol, do you have my book with you still?!"

"Of course!" Carol cried. "I always keep it with me!"

She pulled the book out of her purse and tossed it to Bob.

Bob caught the book and threw it to Quo.

"WE DON'T NEED SPACE!" Quo shouted. "SPACE! NEEDS! US!"

Quo whipped the book up towards the rifts. Somehow, Adam and Glor came out of the now white sky, towards the book. They grabbed the book and landed next to everyone.

"Where's Nova?!" Quo cried.

"Here!" she shouted, as light shot down from the sky, and finally turned into the form of Nova.

"Everyone, we have to get out of here! I am finally running out of power."

Nova looked up, and focused, as everything seemed to go back to normal.

With one more burst of power left, Nova sent everyone back to the exact moment they left, including herself.

Now, back on their third home planet, everyone looked around.

"So, that's it?" Quo asked.

"I think so," Bob guessed.

"Smedge is still defeated, right?"

"Most definitely," Nova smiled. "He is gone. For good. Except, well, he is still a baby. But, chronologically, yes, that Smedge is gone. Forever."

Bob smiled. "You used my book to come back? How did that work?"

"With all of the confusion," Quo said, "I figured if we used something from their timeline in our timeline, they might be drawn back towards the opening to our timeline, as the book itself was drawn to its original timeline!"

Nova smiled. "We were lost. I think the confusion was in all realities. We didn't know if we were going to make it back. Until we realized. We all were trying to get out, but every other reality had opened up on our timeline. We didn't know which one to go through. Until we saw a book heading towards us from the correct rift. The right timeline."

Bob stared at them. "So... basically... my book saved the day!" Bob laughed.

Carol smiled at him.

Everyone talked about what happened for a long time. The Elders, though they had a lot of healing to do from everything, still watched over everyone to make sure they were all happy and peaceful. And with the help of the species they shared their third home planet with, everyone did live happy lives.

Trolk and Gleck went back out to explore space. Apparently, that mission wasn't enough for them.

Nova, Adam, Veronica, and Noah stayed on the planet for a little while but decided to go on a few missions of space exploration with Trolk and Gleck.

Bob and Carol eventually went back to Earth to visit, but they found themselves wanting to stay with Quo and Glor. They even found themselves on a few space missions with their friends. Because, space needed them.

Captain Zot and Gloria decided that, unless they were needed for another mission, they were basically done traveling.

Clory was back and forth, traveling for some time, staying on the planet for some time.

Quo and Glor were the same way, though they just wanted some peace and quiet for a while, so they didn't travel for months. In those months, they decided to get married. They knew they loved each other, and that, no matter what, they would be together forever.

No one ever dared to go back to the time of the collision, as that point in time was dangerously fragile now. They tried not to even speak of the collision anymore.

Everyone was there for Quo and Glor's wedding. It was a beautiful wedding, and it didn't happen without its own adventure surrounding it.

Maybe that story will be told another day. For today, I think we have heard enough stories.

Good has won, as it always does. And even still, yes, even now, the best stories are yet to come…

Epilogue

There are so many more adventures that could be written about. Maybe someday. For now, we have The Elders' Chronicles. A somewhat organized series of events that actually happened, in this exact order… give or take.

How do I know so much about all of this? Well, I married an Elder. And we have grown old together. We have children of our own, who are already grown up. If the time finds me, I'll write more stories for you all to read.

This is Quo, by the way, and that is how I know so much about all of this. I was there. I am here now. I see some of you asking yourselves, how did he write from Bob's perspective? How could he have known what happened when he wasn't even there? For starters, Bob is my friend. Bob even helped me write these stories. But as you all know by now, many of my other friends have telepathic powers. So, I was told everything, yes. And with Bob's permission, I also received some of his thoughts through our mutual telepathic friends. I received many thoughts from each of my friends. That's how I wrote from many different perspectives.

And though you may think it is interesting for a human to write the Elders' Chronicles, Gloria and all the other Elders, including Glor, would beg to differ.

Bob inspired me with his books, to become a writer. Since his book saved my friends, I figured, maybe this book will be that important someday.

Maybe.

And if you're wondering about the aliens that welcomed us all on their home planet, maybe I'll write about them in the next story… if there's time…

But there is always time. Until time runs out. And when time runs out, I guess that is the end.

Or is it?

Book three in The Elders' Chronicles series finds Quo and his friends face to face with a common enemy. This shapeshifting villain has just revealed who he really is. Smedge. He has news for everyone. And he tells them they need to make a choice: Create the weapon that he and his wife Enyo just used to cause the collision of the Elders' home planets, the same weapon that has been weakening the Elders, or, don't create the weapon. If they choose that option, everything changes, creating a new timeline where they never knew each other. A timeline where Quo, Bob, and Carol never met Glor, Clory, their family, or their friends. They wouldn't even remember them. They wouldn't remember anything.

Quo never meeting Glor? That's unacceptable. But staying in the current timeline, creating this weapon, this necklace, just so they don't lose what they have and who they are? That seems unacceptable too.

However, maybe there's a third choice. But is this option worth the risk? Everything seems fine. Everything looks good. Maybe the third choice is the right choice.

Is this revision something everyone can live with? Only time will tell...

About the author

Massachusetts based Keith Imbody is a musician, writer, and the author of The Elders' Chronicles series. After many years of writing songs and stories, Keith decided it was time to start self publishing. He has a passion for science fiction and fantasy, which you might find out after talking with him for just five minutes. His other passion is singing, though these two passions probably wouldn't work well together. Would anybody enjoy a Science Fiction musical?

Made in the USA
Middletown, DE
30 June 2025

77443267R00220